Marked by Gods

The Marked Series, Book 2

Jayme Hunt

This book is a work of fiction. Names, characters, places, and incidents are the product of the author's imagination or are used fictitiously. None are intended as a faithful representation of any one country or culture at any point in history.

Contents

To my grandpa Marty, who never knew me as an author, but supported me in all my endeavors.

To my grandpa Gary, who is also an indie author, and always says that everyone has a story in them.

And to my grandpa Charlie, whose last text to me was about how much he loved my debut novel.

Each of you holds a huge place in my heart, for different but equally important reasons.

I love you all.

Author's Note

Dear reader —

This book has references to parental death, discussions of sexual assault, offensive adult language, violence, gore, and explicit sexual scenes.

If any of this content is upsetting to you, please protect your well-being and do not continue.

CHAPTER ONE

I paced the edge of the dimly lit room for what felt like the millionth time that day. It was a genuine wonder I hadn't yet burned my tracks into the stone floor.

There was a definite chill in the air, as fall was creeping into winter, though it didn't touch my skin. The amount of energy I spent training during the day had no effect on my restlessness at night, so I opted to work myself into a sweat once more. It was easier to focus on physical exhaustion rather than my racing mind.

Lap a-million-and-one involved a slow detour around the bed, while I dragged my fingertips across the blue and silver linens. The bed was large and extravagant, to be sure, but that was its only purpose — to intimidate with grandeur. Sleeping under the blanket felt like crawling beneath a rug made of straw.

A knock came at the door, echoing through the large room. I called for them to enter.

"Does this place not have a library?" I demanded, turning to face the figure. Soren's green eyes widened, surprised by the hostility in my tone.

"It does," he offered mildly, leaning against the door frame. He cocked his head at me with curiosity. "Do you want me to show it to you?"

I nodded and scrambled to join him as he guided me through the corridors. As running my body ragged offered no respite, at least I could occupy my mind with books. Perhaps I could even do some research to help our cause.

Soren had been the one to find me after my hunt for the talismans took an unsuspecting turn. Dagda's cauldron transported me to an upper echelon of Muiranvia, wounded and surrounded by shadows. It had been a mere coincidence that led Soren to stumble upon me. He'd been tracking a flock of *Sluagh* — winged dark Faeries that feasted on souls. Since they flew, they rapidly covered terrain; Soren had been tracking them for the better part of a week before he found them — and me.

I hadn't been able to see anything in the dark, but I'd heard the Sluagh: the slash of their wings cutting through the air, the burning in my chest as they attempted to rip my soul from my body, rendering me semi-conscious.

Soren had used his limited fire magic to keep them at bay as he dragged me, still clutching the cauldron, to the nearest safe haven he knew of — coincidentally, one of Myriam's family abodes. She was wealthier than I'd suspected, with homes dotting nearly every corner of the land. I supposed I should be grateful, but her family's opulence only added to the indignation I already felt at her ignorant mindset.

I was surprised to learn Faerie dust was scarce, reserved for the royal Aes Sídhe and its commander alone. Soren had instead sent word to Blaise with enchanted paper, requesting he come and retrieve us both while I recovered from my injuries. But as days passed and my body healed, we heard nothing. I'd taken to training with Soren and pacing the confines of my room. The unwelcoming energy emanating from the rest of the mansion made exploring as appealing as another jump through the cauldron.

I hadn't had much of an opinion of Soren, other than disgust in his choice of partner, but he'd grown on me over the past few days. While he wasn't as strong as Blaise in combat, his sheer speed challenged me, forcing me to alter my tactics while we practiced. He showed me how he used his signature air element to enhance his physical abilities, something I'd never learned while working on my magic with Darrya. He tested my air shield and gave me some additional pointers, praising the strength of my magic.

"It's truly incredible to see what someone as gifted as you can do," he'd said, and the sincerity in his words surprised and heartened me. Still, I grew uneasy as we waited to hear from Blaise.

"Here we are," Soren said. The large door creaked on its hinges as it swung open. I peered inside, hit by the dusty smell of disuse before my eyes could even adjust. *Exactly how I pictured it,* I scoffed to myself as I stepped inside, inspecting the room.

The walls were pure white, a stark contrast to the wooden bookshelves. Though the shelves were fully stocked, I doubted they had ever been read — likely purchased off a predetermined list. There were popular titles from several genres, many of which were in the palace library, too, though those had been well-worn and maintained. These looked brand new, yet coated in dust, as though they hadn't been touched since the day they first arrived on the shelves. The chairs in the center of the room were detailed with gaudy blue fabric, and looked like they'd be less comfortable to sit on than the actual floor.

My fingertips skimmed the spines of the books as Soren turned to exit the room.

"Can I take Fathom for a ride tomorrow?" I asked.

His horse was housed in the nearby stable and hadn't moved since. My separation from Gray was already grating on me, and I spent most days imagining I was astride him again, feeling connected to both him and the nature around us. The power of Soren's horse likely wouldn't hold a candle to Gray, but still, it would be *something*.

I saw the answer in his guilty expression before the words left his lips.

"That's not a good idea," he ventured softly. "The Sluagh have your scent now, and they relish the hunt. I've been scouting, and I know for certain they haven't left the area. There are too many in this flock to take them on, even with the two of us. If you can just wait until we have reinforcements from Blaise—"

"Yeah. Blaise," I muttered, pulling a book from the shelf at random. "If he ever shows up."

I understood his reasoning, though. Sluagh could not enter houses if the entryways were salted, but if we ventured outside, they would descend upon us with no hesitation. My stomach twisted darkly with that now-familiar pang of neglect. I reminded myself there had to be some reason Blaise wasn't here yet. Even if he wouldn't come just for me, surely he'd come for his best friend and third in command? The abandonment felt a little less personal, then.

A small voice nagged in the back of my mind, reminding me that it wasn't just Blaise who could be looking for me. Kipp, Finlay, and my father had all been there when I'd disappeared with the cauldron. Were they looking for me? I could understand if Finlay wasn't. I had likely been nothing more than a distraction to him. But Kipp had been feverishly determined to protect me, and my father...well, we had *just* made amends. I could only hope that meant he was missing me and aiding in the search for my return. But truth be told, I wasn't so sure anymore.

"He will," Soren said softly, resting a hand on my shoulder. I was startled by the gentle gesture but didn't pull away. "He loves you, you know."

I shrugged. "He's never said as much."

I pulled away to flop on a chair, and a whoosh of musty air rushed up to hit my nose, which I immediately crinkled. The chair, if it was possible, was even less comfortable than my bed.

"Can I bring books back to my room? I swear I'll return them," I promised.

Soren waved his hand dismissively. "I'm sure you can. I doubt Myriam or her family would even know the difference, unless it's merchant logbooks," he replied, giving the room another once over. "I get the feeling they're not much of the...*reading* type."

His admission made me snort, and he tossed me a smirk in return, those emerald eyes gleaming. When he turned to leave, I slowly rose and returned the random book to its position, inspecting the other titles in earnest. I wasn't exactly sure what type of book I was looking for, other than a distraction to pass the time.

I knew there was truth behind Soren's warnings about the Sluagh. The day prior, I'd attempted to slip out for a walk and was halted by the presence of a black shadow soaring overhead. It was much too large to be a normal bird, and I'd felt an immediate, crippling nausea, which had me clutching at my stomach as though it had gone hollow. Every instinctual nerve in my body had screamed at me to turn around, and so, I'd listened.

The second I went back inside and closed the door, the nausea dissipated. Whatever the Sluagh were, they seemed ten times worse than any of the dark Faeries I'd encountered before. And despite Soren's praise of my fighting and magic skills, I was still keenly aware that I hadn't yet summoned fire — the most effective element for fighting the Sluagh.

If there was a whole flock of them, rationally, I had to accept there was no chance we could fight them off alone.

My fingers stilled as I reached a section on the different realms, spotting the word *Annwn* among the titles. Where had I heard that before? I closed my eyes, trying to recall something Kipp had said, though it felt like ages ago now.

"The story says that it was plunged into the chest of a supernatural demon, and it fell with him into the depths of Annwn."

Annwn. The Otherworld. That was where we needed to look for the third talisman: the sword of Nuada. We'd found the first talisman, the Speaking Stone, in Lachlan's castle. And after hunting down the beithir for Dagda's cauldron, that second talisman now lay somewhere in this mansion. I hadn't inquired about it since our arrival. This talisman was supposed to be our next step. Without another thought, I tipped the book back by its spine and pulled it from the shelf.

"All right. Time for some nighttime reading," I murmured to myself, clutching the book to my chest as I hurried back to my bed of straw.

CHAPTER TWO

B laise had to focus on preparing his army for the inevitable. They'd accepted the steep increase in training without complaint, but questions they dared not utter were etched in their expressions. He owed them an explanation, but he wasn't sure how to present it without causing panic. While his unwavering loyalty and immense skill had earned him his position as commander, it had come with other unexpected responsibilities — communication chief among them.

As a result, he was almost grateful for the distraction searching for the sword provided. His stomach clenched as he thought about the urgent reasons behind retrieving it, but he had long ago mastered the art of taking his desperation and turning it into more productive outlets.

"What's the word, boss man?" Larke appeared, his warm, chocolate-brown eyes wide and questioning. Blaise tossed him an appreciative grin at the affection in his tone. Soren had left well over a week ago to hunt a flock of Sluagh, and had not yet returned. In his absence, Larke had stepped up considerably, covering both of their duties and ensuring everything went on without a hitch.

"The Sluagh — lots of them. Increased sightings around Sairas," Blaise replied, wringing his hands together in frustration. It was a wonder he hadn't taken the skin clean off; he had been doing that often lately.

Soren should have returned by now, and as each day dragged on without a word, his anxiety increased. Katherine had disappeared before his very eyes, and all of his attempts to track her had failed. And now this? The gods were intent on testing him in every way, it seemed.

Larke shifted on his feet. "Of course there are. The dark Fae we killed last month would have occupied the surrounding lands they now have free rein to."

Blaise nodded, impressed as usual with how quickly Larke had assessed the situation. He was second-in-command and frequently proved why Blaise had been right to choose him. "And with the days getting shorter, the amount of time they have to hunt is getting longer."

Larke cursed. "Should we enforce a curfew?"

Blaise took a moment to consider. Despite the increasing chill in the air, indicating winter storms that would arrive any day now, the orange and golden colors of the trees surrounding the palace looked harmless. The only traceable sounds were the soft murmurings of passersby and the soft caw of a bird. For all intents and purposes,

Sairas was peaceful, and Blaise was grateful that he had kept the chaos from bleeding into the place he was sworn to protect.

The Sluagh only hunted at night, when the last of the sunlight blinked out from the sky. They were more drawn to dying souls — easier prey than a healthy army surrounding the town, now alert at all hours. Spreading a cautious warning should suffice. For now.

"Not yet," he answered, fixing Larke with a look. "But ensure the army is prepared for them. Provide extra training on how to kill them, what to look for, and how they'll make you feel. You're up to speed on that, yes?"

Larke nodded, straightening. "Aim for the head or the heart. A cut anywhere else and they'll still survive," he recited. "They can be mistaken for ravens or bats in the sky, so always be on alert. Salt the entrances to your home so they cannot enter. And keep close tabs on your emotions. Their incapacitating power presents as crippling despair."

Blaise clapped his shoulder, a sign of both approval and dismissal. Yet before he could take his leave, Larke's next words stopped him.

"Maybe you should tell Finlay," he said tentatively. Blaise's look was sharp, and he flinched. "Look, I know he's not your favorite person—"

"That's an understatement," Blaise muttered. Resentment and jealousy flared in tandem in his chest. Larke ignored him and continued.

"—*but* he's got the strongest fire power out there. It's one of the few ways to kill them, aside from a blow to the head or the heart. If he can offer that protection to our people, it's worth asking."

Finlay's name conjured images in Blaise's mind; images that set his nerves aflame with unchecked fury and more than a little envy. The prince, standing a little too close to Katherine when they spoke, eyes darkened with clear desire as he gazed at her. Katherine's expressions following her interactions with him, flushed with what could be rage — or something else he didn't want to examine too closely. He gritted his teeth as he recalled his pet name for her: *little angel.*

Blaise inhaled a slow, deep breath and shoved the thoughts back into the dark crevices of his mind.

"The queen would never stand for Finlay offering himself on a silver platter to those monsters," he retorted, crossing his arms. Larke pulled his jacket tighter around him and exhaled a deep, hot breath, sending misty clouds spiraling into the sky.

"The way I hear it, he made it pretty clear he'll do what he has to if it comes to another battle, damn the consequences," Larke said softly. "If not for the rest of his people, at least for her."

Blaise winced, catching the reference to Katherine like a physical blow. He knew damn well that Finlay wanted her, but hearing it said aloud was the confirmation he didn't want, alluding his feelings went beyond physical desire. Larke had been spending more time with Darrya, who likely knew Finlay's feelings firsthand. Blaise vividly remembered their encounter with the beithir, where they had both answered "love" to the final riddle. He wrung his hands once more, suppressing the sudden urge to hit something.

"We can ask her father. His magic is strong as well," he grumbled, but Larke shook his head.

"Not nearly as strong as Finlay's fire." Larke's tone remained gentle, but that simply angered Blaise further.

"*Fuck.* Fine. I'll ask him," he snarled.

Larke broke out in a grin and punched his shoulder. "Good deal, boss man. Now. Fancy a quick session?"

He raised his fists and settled into a fighting stance, turning his palm to the air and gesturing with his fingers to lure Blaise in. Blaise grinned, lowering his center of gravity and shaking his arms out.

"I have to make a trip back home...but I suppose I could spare a few min—"

His fist shot out before he finished his own sentence, hoping to catch Larke off guard. But Larke knew him well, and ducked before it could connect with his jaw.

"You talk a big game, thinking you can take me down in just a few minutes." Larke laughed loudly. "I'll have you flat on your back in less than one."

Blaise snorted, thankful for Larke's ability to cheer him up. "You're on, Larke. You have forty seconds left."

The second Blaise landed in Leyteras, his jovial attitude disappeared. The remaining Faerie dust settled in the dirt around him as he began his walk into the heart of town, inspecting the land as he went.

Curious, he thought, how the sun shone in Sairas but not here. It was almost as if Leyteras was meant to be dull; a land where the days were always cloudy, and bright greenery didn't exist. Back home, birds chirped and cawed, and whispers of conversations carried in the wind, yet the silence here was heavy, only interrupted by brief yells or sharp words.

As he approached the heart of town, his eyes scanned the pale greens and dull tans that stretched out for miles: the fields owned by Larke's family. Larke's higher status in Leyteras was owed to it; the stretches of farmland that produced barley, potatoes, and alfalfa hay. He often wondered if Larke's hardworking attitude and fierce loyalty came from that upbringing.

Larke's home had been a haven of sorts, his family a replace-ment for the nuclear one Blaise had so desperately wished for in his younger years. Larke's parents hadn't batted an eye when he and Soren had visited as children, always having food ready to fill an aching stomach and a washcloth to clean up the wounds they both received while fighting. If their little group was a tree, Larke's parents were the roots that held it steady, even in the worst of storms.

He smiled faintly as he reminisced, his feet carrying him automat-ically down the dirt roads of the town, where he stopped at the local market for several items.

Shrugging the bags of produce over his shoulders, he cut down a side alley to an area where the homes were smaller and less tended to. He stopped in front of a small, two-bedroom home, with boarded windows and paint peeling from its exterior. From the outside, it looked uninhabited, but he knew better.

His army wages had allowed his mother and sister to move here, where each finally had their own bedroom. Blaise provided what he could to ensure neither needed to work, though he wished he could give them more. He suspected his sister still sold her body at times, but she would never breathe a word of it to him after their last argument. He knew it wasn't his place to push the subject.

His mother, on the other hand, had gone blind decades ago, rendering any type of work nearly impossible. It was a degenerative disease; even the most skilled healer couldn't keep it at bay forever — not that it made a difference back then. Blaise hadn't made the kind of money to afford their services either way. Even getting to the market was a chore for her, and if his sister didn't accompany her, she became an easy target for pickpockets.

Blaise's dad had left before he understood what a father should be, but between himself, Larke, and Soren, they were able to provide some stability for his mother and ensure his sister, Sera, stayed out of too much trouble. Soren had rescued her once while they were young; she'd been plied with too much alcohol and led into the least desirable part of town for the gods only knew what malicious intent. For that, he would forever be grateful to his third in command.

Blaise wanted to continue taking care of them, so he enjoyed coming back when he could. He tried his best to do some shopping and cooking anytime he came, often slipping some extra coins into his sister's pockets to tide her over. While it didn't make up for his inability to provide more for them earlier in life, it eased the ache in his soul knowing he could now.

"Hey, mom," he called as he pushed the door open. It groaned in complaint, and he had a moment of panic, thinking it would break.

He could cook, but he was no repairman. Luckily it slammed solidly back into place, and he made his way to the kitchen.

"Is that you, Blaise?" his mom called out. He heard her shuffling as he began pulling items from the bags he'd brought. He located a knife and a pan, then glanced up to see her at the doorway. She was still beautiful, with a sharp jawline and striking pale eyes. Streaks of gray embellished her dark hair, adding a tasteful dimension to it.

Blaise began cutting potatoes as she found her way to a kitchen chair, allowing her as much independence as possible.

"You're looking good," he noted casually as he chopped. "How have things been here?"

"Dark," she quipped, and he chuckled. She had the same quick wit he admired in Katherine. "I hope it's been slightly more eventful for you in Sairas."

"A bit too eventful."

While he cooked, he launched into what had happened over the past few months. The only thing he held back was the private conversation he'd had with Ensley, but his heart twisted as he gleaned over it. He'd never been one to keep secrets from his mom. She'd heard all the good and the bad in his life, and hadn't missed a beat. She was his example of unconditional love.

When the meal was cooked and the leftovers had been put away, he pushed a plate towards her, placing silverware in her hand. "Glass on your right," he murmured, moving to sit opposite of her at the table.

Her hand shot out to pick up the glass, and she hummed in disapproval as she sipped it. "Why isn't this wine?"

He rolled his eyes and stood again to get her a glass.

"Don't you roll your eyes at me, young man," she called at his back. "I've lived long enough to earn a glass of wine with dinner."

He chuckled. She didn't need to see him to know him inside and out. "I suppose Sera won't be joining us," he commented as he handed her the wine and sat back down.

His mom waved a dismissive hand. "Who knows where she is," she said, though they both knew. They ate in silence, Blaise allowing her the time she needed to concentrate on her eating and process his stories.

"This Katherine," she murmured at last, glancing across the table to fix him with a serious look. She was uncanny like that, peering into his soul decades after her sight had diminished. "Do you love her?"

Blaise started in surprise. They'd never said as much to each other. But as he envisioned her — with her bright amber eyes, reminding him of the warm natural light cast by the sun during the golden hours, crinkling with amusement every time she defied him — he knew he'd never felt anything this deeply. His every thought was consumed by her; his every action, done for her. There was no other name for it, even if he had never voiced it out loud.

"Yes. I do."

"Good. Then find her. Do right by her," his mother said. She took a long sip of her wine, and Blaise noted the slight shake of her hand as she did. She'd become an expert at hiding her true emotions, but Blaise knew his father's abandonment of their family had left its invisible scars. Once she placed the glass on the table once more, he took her hand in his.

"I will," he promised.

CHAPTER THREE

S oren was uneasy.

I could tell from the change in his demeanor over the past week. The scuffing sounds of his trudging echoed late into the night as he paced his room down the hall. His eyes appeared bloodshot in the mornings, and I often heard him muttering to himself behind closed doors. He'd closed off and refused to even train with me, so I'd gone through the paces by myself until I was tired enough to settle down with a book and my own thoughts.

We still hadn't heard from Blaise. At my request, Soren had sent letters to Darrya, and then Kipp, both of which went unanswered. If it hadn't been for a small black cat venturing into the library earlier this week, I would be completely alone. I had bribed it to stay with offers of bread and milk.

As much from curiosity as concern, I was about to question Soren over breakfast when the door burst open. We both whirled around, my heart leaping at the thought that it could be Blaise. Instead, a slender woman with white-blonde hair stood in the doorframe.

"Myriam!" Soren exclaimed. His chair tumbled to the ground with a clatter in his haste to reach her. They embraced, immediately melting into a ravenous kiss. I clenched my fists and turned away, a hot, irksome feeling coursing through my veins.

Why hasn't Blaise come yet?

"How did you get in here?" I demanded as the two finally broke apart.

Myriam looked surprised to see me standing there. She glanced between me and the entrance, as if I were daft. "Through the front door?"

I shook my head. "No. I mean past the Sluagh." At her blank expression, Soren filled her in on our unwanted neighbors. If possible, she became paler than before.

"I had no idea," she whispered to Soren, her attention fixed only on him. "I was worried for you and used a tracking enchantment on your shirt. I just had to find you."

At that, Soren lunged hungrily for her once more, and I excused myself, leaving my breakfast uneaten on the table. My anger and despair grew so visceral that I could nearly taste it coating my throat. I slammed my fist into the thick spiral wood railing at the base of the stairs, desperate for an outlet.

"Fuck," I hissed, jerking my hand back and cupping it, though the physical pain was welcoming. I hadn't realized a tracking spell was an option — an easy way to find me, should anyone care to look. Which meant that everyone had to be beyond caring.

Perhaps they assumed I was dead. By my calculations, it had been at least two weeks since the cauldron had deposited me in the middle of nowhere. The dust was possibly left as some cruel joke by the last user, but still, it had landed me in trouble only halfway through our talisman hunt. Even the Faerie with the smallest heart I knew had tracked Soren for hours across Muiranvia to ensure he was safe, and yet Blaise couldn't even be bothered to try — or Kipp, or Darrya, or Cas, or Wren, or even my father. Certainly not Finlay.

I stalked to the library, knowing damn well it wasn't the outlet I needed today, but it was the only one I had. I pulled books from the shelves, reading covers and putting them back until my heart rate calmed incrementally.

A light rap came from the doorway, and I glanced up to see Soren peering guiltily into the room.

"May I join you?" he asked, and came forward slowly at my nod. Settling on a chair next to me, he fixed me with a tender gaze, his eyes softening. "I'm sorry that it wasn't Blaise. Truly."

I shrugged; the heat of my emotions earlier had burned their way through me. Now, all I felt was cold.

"Does this mean we can leave?" I asked instead. "Can Myriam help?" I hated the idea of relying on Myriam for any support, but she was my only option.

"She does know how to use her fire magic," Soren mused, rubbing his chin thoughtfully. "Give me a few days to train her against them, and we may have a shot."

I leapt up from my seat without thinking, sending my book flying as I pulled him into a hug. He laughed in surprise and embraced me in return.

"It wasn't a yes. I won't put either of you in any more danger than necessary. But we'll see," he amended, warning against my optimism. I shrugged it off. I was more than willing to face these creatures if it meant I could go home, even if I couldn't aid with my own fire magic.

Soren leaned over to pick up the book that had thudded to the floor, inspecting the title. "Nuada's treasures, huh?"

He turned the book over in his hands, eyes flicking from the cover to me. "You wouldn't happen to be looking for his sword, would you?"

My heart thrummed excitedly. "What do you know about it?" I asked, my voice breathless. He bit his lip, contemplating something for a long moment. I held back the urge to scream at him to spit it out.

Finally, he held out his hand to me, and I peered down in confusion. "Come on," he said. "Myriam is who you need to talk to about this."

He motioned for me to follow, but I drew back warily. While I trusted Soren, I didn't trust his partner enough to share a drink with her, much less discuss plans to dismantle Nemain. Confiding in her went against every fiber of my being.

Soren noticed my hesitation and rolled his eyes. "Look. It doesn't take a Valkyrie to see you don't like her. But I can't help you like she can. If you want answers, you're going to need to listen to her."

We sat at opposite ends of the table, perched on the edges of our seats like two lionesses squaring off against one another. Though it was still the middle of the day, the skies outside had darkened, indicating the start of a storm. Myriam's face was cast in shadows, but her pale gray eyes cut through the darkness as she assessed me.

After a long moment, she turned back to Soren. "And you're sure we can trust her?"

"I feel like I should be the one asking if I can trust you," I cut in, my tone low and threatening. A clap of thunder rumbled from outside, as if to underscore my own stormy mood. She arched an eyebrow and leaned back in her chair, her surprised expression curling into a smile. Soren, who had been tense from our first words, visibly relaxed, breaking into a grin of his own.

"So she does have some bite," Myriam mused. "All right. You may still surprise me yet."

I blinked in confusion, but before I could comment, she continued.

"You may have noticed that our race is disappearing. This isn't a new development. It's been happening for, oh, at least the last two or three hundred years. Someone has been hunting us, picking us off, one by one."

I nodded, having heard this all so many times before. My mind flitted back to what we'd uncovered about the triple goddesses —

two had already died, leaving only the raven-haired woman who haunted my dreams. "Nemain."

Her lips parted slightly, and she leaned forward, visibly excited to tell the rest of the story. "Yes. A tremendously powerful, fearful goddess. But she hasn't been fighting this battle alone."

Again, I nodded, picturing the malignant creatures I'd fought in battle alongside Soren. Faeries that favored the shadows, with inky black blood coursing through their veins. "The dark Faeries."

Myriam slammed her hand on the table with a loud bang, causing me to jump. She was surprisingly strong, despite her slender frame. Her palm curled into a fist, and she pointed a finger at me, grinning with a glint in her eyes.

"Yes! But it's more than that. More than she'd want to let on. She also has the help of the lesser Fae." My lip curled at the term, but before I could comment, she continued. "Faeries across all the lands, from the lowest lines of poverty to within the very royal court. She has help on all fronts."

My pulse quickened. At the royal court? What did that mean for the queen's safety? For Darrya, or Kipp, or Finlay?

"Are you sure?" I asked uncertainly. "I know there are those who are unhappy with the queen's leadership, but she's been more pro-gressive than most. From what I hear, she's integrating all races of Fae at nearly every level, trying to foster equality."

"And that's exactly what they needed! To go from simply re-moving lesser Aes Sídhe to directly impacting the leadership source. That's how they've begun picking off members of the royal fam-ilies." Myriam replied emphatically. "I've been using my family's connections, and now, my proximity to the palace to confirm it. It's more than just a hunch. Now they have direct access to intel. They're infiltrating all the movements of the queen, her acquaintances...her army."

Her army...

Blaise.

I shook my head, trying to piece everything together. I turned to Soren, noting his pained expression.

"Not him," I whispered. He looked helplessly back at me, knowing exactly whom I referred to.

"It's impossible to say. But he did come from nothing. If anyone has experienced the inequality firsthand, it's him. He'd have more than enough reason to want to settle a score," Soren murmured.

My heart jumped to my throat, as though I would throw it up. No matter what Blaise had experienced, entire royal families had been decimated. The Blaise I knew would not take the lives of innocents.

I ran my hands through my hair several times, considering. I imagined Blaise's kind, hazel eyes and the way his full mouth felt against mine. His fierce loyalty to his people, as well as his devastation after the dark Fae invaded the palace. It didn't seem possible Blaise would double-cross anyone. But then again, he had made me believe his feelings for me were real, only to abandon me now...

"Okay. So," I ventured, deciding to move on from that explosive topic. "What does this have to do with Nuada's sword? What do you know about it?"

"I know it's one of the four talismans that, when combined with the others, can lead an army and match Nemain's power as a goddess," Myriam explained, holding my gaze. "But you already knew that, didn't you?"

I nodded, but remained silent. I wasn't offering any more information of my own until she told me what I wanted to hear. The breath I held while waiting for her to continue seemed endless, but it worked.

"Well, Soren and I have been working on two problems that have presented themselves with those talismans. The first is where those talismans are located, and the second is—" She folded her hands together, resting her chin on them and squinting at me thoughtfully. "—who is powerful enough to wield them without crumpling under the enormous power. Now I believe we have solved both problems."

"You know where the sword is?" I blurted, immediately regretting the excitement in my voice. Myriam smiled at my tone, but it lacked any genuine warmth and seemed more from the excitement of having something to hold over me. I bit the inside of my lip as she took her time to respond.

"Yes. It's in the Otherworld," she finally replied, and held up a hand as I opened my mouth. "And yes. It is possible to get there. We just need to get our hands on a silver apple branch."

My brow furrowed as I considered this odd bit of information, but then another thought barged its way into my mind, taking precedence. "Only certain people can wield the talismans?"

Myriam and Soren exchanged a weighted look. "Indeed. Neither Soren nor I can wield them. Soren had thought Finlay was a good possibility, but his proximity to the crown made it a bit too complicated. But now, here you are." Myriam's voice nearly became a purr, and my stomach turned unpleasantly at the sound. "You're even more powerful than him, and you understand what's at stake. That's what I would call a win-win situation."

I leaned back in my chair to avoid her piercing stare, which seemed almost ravenous. I glanced at Soren for help, but was forced to avert my eyes when his hopeful expression became too much to bear.

"I don't know about this," I began uncomfortably.

"Look. You may despise me, but I know a kindred soul when I see one. And part of you is exactly like me. You've always known there was more to this life — more that you were meant to do with it — and you've already started embracing that. You owe it to your friends and family, but more importantly, *yourself,* to become everything you're destined to be."

Her words unlocked a flood of memories from my visit to Lachlan's castle, when the duke allowed me to sit upon his throne and touch the first talisman. The stone's cry had made it impossible to ignore my destiny. I was to be the true ruler, the one destined to lead the armies against Nemain, and to wield the talismans against the goddess of death.

Myriam had no way of knowing all that, but she saw something in me that revealed the truth. And while I didn't fully trust her, she had a way to the talismans, a way I desperately needed after this setback. I couldn't stop now.

It was true. I despised her. But at this moment, what I despised more was how right she was.

CHAPTER FOUR

The blade withdrew easily from the goat's body, and Blaise was left disheartened. Violence was the easiest outlet; the brutal physicality of it allowed him to release his emotions with each stab or punch. He didn't like when it was over quickly.

The goat thrashed a few more times, briefly shifting into a rabbit before shedding tufts of gray fur to die in its original goblin form. Blaise snorted in disdain, stepping back from the inky black blood now pooling around the creature, a stark contrast to the green grass where it lay. In the scheme of things, Púca were relatively easy to hunt, and he had to escape his boredom. The Sluagh, while still hovering too close to Sairas for comfort, were difficult to track without committing entirely to the hunt, hence why Soren had left nearly three weeks ago to fulfill that task. Nevertheless, there were other malign Fae encroaching on the town and the palace, increasing in numbers every day.

He'd asked Katherine's father, Patrick, if he'd wanted to accompany him in his missions to deter the dark Faeries from Sairas' borders. Patrick had refused, opting instead to join Kipp and Castille on their hunts, dive into books, and keep Katherine's stallion, Gray, exercised.

He was sure Patrick hadn't slept in weeks, though he couldn't say for certain. While Blaise had worked tirelessly to track Katherine — dispatching men to scour the area surrounding the cave where she had disappeared, and ordering various tracking enchantments on everything she owned — he still had to split his efforts with his duties as commander. Patrick had taken up residence in the palace, but had not yet searched for employment or made any attempt to fit in with the people of the court. Blaise suspected he devoted his days and nights venturing further out of the palace to scour for any hint of Katherine. And yet, despite both of their efforts, no trace had been found.

Blaise gritted his teeth, stabbing into the Púca once more before jerking the blade back and wiping it clean. He knew his outlet was the least productive of them all, but his intelligence had come to a standstill. He had no leads, and helplessness was not a feeling he was used to. Even worse, it meant he had no excuses left to continue avoiding a conversation with Finlay. With a heavy sigh, he stalked back to the palace. While Larke had made no further mention of the Sluagh coming closer to town, it couldn't hurt to ensure Finlay was willing to help, should the need arise.

He nodded stiffly to the guards at the entrance of the palace, who lowered their heads in deference, and likely a little fear. He noted dully that he was positively splattered with Púca blood, which he hadn't bothered to wipe off his face, much less his clothes. Normally, he attempted to keep his face clean-shaven, his hair combed back, and his expression mild when he addressed the guards. In the past several weeks, though, he simply hadn't had the energy to. He suspected those shifts in his appearance hadn't gone unnoticed.

It used to unnerve him. He'd once feared any move he made would be a misstep, and all would know he didn't truly belong. *You're not royal,* the voice inside him would whisper. *They know, and they will never listen to you.* Over the years, he'd learned to stamp the voice down, but every now and then, it forced its way back up. The helplessness he currently felt stirred up the voice within him, and he quickened his pace as if to outrun it.

As he bounded up the steps to locate Finlay, he heard voices emanating from Patrick's room.

"—really think a Cait Sídhe will help?" Kipp was asking Patrick in a dubious tone. Blaise peered around the doorframe and saw Kate's father shrug in answer, his expression taut.

"It can't hurt. We're running out of options. I've only got a few more books to sift through, and they're not likely to get us any closer to the Otherworld, either."

"Where the hell did you even get one of those?" Cas inquired. There was always a note of humor in his tone, which Blaise appreciated. He was like Larke that way — always able to remain optimistic, even in the darkest times.

Patrick's smile was grim as he answered. "I've had her for a while; she's been my only steady company over the past ten years. I guess a spirit out there sensed my loneliness."

Blaise rapped on the door lightly as he opened it, and every gaze fixed on him. He noted the dark circles sitting under their eyes, ones he was sure had found a home under his as well. Nobody had been able to sleep much recently, and the toll was weighing on them all. Even Castille couldn't fully heal those markers away.

Blaise cleared his throat.

"I take it there hasn't been much progress," he ventured, wincing internally as their gazes all hit the floor. He wished there was more he could do to help — but then, he realized with a start, there was. Fishing in his pocket, he pulled a keyring out and tossed it at Patrick. He eyed Blaise curiously.

"The key to our army library," Blaise explained. Patrick lifted an eyebrow in response. "It mostly contains war and strategy books, but you may find something useful there. That being said, if you get caught, you didn't find this from me. Got it?" he added carefully, and Patrick nodded in understanding, pocketing the key.

"Thank you," he replied.

Blaise nodded. "It's the least I can do."

It was just the four of them there. Darrya had been gone for weeks now, using her envoy skills to weasel any vital information out of the higher-ups while attempting to keep a low profile. The updates they'd received had been laced with frustration and fury. Like Katherine, Darrya was more prone to anger than sadness — a good quality, Blaise thought, for someone on a mission. Sadness led to quitting. Rage was much more effective.

"Do any of you know where I can find Finlay?" He pivoted topics suddenly and braced for the surprise that inevitably followed.

"I think he's in the library," Kipp answered carefully, studying the blood adorning Blaise's hunting attire. Blaise plastered a smile on his face, hoping it didn't look as fake as it felt.

"Thanks," he answered, turning back towards the door.

"What do you need with him?" Cas called as he walked away. Blaise knew their concern was warranted. On more than one occasion, they'd witnessed tension that lingered between him and Finlay over Katherine.

"Just to talk," Blaise said over his shoulder. "Don't worry, I won't kill the prince."

The others chuckled in response.

"Yet," he added softly as he closed the door, its eerie groan covering his words as it shut.

He found Finlay sprawled across a leather couch in the library, the soft glow from the window shining on his blond hair. Despite his lazy posture, Blaise could tell he was stressed from the way his jaw clenched.

Hearing Blaise's clipped footsteps, Finlay glanced up. If it were even possible, he stiffened further, and Blaise slowed, attempting to soften the storm in his expression. He'd taken a quick detour to change out of his bloodstained clothes, but his mind raced as he considered how to treat the prince as a positive acquaintance, even as jealousy reared its ugly head.

The words they'd exchanged before Katherine arrived in Muiranvia had been minimal. Blaise's commands had always come from the queen herself, and Finlay had mostly stayed away from the palace, instead opting to live and train in his hometown. Finlay's reputation grated on Blaise, renowned as a spoiled royal with all the power a Faerie could desire, yet with a penchant for irresponsible pleasures. Since Katherine's arrival — and their joint attraction to her — their exchanges had been nothing but hostile. He certainly couldn't clap Finlay on the shoulder and say anything in jest, like he normally could with Larke or Soren.

Luckily, Finlay spoke first.

"Blaise. To what do I owe this displeasure?" His tone was low and slightly mocking, but his lips twitched into a small smile. A peace offering of sorts. Blaise took the opening.

"We have a bit of a problem," he started, "with a flock of Sluagh."

Finlay's eyebrows raised, and he let out a soft laugh. "Of all the things I thought you would say, that was *not* on the list."

Despite himself, Blaise offered a slight grin, but swiftly brushed aside any feelings of camaraderie. "We can handle a few at a time, but if the flock grows bolder or increases in size, we could really use your help. Not only can your fire magic kill them, but it will give us the light we'll need at night to fight alongside you."

Finlay nodded in understanding and straightened on the couch. "Yes, that makes sense. Of course I'll help. Just send for me when I'm needed."

Blaise must have looked as shocked as he felt, because Finlay's expression turned curious.

"What, did you assume I'd be sequestered amongst my royal rich-es?" he asked, his tone sarcastic.

"No," Blaise admitted honestly, recalling Finlay's steadfast aid in the battle at the palace. "I know you're up for a fight. I just wasn't sure—" he paused, trying to figure out the right way to phrase it. "It would mean you'd always have to be alert, to keep yourself and others safe. Alert and sober," he finished haltingly.

A muscle in Finlay's jaw twitched, and Blaise knew he'd struck a nerve, no matter how carefully he'd tried to word the request. Even if he hadn't seen it firsthand — which he had, on many occasions — stories of Finlay's parties were near legendary, as was the state he was in during them. For decades, he was rarely seen without either a flask or a cigarette in hand, and usually, he had both.

"I haven't been under the influence. Not for a while. Not since—" Finlay hesitated, glancing down for a moment before meeting Blaise's gaze. "Well, you know."

"Yeah," Blaise answered, ignoring the pang of despair. Instead, he envisioned Katherine's eyes, bright and gold like sunshine, with her beaming smile to match. "I know."

Chapter Five

The cat wouldn't leave me alone. Sometimes I was glad for its company, especially when it slept on my chest as the nights cooled, but other times I just wanted it out of my way.

This was one of those moments. My face tickled, and I swiped at my nose, removing the offending black hair. I looked up from my book to glare at the offending creature, which lay on my stomach, swishing its sleek tail.

Despite its healthy appearance, I was certain my new feline friend was simply a stray that had wandered in from the woods. Though it had taken a liking to me immediately, I hadn't seen it interact with anyone else. As far as I knew, Myriam's mansion was the only house for miles; I certainly hadn't seen any other signs of life outside, so we were the cat's best option for food and warmth. Myriam didn't strike me as the type to care for a pet — or much of anything, for that matter.

"Don't you have somewhere else to be?" I demanded, but of course, it didn't respond. It didn't even flinch at my tone; instead, it gave another flick of its tail and fixed me with an intense stare, its pale gold eyes unblinking. I glanced away first, unnerved, but still feel its gaze on me.

"Aren't you supposed to be bad luck?" I muttered, slamming the book closed and placing it under my arm. It was at least the fourth book I'd snagged from the library in as many weeks, and while I'd found some fiction and romance novels, even those were growing dull. I shrugged the cat off as I slipped off the bed, planning to move to the library.

"Actually, black cats are considered good luck here."

I jumped, a hand flying to my chest. Soren stood in the doorway, smiling.

"By the gods," I groaned, "you're just as stealthy as the cat!"

I didn't mean it as a compliment, but Soren's grin grew nonetheless. With a wink, he slid away as silently as he had come. I rolled my eyes and peered down at the cat, who had jumped off the bed to join me. It didn't so much as glance in Soren's direction. That didn't surprise me, though; it completely ignored our two other cohabitants, focusing all its time and attention on me. I supposed I was the only one to feed it, but it still struck me as odd.

For that reason alone, I was baffled when it ran a few paces ahead and then stopped, turning to me with a pointed look. I tilted my head, watching as it paced in circles, meowing.

"What?" I asked, irritated.

It simply meowed louder.

"Oh, fine," I grumbled, tossing the book on my bed. Once I began moving toward the small creature, it became silent and moved deftly down the stairs. On impulse, I went after it, sensing its desire for me to follow. When it scratched the front door, though, I hesitated, thinking of the danger that lurked outside. A dark image flashed across my mind, and I imagined the tiny creature swooped up in the clutches of a Sluagh.

I turned away, but the moment I did, its cries resumed, and it began clawing aggressively at the door. I bit my lip and shook my head, but its cries only intensified.

Finally, I opened the door.

The cat burst outside instantly, making a beeline for the stable.

"What the fuck?" I froze in the doorway and gazed up at the sky nervously.

The peaks of mountains toward the west indicated the whereabouts of Myriam's home — somewhere in Muiranvia, as I already knew, but clearly far north. My geographical knowledge was limited, but from what I recalled, there wasn't much in the way of civilization in northern Muiranvia, except along the northernmost tip, which was home to small port towns that serviced the small channel between Muiranvia and Daersill. The tall forest trees cast shadows on the ground, growing frosty as temperatures plummeted toward winter.

When I determined there was nothing unusual combing the skies, I scrambled after the cat, but still felt the familiar prick of nausea. I quickened my pace to reach the barn, where the cat had leapt through the barn door window and into Fathom's stall.

I slid the barn door open and clambered inside. The nausea didn't dissipate, but when I peered around, I finally located the cat — right on top of the horse's back. Fathom, to my surprise, did not shy away; rather, he seemed pretty content to have the cat perched atop him. The cat stared at me, those yellow-gold eyes wide and unblinking.

I stood there, warring with two voices in my head. The first told me to return to the mansion, to stop playing this dangerous game for no reason. The second told me that, while bizarre, this was a sign to try and get me home, to my friends and family.

On impulse, I grabbed Fathom's halter off the hanger by the stall and tied it on him, leading him out. His steps were sloping, but the cat didn't move from its position on its back. I snorted at the visual, turning to locate his tack.

As I saddled him, I had to pause and rest my forehead against his warm neck, the nausea becoming overwhelming. The cat jumped off Fathom's back once the saddle landed too close for comfort, landing on the ledge of the stall door. It shot me a disdainful look over being displaced and began grooming itself. I watched it for a long moment while waiting for the nausea to subside.

This is a stupid idea, I thought. *I'm risking my life to try and get back to friends and family that don't even want me. Why would I go to them?*

I froze. Kipp, Cas, Wren, and Darrya hadn't even searched for me. My father had abandoned me for a second time, barely after I had come to terms with his first betrayal. And Blaise…

Blaise was the worst of them all. He'd made me fall for him while hiding who he truly was.

They're neither friends nor family. Why would you risk your life to go to them? They don't love you.

I gritted my teeth, bracing my hands against the saddle. My fingers toyed with the cinch, tempted to unsaddle Fathom and be done with this madness. Who did I have to go back to? Who would actually want to see me?

The only person I could think of irritated me half the time, but there he was, appearing in my brain nonetheless. His golden hair, pale blue eyes, and snarky attitude burned into my memory, and I realized with a jolt that I *missed* him. He'd been under no obligation to find me, so I wasn't upset he hadn't come to my aid. I considered him neither friend nor family, and yet, he was the only one I wanted to go back to. The only one who may want me.

Fathom stomped, growing impatient. I grabbed his bridle and threw it over his halter before I could rethink my decision. It was difficult to ignore the nausea, bordering on painful as I left the barn, but it urged me to quicken my pace as I slammed the door shut.

I heard a plaintive meow, and on a whim, I ducked to scoop up the cat, tucking it in the billowy shirt I'd stolen from Myriam's closet. It curled up against my side like it had meant to be there the entire time, and I couldn't help but grin when its golden eyes peeked up at me.

I mounted and turned Fathom southward, ensuring I kept the mountain range to my right. I peered up at the sky, which remained blissfully clear. It was still early in the day, but Soren had said we were several hours from Sairas. Easily a full day's ride, then, give or take. I'd likely arrive after nightfall. But it didn't matter — I had been cooped up for too long, and if I went back inside, I knew I would change my mind. It was now or never.

"Alright, you two," I said, clicking my tongue and urging Fathom forward. "Let's go find Finlay."

Chapter Six

The dreams wouldn't stop. Night after night, they returned — blissful in the moment, but his heart cleaved in two every morning when he woke. Sometimes he laid his head back down on the pillow, squeezing his eyes shut to will the dreams back to him. Other times, he escaped to the fresh air outside, hoping to distance himself from the images that haunted him.

In those dreams, he imagined Kate's honey-colored eyes and the way they crinkled slightly at the edges when she smiled. He recreated their conversations, admiring her sharp tongue and how she fearlessly stuck to her ideals. Mostly, he envisioned the way she'd looked on his lap, as he felt her breathing hitch and her head tilt back, their bodies consumed with the sole need for one another.

With his eyes closed, he could imagine it was something they both wanted. Awake, he knew it was all in his head, driven by the *voitín*. But like a drug, he kept returning to the source, despite the pain it delivered when he awoke.

Lately, he'd been desperate for his cigarettes and whiskey. Without Kate's closeness, that familiar ache deepened again, settling back into him as it had in the decades before her. At least, he reasoned, the dreams that haunted him now were tinged with beauty. A dark kind of hope.

They were leagues better than his previous nightmares — the ones that replayed his parents' demise. Those were rife with images of crimson-stained floors, ominous shadows, and blood-curdling shrieks that made his toes curl in terror. Every morning after those dreams, he woke in a worse state than if he hadn't slept at all. His best bet against such visions was to induce a dreamless slumber.

His fingers twitched, desperate for a surge of nicotine. This was one of those days where he'd escaped outside, and he breathed in deeply, reminding himself of all the reasons to stay sober, their hunt for the sword remaining at the top of the list. It was the only leverage they had so far, the bait they needed. Even so, being sober meant taking life on the chin. And that truly *sucked.*

Finlay blinked, resurfacing from his memories — were they memories, if they were only in his dreams? — as a soft breeze sent a leaf twirling right under his nose. He glanced up to find his cousin sauntering over to where he sat in the courtyard, finally back from her travels. She plopped down next to him, not bothering to shield her powder blue dress from the dirt.

"You're thinking so hard, I can almost hear it," she began pointedly, her brown eyes boring into his. Finlay sent a volley of air toward her in return, but his control over the air element was far clumsier than hers. The leaf he'd picked up with the breeze hit her cheek, and she rolled her eyes.

"Stick to what you're good at, fire prince," she said with a good-natured laugh, and handed him the leaf. He picked at it slowly, thinking.

It made no sense, truly. Kate wasn't his — he wasn't even sure if she was Blaise's — and yet, he continued lusting after her. He'd already admitted he'd give up the throne for her, and though he never truly wished to rule, he would have fought anyone else to keep the position. He was committed to helping her hunt down the talismans, and without a doubt, he knew he'd kill for her. His emotions surged when he was around her, yet they still made no sense to him.

"If she gets hurt—" he started, crumpling the leaf in his fist, and Darrya placed a hand over his.

"—she won't," she cut him off, gently but firmly. He gave her a grateful smile as she ruffled his hair. Darrya had noticed long ago how he'd changed with Kate around, but he wasn't sure she understood the extent of it. Not that he was prepared to admit how much he pined after a woman unlikely to ever return his feelings.

"Her father believes he's found a way into the Otherworld," Darrya continued.

Finlay perked up then, his heart swelling with hope. "He believes, or he knows?"

He'd seen the way Patrick had thrown himself into the cause, yet Finlay still kept his distance from him. Kate's father barely slept, his efforts endless. After a while, Finlay had to admit, it was more than just for his own interests, and he genuinely wanted to help his daughter. Pat had earned a bit of respect back in his mind, but he still remained somewhat apprehensive.

"Right now, it's just a hunch," Darrya admitted. "But he found an ancient text that states heroes can be invited in if they bring a silver apple branch as an offering."

Finlay wiped a hand across his face in exasperation. "Great. And where do we find *that?*"

She shrugged. "I'm not positive. But there is someone who might know," she ventured, throwing a cautious look his way. Her warm brown eyes bore a pleading look that told Finlay all he needed to know.

"No," he said. "No, no, no." He tossed the shredded pieces of leaf to the ground and stood. "I haven't spoken to great-grandma since I forced her hand in allowing Kate and her father to stay here. I doubt she'll even listen to me."

Darrya pinched his arm, and he flinched. "What was that for?"

"There's a reason you were able to convince her before. She *loves* you. Anything you care about enough, she will, too." She smiled warmly. "You're family."

"Ah, but you forget. Our family is completely dysfunctional. Not to mention prone to tragedy." His words rang with a stinging truth, but he smirked in an attempt to breeze over it. He'd never been the type to express his pain; rather, he drowned it in humor to soften its blow. Humor, and various drugs. Kate was the only person he'd felt safe enough with to let those walls down.

It felt as though he'd begun to build something in her presence — a strong and tangible fortress to aid his broken soul. But in the weeks following her absence, he'd discovered that the fortress had been made out of nothing more than sand: fragile, temporary, and easily washed away. The waves came in many different forms, but the strongest was his guilt. If he'd seen the signs, if he had been the one to offer himself to the cauldron instead, perhaps she'd still be here. While sleeping, he was graced with sweet memories of her, but nightmares now haunted his waking thoughts.

Darrya held her hands up with a chuckle, and he grinned appreciatively in return. She never pushed him on things, and for that, he was grateful.

He waved good-bye as he headed back to his room, hoping to steal a few minutes — or hours — with a novel before working up the courage to face his great-grandmother. When he returned to his room, however, he saw the last person he expected.

"Kate."

Finlay blinked, too surprised to even use his nickname for her. She looked...*different.* How long had it been since he'd last seen her? Breathed the same air as her?

"You're safe," he managed to get out. "You're here. How — how did you get here?"

"I have my ways," she replied. Her voice was surprisingly sultry as she shrugged off her overcoat. His eyes traveled over her appearance, just as seductive as her voice. She wore Faerie clothing that clearly wasn't her own — tight black leather pants and a billowy white shirt that laced in the front. She left a large part of the top untied and open, mimicking Finlay's normal style, but it looked leagues better on her. His eyebrows lifted as realization dawned on him.

"What are you here for, Kate?" he asked, his voice brimming with curiosity. He stepped further into the room, and her eyes tracked his every movement. His muscles went taut at the scrutiny.

"Just to talk," she said, but it was in a voice far too innocent for her. Finlay picked up on it immediately. He sat on the side of his bed, but made no move to invite her.

"I see. And why are you not currently...*talking* with Blaise?" he questioned stiffly, hating the jealousy that coursed through his veins at the unbidden image of them together — the memory of finding the pair in Kate's room, clearly having recently been together in more ways than one.

An indecipherable look flitted across her face, but it was gone in a flash, replaced by a slow smile.

"Blaise and I have...parted ways." Her voice was strong and matter-of-fact, perhaps with a hint of anger. He cocked his head, attempting to solve the riddle in that, but she began moving towards him in a way that told him he was in dangerous territory indeed.

He shifted back further onto the bed in confusion, creating space between them as his mind raced. From the brief encounters he'd had with Blaise, there had been no mention of Kate's return. He'd seen him mere days ago. He had appeared disheveled ever since Kate's absence; pained lines etched his face, betraying the weight of the world on his shoulders. Was their parting of ways as recent as tonight? Had Blaise found her, only for an argument to ensue and lead her here?

"I'm pretty sure he always knew how I truly felt about you." Kate continued forward, moving to stand between his legs. She leaned in, her shirt falling open just enough to expose her chest to him.

Despite his other self-destructive habits, Finlay liked to think he had retained some honor. That, however, flew out the window as his eyes traveled downward, reveling in the sight of her lacey black bra.

"You understand me. You understand what I want," she murmured, taking his hands and moving them to her waist. Finlay's throat constricted, and he tested the waters, moving his hands to her backside.

"I don't understand this," he admitted.

She laughed and crawled onto the bed to straddle him. A strangled sound built low in his throat, and his hands began moving of their own volition. She had never been frail or slender; rather, she was athletic and toned, and he relished that fact as he ran his hands over her every line and curve. She was sexy, enchanting, and unbreakable. She leaned in and kissed his neck, and this time he truly groaned at the feel of her lips on his skin.

"Join us," she whispered, hands tracing their way down his chest. "Join us in the fight."

"I already have, little angel," he muttered. Confusion clouded his already muddled thoughts, but he shoved them away. "We all have." His hands trailed over the back of her bra, toying with the clasp.

"No. The others gave up a long time ago, if they were ever on our side to begin with. I'm talking about the *real* fight."

His hands stilled. *What?*

Kate pulled back, fixing her amber eyes on him. Her voice was steady, but lacked the usual passion and fire from when she discussed this in the past.

He took a moment to study her, trying to detect if anything else was amiss. Thankfully, she looked uninjured. Her face was set in a determined line, gaze raking over him in a way that bluntly conveyed her intentions. Her hands followed the trail her eyes had taken, and he moved into her touch on impulse. His thoughts jumbled as he relished the feel of her against him, warm and whole and somehow, in this moment, *his.*

"What are you talking about?" he asked, his interest waning slightly as he nuzzled her neck. Gods, he loved the smell of her, that soft, wild floral scent. It was a scent he associated as much with her as the meadows of clover and primrose surrounding the palace. Both smelled like home.

"The fight against the lesser Fae. They're with Nemain. We need to ensure the survival of our race," she continued, voice dark. "Soren, Myriam, and I are hunting the real culprits. And the talismans will help put us back in our rightful positions, once and for all."

Finlay's hands froze for a final time. What in all the gods' names was she talking about? It was as though she was trying to fit puzzle pieces into an opening where they didn't fit. Something was wrong here; wrong with her. The division of the Fae was a very real issue, often disparaged by those in high ranks, but not Kate. That was not her outlook. Finlay didn't want to lead, but when he — or Kate — inevitably did, that was one of the first changes they would make.

Kate had never once looked down upon anyone in the manner she displayed now. The only times he'd seen her darken like this was to defend those she loved against the malign Fae borne of the shadows. She loved all her friends and family without condition, loved without regard to their race or socioeconomic status. The words she was uttering were not — could not — be her own.

He examined her excited face, cupping her cheek. She pressed into it, and he tried to ignore the movement while his thoughts raced. Her eyes, he now noticed, were tinged with black, and her sultry smile did not quite reach them. He'd only ever read about this, but all signs pointed to it.

Was it possible?

His hand moved off her cheek to her shirt, pulling the open lace gently to the side...and there it was.

Her mark had been entirely covered with a new symbol. The Shield Knot was now a dull background to a new mark; the bright, bold ink over the top of it boasting three interconnected coils. They spiraled out at three angles that loosely interlocked at the center.

Finlay's fingers wrapped around her arm, squeezing tight.

"Fuck," he hissed.

The Triskele.

The Triple Spiral symbol represented all connections that came in threes: death, birth, and reincarnation most prominent among them. It also portrayed the connection between humans, gods, and Faeries. And — perhaps most conveniently — a connection that only a triple god or goddess could leverage for their own whims. There wasn't a doubt in his mind who had been the one to re-mark her.

"Hold on, Kate," Finlay pleaded, his hands moving to tighten on her arms. She squirmed uncomfortably, and he realized he was outmatched if she fought back or attempted to run. He couldn't — wouldn't — raise a hand against her, but she wouldn't hesitate against him. Especially with her new mark.

"Why?" she asked, eyes narrowing. "Why won't you join me?"

"I will," Finlay hedged. He carefully shifted to stroke her arm instead, feigning complicity. "But I think the others should be a part of this conversation as well. They'll want to join you."

Kate scowled and shifted off him. He bent over, tactfully covering the evidence of his arousal — not that she hadn't been able to feel it herself only moments before.

"Why should I?" she demanded. "They didn't even care enough to look for me. They wouldn't understand. They aren't like us."

"Because this isn't you!" he burst out, running a hand through his hair in frustration. "Gods dammit, Kate."

Her eyes widened as she stepped for the door, opening it a fraction of an inch. Finlay jumped up, fingertips flickering with sparks. Perhaps if he lit the door on fire, she would be forced to stay...? He shook the thought away almost immediately. She would force herself through it, and he couldn't stand the idea of hurting her, even if it wasn't really *her* right now.

"I thought you wanted me," she said, voice low voice and tinged with genuine hurt.

Finlay bit his cheek, considering his next words. "I do, little angel," he replied earnestly. "I want you so badly it haunts my dreams. But not like this."

"Like what?" She raised an eyebrow, unaware of the profoundness of the situation. In that moment, he noticed all the minor details he hadn't noticed before — the manic tint in her darkened eyes, the lack of responsiveness in her body, the emotionlessness of her words, and even her unusual wardrobe. When he'd imagined this moment, he'd imagined a different scenario, a different...Kate.

"I want you to care." His words were soft and truthful, despite the larger issue at hand. His shoulders sank, however, as no emotion registered in her expression.

"Well. I'm sorry you feel that way," she responded flatly. Finlay felt his heart crack at the words. He didn't know if this exchange conveyed Kate's true feelings or if it was the result of being re-marked. He wasn't sure he wanted the answer.

Finlay closed his eyes and ran his hands over his face, blowing out an exasperated breath. By the time he looked back up, Kate had disappeared, and he was alone once more with his pounding heart.

The only good thing to come out of their interaction, Finlay reasoned, was that his decision was solidified. He'd gather the others tonight, and the next morning, he'd pay a visit to his great-grandmother. He only hoped one of them would have the answers that could save Kate. That could save all of them.

CHAPTER SEVEN

Finlay was the last person Blaise expected to see when he stumbled from his bed to answer the aggressive banging on his door. He opened his mouth to question him, but Finlay grabbed his wrist and dragged him halfway out the door. Blaise's wrist seared from the touch, Finlay having clearly forgotten to dampen his fire magic in his craze.

"Shit, man," Blaise snapped, yanking back his wrist and wringing it. "What the hell?"

"We need to get the others," Finlay said, his voice broken and frantic. Blaise met his gaze and noted the panic in it. He raised his hands.

"Okay, okay, I'm coming," he replied gently, darting back into his room to grab a shirt, shoes, and pants. He pulled them on as they left, struggling to keep up with Finlay's pace. "Do you mind telling me what this is about?"

"Kate." Finlay's reply was short, and the anguish in his tone had Blaise's heart racing. Before he could reply, however, Finlay was banging on Darrya's door, repeating a version of the same frenzied show he'd put on with Blaise. He did the same with Kipp and Patrick, and when they were all gathered, Blaise lost his last scrap of patience and forced the prince to sit in Patrick's room.

"Okay, Finlay. Everyone she knows in the palace is here," he said roughly. "Now, *what* happened?"

Finlay looked over at him helplessly. His long, golden hair sprawled out at every angle, and he wore the same burgundy leather pants and tan, laced shirt from earlier, indicating he hadn't so much as changed for bed. Frantic exhaustion was rife across his face, but his eyes shone clear, indicating that whatever had happened, he was stone-cold sober.

"She's been re-marked," he said, "with the Triskele."

The tension in the air snapped, even as Blaise's mind raced to place the familiar-sounding word. Kipp swore loudly, and Darrya clutched his hand, eyes swimming with alarm as she turned to comfort him. Behind Blaise, there was a loud bang as a piece of furniture slammed into the wall, the splintering crack of wood resounding through the room. He didn't have to look to know Katherine's father had taken his rage out on the nearest inanimate object. Finally, the words clicked in his mind.

"So, we were right. Nemain got to her," Blaise stated quietly. His emotions threatened to drown him, and it took all his training to shove them aside. As commander, he had long since learned to fully disconnect from them, treating them as a foreign entity his body needed to expel. If he didn't, he would crumble from the sheer weight of them. If there was a time to keep his wits about him, it was now. Perhaps he'd revisit them later and deal with them then — but the odds were better that he wouldn't.

"That must be what happened when you all made it to the cauldron," Darrya breathed, dumbfounded. "Nemain knew you were going for it and made it there first. She was going to capture whoever had been working their way through the talismans."

"It must have been covered in Faerie dust. Enchanted to send whoever touched it right into her grasp. Fucking hell, I *knew* it was too easy to get to it!" Kipp exclaimed, his voice rising as he spoke.

Blaise glanced over to see Kipp trembling, a low growl beginning in his throat. Darrya sidled a few steps away as the whites of Kipp's eyes began disappearing, replaced by a more lupine expression. With a start, Blaise realized he was starting to shift.

"Keep it together, Kipp," he warned. Dealing with an emotional wolf was the last thing they needed right now. At Kipp's sidelong glare, he tried another avenue and added gently, "We need you here. *She* needs you here."

It took a moment, but Kipp nodded, and his eyes slowly returned to normal.

"We were all played a fool," Patrick said finally, his voice low but steady. Annihilating the chair must have helped, and Blaise couldn't judge; he was certain many things in his own room would meet their demise later tonight. "How did you find this out?"

They all turned to Finlay, who spoke. "She came to visit me. When she began talking about our superior race, and how the lesser Fae were to blame, I knew it wasn't her. It seems like Soren and Myriam are in on it, too."

Blaise saw red.

Soren had sent him a note, explaining his hunt as the reason for his extended absence — it made too much sense to disregard. He didn't think Soren would let his guard down enough to be re-marked himself, but...Blaise had seen the way his friend looked at Myriam and knew he had open wounds, left from a life deprived of the kind of love one needed growing up. Myriam could have spotted that weakness, too, twisting love over time to work in her favor.

Blaise clenched his fists, nails cutting into his palms and drawing blood. Kate had seen that malice in Myriam from the start, whereas Blaise hadn't. He'd been blinded by his trust in Soren and had no opinion of her at all, past his approval of Soren's happiness. While a part of him understood how it could have happened, it didn't take away the fury he felt at Soren's betrayal. He filed away the mental hit to satiate his rage.

Kipp let out a soft snarl, but didn't begin his shift again. Instead, he asked, "I know we can't track her with magic, because she's been blocked, but if she's been able to leave this whole time, why didn't she come find one of *us* right away?"

"Because she would have been ordered not to visit family or friends," Patrick said flatly. "And some regular emotional manipulation was likely tossed in for good measure."

"She did say you didn't care enough to look for her," Finlay admitted, a grief-stricken look on his face. Blaise's heart twisted at the thought of Kate feeling abandoned by them all, as though they hadn't been looking for her this whole time. He allowed himself to feel the despair over that, letting it fuel him.

"But she wouldn't really consider you a friend. You were the loophole Nemain didn't expect," Darrya added thoughtfully.

Blaise tilted his head, considering Finlay as a slight flush colored the prince's cheeks. His fists tightened once more in realization. Blaise had seen Katherine's mark several times and had even suggested its placement. He could wager a guess at how Finlay stumbled upon the new mark.

He knew Finlay wasn't opposed to the idea of seeing Katherine undressed, but it told him something he'd been avoiding — something worse. Perhaps Katherine considered Finlay as neither friend nor family, but as something else entirely. And tonight, she'd come to see that through. All it had taken was magically removing him from the equation. Blaise practically choked on his rage, and Finlay averted his eyes, clearly sensing the venom clouding the atmosphere.

"Why didn't you go after her, Fin?" Darrya demanded, and Finlay tossed her a guilty look.

"I thought about it. I really did,' he replied. "But with that mark and the way she was acting, I was certain she would fight me with everything she had. And I wouldn't fight back."

At least, Blaise thought, they agreed on that. Neither could lay a finger on her. He relaxed slightly, realizing that whatever Finlay felt for her, it meant he wouldn't hurt her.

"So, we go after her now," Kipp said eagerly, turning to the door. "She can't have gotten far."

Patrick shook his head. "As much as I'd love that, Kipp, she's probably long gone by now. And we still have no way to track her." He paused, and the entire room visibly deflated.

"The way I see it," Patrick added, "we just need to make slight amendments to our original plan. We now know that Katie's safe, and whom she's with." His voice trembled slightly. "Which means our main plan to find the sword will still lead us back to her. Nemain is clearly hunting the talismans, too, and if she has the choice, she'll trade Kate for the sword. That's what she really wants."

Blaise nodded emphatically, feeling a sense of relief. The plan they'd all been working feverishly toward was now solidified and would not go to waste.

"But now, we have to figure out how to remove the Triskele and its magic. Or else, she won't even want to come with us," Darrya added softly, her eyes flicking between Finlay and Patrick.

At her words, Kipp let out a soft whine, and Blaise felt a pang of sympathy for him. Despite their storied past, they'd long since resolved their petty disagreements to put Katherine first. Kipp and Katherine's friendship was strong, and he felt a duty to protect her after bringing her into this realm. Blaise knew all too well that overwhelming sense of responsibility for others. As much as he tried to avoid it while awake, his dreams were haunted by those he led to battle that came back injured — or worse, those that didn't return at all.

"I'll ask my markman tomorrow," Blaise said. He shook off the memories and bit down on his emotions as they threatened to rush forward once more. *Deal with them later.* "If he doesn't know outright, he'll surely have a connection to someone who knows how to remove it."

"And I plan on asking the queen what she knows about the silver apple branch tomorrow," Finlay added.

"I'll fill in Cas and Wren tomorrow as well. Maybe they'll have some more ideas, or even some way Cas can help by healing the mark?" Kipp's suggestion was more of a question, to which everyone nodded their agreement. He'd never heard of such a solution, but it could never hurt to have a healer involved, Blaise thought.

"So, we're decided," Darrya chimed in hopefully. "By this time tomorrow, we could be on our way to the Otherworld."

They exchanged apprehensive smiles, not quite feeling cheerful, but having a way forward nonetheless. The only one whose lips remained firmly downturned was Patrick. Blaise was certain he wouldn't smile again until he had his daughter back. He had avoided watching her grow up, missing crucial moments of her life to protect and keep her from harm, only for her to fall into its clutches shortly after his return. The heartbreak was written in every frown line and every mark of tension on his face. Blaise couldn't tell if the news today had alleviated his pain, or merely deepened it.

As they all departed Patrick's room and returned to their own, Blaise pulled Finlay abruptly to the side, shoving him against the wall and waiting until he was certain they were alone.

"Look, man, it all happened so fast. I need you to know that, if I had the whole story, I wouldn't have done that to her or to you—" Finlay rambled, lifting his palms helplessly.

"Shut up. It's not about that," Blaise hissed, though his palm twitched, itching for a release from everything he held inside. If Finlay kept talking, it was entirely possible his face would end up on the receiving end of that, royal consequences be damned.

Luckily, the prince listened for once, falling silent and allowing Blaise to continue.

"I need to know. Do you love her?"

A baffled look flitted across Finlay's face, quickly replaced by contemplation. After a few heavy moments, he gave a slow nod. Blaise studied his expression for any signs of dishonesty, but found only nervous truth. Part of him broke at that, but he took a deep breath.

"In that case, I need you to listen to me. Listen carefully and tell no one. Can you do that?"

Finlay nodded, and Blaise launched into his story.

Finlay's sky-blue eyes had widened to the size of saucers by the time Blaise finished. He gave the prince several long moments to absorb the information.

"Blaise..." Finlay hesitated. "Are you sure there isn't someone else you should be telling this to? Asking to do this?"

Blaise shook his head emphatically. It had taken him a while to put the pieces together, but he was certain this was the right path. The right way forward.

"It has to be you. You're a pain in my ass, but I trust you. Do you trust me?" He turned the question on its head, and Finlay returned the nod without hesitation. Blaise reached into the back of his pants and produced a small blade, similar to the one he'd originally given Katherine.

"By the gods, do you always carry a blade on you?" Finlay asked, eyeing the dagger. Blaise let out a choked laugh.

"Indeed. In fact, I think it's time you start," he replied beseechingly. In one deft movement, he grabbed Finlay's palm and slit it open. Finlay exhaled sharply but didn't move. Blaise sliced his own palm, and after letting it bleed for a moment, pressed his palm to Finlay's. They met each other's gaze.

"Will you uphold this promise?" Blaise asked.

Finlay's response was immediate. "I will."

Blaise murmured a few words, and a glow rose between their palms, disappearing as quickly as it came. When their hands disconnected, the cuts had disappeared, replaced by a small, white scar in the shape of a Trinity Knot marking both of their palms as a sign of their promise, bound by magic. Their shared look was weighted.

"This doesn't mean I like you," Blaise muttered, but only half-heartedly, to sever the heavy moment. In any case, it worked, and Finlay offered a sad smile in return.

"Perhaps someday, I can prove myself likable enough."

Blaise clenched his jaw, thinking through what he had just shared. "For the both of us, I hope so."

Chapter Eight

Avalas was a strange pocket of land, settled at the southernmost edge of Muiranvia. It was lush and green, a stark contrast to the largely infertile stretch of land covering Leyteras to the east, likely due to the large lake that separated the towns. It was tucked low in a valley, surrounded by stretches of orchards. Finding the silver apple branch would be like finding a needle in a haystack.

Blaise straightened when they landed, dusting his leathers off as he gave a sidelong glance to Patrick and Kipp. They wore the army's fighting leathers, too, though both appeared uncomfortable in them. He bit back a smile at the comical sight.

It was a strange group, to be sure. He'd ordered Larke to stay behind — the only one Blaise trusted to keep things running smoothly in his absence; he didn't want any other soldiers finding out the truth of this errand in case any were compromised. Finlay had suggested retrieving the silver apple branch here, on a hunch gathered from his great-grandmother. Yet much to Finlay's dismay, he was put under strict orders from the queen to stay behind. Blaise understood his disappointment — there was a chance, no matter how small, that they might run into Kate. His mouth went dry at the mere prospect of seeing her again.

Three people were more than enough for a quick search of the orchards surrounding Avalas, so ultimately, Katherine's father and Kipp were the only two to join him. They stared at the endless rows of trees; red and yellow apples dotted their branches and stretched out for miles in every direction. Blaise knew they all shared the same thought: it would take the three of them ages to locate what they were after.

Despite his deflation at the sight, he still felt a pleasant buzzing in his soul. Trees carried an energy of their own, and the older they were, the more magic they absorbed from the earth. Even without any of the elemental magic that coursed through the veins of the Aes Sídhe, Blaise could feel the gentle hum in the atmosphere, vibrating from the trees themselves.

"Where is the highest point?" Patrick asked at last.

Blaise turned to him curiously. "Why?"

"Because that's where lightning would be most likely to hit," Kipp guessed, looking to Patrick for confirmation, who nodded. "In that case...there."

He pointed, and as they set off for higher land, realization dawned on Blaise. Yes — all trees had energy, but those struck by lightning became sacred, their wood then used for charms. The last time he'd heard of an oak tree struck by lightning, many of his soldiers had requested temporary leave and traveled endless miles to collect pieces of it to save for enchantments, or to simply carry for protection. The oak tree was considered the most powerful, but the apple tree was a symbol of the Otherworld. It made sense that the offering had to be a lightning-struck branch.

They crested the hill for a better vantage point to survey the surrounding orchards. Off in the distance, Blaise spotted a trail of smoke floating above the small town of Avalas, but—

"There." He gestured ahead. "That's the highest point."

They were only one hill away from the tallest point, separated by a small stretch of trees, perhaps a half-mile away. From this short distance, Blaise could see a discolored tree standing at the center. It was split down the middle where the lightning had struck. Instead of the usual lighter, raw wood exposed underneath, silver threads webbed across the trunk and branches. His pulse quickened.

The others saw it too, and he heard Patrick exhale deeply. They began down the hill in unison, a sense of relief washing over him at how easy the task had turned out to be.

As though life wanted to play a cruel joke on him, a crackling sound split through the air. Everyone tensed, and Blaise's hand instantly clasped his dagger, ducking into a fighter's stance. Their eyes snapped to the source of the sound, a cloud of ash flecked with gold that rose in the distance. Faerie dust.

A single form stepped out from the dust, heading directly toward the same tree they'd been hunting.

Kipp growled. "We aren't alone."

They sprinted their way through the remaining row of trees, cresting the hill at the same time as the stranger who had portaled in. The form was clearly Myriam, and after a quick sweep across the landscape, Blaise determined she was alone. She slowed as surprise etched across her pale face — she was not expecting company, either.

"Where is Kate, Myriam?" Blaise demanded, clutching his dagger. The soft breeze signaled Kipp's shift behind him, and the ground trembled beneath them in warning — Patrick's earth magic, to be sure.

Myriam's cool face gave little away. She simply eyed him reproachfully, a hand moving to her own sheathed blade. "I suppose you'll just have to keep me alive to find out," she replied lightly.

It was all the confirmation Blaise needed: she had Kate. Perhaps he couldn't *kill* her, but he could injure her, take her hostage, and force the answers from her. He charged.

She ducked his first swipe with surprising ease and drew her sword. Blaise acknowledged her bold move curiously. Surely, she didn't think a fight against the three of them would be fair?

As if in answer to his question, four figures appeared from the shadows. Blaise didn't have time to evaluate the kind of creatures they were — only that they were dark Faeries — before the glint of a blade singing through the air drew his attention.

Myriam struck, the blade coming down with surprising speed and force, given her light frame. Blaise darted back, just a second faster than the unexpected strike. *Okay, reevaluate,* he thought as he danced away, pulling her back with him into a one-on-one fight. She swung again, and Blaise bent at the waist as he retreated, feeling the air brush against his stomach as the blade swung by. Perhaps she didn't think Blaise would kill her, but her blows were precise. Her intent was lethal.

Unnatural purple flames lit up the corner of his vision, and he glanced over to see Patrick blocking the dark magic with a stone barricade, summoned from the earth. Myriam saw the opportunity and swung her blade horizontally, but Blaise blocked the strike with his right forearm, stalling her swing. As he did, he deftly switched his dagger from right hand to left and whirled, striking her opposite shoulder with his back turned. She cried out, stumbling backward as he spun to face her once more.

"Oh, you're good," she hissed, clutching at her bleeding shoulder.

He said nothing, taking silent note of how his companions fared. Patrick still parried with the fire-wielder. Kipp was a reddish blur as he leapt and tackled one of the creatures to the ground. The sickening crunch that followed told him it had likely lost its head.

Myriam followed his line of sight and snarled, a violent sound that told him she hadn't expected her malicious soldiers to be dispatched so easily. She veered away from him and stalked toward the apple tree. Blaise mirrored her steps and placed himself firmly between her and the tree.

"Nobody else needs to get hurt," he said, voice low with warning.

Myriam's eyes flashed, an unnerving darkness spreading in them. "There will be plenty more hurt. This is only the beginning, commander."

He glanced behind him to see Patrick and Kipp, squaring off with the last dark Faerie. It was three against two, soon to be one. All they had to do now was regroup and get away. In one swift motion, he snagged a branch beside him — the only one he'd seen with silver streaking through it — and used his blade to cut it off at the base.

Before he could adjust his grip on the branch, however, his feet snapped together and tugged forward, sending him flat on his back. The air rushed out of him, and he spluttered, struggling to breathe as Myriam dragged him toward her. She grinned wickedly at him, flicking her palm to use whatever magic it was — earth, maybe air? — to drag him closer, feet bound. She raised her sword, releasing her magical hold on him momentarily as she gripped the hilt with both hands to bring it down over him.

He rolled in time to avoid the blow, but a second passed as he scrambled to his feet, the sword slashing his side. He winced, stumbling back, and dimly heard sounds of alarm from Patrick and Kipp.

She continued toward him, and he made the split-second decision to drop his dagger and catch her arm mid-swing. Blaise twisted, and she shrieked, dropping the blade. Footsteps alerted him to Patrick and Kipp's approach, and he dropped her hand, fishing frantically for the Faerie dust in his pocket. Myriam seized the opportunity to grab hold of the other end of the branch.

They locked eyes, anger and frenzy channeling through the look as they clutched either side of the branch. The wind picked up, shadows swirling around them. Blaise didn't want to stick around to see what creatures were coming next.

With a final roar, he yanked back on the branch, throwing the dust as he went, praying to the gods that it covered Patrick and Kipp as well. There was a snap and a scream, and then he was tumbling back through the dust to Sairas.

Chapter Nine

"We should find it along the outskirts of a little southern town called Avalas. It's known for its apple trees. I'll go scouting and be back by nightfall." I heard Myriam say, but I was barely listening.

Her research had helped locate the silver apple branch, and I thanked the gods for her impeccable timing. She hadn't realized I'd been gone the entire day, immersed instead in her investigation. She had only just come to look for me once I resurfaced. Soren, on the other hand, gave me a curious look, clearly having noted my absence.

I avoided his gaze tactfully as Myriam gave us a debrief, spreading a large map across the kitchen table and pointing somewhere south. Visiting the palace had been a mistake, and for the life of me, I couldn't understand my own reasoning. All I knew was that the last person I'd hoped would be on our side had refused me. Rejected me. Just like the others. Embarrassment and rage coursed through me, flushing my cheeks, and I clenched my hands into tight fists.

The slam of a palm against the table jolted me back to the present.

"Are you two even listening?" Myriam hissed, splaying her fingers flat against the map. I nodded, swallowing, while she fixed me with a dark look.

"Soren," she turned to address him directly. "Keep an eye on her. I want to make sure she's ready for when we get back."

He nodded, meeting my gaze. A twinge of irritation coursed through me as she spoke over me like I wasn't there, but it passed quickly, and I stared unflinchingly as Myriam exited the room. Finally, Soren spoke.

"How did you do it?"

"What?" I replied, surprised by his question. *Where,* I had expected, or *why,* but certainly not *how.* There was no way I could answer honestly, and explain I'd been nudged into the decision by a simple, albeit irritating, black cat.

Soren's intense look furrowed, but he shifted gears smoothly. "Thank the gods you were spared by the Sluagh. Who did you visit?"

"Finlay," I answered warily. Unease coated my skin like cold armor, but I wasn't sure why. I wasn't in trouble, and certainly not with Soren...? Nobody had come for either of us, and he knew my feelings about Blaise's betrayal. Being here for this fight, with him, felt more important. I'd chosen my path. "Is there something wrong with that?"

Soren jerked his head back. An emotion like surprise flitted across his face, yet it was smothered so quickly, I was unsure I'd even seen it.

"Not at all," he replied mildly, flashing me a grin. "But you can't go worrying me like that. The Sluagh are dangerous. You wouldn't stand a chance alone against a whole flock on your own, especially without any fire magic."

His words grated against that part of me that held the insecurity over my magic, and my hands curled into fists once more.

He knew. He knew, just like he knew the unhealed wounds in Blaise's past. Underneath that boyish charm and bouts of compassion, Soren had a knack for finding a person's vulnerability and exploiting it without mercy. I wondered if he understood the power that particular weapon held; a power as potent as his own magic or skill with the blade.

I dismissed those thoughts, instead muttering, "I know. It was a mistake. It won't happen again."

I didn't give him a chance to respond. Instead, I turned to head upstairs for bed. I hadn't slept the entire time I'd been gone, and exhaustion pressed against my consciousness, bidding me to finally rest. With a huff, I flopped onto the bed, hoping to nap as we awaited Myriam's return.

When she did, it was a whirlwind.

A resounding crash had me shooting up from my bed, and I rushed downstairs. From the sun's position, I determined that at least a few hours had passed while I slept, and Myriam must finally be back.

Sure enough, she had crashed into the kitchen table — presumably arriving back by Faerie dust — and sent everything atop the table clattering to the floor. Soren arrived moments later, and our eyes widened in tandem as we took in her appearance.

She was covered in blood, white clothing smattered in crimson and black, like some tragic painting. The urge to protect her rushed up, a powerful force that urged me forward in concern, grabbing for a clean cloth. Myriam pointedly ignored me and wiped her face, smearing the browning red blood across it. She wasn't faint or disgusted; instead, she was furious, and the fury was directed at me.

"Your people," she spat, "were there."

I raised a brow, my mouth falling open in shock and confusion. "*My* people?"

Her words were nearly a hiss. "Blaise, Kipp, and your *father*."

I paled, exchanging a glance with Soren.

"They were searching for the silver apple branch as well. We both found one, just one. So, they came for me," she seethed. "Between them and a few dark Fae, I barely escaped with my life."

My eyes traveled to a rip in her shirt, where fresh, scarlet blood gushed. Soren cursed and turned to the cabinets, rummaging for bandages. Again, Myriam didn't seem to notice; rather, her anger oozed from every pore, filling the air with an almost tangible rage. I felt the anger spreading to me, too, as I realized what this meant.

If we lost this opportunity to get to the Otherworld, to retrieve the sword, we could lose everything we'd worked so hard for. My mouth felt dry as I asked, "Did you — did you get the branch?"

Myriam pursed her lips and turned, motioning behind her. On the table lay a slender branch, webbed in white silver, with golden apple buds lining its curves. It was surprisingly short, however, and I noticed it was snapped on one side, ending in pale, frayed bark.

"Yes, and no," she answered me, as Soren worked his way around her, tending to her wounds. "The branch ended up splitting, at which point I cut my losses and took off with what I could."

I bit the inside of my lip as I assessed the mutilated branch. Anger and abandonment twisted uncomfortably within the pit of my stomach. Three people I had once cared about had joined forces to locate this branch, yet no one had tried to locate me. And with them having half of it, it potentially ruined all our chances.

"What does this mean for us?" I asked. Myriam turned her eyes on me, their pale gray tones turning impossibly dark.

"What does it mean? It means we're in a race to the sword now." She shooed Soren away and picked up the silver apple branch, grasping it tightly. "We leave in ten minutes. Get prepared."

At her clear sign of dismissal, I exited the room, but my hands shook as I went through the motions of putting on leathers and sheathing my sword. Kipp and the others were constantly on my mind, no matter how much I didn't want them to be. Facing such direct betrayal from them all was an overwhelming prospect. Not only did it make me tremble with rage, but that nagging, vulnerable part of me wondered why I wasn't worth listening to or worth fighting for. Or fighting with.

When I reappeared beside Myriam, I was armed, but teetering somewhere between fury and anguish. She fixed me with an assessing stare.

"Are you ready?" she asked, spinning a throwing knife in her hand. She had changed her clothes but left the blood smeared across her face, as though she relished the clear message it sent to those who dared cross her.

"Yes," I replied, shifting on my feet. I swung my arms and shook my legs, warming my limbs up. My only task was to retrieve and carry the sword, but I had to prepare for a fight, on the off chance there was one. She raised a brow at me.

"I don't mean physically," she replied flatly, and my heart plummeted. She read me like a book.

"I'm not sure I can face them," I admitted, chewing on the inside of my cheek while considering my next words. "They abandoned me. Clearly, I wasn't worth the fight. And maybe they're right. I'm not good enough to be an asset here."

Myriam's expression hardened, and she leaned forward. Her mouth pressed into a thin line, but when her nose met mine, she bared her teeth at me.

"Gods spare me. Your human side is insufferable," she hissed, then yanked her head back. "Only you would take this so personally." With a roll of her eyes, she snapped her fingers out and snatched my sword from its sheath.

"What the hell?" I demanded, my hands reaching to grab it back. She whisked it out of reach, so fast I blinked in alarm. I'd never so much as attempted to brush against her power, but something told me it was lethal. Her fighting skills were nothing to scoff at.

"It's despicable how we're raised to believe a woman's worth is tied only to others deeming her worthy. Human, Faerie, or Goddess, this mentality remains the same — we're preferred as creatures who seem powerful, but do not use that power. Even the queen now rules mostly out of lingering adoration for her late king."

Myriam leveled the sword in her hand and lifted it to my neck. My heart pounded, but not from the blade at my throat. Her words rang through my ears, the truth in them making me blaze with the same rage I saw in her.

"I *could* remind you how powerful you are, but you shouldn't need to hear it from me. You should know it deep down. You don't need anybody to see your worth except yourself."

She flipped the sword deftly in her hand, so that she held the blade flat and extended the hilt back toward me. As I grasped it, Soren entered the room, and she leaned in to whisper her next words.

"Your truest power is what lies within you. When you learn how to harness *that,* without using others as a crutch..." Her gray eyes flashed, a stark contrast against the dark, dried blood across her cheek. "You can activate the talismans, and then, you'll truly be unbeatable. Kill, bring back the dead, make others do your bidding, even make them love you. But it all starts from within."

My heart pounded at the promise in her words, the sound re-verberating through my ears. She was right. I didn't need others to tell me the impact I could have on this world. I was strong, and powerful, and yearned for so much change. But a great deal of that change was tied to others. I needed to begin thinking of changes that would benefit me — and once I had all the talismans, I could do everything Myriam had mentioned. All of that, and more.

Myriam must have seen the shift in my expression, because she straightened and nodded to Soren, pulling a fistful of Faerie dust from her pocket. I stepped closer, attempting to calm my racing pulse and steel my resolve for what lay ahead.

"Time to pay a visit to the Otherworld," Myriam said darkly, and flicked the dust in the air.

CHAPTER TEN

The pieces were falling into precarious place, though it did nothing to calm Blaise's concerns. He fidgeted as Castille tended to his wounds, earning various flicks from the Pixie, who reminded him to stay still. Blaise obliged, using only his eyes to survey the Faerie's warm, quiet home in Sairas. Castille was an incredible healer, with power and empathy in spades. He rivaled the army's own healer, and yet had somehow kept his magic under wraps. Blaise suspected it had something to do with Castille's personal choices, not wanting to be at anyone else's beck and call. If he'd had any say in the matter, Blaise had to admit, he'd have done the same.

"Keep still!" Castille reprimanded, continuing his careful work of lifting the bruises and cuts from his skin. Blaise stilled, but he wasn't flinching from pain; he'd experienced much worse. He was shifting from impatience.

He knew after their paths crossed with Myriam that time was of the essence. Neither would be wasting precious time, now that they both had a piece to grant them entry into the Otherworld. They'd slain the dark Faeries that had joined her in her quest for the silver apple branch, but she'd still escaped — and with half the branch, nonetheless. He could only hope that their hunch was accurate; that she and Soren needed Katherine to harness the sword's power for herself.

"If she wasn't of value to Nemain, she'd be dead already," Finlay said softly, meeting his eyes. Blaise grunted in answer, shifting once more.

Though Finlay had been ordered to stay at home while they located the branch, Blaise knew there wasn't anything anyone could say to keep him or his spitfire cousin from joining them in the Otherworld — especially if they had a chance of bringing Katherine back. He had begrudgingly chosen to trust the prince, but it still didn't quite sit properly with him, knowing the feelings he shared for her. Blaise planned to spend shove that piece of information into a deep pit inside him, right next to the other mounting feelings he was sure he'd never face. Permanently compartmentalized.

"Done," Castille announced, stretching his fingers. Blaise stretched his arms and murmured his thanks, but the Faerie cut him off.

"Don't thank me yet," Castille continued, glancing at Kipp, who sat in the corner of the room. The chestnut-haired Urisk returned his look curiously. "I'm coming with," he asserted, and Kipp scrambled to his feet, instantly perturbed. The Pixie waggled a finger at him, his eyes shooting daggers as he continued.

"You're going to need me. If things go awry, or you need to resort to your backup plan, you'll need a healer on-site. I won't have you rescuing our Katie-cat only to bring her lifeless body back to me."

The heated standoff between Castille and Kipp seemed to lessen as Kipp considered the truth of his words. He lowered his head, his ice-blue eyes dropping to the floor as he murmured his agreement. Blaise's own eyes trailed unwittingly to Finlay, to see if he'd witnessed the same charged tension in their exchange. Finlay's eyes were unreadable, fixed with the same soft amusement as always. Blaise rolled his own and glanced at the clock.

"Patrick should be back any minute with Darrya. We'll certainly have a large group going with us, but better to be over-prepared than under. Do you all have the words memorized?" Blaise tried his best not to bark the orders, as he would with his own army. The group in the room nodded along willingly, and right on cue, the door opened.

Patrick strode through, followed by Darrya, outfitted in her bow and arrows, her expression fierce. It was the same expression she'd worn when she had demanded to come along on this expedition, long before they had even gotten their hands on the silver apple branch. Blaise had seen her skills with that bow; she rivaled even the best archers in his army. There would be no complaints from him.

"Katie's not here to tell me not to risk myself," she had said with a mischievous grin, a look Blaise was certain had captured Larke's heart during their training. An ache he couldn't push away thrummed painfully in his chest as he remembered similar moments shared with Katherine during their training together. He could practically feel the brush of her body against his, the ones that had teased his mind and sent his body into a frenzy long before he'd allowed himself to truly touch and claim her.

"Blaise?" Darrya said now, cutting into his memories and bringing him back to the present moment.

"Err, yes?"

"The lights are on, but nobody's home," Castille chided, softening the light taunt with his wide grin. Blaise flushed slightly and forced himself to assume his role as commander once more. He grabbed his pouch of Faerie and cleared his throat.

"Right. Patrick — you have the branch, yes?" he asked.

Patrick flashed the snapped portion of the silver branch in response.

"We can only hope this will grant us the entry we need, but just in case, I need you all ready on the off chance things go awry." *More than an off chance,* he thought, but chose not to voice it. "I'll have another handful of Faerie dust ready to take us out of harm's way. And Finlay—" He looked at the heir, whose jaw twitched. "You know what your role is."

Finlay dipped his head almost imperceptibly. The others exchanged unnerved looks while Blaise took a deep breath. He motioned for everyone to gather closer, and once they surrounded him, he clutched a large handful of Faerie dust. "Here's to getting her back."

With that, he thrust the powder in the air, and they disappeared.

Blaise braced for the unexpected, but was still jarred when they landed. Vast expanses of taupe rock stretched in each direction, so tall he had to crane his neck to glimpse skylight beyond the peaks. It made little difference, however, seeing as the sky above was cloudy and dark, nearly as gray as the stone that stretched high to touch it.

Though it appeared they stood in the middle of a gorge, there was no sign of a river to have carved the walkway. Instead, a statue of a man stood before them, with three hounds at his feet. On either side loomed massive gates, easily thirty feet high. They were carved top to bottom with Faerie creatures of all shapes and sizes, intertwined with one another and looking in different directions. Though he saw nothing behind the gates that indicated any paths beyond, he knew instinctively that once they opened, a whole other world stood behind them.

"Who is that supposed to be?" Castille asked, staring at the stone figure. He sat atop a large throne, donning a long fur cape, hands outstretched, each clutching a long blade. His head was covered by a large deer skull, with antlers that boasted more points than any normal deer, stretching and weaving their way into a foreboding crown.

"The god of death," Blaise murmured in answer, clutching the hilt of his hidden knife tighter. As if that would do anything. "Arawn."

Despite the title, Arawn was known as a fair and just god, sorting the souls between heaven and hell and presiding over them both. Blaise was more than familiar with death. He breathed it, lived it, *dealt* it. He wondered absently what it would mean when his time came. Where Arawn would choose to sort him, based on his morality and his deeds. He wouldn't be surprised if he ended up with some of the very Fae he'd killed.

"Which way do we go?" Darrya asked breathlessly, surveying the gates on either side. She sidled to Finlay and gripped his hand. He leaned into her and squeezed her hand in reassurance, though his own expression remained guarded, giving nothing away.

"Where else would hell be?" Kipp answered with a grim smile, gesturing to his right. "The one with the figures looking down."

The moment they moved, however, the statue began rumbling. Loud cracks echoed through the gorge as the rock split and crumbled, revealing another solid figure underneath — a figure that was very much alive and moving.

Blaise watched, eyes widening, as Arawn himself stood before them, mildly brushing dust off of his fur cape. The three hounds at his feet followed suit shortly after, shaking rubble from their coats. Even as Blaise felt the energy of Kipp's shift beside him, his eyes never strayed from the beasts.

They matched Kipp's wolf form for size — at least, from what Blaise could see. The animals seemed to shift in and out of the shadows, disappearing and reappearing like mist on water, not entirely tangible beings. The only things that remained solid were their eyes, gleaming like embers on a fire. Those blazing eyes remained pinned on their group even as they circled their master. Blaise and Kipp instinctively made their way to the front of their group, guided by their protective natures.

"No need for that, my friends," Arawn boomed. His gravelly, amused voice encompassed the entire space around them, consuming them. His tone wasn't harsh, and yet, the power behind it nearly made Blaise shiver. "I see you've brought the silver branch. My nightmare hounds and I will do you no harm."

"Nightmare hounds sound pretty harmful to me," Finlay challenged, and Blaise flinched as he watched the god of death tilt his head at the fire prince. After a long moment, a low chuckle emanated from under the deer skull. He swore if he could see his face, Arawn would be grinning.

"Yes, well," he drawled in answer, "they do boast a particular talent for drawing out your memories and relaying them to me. How else would I be able to decipher where your soul belongs when the time comes?"

Before anyone had time to ponder his words, he continued. "But you, little heir of fire — my hounds tell me you don't fear death. You even welcome it. How curious."

Blaise shot a startled look at Finlay, and saw the others do the same, but the prince's face remained impassive. The kid was an excellent gods-damned actor, Blaise had to give him that. Arawn's sigh brought Blaise's attention back to him, and he continued.

"As interesting as it is to see so many souls at my gates with so much life ahead of them, this is not the purpose of your visit. You seek the sword, and the sword you shall find. Continue straight down the main path. Do *not* stray, lest you wish to learn what souls are like in the pits of hell." The god set down a blade and outstretched his hand.

"Give me the branch. I will ensure your passage out of hell remains open."

Blaise gestured, and Patrick passed it forward. Blaise approached Arawn tentatively to place it in his hand, which shimmered with the same silver hue as the branch. Before he could turn to rejoin his group, the god leaned in, and the skull he wore brushed against Blaise's skin. He whispered lowly in Blaise's ear.

"I can assure you, commander, that this will be your only trip through those gates. When your time comes, you will be headed in the opposite direction."

A lump formed in Blaise's throat, unbidden, and all he could think to do was bow his head in gratitude. As he returned to his group, their curious and expectant eyes on him, relief washed over him in waves. He hadn't realized how much that question had weighed on him until then, but Arawn had. The act of selflessness — to ensure Blaise had his answer — was the mark of a true and just god. He would be forever grateful.

None of them commented on the brief exchange, but right before they entered the gates of hell, Arawn spoke once more, this time addressing Katherine's father.

"Grandson of Cú Chulainn."

Patrick rose to attention, his eyes fixated on the god. Blaise's heart clenched at the look in his amber eyes — Katherine's eyes. He took a deep breath, twisting the hilt of his knife. They were so close.

"I am one of very few gods left here in this realm to continue my duties," Arawn continued. "They include ensuring an order to life and death."

The god strode back to his throne, calling his hounds back into place. As they settled at his feet, they locked eyes with Blaise once more, a knowing gleam in their solid gazes. The stone began gathering around the god once more as he sat back down and delivered a final command.

"Do not let Nemain continue upsetting the order of things. It will mean the end of our world as we know it. Your daughter is our only hope."

Chapter Eleven

He felt his cousin's burning gaze as they walked through the cavernous paths of hell and pointedly averted his eyes. He knew exactly what she was thinking. The words spoken by the god of death rang in his ears as well.

You don't fear death. You even welcome it. How curious.

He had long worked to push away those feelings, keeping them beneath the surface. In fact, he'd forgotten them entirely when Kate had entered their lives — giving him something to focus on, something light. But with Kate's absence, his fears had crept up once more. And even though beautiful dreams of her broke up the appearances of his nightmares, he was still haunted on many a night.

He had felt those hounds sifting through his memories, the touch of their magic faint but present. Finlay knew why they targeted him, too. His memories were as dark as their own shadows; it was a sadistic type of food for them, he assumed.

Screams shattered through his thoughts, echoing through the tunnel and causing him to wince. Whatever suffering the poor soul endured doubled as torment for others, listening while awaiting their own punishment. It stood to reason that torture down here would serve multiple purposes.

He clenched his fists, trying to block out the sounds, and watched as Castille gripped Kipp's arm. Kipp, who had shifted back into his human form, leaned into the touch to reassure him. The sight reassured Finlay slightly as well.

It seemed Arawn had kept his promise of safe passage on the main path, though, and after a few more agonizing turns, Finlay's magic flared, as if attempting to locate its own missing piece. He turned his hands over, allowing the flames to grow across his palms. He grinned at Blaise, who simply raised his eyebrows.

"Well, we guessed correctly. It seems like calls to like." Finlay said, and with their next turn, his flames expanded as they approached what had to be the sword of Nuada, nestled in the chest of a decayed, frightful-looking beast. The sword shone, a stark contrast to the grays and blacks surrounding the rest of the cave.

The sword was forged in Fionnias, the lost fire city, crafted in the blazing temperatures only their shops could produce. If that fire still existed in the sword, they reasoned, the only person other than Kate with the power to safely wield it was Finlay.

The group stood frozen, taking several long moments to admire it. Before anyone could move, however, footsteps rang out in the tunnel behind them, and Finlay heard the voice that consumed every good dream he had.

"I don't understand why he wouldn't let Myriam through the gates."

Finlay's eyes shot to Blaise to gauge his reaction. Every muscle in Blaise's body had stiffened, and his eyes shone darkly, likely consumed with rage and hope; Finlay was sure they mirrored his own. The others straightened, recognizing Kate's voice, and Patrick let out a soft, strangled noise. Finlay glanced over to see his expression brimming with emotion.

Blaise pulled his knife out, tracing his fingers across it and muttering the words they'd all memorized. The enchantment that, once placed on the blade, would allow it to cut her new mark and break the claim Nemain had placed on her. For a moment, Finlay feared what would happen if Blaise missed and plunged the knife a few inches lower, directly in her heart.

No. He shook his head, dismissing the dark thought. Blaise would never miss. But as he observed the set of Blaise's jaw, he knew they both worried regardless.

A few more steps around the corner, and she was there. Clearly, she had anticipated the possibility of seeing them there, but she froze nonetheless, taking them all in. Finlay's heart raced, and he forced his gaze away from her for a moment, searching for the person she had been speaking with. Yet there was no one, and he wondered for a moment if it could really be this easy. They were so close to getting her back. But—

She inched around their circle, eyes full of mistrust as they darted rapidly between them and the sword. It shone even brighter in her presence — clearly, it called to her, and her to it.

"Katie," her dad murmured, reaching a hand toward her. Finlay watched, hope he shouldn't dare have flaring in his chest as Kate's fingers twitched, as if she wanted to take his hand. But he should have known better, given her new mark. Kate didn't take his hand. Instead, she turned back toward the sword.

"Kate, please," Darrya begged, nocking an arrow. Kate tensed, magic dancing across her palms, now burning near-white. Finlay shot Darrya a look of warning. He understood why she'd come along, but it didn't mean she needed to be reckless. Kate's power, paired with her current state, could easily knock even Darrya on her ass.

"What don't you understand?" Kate ground out. "I thought this is what we agreed on. We *need* this."

"Not like this," Castille pleaded softly, standing behind Kipp. His wings were out, but taut against his back, as if ready to either fly toward or away from her at a moment's notice. Finlay felt the energy pulsating from Kipp as he restrained himself from shifting once more. Finlay mentally pleaded with Kipp to refrain. This was a delicate situation, and Kate was willing to fight it out, putting everyone — including herself — in danger.

"How else, then?" Kate demanded, balling her hands into fists.

Wisely, nobody responded. But when she stepped forward to claim the sword, her attention elsewhere, Blaise seized the opportunity and crashed into her. He didn't get a good shot at her collarbone, but it still sent her tumbling. Finlay forced his feet to stay put, fighting the instinctual urge to rush to her side. He feared for her, but with this new version of Kate, he also feared *her*.

As if to underscore his point, Kate steadied herself and released a snarl entirely unlike her, pulling a knife from a strap on her leg and glaring at Blaise. Her eyes had gone entirely dark. Blaise paused and tucked his knife away, raising his palms instead.

What are you playing at, Blaise?

"Come on then, sunshine," he growled. "Show me what I've taught you so well."

Before they could launch themselves at one another, Soren appeared from the shadows. Finlay watched as Blaise hesitated and paled, but regained himself fast enough to duck the punch Soren sent his way. As they began a battle between themselves, Finlay's eyes returned to Kate as she inched back toward the sword of Nuada.

Not a chance, little angel. Time for plan B.

A torrent of flames engulfed the sword, and Kate pulled back with a hiss.

"Finlay," she growled, those dark eyes turning on him. His heart plummeted; they were devoid of the liquid gold he'd come to love, swallowed by darkness. He wondered helplessly if she was too far gone, too enmeshed with the mark to even come back to them.

"I'm sorry, little angel," he said grimly. "I can't let you do this."

Her fist clenched around the knife, and Finlay braced himself. This time, he'd have to fight back, potentially hurt her to save her. But before she could approach, Blaise lunged for her, grabbing for her hand.

Finlay seized the moment to race for the sword, grasping the hilt with both hands as he tugged it from the chest of the demon. It seared his hands for a brief moment but settled as he willed the fire into his very being, entwining it with his own magic. The powers danced deliciously together, an homage to his own fire god, but he didn't spare a moment to savor it.

"Do it, Kate." Soren's voice was dark as he turned to face them. "You know we have to."

Flames roiled around Finlay as he ran his hand down the blade, muttering the necessary words. Glowing notches appeared on the sword, dashed in the pattern he'd learned for this exact scenario. His eyes flicked up to the scene before him as he spoke. Kate's knife was raised as Soren held Blaise in a chokehold. Finlay prayed he could complete the enchantment in time.

Soren's eyes met Finlay's as he finished uttering the words, his eyes widening as he yelled, "Kate — look out—"

Kate whipped around to face Finlay. He took a precious moment to meet her gaze, flecks of amber now replacing some of the black. It gave him the hope he needed that this would work, and this would be the only chance they would get.

Their eyes locked, and he lined the blade up with where he knew, from their brief moment in his room, the mark lay. He sent two prayers into the ether as he plunged the sword down.

Please, gods, let my aim ring true.

Please, gods, let her forgive me.

He held his resolve long enough to follow through with the strike, but crumbled as he heard her scream.

CHAPTER TWELVE

The washroom had been my best friend for the past hour. I wiped my mouth, trembling from the effort it took to purge my body of the absolute nothingness left within it. I wondered when my body would take the hint it had nothing more to give to the porcelain bowl. But every time my mind ventured to the events of the past month, my stomach roiled and threatened to spill its contents once more.

I felt thoroughly, utterly violated. I only vaguely remembered Blaise's words before we left, as he held a blade to Soren's neck. "I should kill you for your betrayal, but this is for Sera. Consider us even." Even less clear was the way my father carried me after we used Faerie dust to escape the pits of hell, and the waves of pain in my shoulder with every step back to the palace.

But I remembered everything that happened before then.

Every action and every thought while with Myriam and Soren still stuck with me, and the visceral feelings accompanying them. My mind — my thoughts — all belonged to me, and at the same time, they absolutely didn't. I felt weak and disgusted, though I'd been told repeatedly there was nothing I could have done to fight against it.

The only person I'd allowed to see me since arriving home was Cas. He'd been gentle and quiet, his deep brown eyes assessing, but not judging. His explanation was soft and careful as he relayed what had happened to me: the destruction of my initial Shield Knot, the re-marking with Nemain's Triskele, and how Finlay had severed the ties with an enchantment on the sword of Nuada. He hadn't asked a single question of me, and I sensed none of them would, not until I was ready. It made me feel even worse, though, knowing they were treading on eggshells around me.

Instead, he'd inspected my shoulder, healing what he could. Due to the now impressive stack of enchantments that had afflicted the area, he could only heal the damage from the sword. His tone was apologetic as he skimmed over the scars of the mangled marks, but I muttered how I'd prefer to keep them as a reminder. After a pause, he nodded and slipped away, leaving me to my own mind for the past hour.

Physically, I was already back to health, aside from the superficial wounds on my collarbone, which ached only slightly. But as I sucked in a deep breath through my nose, partially to calm my tremors from retching and partially to avoid hyperventilating, I wondered how long I would feel the mental aftershocks from this.

I should have felt positively furious at Myriam and Soren — and a part of me was, to be sure — but more so, I was *frightened.* Not of them, but of myself. It was an unnerving feeling, to distrust my own mind. They had fed me lie after lie, and I believed every word. It was easy for the others to blame the magic, but they had not lived it. For weeks, I had blindly followed Soren's version of the truth, pitting myself against those I loved. I had even begun to see Myriam's side; understanding and even *liking* her. It was hard to ignore my personal failure in that.

My knees complained from their time on the bathroom floor, and I took another deep breath. I couldn't stay like this forever. The only way forward from this mess was to wade right through the shit. I stood, knees cracking, and stabilized myself against the wall. One more minute. I allowed myself one more minute to wallow in it. Then, I closed my eyes, steeled myself, and shoved the door open.

I was met with an arrow flying into the wood next to the bathroom door, embedding in the frame with a dull thud.

I whipped my head around, eyes wide as I located the archer. Cas sat in a chair across the room, gaping at me, his hands frozen on Darrya's bow.

"What are you doing?" Kipp growled, grabbing the bow from his hands and returning it to its rightful owner. "Do you *want* to turn this room into a crime scene?"

"Your bedroom is a crime scene," Cas replied without missing a beat. "This was simply an accident."

In the hour I'd been healed and emptying my guts, none of my friends had moved from my dad's room in the palace. Darrya was the first to approach me, but her usually fervent embrace was now tentative. She pulled back after a moment, playing with my hair while analyzing my face. Whatever she saw there compelled her to smile softly and whisper, "We're so glad you're back here safe, Katie."

I tried to smile back, but failed, and covered it with a full scan of the room. My father, Kipp, Cas, and Blaise all looked back at me with quiet caution.

"Wren?" I questioned hoarsely, remembering her absence in the Otherworld.

"Frustrated, but keeping lookout. I'll go get her whenever you want," Cas said warmly. "We needed someone to stay at home and ensure chaos didn't descend while we were away."

I nodded, my gaze traveling back over the others. "I don't know how I could've ever imagined it. That you all betrayed me. That you forgot me." My eyes welled, and I blinked furiously to keep the moisture at bay.

My father was the first to spring up. He reached me in two strides, circling me with his strong, warm arms.

I staggered back, momentarily caught off guard. Ever since his reappearance in my life, we had been toeing an invisible line, choosing to play it safe. He gave me time, and in turn, just before my capture, I'd given him forgiveness, but this — this was the most open affection he'd shown me. It was as if the wall containing all the negativity of our relationship shattered with his embrace. I found myself slowly melting into his arms, welcoming the feeling of unconditional love that enveloped me.

"Never, Katie," he murmured into my hair, rubbing my back. The gesture unlocked memories from long ago, and my throat tightened painfully. "We tried everything we could. We kept trying."

"He even sent his cat to try and find you," Kipp smirked, attempting to lighten the mood. I gave him an incredulous look.

"Was it a black cat?" I asked, thinking back to the furry creature who lured me away from Myriam's mansion and guided me back to the palace.

My father chuckled. "Yes! So, she found you. I'm glad to hear it."

"She's yours?" I asked, and pulled out of the embrace to study his face.

"Yes. She's a Cait Sídhe. A Faerie cat, of sorts, sent by the spirits in times of need. Shadow was my only companion for quite some time."

Cas snorted audibly. "By the gods! I see the terrible pet names run in the family."

A small, genuine smile blossomed across my face, and my heart warmed as everyone laughed.

"I think I need to rest," I said, hating the meekness that found its way into my tone. I swallowed and tried again, my voice stronger this time. "I need to bathe and get some sleep."

Everyone nodded, their faces all mirrors of concern. My dad placed his hand on my shoulder, and I turned to face him.

"Are you sure you're okay, kiddo?" he asked gently. I nodded, forcing the small smile on my face to widen as I extracted myself from his arm and exited the room.

I was just beginning to run water for the bath in my own room when a soft tap came at the door. I opened it a crack, glimpsing Blaise on the other side. Though I could only see half of his face, I could tell his expression was strained — his jaw taut, eyes crinkled with worry.

"May I come in?" he asked gruffly, and after a moment, I nodded, widening the door for him. He slid his way in, assessing me carefully, and tilted his head as he heard the rushing of the bath water.

"Continue whatever you need to do," he said. "I just needed to see you." He was still standing by the door, studying me as though I might break at any moment. I wasn't sure how to feel under his scrutiny. "And — if you'll have me — I'd like to spend the night," he added, dipping his head.

I flushed, realizing how long it had been since I'd touched him. A part of me was still confused by the ideas Myriam and Soren had put in my head — whispers of his disloyalty, his abandonment — but I shoved them aside. Blaise had never faltered and never truly turned his back on me. This whole time, he had been looking for me, ready to fight. And here he was, ready to help put me together again.

I strode up to him, placing a hand on his cheek and running my fingers along his jaw. I noted the roughness of his stubble as I grazed my thumb across it, a clear indication that shaving had been the last thing on his mind. His eyes softened at my touch, and he wrapped his hands around my waist, pulling me in close. He breathed in deeply, as if he were afraid even the scent of me would disappear, and I turned my head to capture his lips.

His kiss started cautiously, but deepened as I latched my hand behind his neck and pulled him closer. The fullness of his kiss threatened to drown me in its pleasure, and I was all too willing to sink into that feeling as it overwhelmed every other emotion.

We broke apart for a brief moment, panting, and in a bold move, I began shrugging off my clothes. Blaise's hands stilled as I stripped, and he took me in ravenously as I stood before him. A memory flashed through my mind, unbidden — the way I'd attempted this last with Finlay.

But no — I brushed the thought aside, casting it off as a lust-driven accident, fueled by the mark. The prince was attractive, that was undeniable, and when my inhibitions were lowered, my own body made that clear enough. But Blaise was who I truly wanted to be with. My nipples peaked as Blaise's eyes raked over them. I couldn't hide my desperation; I wanted his hands on me instead of his eyes. But then his gaze landed on my collarbone, and he visibly paled, averting his eyes.

"Your bath is probably ready," he murmured, stepping back. The distance felt much larger than the few steps he took. I covered myself with my arms, suddenly embarrassed, but at the sound of rushing water, threatening to spill over, I realized he was likely right.

I settled into the bath, enjoying the hot water for several long minutes before washing up, eager to return to Blaise's touch. But when I had, I saw that he had laid out my silk pajamas and was already curled up in my bed. I threw the pajamas on and sidled up to him. He drew me in close, but simply dropped a kiss on my forehead with a murmured "Sweet dreams" in a clear sign that he would pursue nothing further.

I tossed and turned for half an hour before clambering back out of bed. I draped a blanket over my shoulders to cover myself, and slid out the door, heading for the courtyard. My bare feet were light while I padded down the steps, but as I rounded the corner into the yard, I tripped ungracefully over a figure on the ground. My blanket went flying, and I had just enough time to brace myself against the impact of the fall.

"What the hell?" said a muffled voice, one I immediately recognized as Finlay's. He lit a small flame in his palm, recognition flitting across his face as he spotted me. He was dressed in plain dark lounge pants and a loose, cream-colored tunic. Anyone else would look mad dressed in so little clothing as the weather turned cold, but I figured his magic likely acted as a built-in heater.

"Little angel. What's a lady like you doing out here, so late at night?" He nodded at my skimpy, silken pajamas, now exposed with my blanket splayed across the grass. I didn't miss the lustful expression that flitted across his face. "And dressed like that, no less?"

"I'm no lady," I seethed, gathering my blanket back around myself. "And I just needed...a breather." Finlay opened his mouth to question me further, but I quickly added, "And what are you doing out here?"

Our eyes met; I noticed his were darker than normal, slick with the haze of consumption. The lack of sobriety was unsurprising, but there was a tinge of darkness — something was weighing on his very soul, more than his usual when he drank. Clearly, whatever it was, the drugs weren't quite cutting it.

"The same. Avoiding the third degree from my cousin. It was a rough day." He lifted his golden flask in cheers, taking a large swig. "I'm truly sorry for what I did to you," he added, faltering slightly. I looked up in bewilderment, seeing the truth in the sadness of his expression. While it was irritating finding him back on the bottle, it tugged at my heart to know his pain was in part due to me. Though I only vaguely recalled what he did, I was grateful that he did it.

"You needed to," I murmured, rubbing absently at the marks. His gaze followed the movement.

"That's not why you're out here, is it," he commented. It wasn't a question. "You have someone in your room you could talk to about that, if you wanted to."

I opened my mouth to ask how he knew that, but he tilted his head and continued. "Something else is bothering you."

I snapped my mouth shut, unwilling to answer, but he waited patiently until the silence grew unbearable. I shifted to sit beside him, rolling my eyes.

"Fine. If you must know, it's because I have...an itch, and Blaise is refusing to scratch it."

Finlay's eyes widened, and he leaned back, taking in the information. "I see."

"I think he's afraid I'm *fragile* right now," I huffed, voice dripping with irritation. Finlay bit his fist as a grin spread across his face.

"It's not funny!" I insisted, punching his shoulder. "He's afraid it'll break me or something. But I'm not like that. In fact, I think I need it, so that I don't have to focus on — everything else."

"Using sex as a distraction," Finlay remarked, eyes sparkling darkly. "Some things never change."

I scoffed, narrowing my eyes at him, and he held my gaze unwaveringly. It was in that moment that my mind flitted over our own moments of passion, spilling together in my mind. My breath caught as I remembered the way he'd spoken to me in the forest as we'd captured the dark Faerie; the brief moment we shared at the river, riding high on *voitín*; the way I'd approached him the night I escaped Myriam's mansion, betraying more of my body's reaction to him than I'd like to admit.

"For the record, you're probably the least breakable person I know. You're like a rose." His words tore me from my memories. My face must have betrayed my bewilderment, because he elaborated, leaning forward.

"Stunning to look at on the surface, but your roots keep you grounded even in the harshest conditions. It takes a wise person to know how to handle you, because you have some serious bite if they do it wrong." He winked as he said the last part.

"Ah," I blinked, digesting the information. He studied my expression, and I wondered if he was remembering our moments together, too. If, like me, he was dissecting them and trying to decide if our close calls were due to outside factors, or something earnest. A dangerous temptation flitted inside me, wondering what it would mean for it to be...*more.*

"So, what do you suggest this rose do next?" I asked recklessly as I leaned forward, my breath catching in my throat. The question was laced with multiple meanings, and I wondered which he would answer.

Who do you suggest I choose?

He regarded me for a long moment, his flame still shimmering in one hand. I wondered if he had caught on to the insinuation. I felt a brief twinge of guilt as I recalled where Blaise was at this very moment, while I was down here doing...gods, what *was* I doing? Finlay's other hand twitched, as though he was about to reach for me, but I pulled back, and he didn't finish the movement.

"Have you ever taken matters into your own hands?" he asked instead, expression turning to one of bemusement. His eyes traveled low, and then back up to mine. "I mean...literally."

My cheeks burned as I grasped his meaning, and my mind flickered to the last night I had almost done so, thinking of only him.

"Maybe," I hedged.

"Mmm. I'll take that as a yes." His eyes danced in tandem with his flames. "I suggest you go back to your bed and do just that. Any man sharing your bed, no matter how noble, will be unable to resist joining in on that fun."

I nodded, gathering my blanket around me as I rose. My cheeks were flushed with embarrassment and more than a little arousal. Had I just been rejected *and* complimented at the same time?

"Kate," Finlay said, stopping me in my tracks. I glanced back at him, and his gaze was piercing.

"Blaise is a good man," he murmured. "I doubt even you can understand the depths of his love for you. But I certainly hope he can show you."

I blinked, confused by his kind words, but before I could probe further, he bolstered the flame in his hand and added, "And if he doesn't, well, I'll leave the light on."

I snorted, feigning irritation, though I was happy we had returned to our normal banter. His momentary seriousness was unnerving.

"You're a pig."

"Nonsense. I just find your lack of sex life much more entertaining than my own."

He winked, but once I reached the steps and glanced back, he was once again frowning, flask back in hand.

Chapter Thirteen

Blaise was awoken by uneven breathing next to him. After blinking for a few moments, he whirled around in bed, the room and who was beside him registering piece by piece.

"Katherine?" he asked, his voice raising an octave. "Are you okay?"

When she turned her head to look at him, his breath caught in his throat. Her golden eyes were half-closed, back arched as the blanket moved between her thighs. She bit her lip as she considered him, but didn't stop her movements. She let out another breathy moan.

"What are you doing?" His eyes widened, but he already knew. And oh, what a troubling and arousing sight it was.

"We had some unfinished business earlier. I'm just...finishing it myself," she said, voice dripping heavily with suggestion.

"You..." his voice trailed off, eyes roaming hungrily to where her hands worked below the blanket. He bit the inside of his cheek, an internal war commencing inside him. He wanted to rip the covers off and replace her hands with his own — and then his mouth, and cock — but his mind flitted to Kate's haunted look from earlier, her faraway expression as she'd mindlessly touched the scarred piece of flesh where her marks had once been. "I just don't want to hurt you further."

She paused her movements, rolling to her side. The motion displayed her breasts perfectly underneath her satin tank, and he licked his lips. She smiled slowly, acknowledging the motion. "But this is exactly the hurt I need," she murmured, the challenge in her words clear.

Those words were his undoing.

He loosed a deep groan and grabbed for her, disregarding any notion he'd had before of being gentle. Her gasp only furthered his desire, and in one deft movement, he sent the blankets flying, exposing her to him.

He was delighted to see the work she had already begun as nothing stood between him and the beautiful skin below her navel. Even so, he was determined to show her he could offer so much more than her hand. He shifted to lie over her, resting on his knees while he removed his shirt. He never broke her gaze as he grabbed the edge of her own shirt, tugging it over her head.

His heart bobbed in his throat as he took in her fully naked body, dutifully ignoring her wound, instead trailing his eyes over her physique: muscles and curves fleshing out every piece of her perfectly. He'd imagined her divine body countless times over the past few weeks — he craved it, even, teetering somewhere between frustration over her absence and arousal every time he recalled her in those moments. But the fantasies didn't do her body justice. He bent over her, trailing kisses down her throat, relishing the small sounds she made as he worked his way over her body. It invigorated him further, but he stopped when her hands fisted in his hair.

"No," he growled, grabbing her wrists and placing them above her head. He shot her a mischievous glare, adding, "Those hands have done enough already."

She obeyed, eyes wide as her beautiful chest rose and fell with every breath. His eyes were drawn to the motion, and he claimed a breast with his mouth. Cupping her other breast with his hand, he lightly pinched her nipple as his tongue flicked over the other. She arched under him, and he grinned wickedly at how receptive she was to his touch.

He pulled back from her chest begrudgingly after a few moments, and moved lower. Her stomach went taught as he trailed kisses near her hip bone, her breath growing raspy in anticipation. He sighed against her thigh as she parted herself for him, trailing his nose up one leg while planting kisses until he settled between her thighs. There, he dragged his tongue along her.

Her legs shot out instantly in response, and she bucked her hips so hard, he feared he might have broken his nose.

"By the gods, Katherine." He let out a breathy laugh, massaging the bridge of his nose. She gave him a guilty look, her cheeks flushed with shame.

"Sorry, it's just, I..." she trailed off, cheeks reddening further. "I've never had someone do this to me before."

"Never had anyone do what?" he asked as he blinked away the sting. Her eyes traveled to where his mouth had been mere moments before.

"Wha — oh. Oh," he chuckled softly. "You know, for someone who just taunted me into this, I would've expected you to be a sexual deviant." He pinched her leg, grinning as she jumped again, and leaned over to whisper in her ear. "But I'm delighted to be your first."

Before she could respond, he was back between her thighs, lifting her legs over his shoulders. He splayed one hand flat against her stomach and used the other to cup her ass, keeping her still as he continued with renewed vigor, pressing his tongue flat against her core before licking up languid strokes. He held her still as she attempted to arch her back, and grinned as he heard her soft cry of complaint, swirling his tongue in response.

He continued relentlessly, exploring with alternating lashes of his tongue and sucking kisses, drinking in her sounds of pleasure as they crested over his ears, until she reached the point of oblivion. His cock jerked to attention as her thighs tightened around him, and with one final flick of his tongue, she was there.

He delighted in the sound and feel of her climax for a few precious moments, before his resolve gave way and he pushed his own pants down, claiming her where his mouth had been moments before.

"Fuck, Katherine." The words slipped out as a groan as he felt how wet she'd become for him. She arched to meet him, fingers clawing clumsily at his back as she tried to pull their bodies closer together. Her legs wrapped around him, hips lifting, and he thrust harder, trying to take as much pleasure as possible from her as he gave.

He pounded into her, palming her perfect ass as she lifted her hips further to meet his movements. Her head rolled back in delight, and he felt a power unlike any before, outdoing any glory he'd felt on a battlefield or fighting arena. He could watch her like this forever.

He picked up the pace, eyes fixated on her lips as she bit them, trying to contain her screams of pleasure.

"Let it out, sunshine," he growled between his thrusts. "Let the world hear us."

"Oh — gods — oh — *please,*" she cried, and the sound of her drove Blaise wild with need. He slammed into her with renewed force, and the movement sent them both spiraling over the edge, gasping curses as the pleasure seized them both.

Blaise collapsed over her, and they panted in tandem as he worked to reorganize his thoughts, as scattered and ruined as he was. He stared down in amazement at Katherine underneath him, who shot him a wicked, sated grin. She pushed him off playfully, but then turned to face him once more, her grin softening into a blissful smile as she gave him one last long look. Her eyes closed, then, seemingly lulled into drowsiness at last.

Blaise scooted closer and rolled onto his back beside her, grateful to see her at peace once more. He sent a silent wish into the ether that it could be like this forever.

But he knew it couldn't. They were nowhere near out of harm's way. However, one thing he knew for certain was he would fight tooth and nail to keep her safe.

"Blaise." Larke's tone told Blaise everything he needed to know before he'd even turned. He braced himself, and sure enough, Larke's face was grim as he entered the armory. It was late in the morning, but Larke didn't comment on the time. For that, Blaise was grateful. He had slept in with Katherine, relishing the feel of her warm body safe beside him and watching her soft, steady breathing as the sun rose. The contentment had felt too short-lived, so he greedily stole every second he could before returning to his duties as commander.

"There were several attacks last night along the outskirts of Sairas. The Sluagh."

Blaise squeezed his eyes shut, face darkening. So, he had the answer he'd feared. The Sluagh were working with Nemain, who had used them last night to send a message. She wanted the sword back, and most likely Katherine with it.

"How many?" he asked, his gut wrenching.

"Two. The others were able to get inside and salt the entrances before any more damage could be done."

Blaise knew he should be relieved, but the loss still weighed on him. Two lives he was personally responsible for. He strode past Larke, making his way out of the armory and listing off orders as he went.

"Station more men evenly across the town, so no side is left less protected than another; enforce the curfew for sundown. Spread word on the best ways to combat their attacks."

Larke nodded, making mental notes. He had stopped by the other night to ensure Katherine's safety, and while she was in the bathroom, Blaise recounted the events, including Soren's treachery. Larke had been — and still was — furious at the news.

"He was like a brother to us," he'd spat out in dismay, knuckles turning white as he clutched the hilt of his sword. "But a brother would never do what he's done."

Blaise couldn't agree more. Growing up, the trio had been inseparable; Larke and Soren had filled the pieces of Blaise's life that had been missing with his own family. They had risen together, and when they fell, they picked one another up. Sure, they'd had disagreements, but this — this went far beyond that. Blaise saw the same pain and betrayal etched across Larke's face that was surely mirrored in his own, but as they looked at each other now, he knew they had said what they needed to on the subject. There were other issues at hand.

Larke shifted on his feet, fingers tapping at his sword as he considered their next steps. "Anything else?"

"I'll handle the rest," Blaise grumbled. "This is a direct retaliation for us claiming the sword of Nuada. I'll have to figure out how to leverage that as a checkmate; use it as a threat to get Nemain to call off her army."

"Better yet, we figure out where the bulk of her army is and cut the snake off at its head," Larke added.

Blaise grunted. "Wouldn't that be ideal."

Larke studied him for a long moment, and then slipped away, leaving him again with his own thoughts. Blaise was grateful for it. It wasn't often he was stumped, but recently, things had gotten a lot more complicated.

Chapter Fourteen

Listening to Kate talk was an excellent distraction from the prior day's events. Finlay and Kipp had joined her and Darrya for lunch, finding a table in the dining hall. They all listened breathlessly as Kate tentatively opened up about what she had endured the past month.

Everyone visibly deflated when they heard that Myriam and Soren had kept Kate at arm's length; she had seen no trace of Nemain anywhere on the actual premises. The three of them were just glorified puppets, while Nemain was somewhere in the distance, pulling the strings. The thought of her still out there, lurking in the shadows, sent fear twisting through Finlay's gut. It was much easier to prepare for the devil you knew. That was half the reason Finlay preferred to dance with his own devils regularly.

The most interesting information she offered was also the most worrying.

"The thing I hate the most is that some of it made sense," Kate huffed in exasperation. "Even when Myriam was angry at me, she was telling me things like 'your truest power lies within you,' and 'you don't need anybody except yourself.'"

Silence hung in the air at her words, and Finlay exchanged nervous glances with Darrya and Kipp. Was it possible that traces of the enchantment still lingered in her mark? Darrya bit her lip, but Kipp simply sighed, putting down his food.

"Most villains don't get very far if all they ramble on about is nonsense," he said pointedly. "Her objective, while a manipulation of the truth, is at least somewhat rooted in a cause people want to believe in. If Myriam can speak that eloquently, she's the perfect recruiter for Nemain. But it's curious that she took such an interest in fostering your power specifically."

Kate stilled, and the fork she was holding hovered midair.

"Yeah, about that," she began uncomfortably. Everyone leaned forward, encouraging her to continue. "It sounds like Nemain will need my power to activate the talismans. Myriam said something about them harnessing the power to bring back the dead."

Finlay stiffened. He knew Kate's lineage was personal to Nemain, and that her bloodline rivaled his own claim to the throne, but...this added another wrinkle to the already complicated tapestry weaved by Nemain in Kate's life. In all of their lives, because this also meant...

"The very things that you need to defeat her are also what *she* needs to bring her sisters back?" Darrya breathed, finishing Finlay's thought process out loud.

Kate grimaced, but nodded. "Apparently. So, it really sucks for her that I would never wield them for that purpose."

She plopped a piece of cheese in her mouth, clearly unbothered by the unsaid truth: Nemain would be even more dangerous now that both Kate and the sword had been ripped from her grasp. Finlay's throat constricted as he considered the size of the target Kate had on her back. He exchanged a nervous glance with Kipp, who clearly followed the same troubling train of thought. They'd lost her once already, yet it seemed Nemain was just getting started with her. Who knew what lengths she would go to in order to get Kate back? A wave of protective fear washed over him, his body chilling despite the fire magic burning beneath his skin.

Kate, however, had moved on. She leaned in and whispered something to Darrya. Finlay and Kipp exchanged another glance, this time one of curiosity, and then jumped as Darrya squealed.

"You've never—" She lowered her voice, realizing her volume. "You've never had someone do that to you before?"

With a jolt, Finlay realized they were discussing something Kate had done last night; from the look on her face, it was clearly something sexual. A spark of unwelcome jealousy burned in him, but he watched closely as Kate's cheeks flared a shade of crimson. "Well, it's not like I've lived centuries, like you lot," she muttered. "He's only the second person I've ever slept with."

Just as Finlay wondered who her first was, Darrya asked the question for him.

"Some guy in my high school. In the human realm," she answered, pushing food around on her plate. Finlay's eyes narrowed, sensing more to the story. But as quickly as he noticed her expression, she changed it again, snorting a quick laugh. "And it was done in what felt like *seconds.*"

Finlay's lip quirked. Poor bastard. He probably had no idea what to do with a gorgeous Faeling like Kate. If it were him, he would take his time, exploring every inch of her flesh, listening closely to understand exactly where his touch made her breath hitch, and where his mouth could elicit a moan. He'd never be done with her.

"So...what did you think?" Darrya teased. She leaned forward, eyes gleaming with mischievous interest. She seemed to catch herself as soon as she asked, though, tossing Finlay a guilty look. He shrugged, doing his best to feign indifference. Gods spare him.

Kate's amber gaze darted between him and Kipp. Kipp was clearly doing his best to look nonchalant, too, though curiosity brimmed in his eyes.

"I didn't realize—" She flushed further, her voice lowering so it was barely a whisper. "I didn't realize I could come just from his tongue alone."

Kipp howled with laughter, and Darrya couldn't help but smirk, despite the sympathy that shone in her eyes as she looked at Finlay. Finlay did his best to fake a smile, even as his mind raced and his heart thrummed.

His words had sent her back to Blaise. He'd known, of course, what she was really asking the night before, and yet he'd chosen the high road. Let the better man win. And that decision was the reason she had experienced this for the first time, with someone else's mouth bringing her to ruin. For a moment, he allowed the thought to drive him mad.

He wanted, with every bone in his being, to be the one who made her flush like this. He wanted his tongue to be the one on her, tasting her, *his* name she screamed in pleasure. He shifted in his seat, readjusting his pants, now tightened as the image of her splayed out beneath him raced across his mind, naked and writhing as he feasted on her. He glanced down at his plate, his appetite for food suddenly lost.

"Don't laugh at me like that. It's not like he was biting me like some animal." Kate was busy chastising Kipp, but the comment only set him off more.

"Yes, well, as Cas would say, that can sometimes help," he replied, baring his wolfish canines jokingly. He ducked as Kate threw cheese at him.

Indeed.

Their conversation shifted as Larke approached, and Finlay watched as Darrya's eyes tracked his every movement. He knew Larke felt the same burn for her as she did him. It was only a matter of time before they admitted it to each other, and he looked forward to watching it play out. If he couldn't have the person he lusted after, he only hoped his cousin would have that chance. She deserved it.

He took the moment to excuse himself, heading to the kitchen to return his plate. As he walked, he replayed their conversations, fear and envy warring anew within him. He brushed his hand absently over his pocket, reassured by the presence of his flask. A liquid meal for him today, he decided.

After he dropped his plate off, he pulled the flask from his pocket and turned to find himself face-to-face with Kipp.

"If you're hoping to ask me out on a date, a jump scare isn't the best way to start," Finlay drawled, covering his heart with his hand.

Kipp rolled his eyes, but ignored the remark, instead glancing down at the golden container of whiskey. He crossed his arms.

"You know," he began, his voice soft but firm, "if you're ever going to have a chance with her, you might need to lay off the liquor."

"Ah, but my best comments come when I'm half-cocked. Without sarcasm, I only have my good looks to rely on. And where's the fun in that?" Finlay's voice didn't falter on the flippant answer, but his heart pounded as he realized how accurately Kipp had pegged the situation. At Kipp's raised brow, he added, "Plus, she has her person. Clearly, he makes her *very* happy."

Kipp shuffled his feet, glancing back to ensure Kate was still at the table. "Look, I like him as much as the next person. He's the best commander the queen's army has ever seen. But I've been around a long time; a lot longer than you. And you know what that means?"

Finlay shrugged. "You've moved on to padded underwear?"

"Why do you have to make it so difficult to be nice to you?" Kipp groaned, though his smirk betrayed his amusement. "No. It means I know the difference between simple sexual chemistry and something more. I've heard her talk about him, and I've heard her talk about you."

He paused, looking behind him to ensure she was still preoccupied with Darrya and Larke before he continued. "She may talk about how he makes her feel physically, and she may not know where to place either of you in her heart…but she opens up with you in a way I've never seen her do with Blaise."

Finlay considered his words, briefly letting his thoughts go somewhere he rarely allowed — a world where she was his, and not in the arms of another.

What if?

No.

Even if she doesn't love him, he loves her. And she deserves better. She'll be happier with his love.

And his tongue.

He shook his head. His thoughts were torturous enough without adding unnecessary hope into the mix. "If you know so much about this," he ventured, "then why are you not with Castille?"

Kipp jolted in surprise, his piercing eyes meeting Finlay's. Finlay stood firm. The question was a deflection, sure, but he'd been paying attention. He'd seen Kipp's interactions over the past few months, and none of those mild flirtations came close to the looks and touches he shared with Castille. Judging by his reaction, Finlay had hit it right on the money.

"I don't want to sacrifice what we have as friends," Kipp answered stiffly. "Besides, he's not the relationship type."

"Maybe for you, he would be," Finlay offered, and watched as a flicker of hope danced across Kipp's expression. By the gods, they were both in the same, pathetic boat. Finlay unscrewed his flask, taking a long swig before leaning in.

"How about this," he whispered. "I'll make my move when you do."

With a wink, he sauntered back to where the others still sat. Kipp joined them shortly after, the fluster still apparent on his face. Nobody noticed, however, too preoccupied with the latest arrival — Blaise. His face was grim as he approached, and his eyes traveled to Finlay. Finlay met his gaze, doing his best to block out the image of him and Kate together.

"It seems we may need your powers after all, Finlay," Blaise remarked, and Finlay blinked in surprise. "The Sluagh. They've invaded. It seems Nemain is using them to send a message about our involvement with the sword."

"Blaise," Larke cut in, clearing his throat. Blaise shot him a surprised look, but tilted his head to listen.

"Kate might be able to help. Remember what I said earlier? About cutting the snake's head off?"

Blaise nodded and sat down while Larke continued. "Well, she might not have any information on Nemain's army now. But she's someone who could safely get it."

Finlay furrowed his brow, puzzled, and as he shifted his attention to the others, he saw confusion reflected in their faces as well. Kate jumped in.

"She knows you injured me, and that you took me along with the sword. But she doesn't know that the mark is severed. I could still go back; pretend I managed to escape and get back to her."

Finlay opened his mouth, an instant rebuttal on the edge of his lips, but Kipp beat him to it.

"That's a *really* dangerous gamble, Kate," he put in hesitantly.

"Not just that, but how would you being in the beast's belly help us get intel? How would you report back? How would we know you were okay?" With each question Blaise posed, his voice grew louder, betraying his emotion even as his face remained impassively in the commander façade. Finlay knew, without needing to read his face, the deep-rooted fear within him. It was the same visceral fear Finlay shared for Kate's well-being.

"I'll be fine. They need me just as much as they need the sword. That desperation might just cloud their judgment." Kate's tone was matter-of-fact. "And I'll have to come back to work with the person on my side that set me free from your captivity."

She read the confused expressions around the table and added, "The one Soren and Myriam wouldn't have seen enough to know definitively which side he's on — someone with a *lot* of power; someone they would be ecstatic to hear is joining their fight."

Finlay paled as he realized where this was going. "The one person you could visit as part of the loophole," he murmured, and watched as realization swept over the others.

"You're suggesting you play the double agent?" Darrya asked, eyes wide. Kate nodded seriously, and Finlay knew that look. There was no changing her mind — she was decided.

"We'll hide the sword from them. Kate will need to keep coming back to plot with Finlay to see what progress he's made in 'relocating' it," Larke added.

Finlay hated to admit it was a solid plan.

"And if they don't give up any information? What will you be risking this for?" Blaise demanded, expression pained as he realized everyone was slowly getting on board.

"Nemain will call off her Sluagh once she has Kate because she'll have a better way of accessing the sword. It would remove that threat for the rest of Sairas," Finlay put in, earning a grateful look from Kate, even as the one he got from Blaise was searing.

"If it saves lives, we have to try it," Kate pleaded.

Darrya sighed, turning to Blaise and admitting, "I don't see a better option, Blaise."

"Your father isn't going to like this at all," Kipp interjected.

"Respectfully, he has to let me make this decision myself," Kate said, "especially since this problem is so much bigger than just me."

Finlay's heart went out to her. No one seemed to understand this wasn't about her — it never had been. Her capacity for love, even for a folk she'd only begun learning about, astounded him. She was everything a true leader should be, and it was exactly why he hadn't balked the moment he learned her true destiny. She'd make ten times the leader he would, even on her worst days.

Blaise curled his hands into fists, realizing the battle was lost. His jaw twitched, and he turned abruptly to stalk away, fury emanating off him as he left.

The table went silent, and Finlay recognized the moment as one his talents suited well. He let out a dramatic sigh to crack the tension and faced Kate.

"Well, little angel," he said, voice forcibly jovial. "Shall we discuss the logistics of how I coordinated the world's most heroic jailbreak for you?"

Chapter Fifteen

Despite not wavering once on my decision, the terror didn't loosen its grip on my heart. It held tight as a vice while I talked through my plans the following morning. Luckily, the only ones who took some serious convincing were my father, Blaise, and Wren.

Wren, in particular, was very upset; she had been intentionally sequestered from the action. Though others had their commitments, like Cas with his clients and Darrya with her envoy duties, Wren was the only one whose job at the stable was consistent. She also had no real training in either fighting or defense.

When I found her in the stable, she wrapped her slender arms around me in greeting, and I was reminded again just how breakable she was. She wielded earth magic beautifully, and she was probably the only one Gray liked aside from my father and me. But she was no fighter. When I relayed my plan to her, her look of furious dismay still appeared as sweet and innocent as she was.

"But we just got you back," she huffed, tossing her sleek ebony hair over one shoulder. I leaned into Gray, willing the strength of the stallion's solid frame to bleed into me.

"I know," I sighed, "and I don't want to leave, either. But this is the kind of opportunity we can't pass up. They have the cauldron, and we have the sword, and right now, I'm the only card we have to play."

Wren hummed her disapproval, eyes scanning between Gray and me. "Are you at least taking him with you? For protection?"

I shook my head, running a hand down his strong neck. I wished desperately to take him with me, but it would be silly to put him in harm's way, especially when his presence, as far as I knew, remained secret from Nemain. He was her sister's war horse, gifted to my great-grandfather, intended to be led into the throes of battle. Yet this type of battle was different — insidious, built on whispers and clever phrasing, as opposed to brute force. It was a mission I had to embark on alone.

"Well. Either way, he'll know," she said firmly, stroking his large, velvet nose. "Now that her mark is gone, I'm sure he'll know if you're in trouble."

I smiled, looking up into the depths of one of Gray's dark, piercing eyes. I wasn't sure how much truth there was in that, but Wren sounded confident enough that her words gave me a small sense of reassurance.

"Well then," I ventured. "I'm counting on you to keep an eye on him for the both of us."

Wren promised as much emphatically, and joined me as I saddled another horse, strapping a few essentials in the saddlebags. We exited the stable together, but were soon met by Blaise, his posture stiff. Wren took in his severe expression and turned to me, pulling me into a quick embrace and whispering, "Be safe!" before slipping back into the stable.

"This better not be a last-ditch attempt to get me to stay," I cautioned warily, clutching the reins on the little red horse tighter.

Blaise simply offered a small, resigned smile.

"No, sunshine. I knew long ago that you'd never take orders from me." His smile faltered slightly. "Though I do wish you'd take my requests into consideration every once in a while."

I lowered my gaze, shame spreading from my chest through my entire frame. Blaise took a moment to glance around, ensuring no one else was nearby, and then stepped up to me. He grabbed my chin and lifted my face to meet his. His eyes were dark, filled with apprehension and sadness.

"Just be careful," he rasped, "and come back safely."

I nodded, and his lips captured mine, the kiss heated and desperate. We sank into it for several long moments, using the time to escape what came next and chase the apprehension away with pleasure.

Finally, Blaise stepped back, his face turning grim as the chilly air overtook the space between us.

"You'd better go. I don't want to risk anyone else seeing us together, in case information is getting back to those two somehow." He peered around again, as if to assure himself nobody lurked in the shadows. "Finlay will meet you at the outskirts of town. I know it's not dark yet, but I'd still rather be careful."

I murmured an acknowledgment and turned to mount the chestnut horse. I had already forgotten his name, so mentally, I dubbed him Red. When I turned back to wave goodbye, Blaise seemed about to say something.

I reined Red in, waiting for his words, but finally, he simply said, "I'll see you soon."

I smiled, nodding. "Soon," I promised, and took off towards town.

When I approached the edge of Sairas, I noted a small flame burning in the distance, marking Finlay's presence. I guided Red in that direction.

"There you are," he said as I approached, dousing the fire in his palm. He rested a book in the grass beside him. "I was beginning to wonder if I'd finish this entire book before you'd arrive."

I smirked at him. "And what do you read, exactly? *How To Get Laid For Beginners?*"

He didn't miss a beat. "Nah. I read that one ages ago. A bit of a snooze, actually. I always meant to write to the author and provide a few edits based on my personal experiences."

I huffed a disbelieving laugh as he stood, straightening his jacket. He wore a loose hunter-green shirt, tucked into black leather pants. He'd donned a thick black leather jacket over the top to combat the chill, complete with several buckles that he hadn't bothered to close. The pop of green underneath brought out the light, ocean-blue shine in his eyes.

"How do you do that?" I asked.

He stilled, an unreadable expression flitting across his face for a brief moment. "Do what?"

"Manage to make me laugh, even while you're irritating me."

"Ah. That. Well, I can't give away all my secrets." He shot me one of his lopsided grins and crossed his arms. "You look good. Those clothes — you look...at home in them."

I glanced down in surprise, shifting slightly in the saddle. I'd begun to swap my wardrobe for more authentic Muiranvian wear, but I still preferred pants over dresses, despite the amount Darrya had delivered to my room regularly. Therefore, I'd been slowly gathering what was considered fighting attire: leather pants and loose cotton shirts to be cinched at the waist with leather belts. Since it was growing colder, I'd opted to drape a woolen shawl over the top and don a pair of leather riding gloves for the trip. "Thanks," I returned, smiling. "I *feel* at home in them."

He returned my look warmly and cleared his throat. "So, what's the plan again? Meet back here in three days' time?"

My smile faded as I remembered where I was headed. "Yep. Every three days, like clockwork. Keep it consistent."

"And you've got the Faerie dust?" he asked, motioning to a saddlebag. I patted it firmly.

"I'll be back in the blink of an eye. No more rides than necessary for Red here," I replied, earning an exasperated look from Finlay.

"You didn't."

"What?"

Finlay eyed the small chestnut horse pointedly. "I'm almost positive that the horse's name is Kane."

"What's wrong with Red?"

"Gods fucking spare me. I can't wait to tell Cas and Kipp about this one." He rolled his eyes and uncrossed his arms, his expression turning more serious as he studied me now.

"Well. I know everyone else has told you to be careful, so I won't bother with that. But I suppose what I said the other night applies here too."

When I arched a quizzical brow at him, he reignited the flame in his palm in response. "We'll meet here, on the outskirts of town, every three days. If you don't know exactly where I'm at, just look for my flame."

He leaned in, his voice lowering as those intense blue eyes bored into my own. "If you ever find yourself in a bind, just come looking for this. I'll do everything I can to make sure you're safe." He pulled back, adding, "Like I said before. I'll always leave the light on for you."

I opened my mouth, and then closed it, unsure how to respond to that. Instead, my gaze caught on his book, and I nodded at it. "You'd better be finished with that by the time I get back," I said feebly.

It was a poor joke, but he took it in stride, offering me a nod and a wink. "I'll take careful notes, just for you."

I gathered my reins, taking a deep breath as I faced forward. I had a long ride ahead of me, and far more to do once I arrived. I shot a final look at Finlay.

"See you in three days."

"Three days, little angel. I'll be here."

CHAPTER SIXTEEN

I rehearsed my story on repeat until I had nearly convinced myself of its truth. I'd intentionally left early, and while the sun remained high in the sky, the mansion was several hours north. I only hoped to reach it before sundown.

I was intrigued by the changing landscapes while I rode. I passed a forest packed with deciduous trees while leaving Sairas — maples, oaks, and hickories, all shedding their leaves for winter — into vast expanses of fields and valleys, and eventually into another forest, this time filled with hardy evergreens, lush with emerald needles. Those familiar mountains rose up on my left to greet me once more, and my hips swayed slowly with Red's steps, the sound of his hoofbeats lulling me into a false sense of security.

When I was in middle school, I joined a group of kids that had snuck into a horror movie. By the end, though we all pretended it had been the coolest thing, most of us were traumatized. I slept terribly for weeks, but when a boy I had a crush on invited me on a haunted hayride for Halloween — with that same group of friends — I accepted.

I squeezed my eyes shut against the current chill of the evening and remembered that night, similarly frigid in temperature. I'd taken my irrational fears from that film and turned them into my own personal competition. Could I survive the first scare without jumping? Even though I'd bit the inside of my cheek to keep from screaming, I didn't jump, and then it became a game. How many scares could I make it through? I'd survived the first one; every terror that followed after couldn't be any worse.

I felt so proud by the end, even enjoying it, though the boy never asked me out again. Now, I realized, he'd probably been looking forward to consoling me — perhaps I'd even embarrassed him in front of his friends when he jumped and I didn't. But it had been a pivotal moment for me — a moment I learned the biggest walls I had to climb were the ones in my own mind.

Fear threatened to consume me now, almost a decade later. I knew the unease I felt here was warranted — the terrors that awaited, should I misstep, were very real, unlike the mediocre acting in the horror I'd watched as a teen. But if I could convince my mind, the rest would be that much easier.

I took a deep breath through my nose, the chilled air sharp against my nostrils. The mansion approached, fogged through my long exhale.

Get through the first explanation, and every lie from there on will be easy.

A figure darted across the grass, startling Red, and I glanced down to see a black cat. Its golden, knowing eyes gleamed up at me as it trotted alongside the horse, reminding me that this was no normal cat.

"Shadow," I said with a grin, and its tail swished in response to its name. "Glad to see a friendly face here. I'm going to need it."

I went quiet as we approached the door of the mansion, and before I could so much as dismount, it swung open. Myriam stood there, eyes blazing, as Soren stood in the shadows behind her. My stomach dropped for a moment, feeling the weight of the lies and betrayal that lingered between us before I switched gears.

I swung a leg over Red and leaped down, rearranging my expression into one of exasperated fear. I allowed an ounce of the emotions brimming inside me to seep out in the form of tears as I approached.

"Thank the gods you're both here! You're both okay!" I gasped, gripping Red's reins tightly in one hand. "I was so worried they had somehow found you."

The next few moments hung heavy in the air, splitting with tension as I observed their expressions. My free hand twitched, ready to will the earth between us into a wall if need be, providing me precious time to remount Red and race away. Only when Myriam's face twisted in confusion as she glanced back at Soren did I release the breath I held.

Step one, complete...many, many steps to go.

"How are you here?" Myriam demanded. The whites of her eyes flashed as they darted to either side of me, assessing if I had brought anyone with me.

"It was Finlay," I said, attempting to imbue my tone with awe and relief. "He's on our side. He snuck me out."

A heartbeat of silence followed my explanation; I analyzed their expressions, trying to read their thoughts. My muscles tensed.

"He's the one you visited while you were here before," Soren interjected thoughtfully, sharing another weighted look with Myriam.

Did I really not see this before? I nodded empathically. "Exactly!"

"But I watched him stab you," Soren's tone remained apprehensive.

"Yes." I winced, drawing on real emotion with the memory as I gave my answer. "But we talked that night about everything. He was proving himself to the others, biding his time — still is, in fact. He's gathering as much intel as he can, bit by bit." I paused, gauging their reactions before continuing. Sensing more intrigue than suspicion, I pressed onward.

"Smuggling me back out was the first time he'd taken action. He knew I'd be more help here than there."

The words spilled out, but I stopped myself short of rambling and feigned mild eagerness at their response. Soren seemed receptive, but it was Myriam who concerned me. Her face was impassive, but I refused to break. I was the one who had been able to prepare, practicing my exact tone and facial expressions to ensure believability. Caught off guard, she could only take them at face value.

"And you believe we can trust him?" Myriam asked slowly.

I bit my lip and shrugged, as if it was a question I didn't expect. "I mean, yeah. I saw the way he reacted when we talked before. I know how he feels about his family. And if that wasn't enough, he rescued me to give me the opportunity to get back to you. He even offered to pass along intel, if you're receptive to the idea."

There it was, perfectly placed, as though it were merely an afterthought — a dangling carrot that even Myriam would have a hard time resisting. I watched her eyes widen and blink in surprise as the wheels slowly turned.

Soren leaned in closer to her. "It would be the best plant we could ask for," he murmured. "Information from the prince himself."

Myriam hummed in agreement, fingers tapping thoughtfully against her thigh. "I haven't seen him take a stance one way or the other. If he has opinions, he's excelled at appearing impartial."

I shifted, my knees cracking from the long ride in the cold. The sound broke through Myriam's contemplative state, and she motioned for me to approach. I obliged, tugging Red forward with me, but as I drew closer, she held up a hand. I froze mid-step, heart leaping to my throat.

She held my gaze for a long moment before asking, "And what about Blaise?"

My brows knitted together. This, I hadn't been expecting. "What about him?"

"Did you see him again?"

I paused, then shook my head. She made a small, inquisitive noise in the back of her throat before unsheathing a small dagger from her waist. My pulse quickened as I sized it up carefully.

"And if you had?" She flipped the dagger in her hand before dragging her eyes to mine. "If you had, what would you have done?"

The question seemed innocent enough, but as my lips parted in surprise, I realized the dark request laced underneath. I quickly rearranged my expression, peeling my lips back to bare my teeth. I only hoped the rage emulated my expression from the night I fought against Blaise for the sword — when the evil enchantment of the Triskele mark had nearly prevailed.

"I would have killed him."

Despite the sick twist in my stomach, the venom in my tone dripped off each word. From the cruel curl of Myriam's lips, I knew my answer was satisfactory.

"Come, let's get you inside." She sheathed the dagger and offered me her hand, which I hesitantly accepted. Soren approached and took Red's reins. I slid his saddlebags off in one deft movement, my eyes scanning the surroundings for Shadow. True to her name, she had disappeared, but I had no doubts that she would appear in my room later.

By the time I had settled the items in my room — and given my furry roommate an affectionate scratch behind the ears — Myriam and Soren had clearly made a decision. I came downstairs to find them waiting at the base expectantly.

"Can you arrange regular meetings with Finlay now that you're back here?" Myriam asked brusquely.

I nodded. "He supplied me with a bit of Faerie dust in case you agreed. He's willing to meet every few days — more or less — based on what's happening in the palace," I said.

"And the others? Your old friends and family?" Soren inquired. This, I was also prepared for, and I made a show of curling my lip in distaste at the mention of them.

"Finlay has a safe, secluded location on the outskirts of town." I answered, then added for good measure, "He assured me we wouldn't be seen. That *I* wouldn't be seen, so I can remain — free."

I tripped over the last word, disgust washing over me as I remembered just how trapped I was. Luckily, it came across as a reference to my recapture from the Otherworld, and Myriam nodded in approval.

"You'll need to be careful. We have other spies in the palace, so they'll let us know if the others continue hunting you."

Interesting. I made a mental note to try and weasel some names out of her at a later date.

Her eyes wandered to Soren, and she added, "Soren will accompany you for the first meeting. I need to ensure everything goes according to plan."

I nodded, unsurprised. We had been prepared for this, too. The others would wake up following my departure, feigning rage and confusion over my 'escape.' Finlay wouldn't bat an eye once hearing I had an addition to our first meeting — and would hopefully have an arsenal of simultaneously interesting, but ultimately useless, information on the army and the queen's decisions.

"Do you know what happened to the sword?" Myriam asked, pivoting topics. I shook my head. This was an honest answer. I had purposefully asked not to be made aware of its whereabouts, in case I was re-marked against my will. Subconsciously, I crossed my arms and pulled my shawl tighter across my collarbone, thanking the cold weather for giving me a reason to cover my scars with plentiful clothing.

"And Finlay?" Soren added hopefully, but I shook my head again.

"Neither does he, unfortunately." I forced a mask of shame and lowered my eyes. "I'm sorry I didn't come back with more information. But I hope to find out more soon."

My eyes lifted to meet Myriam's, and then Soren's, conveying the sincerity of my words. They smiled hopefully at me, greedily even, in approval of the plan. I flashed a grateful grin in return.

I was back in. And with a little luck, I would soon find out more — straight from these traitors' mouths.

CHAPTER SEVENTEEN

The days that stood between my first meeting with Finlay were filled with strategic planning. I no longer felt wary about wandering the rest of the mansion, and nausea didn't strike the moment I left the front door, though I made sure to do that only when others weren't present. I strode boldly throughout the place, tracing and retracing my steps until I'd memorized every squeaky floorboard and checked every wall for vents or grates, where words could carry.

"Nerves," I supplied upon receiving curious looks from Myriam or Soren. "I'm not sure what else to do while I wait to meet up with Finlay, so I'm walking it off."

I took to carrying a book with me, plopping rapidly on the nearest chair when I heard someone approaching to lessen the number of times they caught me pacing like a madwoman. I'd only found one book in the library that seemed of any use — a book on espionage, where some long-ago rulers of Muiranvia and Brytham had feuded for the better part of a century. I skimmed the political details, grateful that we now had the level-headed Lachlan as an intermediary between the two lands.

Instead, I focused on any pointers it provided on spying. Aside from mentions of enchanted lock-picking and some clever political moves, I found little of use, but it did give me some ideas of places in the mansion I could check for further information.

When the time came for our first trip back to meet Finlay, I was beaming internally with pride. The moment felt like a small battle won, though I dulled it down to conceal my true emotions from Soren.

Finlay immediately embraced me, his relief evident. I drank in the smell of him. His scent had turned more earthen, likely from sobriety; he no longer carried the scent of vanilla and smoke. Instead, he smelled more like an herbal soap — cedarwood and thyme — and reminded me slightly of crisp, fallen leaves that now surrounded us in the forest, coated in a soft dusting of winter frost.

"You did it. You really did it," he breathed. A small laugh of dismay fanned over my hair.

"Did you ever doubt me?" I murmured into his shoulder before pulling back. I realized it was the first time we'd truly embraced, acting as though we were friends — which we were, now, I supposed. The precarious act of playing liaisons bound us together.

"Doubt you? Never. But them?" Finlay paused, his pale eyes rising to Soren, who stood a short distance away. He nodded subtly in greeting, his face betraying nothing. "I doubted them quite a bit."

"No need," I replied lightly. "I'm safe. I swear it." *Let them know I'm safe*, the words conveyed, and from the soft smile that played across Finlay's lips, I knew he would pass it along.

The rest of the meeting passed relatively uneventfully, with Finlay dutifully relaying the numbers and movements of Blaise's army. He played the part well, feigning disgust where needed and animated commitment to Soren's cause, which Soren ate up. He mentioned that the Sluagh had moved on, his eyes sliding intentionally to me as I breathed a sigh of relief. My strategic shift to rejoin Myriam and Soren had the intended effect, potentially sparing some innocent lives. The knot in my stomach lessened slightly at the news.

This also meant Blaise's army had returned to their natural posts, making them more predictable and easier for Finlay to continue his 'sleuthing'. I analyzed Soren's expression closely, but he didn't bat an eye; he gave no indication he had anything to do with the Sluagh.

The queen was planning a meeting with Lachlan in the next week, so more guests from Daersill and Brytham were expected to fill the palace. Finlay promised to gather even more information, this time from his own conversations as opposed to those he could only overhear.

It was a clever move, I realized, to allude there was more coming, likely of even greater value. He was buying me more time while keeping Soren and Myriam hopeful, and I knew he'd come up with something to look forward to again after next week, if need be.

By the time we were readying ourselves to leave, I could tell from Soren's relaxed stature that he felt no more need to tag along to our next visit.

"You two aren't — together now, are you?" he asked when we arrived home, quirking a brow at me.

"Finlay and me? Definitely not," I scoffed.

"I just thought, maybe — with the way he looks at you—" Soren shrugged, letting the sentence trail off.

"What do you mean? How does he look at me?" I asked, puzzled.

Soren took a moment to consider, as if drawing the image back up in his mind.

"Like you're the only beautiful thing he's truly *seen* in this life."

I flushed, hot and uncomfortable. "Well, isn't that romantic of you," I muttered.

"Well, all I'm saying is, you make a good team." Soren's reply was gruff as he walked away, leaving me to smile to myself, despite what I was going home to. If we made that good of a team, perhaps we'd pull this off after all.

The adrenaline from pulling off our façade faded from my body slowly, like dew lifting from the early morning grass. As it dissipated, exhaustion set in. The next few days were a struggle to stay awake; I waited to sleep until after the others went to bed, and attempted to wake before them, desperate not to miss any conversations.

I slid through the hallways, mindful of my breathing and footwork as I followed Myriam and Soren's voices through the walls. The voices stopped outside the office, and I scrambled to find the nearest vent, propping myself up to listen.

"...wonder if Blaise is the one who hid the sword." Myriam was saying, irritation running rampant in her tone.

"If he is, you know there isn't much we can do if we don't find where he's hidden it. He's got the entire army behind him, ready to jump at his beck and call."

Though Soren had betrayed Blaise, I was almost certain there was an element of respect in his tone, and perhaps a touch of wistfulness.

Good, I thought. *I hope turning his back on his best friend keeps him up at night.*

I heard Myriam snort. "Please. Finlay confirmed what we already know from Kashden and Jamara. He has one-tenth of the manpower that we have with our dark Faeries alone."

My heart plummeted. They continued murmuring, but I barely registered the rest of their exchange, replaying and considering her words. One tenth? Blaise's troop at the palace contained roughly sixty soldiers, but if they were counting the entire brigade in Muiranvia, there were three separate battalions, comprising around seven thousand soldiers, if I recalled correctly. As commander-in-chief, if they assembled into a brigade, Blaise would be the one to lead them all. I hoped it wouldn't come to that.

The conversation ceased, and I darted away to avoid being discovered. For the first time that week, I slept peacefully, feeling accomplished for having heard something useful.

Chapter Eighteen

Finlay enjoyed plays and theater as much as the next Faerie, but he was certain the best acting ever witnessed had taken place this past week, right in the palace. Kate's father, Blaise, and Kipp all seemed as angry and distraught over her disappearance as they had been the first time — perhaps more so. Darrya and Wren acted confused and helpless, while Finlay leaned heavily into his cocky indifference, grateful that it was second nature for him.

He was, however, surprised by the way it tugged at his heartstrings. He hadn't considered himself super close with Kate's friends, yet to be ripped away as the group had begun embracing his presence left him empty in a way he'd never experienced. A consequence of his own actions, he supposed. If he never allowed himself to get close to someone, he'd never feel lonely at the loss of their presence.

Instead, he busied himself with becoming the palace shadow, listening for murmurs and conspiracies through walls. While he knew the names of some of the queen's spies, it had been ages since they'd allowed him to tag along, for their own sheer amusement as much as his. He doubted he had the same charm to learn their secrets as he did when he was a curly-haired, chubby-faced child, too young and stupid to pose a genuine risk to their careers.

He relearned secret entrances through the palace, navigating through corridors in the back walls and making his way from place to place without the tracking of eyes and ears.

Larke became his liaison to Blaise, coordinating meetings for them, which Blaise passed along to the rest of the group. Whereas Finlay became the palace shadow, Larke became the commander's — following him everywhere as the two of them exchanged endless conversation in hushed tones.

Finlay waited expectantly in the corridor that led to a vacant room. Kate's presence as she stood beside him left him buzzing. He was hard-pressed not to extend his energy to tap against hers as he had once before. That feeling — so long ago, now — had been exhilarating. Finlay was sure Kate hadn't yet tapped into the full extent of her powers, but when she did, he had no doubt it would be exceptional. And he could think of no one better equipped to wield it than her.

"Finlay?" Blaise's hushed voice called out in the corridor, and Kate perked up at his side.

"Here," Finlay responded softly. As Blaise rounded through the doorway, Kate rushed forward to embrace him, and his head nestled on top of hers.

"I'm so glad to see you're safe, sunshine," he murmured, pulling her closer. As she melted into him, Finlay's chest tightened, remembering their embrace the week prior: friendly, but nothing like the intimacy he witnessed here. He cleared his throat.

"Kate has some news to share," he said, catching Blaise's eye. Blaise loosened his grip on Kate, holding her at arm's length before peering down at her.

"What have you heard?" he asked, his posture stiffening.

"Myriam and Soren have intel on your army. From a…Jamara? And Kash…" she trailed off, blinking as she tried to remember their names.

"Kashden," Blaise finished flatly, running a hand through his hair. His tense expression bordered on one of chagrin. "Interesting. They're both a bit aloof, but I never would have guessed. I'll ensure any important information is withheld from them."

"That's not all," Kate pressed on. "They also mentioned numbers. Ten times your army, Blaise. All dark Faeries."

Blaise chewed on the information for a moment, his wheels turning, and then let out a heavy exhale. Finlay and Kate both watched him tensely, exchanging a glance.

"I wasn't sure if she meant your troops here at the palace or across all of Muiranvia," Kate added warily.

"Oh, she definitely meant all of Muiranvia," Blaise answered with a grimace. "Which means she has about…seventy thousand dark Faeries at her disposal."

"From where?" Finlay blurted, confused. His heart rate quickened as he imagined what seventy thousand dark Fae would look like lined up and prepared for battle. Hordes of Sluagh, Gancanagh, Nuckelavee, and more…all bloodthirsty creatures, wielding lethal powers borne from the shadows. All partnered in one army.

The dark Fae were naturally solitary creatures, and tended to leave bustling Faerie cities and towns alone. What had Nemain said — or done — to gather so many of them together? Furthermore, how could a mass of dark Faeries *that* large exist in Muiranvia without them knowing? Their presence would look like a blemish on a map; tens of thousands of Fae creating a sea of endless darkness.

"We can't take on an army that big," Kate said, her voice nearly pleading, as though begging Blaise to contradict her. He delivered, his eyes dark.

"Not without more training, no. But although the dark Fae have immense and unique powers of their own, their natural tendencies do not allow for camaraderie. They'll just as easily fight each other as us. That chaos gives us an edge."

Blaise rubbed his chin, pondering for a moment. "I'll have Larke ask for reinforcements from Daersill. Discreetly, of course."

The knot of panic in Finlay's chest lessened at the realization that Blaise had a plan, but he tensed as the commander's gaze turned on him.

"Lachlan's sons are visiting with him this week, are they not?"

Finlay bit the inside of his cheek hard enough to draw blood.

"Yes," he answered tersely. Neither he nor Darrya was thrilled by the prospect of their visit; Darrya already planned to make herself as scarce as possible. Finlay didn't blame her — if they even looked at her for too long, he wasn't sure what he would do. His fingertips sparked with whispers of angry flames at the mere thought.

"Could you ask them about their forces in Brytham, and if they would be receptive to offering their aid in times of need? If we had an idea of their numbers and willingness to help, it could give us the advantage we need." He paused, hazel eyes reaching Finlay's before he continued. "I would ask, but they are...difficult to get an audience with. They would not refuse you, however."

Finlay bit back his automatic refusal, eyes skating to where Kate stood resolutely. If she could march back into the lion's den, head held high to face her demons, he could do this. He nodded, plastering a smile on his face.

"Only if I can throw those two into the fight as well. Maybe have Darrya accidentally shoot them, while we're at it."

Aerrin and Thaddeus Byrne were opposite sides of the same coin. Aerrin's dark red hair was short and trim, the shadow of his beard neatly kept and punctuated with the permanent broad smile on his face. Thaddeus was the solemn to Aerrin's silly, his own dark-colored hair long and straight, blue eyes distrustful. His lips were permanently pressed into a thin line, as though observing the world and always finding it wanting.

Finlay surveyed them both as they entered the throne room to address the queen. They walked side by side, yet trailed a few respectful

steps behind their father. It was a gift to have multiple children —
a gift his parents never had the chance to experience. Despite living
for multiple centuries, Faerie parents were considered blessed if they
had two children, let alone three or four. Siblings were a unique
experience, one even more complicated by titles and crowns.

Finlay considered his cousin as close as a sibling, having been
raised alongside her, but it was different for royal blood. Even if
she had married one of the Byrne brothers, solidifying the relationship between their lands, she'd never be in line for the Muiranvian
throne, as long as Finlay lived. Their relationship had never been one
of animosity, though, as neither truly wanted the title.

His ears blocked out whatever kind words were exchanged between Lachlan and the queen, eyes narrowing at Aerrin. Intrusive,
violent thoughts flooded his mind as he took in Aerrin's devilish
grin. He'd been wearing the same grin while looking between Finlay
and Darrya all those years ago, when Finlay had been all of eighteen
years old and barged in at the sound of his cousin's distress.

Finlay distinctly remembered the way everything had registered
with him, one at a time: the ragged sounds of Darrya's sobs, the
bright crimson trickling from her lower lip, the hanging sleeve of her
dress, torn from her shoulder. And finally, the way he'd lit the entire
room on fire with his rage, unable to bring it back under control.

Aerrin had disappeared the second Finlay sent the room up in
flames, with Lachlan appearing eventually to douse it. The duke had
taken one look at Darrya and whisked her under his wing, curtly
ordering Finlay to walk off his anger. She'd emerged from a room
on the other side of his castle a while later, healed, somber, and

quiet. Lachlan, to his immense credit, had promptly announced the dissolution of her engagement to Aerrin with quiet fury.

Finlay had never discussed the incident with Darrya in depth, but she'd expressed her gratitude to him multiple times in passing over the past century.

While he knew he'd arrived in time to save her from further harm, it didn't keep him from nearly boiling over in rage every time he was forced to share the same air as Aerrin — times like this. It was all he could do to rein in his power enough to keep the room from rising in temperature by several degrees.

He shook the memory off, bringing himself back to the present moment. Aerrin was the eldest of the two brothers, in line to take over leadership of Brytham. It was currently led by the regent who reigned in Lachlan's stead, because Lachlan opted to remain as ambassador between their lands and stay in Daersill. Unfortunately, all of this meant Finlay had to address Aerrin directly.

He leapt into action as they exited the throne room, hoping to catch Aerrin and Thaddeus together. Aerrin and Finlay had spent much — mostly forced — time together, whereas Thaddeus was younger and kept mostly to himself. Finlay didn't know him too well, but with what he did know, Thaddeus was reserved and relatively unproblematic, underscored by the sheer lack of rumors regarding him. He would be an excellent buffer for Finlay's rage.

Lachlan cast Finlay a curious glance as he breezed past. Finlay had the presence of mind to flash the duke a small smile, tilting his head respectfully as he passed.

"Thaddeus. Aerrin. I was hoping for a moment of your time." Finlay's voice rang out, surprising himself with the confidence it held. They paused in unison and turned to face him. Both were dressed warmly in the colors of their land, thick royal blue tunics and overcoats, made of linen and embroidered with silver.

"By all means," Aerrin replied coolly. His voice retained some of the lilt Lachlan had, yet was marked by stringent language education, similar to Finlay's.

Finlay stopped a few feet from them, clenching his jaw as they surveyed one another. He tilted his chin a touch higher, reminding himself — as much as the brothers — who was in control.

"We had a surprise attack from a rogue group of dark Fae a few months back. It seemed isolated, but recently, we've had a few incidents with Sluagh, which have pressed our local troops thin." Finlay chose his words carefully, tapping into the crumbs of political prowess he possessed. Aerrin tilted his head, listening intently.

"It seems to have resolved itself, but it did bring up some questions we haven't needed to ask previously. Most prominent of which being, if we needed to request aid from your land, would you provide it?"

"Naturally." Aerrin's answer was instantaneous, and Thaddeus reaffirmed the answer with a nod of his own. "As I'm sure you would do, should the situations be reversed," Aerrin added — a political comment if Finlay ever heard one.

"Without question," Finlay's reply was smooth. "Which leads to my second question. What kind of numbers could we count on, in such a time of need?"

Aerrin considered the question for a moment. "Around three thousand. Thirty-five hundred, if we include troops from our residence and Aes Sídhe who would join the fight." Thaddeus jerked in surprise at his answer, shooting his brother a questioning look before averting his gaze.

It was a small move, but Finlay marked it. It seemed Aerrin did as well, judging by the muscle that feathered irritably in his jaw. Neither of them chose to comment on it, and Finlay nodded slowly in approval.

"Well." He allowed the single word to hang for several moments before continuing. "Let's hope there is no need for it. But I appreciate the validation in the unity of our lands, regardless." Finlay curled his lips in a polite smile. "I hope you have a wonderful stay here in Muiranvia."

Aerrin lobbed a grin his way while Thaddeus murmured his thanks. Finlay turned on his heel, proud of the cordial exchange, but heard Aerrin's voice echo down the hallway before he turned the corner.

"Give my best wishes to Darrya as well," he called.

Finlay's fists clenched, tightly enough to cut crescent shapes into his skin, flames instantly springing to life and rolling across his palms and over his knuckles. He willed himself to keep walking. He was no longer a teenager, unable to control his emotions or powers. To turn around and show his rage was to relinquish his control, and Aerrin knew it. He continued, mind racing.

Brytham would not help them, that much was clear. Aerrin had blatantly underreported their numbers, which likely meant he'd also lied about their support overall. Though Finlay couldn't fathom the reason, he planned to find out exactly why Aerrin had lied to his face.

Chapter Nineteen

Confidence flooded my veins as my sleuthing went undetected for the next full week. Despite my copious eavesdropping, I learned no new information, but the attention had faded from me as well. As Finlay relayed it to me, Lachlan was wholly committed to the queen and her views, which I promptly relayed to Myriam and Soren. What I didn't include, however, was his recounted discussion with Lachlan's sons, who I didn't realize existed.

"They're utterly useless," Finlay had told me. "His eldest promised their support, but it was..." With a pause, he sighed and shook his head. "I could tell it was a complete and utter lie. We can't trust them."

The interaction had clearly left a sour taste in Finlay's mouth, so I didn't press the issue. It made my heart sink to hear, but I kept it to myself. It was a weakness in our armor that Myriam and Soren didn't need to be privy to.

I stifled a nervous yawn as I considered the implications of a potential war between our army and Nemain's. Lack of sleep had taken its toll on me as I maneuvered the empty rooms in the dead of night, with only the moonlight as my guide.

I crept from room to room, stretching my legs and reaching with the balls of my feet to pass over creaks in the floor. I felt along for any imperfections in the walls that may indicate a hidden opening. A soft chirrup sounded as Shadow darted across my path, bringing me to a halt. I raised an eyebrow at her, but kept my mouth shut — if there was something the Cait Sídhe was trying to convey, I needed to stay quiet and watch her closely.

Shadow approached the fireplace in the room, curling up in the pit. I suppressed my alarm as realization dawned on me; she sprawled out, gathering not a single spot of coal on her black coat. Though every other fireplace had been lit in this house to combat the colder weather, this particular fireplace had never been used. Slowly, I approached, running my hands over the brick and pushing.

We were in a large guest room, far away from where Myriam, Soren, and I slept. I was grateful for that as the fireplace groaned in complaint, but gave way, shuddering as I pushed. I paused, waiting for a full few minutes in silence, willing myself not to breathe as I awaited any sign the others had woken from the sound. Nothing came. Emboldened, I pressed again.

I opened the space just wide enough to scan what lay behind the faux fireplace. When I saw what it was, I pushed further.

Far enough to bring Dagda's cauldron into full view.

I glanced around anxiously, whipping a blanket off the nearby bed and wrapping it around the cauldron in an abundance of caution. I squeezed my eyes shut as I pulled the cauldron out, a moment of panic washing over me as I remembered the last time I clutched the talisman. Nausea rose in my stomach, threatening to climb up my throat, as a phantom pain burned through my ruined marks.

When nothing more happened, I breathed a sigh of relief and willed myself not to waste any more time. I moved as quickly and silently as possible, bringing the cauldron back to my room and replacing the blanket with my own. Darting back downstairs, I re-arranged the blanket into its original position on the guest bed and pushed the fireplace back into place. This time, I didn't wait to hear if anyone else moved; instead, I scurried back to my room to curl up with Shadow, waiting breathlessly.

Five minutes passed, then ten, as I waited for someone to come for me and demand what I had done. When fifteen minutes passed, I finally released a long breath and reached for the bag of Faerie dust I kept beside my bed. I wasn't scheduled to return to the palace, yet, but I couldn't keep this in my room any longer than necessary. I had to deliver the cauldron to Finlay before they discovered it was missing, and the moment to try was now.

The forest was dark and disorienting as I landed. It took a moment for my eyes to adjust, and I blinked rapidly before turning to locate the direction of the palace. My pace picked up as the cold night air assaulted my face, and I tucked the blanket surrounding the cauldron closer to my face to combat the chill.

Leaves crunched under my feet and owls cooed as I neared the palace, and my eyes scanned the perimeter for any signs of movement. They landed on a flicker of light in a corner of the palace; it stood out, simply for its random location. I blinked in surprise, and realized it was near the hidden passageway Finlay had snuck me into the last time I had visited. I set off toward it.

The heir was asleep, propped up against the side of the palace. Only a light blanket sat beneath him for comfort against the cold, hard ground. He wore all black, from his leather boots, loose pants, and tunic, to the oversized fleece coat over top. His hands were intertwined in his lap, his palms burning in a reddish-orange glow that rose high in the air. I was amazed to see that he could keep the flame ablaze in his sleep. It rested in his lap, and yet refused to burn his skin or clothing. I was certain he was exerting only a lick of his power.

I leaned forward, my nose brushing against his rumpled golden locks as my lips nearly pressed to his ear.

"Wonders never cease," I whispered, and watched as his eyes fluttered open. It was always intimate to see someone asleep, but especially him — he wore none of his normal expressions that typically alternated between benign amusement and cocky observance. His sleepy look was soft, bordering on tender, even.

"Mmmm?" he murmured as he came to consciousness, flames sputtering with uncertainty.

"Leave the light on, huh?" I asked, motioning to his hands. "I didn't realize you kept your promises so well. Or so...literally."

He blinked and looked down at his hands, lowering the arching flames into a dull glow, almost like a night light. Now fully awake, his expression widened into his classic lazy grin. "There's a lot you don't know about me, little angel."

"Noted. But right now, I only have one question. What are you doing freezing your ass off in your sleep out here?"

"I don't know if you've noticed, but I have an eternal flame inside me. It burns pretty hot. It would take an active effort for me to freeze."

He stretched and stood, glancing at the palace behind him. "I figured it would be easier for you to find me undetected if I stay outside of the palace walls. Not to mention, the brothers Grimm still haven't gone back to Brytham."

Finlay's tone dripped with disdain, an echo of Darrya's sentiments. She had also been absent from the palace for the past week, and I missed her radiant optimism. In fact, I missed all my friends. It still surprised me sometimes — I'd spent most of my life forging my path independently, and yet here I was, aching for companionship.

I raised the cauldron, still swaddled around the blanket, and received a curious look from Finlay.

"What the hell is that?" he asked. "Did you steal a lumpy baby?"

"It's a massive win, and also a massive problem," I replied, unraveling the blanket. Finlay's eyes widened as he took in the cauldron, and he choked out an incredulous laugh.

"You fucking did it, Kate," he breathed, and I smiled as he used my real name with pride. "But I see what you mean. Once Nemain finds out it's gone, and she's left with no safeguard against the power you can collect from all the talismans..." He trailed off, leaving me to finish the sentence for him.

"She'll tear the world apart to get it back."

A tense silence hung in the air as we considered the implications. We had put everyone in danger by reclaiming the cauldron, should Nemain come looking for it here. My mind flitted from face to face as I considered those I loved, sleeping soundly in this very palace — Darrya, Blaise, Kipp, my father. Everyone Nemain would target.

"So, we'd better find a damn good hiding place," Finlay said with conviction, blowing a stray piece of hair from his face. The hot breath swirled white in the cold air, and I watched it rise as I sorted through my thoughts.

"I have an idea, but it might be risky," I hedged. Finlay leaned forward expectantly. "What if we give it to Lachlan?"

"Lachlan?" Finlay echoed. "Why him?"

"I mean, he has the Speaking Stone, and I haven't heard any mention of that from Myriam or Soren. He's kept one talisman concealed for who knows how long."

"But he told you the first time he met you. Who is to say he's not blabbing to others as well?" Finlay retorted, crossing his arms. The dull glow dissipated entirely, leaving us basking only in the light of the moon.

I had to admit, it was a good point. "Then we give it to him with the addendum that both are to be kept secret from here on out," I ventured, before adding, "He knows what happened when I touched the stone. He heard the call, and he respected it."

Finlay sucked his bottom lip between his teeth and chewed, thinking. I tried not to focus on his mouth — one that I'd come close to kissing more than once.

"It would be a good strategic move to get it out of Muiranvia entirely," he mused. "Split the talismans, even from us. She wouldn't suspect that at all."

"So, will you give it to him? Before he leaves?" I asked, and he nodded slowly. I flashed him a grateful smile and plopped the blanket-wrapped cauldron down next to him.

"Thank you," I said gratefully, rubbing my hands together. "Okay. I'd better get back before there's any suspicion."

As I turned to leave, Finlay stopped me, grabbing my wrist.

"Little angel."

I turned, and when he met my gaze, he asked, "Are you sure you want to go back?" A note of fear cut through his voice. "We have the cauldron. We know the numbers for her army. You don't need to play their side anymore. I can't stand to think that you'll get caught in the crossfire when Nemain realizes the cauldron is missing."

His protective words tugged at me, and I reeled with the stark realization of how much he cared for me. My eyes lowered to where his hand still gripped my wrist; the heat emanating from him was warm, but not uncomfortable. I flicked my gaze back up to meet his own, intense and unwavering. His thumb trailed over the tender inside of my arm, softly, and I shivered at his gentle touch, my toes curling inside my boots. If I didn't step away now, I wouldn't leave. And I needed to — for everyone's sake.

Finlay must have sensed the shift in my resolve, because his expression tightened. A muscle feathered in his jaw. "Please."

"She has no reason to come back for it until she has another talisman," I assured him, as much for his sake as my own. "I've almost combed through every room. A few more days could give us that final chess piece, so we know *where* to strike. It's the leg up we need, especially since we're so outnumbered."

Finlay looked ready to argue more, but decided against it. He sighed and dropped my hand, leaving it open to the cold night air once more. "Fine. But once you've combed every room, come back. We need you here."

"I will," I promised, and motioned to the cauldron. "Just make sure that the cauldron gets out of here safely."

He echoed my words. "I will."

I reached for a handful of Faerie dust, and his soft smile was the last thing I saw as I departed in a flash, landing alone in my room in the mansion. Shadow looked up from the bed expectantly, and I moved to join her. For now, I needed to sleep, but first thing tomorrow, my hunt would start again.

Chapter Twenty

It was only a matter of time before the misdirections and half-truths stopped placating Myriam and Soren — and time was something we were preciously short on. That urgency drove me to recklessness as I explored the remaining rooms over the next few days.

The room Soren and Myriam shared was suspiciously, albeit unsurprisingly, devoid of useful information. I bided my time, hitting the rooms during their training times with one another, heart pounding in my ears as I sifted through their drawers and ran my hands between their sheets. I felt relieved and frustrated by the realization we may have all the information we could gather from this place.

Now, I sat in an abandoned study, debating whether the darkness warranted the risk of lighting a candle. The room had clearly been passed over for the larger office, which I'd combed over the week prior, and defeat settled over me like the layer of dust in this room.

It was the last unchecked space, but I had already resigned myself to the fact I would not find any more clues.

Absent-mindedly, I pulled the desk drawers open once more, as if willing something to appear. When I opened the bottom right drawer for the second time, however, I noticed something...*off* with the drawer dimensions. A passing scene from the espionage novel I'd read came to mind.

"False bottom drawer," I murmured, tapping lightly against the wood at the base. Hollow. I trailed my finger along it until I found a divot and pulled. My breath caught as the plank gave way, and I placed the faux bottom softly on the floor to pick up the papers that sat there.

A map lay below, crudely drawn but clearly marked. I squinted against the darkness, my eyes following the paths of red and blue ink; after a moment, I realized they were army movements. I did my best to memorize the maps for several long moments before rifling through the other papers, consisting mostly of coded lists and correspondence. Yet I paused on one handwritten note, reading through it with curiosity.

M —

Indeed, the numbers are looking excellent, and we await your next move with bated breath. However, regarding your request for additional allyship, we must unfortunately refuse.

I need not remind you that we have provided many sureties on our end throughout the years, not the least of which being our elimination of royal threats. For this reason, we pray you can understand our hesitancy with more action until sureties are provided on our end, perhaps in the form of a royal dispatchment in turn.

-A & T

A throat cleared behind me. I leapt up, spinning in alarm. My hand flew to the hidden dagger strapped under my pajamas, and I straightened to face Soren, his expression wary and confused.

"What do we have here?" He leaned against the doorframe, assessing me. "A little lost lamb who seems to have stumbled into something she shouldn't."

My heart thundered.

"I was — I didn't —" I fumbled for the right words to say, the moment moving too fast for my thoughts to catch up.

"—You...didn't mean to sneak into the office and find documents hidden in a secret compartment?" he finished for me, stepping closer. I automatically moved back and risked a calculating glance beyond him. If I could make it past him, there was a chance I could safely get to my room and the Faerie dust by my bed. Magic prickled at my fingertips, but I shoved it down. Soren and I had practiced endlessly during my first few weeks here; he knew my every move with magic. Moreover, he wielded fire, something he was very aware I had not yet mastered.

"I'm a very lively sleepwalker," I retorted, eyes sliding back to Soren. I twisted my body, keeping one hand tactfully out of sight. "Don't you know it's not wise to wake a sleepwalker?"

"Somehow, I don't believe you." His response was curt, and when he reached out to grab me, my aim was true. My dagger plunged into his arm, sending him stumbling back.

"You stabbed me!" he exclaimed, aghast, as I shifted to angle past him. We moved around each other, squaring off in a dangerous dance.

"And I'll do it again if you don't move," I warned, flipping the dagger in what I hoped was a threatening move. Despite all he had done, I didn't think I could kill him — but I had no qualms about leaving some damage on my way out.

"No need for that."

I cursed, immediately recognizing Myriam's voice. Her footsteps stopped as she curled around the doorway. I lifted my gaze to meet hers and was startled to see how her abnormally pale eyes swirled with darkness, as though black ink was spilling across white paper.

I gasped as the air was sucked from the room, the weight of her magic pressing down on my lungs like an anvil. The dagger slipped through my fingers as I clawed at my throat, desperate for oxygen. It clattered loudly as it hit the ground.

"I don't foresee you going anywhere," Myriam crooned. "We have you right where we need you."

CHAPTER TWENTY-ONE

Juggling communications between the land's battalions was not an enjoyable task for Blaise, but it passed the time — a welcome distraction from Katherine's absence. And, he reasoned, at least he was able to continue working openly with Larke, Patrick, and the others. He felt Finlay's absence more vividly than he'd expected, given that Blaise had never considered him a friend.

Perhaps he felt guilty, spending time with Katherine's friends while keeping Finlay on the outskirts. Their presence lessened the hole in his stomach, growing each passing week without her. They were the pieces of her that remained in Sairas while she worked recklessly in the shadows.

He smiled into his mug as he surveyed them now. Their banter surrounded him like a cozy blanket as they congregated in Castille's house for breakfast, a luxury Blaise hadn't allowed himself to indulge in for what felt like ages.

"Cas! How did it go with the mysterious suitor last night?" Darrya asked Castille, flopping down on a chair next to Larke. She poured herself a cup of coffee. "Is he joining us for breakfast?"

The Pixie stretched his wings alongside his arms as he emerged from his bedroom, the colors shimmering like a sunrise against his bare chest. He let out a big yawn before tucking them away and shrugging on a robe. A tired grin danced across his face as he warmly regarded the guests in his home. Blaise couldn't fathom how Castille coped with having so many guests flitting in and out, but he seemed to thrive on it.

"Come on, D. You know I don't let them spend the night. Even last night's tasty snack."

The table burst out in laughter, confusing Castille, until Larke lobbed his hand over to Darrya, wiggling his fingers with a grin. "Pay up."

Darrya groaned and rolled her eyes in response, but pulled out a few golden coins and smacked them into his open palm.

"You all were taking bets?" Castille gasped, feigning horror even as his eyes twinkled. Blaise smirked, though his eyes wandered to Kipp, who was the only one noticeably not joining in on the laughter. He smiled, but it didn't quite reach his eyes, which were resolutely fixed on his fresh mug of coffee.

They had just begun refilling their coffee when the door burst open, and Wren stumbled through. Her normally calm demeanor was nowhere to be seen, replaced with a look of sheer panic. Blaise was alarmed when her eyes locked straight onto his; he was on his feet before she spoke.

"I think Katie needs your help," she said, and that was all it took. Those six words had him out the door with her, his hand on the hilt of his sword. The others weren't far behind as Wren motioned them out of the house.

"Tell me everything," Blaise demanded, stalking briskly alongside her.

"Everything was fine last night when I wrapped up at the stables, but this morning Gray was going nuts. I've never seen him like this. He's pacing, whinnying, practically bursting the fence down."

"Which he could," Kipp added thoughtfully, "if he wanted to. Which means he's *trying* to tell us something."

Wren nodded. "Exactly. It took me a minute to connect the dots, but when I did, I came straight to you. Apparently, reinforcements are needed."

Blaise's thoughts whirled with countless possibilities. If Gray felt she needed more help than what he could provide, what did that mean for the danger she was in? His heart raced, and he closed his eyes, taking a deep breath and forcing himself to calm down. He needed to think rationally. If Gray hadn't forced his way out, that meant Kate was — hopefully — still okay. Blaise needed to keep his composure to ensure it stayed that way.

"Kipp, go find Patrick. Larke, bring us weapons. And Darrya—" Blaise paused, the order stuck in his throat. "—go find Finlay."

They all nodded, racing toward the palace as Blaise and Wren continued to the stable. A soft thud alerted them to Castille landing nearby, now fully clothed and wearing an uneasy expression. The disgruntled whinnies reached Blaise's ears before the fields came into view.

He hadn't seen much of Gray since Katherine had first come to Muiranvia, and he hadn't paid much attention to the stallion. Instead, her beautiful face — and that wickedly clever tongue — had been his only focus. But now that he looked closely, he was stunned he hadn't noticed how unique the stallion truly was.

He surpassed every horse Blaise had seen in sheer height and muscle, even the horses in the cavalry. The gleam in his dark eyes was unnervingly wise, and the way he moved betrayed his lethal, godlike power. He flowed rather than trotted his way down the fence line, thick neck arched and nostrils flared in his frenzy.

"Hey boy," Wren murmured, and the horse paused long enough to inspect their group. Wren extended her hand slowly to him, but he tossed his head and whinnied once more, prancing away.

Blaise pursed his lips. "Can you bring us your fastest horses?" he asked.

Wren nodded, slipping away with Castille following behind. Blaise ground his teeth, pacing to work through his impatience. He desperately wished they could use Faerie dust to reach her, but they had long ago surmised that the area was enchanted with explicit restrictions on who could portal in and out. Riding there would have to suffice, and he only hoped they would arrive in time.

Wren and Castille arrived back with several horses, and they all worked together to saddle them. The others arrived in time to pick their horses, and when Patrick went to Gray, the stallion settled for him. Blaise wasn't surprised — Katherine's father had been tending to him in her absence. The fact that Cú Chulainn's blood ran through his veins likely helped, too.

"Larke, stay behind. I need someone here in case the army needs orders in my absence," Blaise commanded. Larke nodded without question, sheathing his sword. Blaise's eyes slid to Finlay, who met his gaze, though quickly averted his eyes.

Blaise and Larke felt Soren's absence keenly. In any other circumstances, Blaise could count on Larke on a mission such as this, while leaving his third to oversee other tasks. But with Soren's betrayal and the other events they'd been dealing with, Blaise had yet to name a new third. It would bring up questions he wasn't prepared to answer. Should they need to fight, he would have to put his faith in Finlay and the others.

"Wren—" he began, but Wren waved him off, offering a resigned smile.

"I'll stay behind. Maybe I can convince Larke to teach me a few things," she replied, and Larke nodded in agreement. When Blaise turned to Darrya and opened his mouth, however, her face clouded with anger.

"Don't even start with me, Blaise. I'm not staying behind," she snapped, and mounted her horse, adjusting the bow and quiver across her back. She straightened in the saddle and gave him a pointed look that left no room for discussion. Despite the circumstances, Blaise had to bite back a smirk.

"Play nice, cousin," Finlay said, mounting his own horse. His tone was teasing and light, but his expression was undeniably tense.

"Let's get going," Katherine's father boomed, leading the way atop Gray. The stallion's head curved, chin to chest, as Patrick attempted to rein him in. He pranced in place, like a racehorse ready to explode from the gates. "He'll lead us there."

As they took off, Blaise brought his horse in line with Finlay's. The prince's eyes met his. With the others ahead of them, they took the moment to openly convey the true dread they shared. Blaise knew if Katherine was hurt, they would both move mountains to see her avenged. And if she was — Blaise swallowed forcibly. He couldn't even go there.

He pushed his horse closer to Finlay's, close enough that their stirrups touched.

"Don't forget," he rasped, voice raw with unchecked emotion and all the threat he could muster. Finlay's jaw twitched, but he nodded, his blue eyes surprisingly dark.

"I haven't. I won't," he swore. Blaise watched as the fist that bore their matching mark clenched momentarily against his reins. With that, they urged their horses into gallops, praying they reached Katherine in time.

Chapter Twenty-Two

H ere's what I've learned about war.

In the human realm, it's as much about resources as face-to-face combat. Everyone dances around their most destructive weapons, dangling them as a last resort power play. But that's not *really* where the power lies. It's a high-stakes political game, where the power is hidden in backdoor conversations whispered between governments and pockets being lined with money.

War in the Faerie realm, I've come to realize, has some similarities; whispers direct and misdirect those in charge, to be sure. But nobody's pockets are filled solely with coin. Instead, magic is touted as the biggest currency — *magic* is where the true power lies. It's dangled as their power play, and they're truly not afraid to use it to their advantage.

And somehow, I became their nuclear weapon.

My gifts were the only thing keeping me alive. Even if I admitted nothing, they could not kill me, as I was more valuable alive than dead.

I repeated that fact to myself over the next several hours, as I twisted and strained against the rope holding my wrists above my head. It was plain rope and not chain, an intentional and stark reminder of how little power I had without the talismans — the tiny sparks I could summon made no difference to the material.

Not that it mattered. I would still be left with both Soren and Myriam to face, and in my state, I stood no chance against either of them. I had no weapons and had wasted the last of my magical energy hours ago, blocking the torturous blows with my air shield, diminishing my gifts to nothing. I had wanted to hold off and use my magic to fight, but the pain she inflicted had instantly eddied every strategic thought from my brain, leaving only the basest urge for survival.

The pounding of my blood resounded through every single wound, throbbing with each heartbeat. I struggled to pinpoint which wound hurt the most, but trying to do so passed the time and somehow softened the overall pain I felt. I stood on the balls of my feet to avoid a tormenting stretch in my shoulders, and the alternative left my calves trembling. By some miracle, however, I had long since lost all feeling in them.

My vision swarmed intermittently with black dots, only clearing when I concentrated on something tangible — most often, the sharp tang of my own blood in my mouth. There was nothing else in the room to distract me; we were in the basement of Myriam's mansion, surrounded only by dirt and stone. I inhaled deeply through my mouth — my nose had long since been ruined for breathing — and tried to focus on the words echoing down the stairs as they approached once more.

"I won't re-mark her yet," Myriam was insisting in response to something Soren said. "She would only be confused by what I plan on doing to her. And I don't want her confused."

"She hasn't given us any answers. What is it you want from her at this point?" Soren asked as they came into view. I raised my eyes in time to see him run a hand through his hair in frustration. I would have grinned if it didn't hurt to do so. There was a satisfaction in how much my silence bothered them. I wouldn't respond to their questions; I wouldn't beg.

"I want her hurting," Myriam hissed, scanning me with her icy glare. "I want her *afraid.*"

I narrowed my eyes. The ropes kept me dangling high, and I looked down the bridge of my nose at her, sneering with as much disdain as possible.

"The only thing I'm afraid of is what your fist will look like tomorrow from all this pointless torture. That purpled, puffy thing will be terribly unbecoming for a lady like you."

Myriam snarled, but it was Soren who spoke. "Watch your fucking tongue before I cut it out."

"I don't think you will," I seethed. "Myriam won't even let you get a hit in yourself. Is it because she has your balls in a drawer somewhere, or is it because you never had them to begin with?"

Before I could gauge the damage of my insult, Myriam moved in my peripheral, and a crack rang through the air. I heard it before my other senses registered the hit, but an instant later, my entire world exploded in agony. A scream built inside me, but all that came out was a whoosh of air. There was no energy left in my body to scream; only enough to harness the assault and overcome it. As the pain gradually subsided, I dimly noted a steady dripping echoing somewhere in the room.

Red and black dots clouded my sight, and when the world materialized once more, I stared down at the ground. With a start, I realized the dripping was coming from my face; thick, scarlet blood pooled onto the ground like the start of an abstract painting.

The funny thing was, the pain didn't deter me. For the first hour or so, I had teetered on the brink of breaking, but somewhere along the line, I made a subconscious, self-preserving decision to channel it into rage. From that point on, every strike made the pain last mere seconds, blossoming shortly after into fury as something inside me retreated to darkness, feeding my resolve.

I attempted to speak, but the endeavor resulted in garbled words and sent white-hot agony searing through my face. I squeezed my eyes shut and choked back a whimper; my jaw had likely been broken from that final strike.

"What was that?" Myriam purred, grabbing my chin. A cry peeled from my lips, unbidden, and I jerked my eyes open to glare at her, attempting to take back the tiniest kernel of control. Dots — *those little shits* — danced across my vision once more, now blinding white. I almost wished they would take over, drowning me in total darkness. But Myriam wouldn't allow that. And I wouldn't, either. Not when I had so much anger to hold on to, tethering me to the present.

"I. Will. Kill. You." I finally growled, over-enunciating as I worked to use as little of my mouth as possible to force the words out.

Myriam raised her eyebrows, but before she could respond, a bang sounded from above. She dropped my chin as she and Soren both spun to face the stairs. I took the moment to recollect myself, allowing quiet gasps as I got my breathing back under control.

"Soren," Myriam bit out. "Go check the perimeter."

He nodded and slipped away as she turned back to face me. "It's precious, really. That someone as young and...inexperienced as yourself would make such a proclamation. But it's mostly sad."

She tutted, striding around me. I made no attempt to follow her movements, choosing instead to listen to her footsteps and track the sound of her voice.

"I told you once how powerful you could be, yet you still chose that disgusting, human side of yourself. You chose to allow love for others to be your crutch. Look where it's gotten you?"

I couldn't see her, but her tone was filled with distaste, giving me a good idea of her expression. I closed my eyes in disagreement, and her footsteps stopped.

I braced for another strike, but when the next sound came, it wasn't followed by pain. Instead, the noise continued, a strange thumping from upstairs. Myriam cursed, and my eyes shot open. I struggled to raise my head, inhaling sharply as my muscles ached in protest.

The first thing I saw was Soren tumbling down the stairs, his limbs sprawling unnaturally as he landed. He didn't move, and it took a moment before I registered the blade lodged in the back of his neck. There were very few people who knew how to use that move — a single strike to sever the spinal cord. I lifted my gaze hopefully to the top of the staircase, and my heart leaped.

Blaise.

He stood stiffly, gaze shifting between Myriam and me. The expression on his face conveyed pure, unrelenting fury, ready to decimate fields of enemies. He gave me a militant scan, acknowledging my consciousness, before turning his focus on the enemy. A muscle in his cheek worked as he made his way sideways down the stairs, gripping another blade in one hand, while the other rested on the hilt of his sword, still sheathed.

Before Myriam could react, the air in the room heated, so dense that my breathing labored further, and I broke into a light sweat. It could only mean one thing — Finlay was here as well. I tore my gaze from Blaise and back to the staircase, taking in Finlay's stature.

In stark contrast to Blaise's lethal posture, Finlay leaned gently against the door frame, expression schooled into near boredom. Though he looked nonchalant, I immediately saw through his clever mind game. The devil-may-care stance was an illustration of the true power he held. If he could change the temperature of the room without so much as lifting a finger, it was a dare to test him further. While Blaise kept his eyes locked on Myriam, Finlay's were focused on me — clear and bright, indicating his sobriety. From the tightness of his mouth, I knew it was taking considerable willpower to restrain his fire further.

The display did nothing to deter Myriam, however. She glanced at Soren's unnaturally still body without so much as a flicker of remorse. Instead, her cold expression passed over him to look between Blaise and Finlay, then back to me with a sneer. "Exactly as I said. You could've been so powerful, Kate. And what do you have to show instead? A few men chasing after you?"

Blaise's scowl deepened, and he clutched his knife tighter, stepping deftly over Soren's still body on the basement floor. He stilled for a moment and glanced down, a flicker of sadness crossing his face. Something in my heart cracked, then, guilt curling in my stomach at the realization that it had come to this — Blaise, killing someone he had once loved and trusted, someone he considered family. The movement had Myriam sliding between the two of us, shielding him from my sight. I twisted to get him back into view, wincing as the movement strained my wounds.

"Let her go, or I'll make you," Finlay warned, his voice a dangerous growl I'd never heard from him. He moved down the steps, slow and deliberate as he eyed the rope that held me prisoner. Solid flames rolled over his hands. Myriam followed the path of his gaze, then turned back, tilting her head to inspect him.

"Ah, the orphaned fire prince," she crooned, dark lips curling into a deadly grin. "I had high hopes for you, but it seems you've taken after your parents with your beliefs."

The words jumbled in my head, and I blinked, trying to make sense of them. She spoke like she knew him and his history so...personally.

She paused, scanning him from head to toe. "I didn't have the chance last time we met, but now, I look forward to killing another misguided heir."

Finlay's stone-faced expression broke as his head jerked back slightly in confusion. He said nothing, but his eyes darted to mine, shock mirroring shock.

"Ah, yes. I suppose you wouldn't recognize me like this. Let me make things clearer for you."

Before any of us could make a move, the space around her began to ripple, like the heat and light of the room were bending into a mirage — just as it did when Kipp shifted his form.

I blinked, and a completely different woman stood before us. Long, jet-black hair had replaced the white blonde of Myriam's locks, her youthful appearance now the weather-worn, wrinkled skin of an older woman. She wore a long, black dress, which flowed in stark contrast against her pale, nearly translucent skin. Despite her lanky form, she moved with lethal grace, her mere presence instantly foreboding.

The shift of energy in the room was instant, flooding my senses with the sheer power emanating from her. She glanced at me before facing Finlay again; her eyes were as dark as her hair, an inky extension of the shift that had started when she caught me earlier. My stomach dropped.

This was the woman whose face had haunted me from the moment I sat upon the Speaking Stone. She was the woman Ensley had prophesied. She was—

"Nemain," I croaked.

Something whizzed through the air, and I dropped to the ground. My shoulders lit with relief as they dropped to my sides. Without another thought, I used my teeth to tear the wretched rope from my wrists, aching to have my body back as my own.

Myriam — *Nemain* — whirled with a ghastly snarl, and I scrambled to gain distance from her, cursing as my legs, fatigued from the position they'd been in, refused to work. With her back turned, Blaise took the opportunity and threw his smaller blade. It bounced off what was presumably a well-fortified air shield and struck the stone wall. It clattered to the floor, landing next to the item that had cut me from the ceiling — an arrow.

Darrya? Who else is here?

As if in answer, a russet-colored blur tore down the stairs, diving past Finlay and Darrya. Finlay had paled, yet the flames continued to roar in his palms. Darrya already had another arrow notched in her bow, trained on Nemain. Her lips were pursed, eyes narrowed in concern as she considered the added complication of the air shield surrounding the goddess. Kipp was by my side in an instant, his wolf form solid and broad against me. I wrapped an arm around him on instinct. Blaise was at my other side a moment later. Nemain hissed, twisting to face us.

"Let her go, or the flames on this one will be too strong for that little shield," Darrya warned. Without missing a beat, the fire in Finlay's palms climbed to the ceiling, circling and licking its way across the stone. The heat which emanated from it was nearly unbearable, rising in seconds.

Nemain's eyes shifted slowly between the two of them, then down to Soren's limp body at the bottom of the stairs, before assessing Blaise, Kipp, and finally, me. She pursed her lips.

"Alright, then. Go. I may have lost this battle, but be warned: you will lose the war."

Kipp nuzzled me, and Blaise wrapped an arm around my side. I clutched the two of them, grimacing as we slowly made our way up the stairs. Finlay and Darrya remained, eyes and weapons trained on Nemain, looking torn between trailing after us and attempting to end this once and for all. I pondered it, too — nearly overcome by the temptation of finishing this. But every movement unearthed a new complaint in my body, the wounds resurfacing with newfound vigor.

I didn't dare breathe until we were outside, where I saw Cas and my father waiting. Both lunged for me the second I appeared, and I half-cried, half-groaned as they dragged me away from Blaise and Kipp, first from the ache of the movement and then from the blissful reprieve of Cas's healing hands.

"Katie-cat," Cas uttered softly, his voice laced with pain. I wondered dimly if he experienced other's agony while he healed, or if I simply looked as terrible as I felt. The deathlike pallor of my father's face told me it might be the latter.

"Nemain," Finlay gasped as he exited the mansion, Darrya following closely behind. "It's Nemain."

My father jolted in surprise. He shifted to clutch me tightly under the arms, lifting me up in one swift movement. I bit my lip so hard I drew blood, my still mostly unhealed body screaming.

"Come on," he commanded roughly. "Get on Gray. We need to get you out of here."

Blaise nodded and peered up at the setting sun. "Pretty soon, we'll have more than Nemain to worry about. We need to get back before the Sluagh begin their movements."

"Gray?" I muttered, my head lolling slightly as I glanced around to locate him; he pranced nervously nearby. The sight of him grounded me long enough that I was able to mount him with some help from my father.

Before the others could mount, however, a burst of dark clouds erupted in the middle of our group. When the shadows cleared, there Nemain stood: tall and foreboding, a sinister smirk plastered across her face.

She flicked her hand upward, and a large, piebald raven came hurtling from the skies above to land on her palm, ruffling its wings before tucking them in close. It disappeared a moment later, dissolving into a long line of black shadow and joining the rest of the clouds trailing around her.

"I forgot to clarify," she droned, black eyes gleaming. "I don't lose."

CHAPTER TWENTY-THREE

Panic emanated from our group, so thick I almost believed I could taste it in the air. Cas and Darrya inched closer to me, but Blaise was the one to break the silence, brandishing his sword.

"I'd be more than happy to end this right here," he said, and my father and Finlay lined up beside him. Kipp prowled in the background, snarling. On the surface, the standoff seemed almost ridiculous: three sword-wielding, muscular warriors and a wolf against a slender, older woman with only shadows as weapons.

But...this woman was a full-blooded goddess of death. The shadows surrounding her fluctuated as if they had a mind of their own. The setting sun was now obscured, casting shade across the ground, as though Nemain's very presence had led the light to flee in dread. The wind picked up, and her shadows swirled faster, like they were readying themselves.

Terror coursed through me, and Gray pawed against the ground, clearly feeding off my anxiety. Nemain's black eyes shot to us and widened in shock, the first indication she'd given of anything other than disdain and cruel amusement.

"It can't be," she breathed. Gray's ears pinned back as the weight of her stare pressed upon the both of us. He tossed his head, and his pawing increased in urgency, reflecting his desire to charge. I pulled the reins taut, willing him to stay still. If he took off, I wasn't sure that I had the strength to stay astride, much less aid him in the fight. He trembled beneath me, baring his teeth, but stayed put.

This time, it was my father who took advantage of Nemain's distracted state, sending the earth trembling and cracking below her. She had no time to react, falling into the gaping hole with threads of dark clouds trailing behind. With a grunt and a heave of his arm, my dad slammed the earth shut, the soil covering her completely. A sudden silence hung in the air.

The wind died down, and my breath caught as leaves settled on the ground, though I wondered for a moment if it would really be that easy.

It won't end here, I realized, thinking of Ensley's prophecy. *The war is already inevitable.*

For that reason alone, I was unsurprised by her reappearance a moment later. Tendrils of darkness emerged from the earth, swirling to solidify Nemain's figure above ground. I clutched the reins tighter with my palms, now slick with sweat.

"I can only be merciful for so long," the goddess growled, tilting her head. "Now hand over what's rightfully mine. The cauldron, the sword, and the girl."

Finlay exploded. Flames raced to surround her, heat bursting from the blaze. Even at a distance, my face burned from the extreme temperature alone. The soft layer of frost on the ground skipped melting and went straight to evaporating.

I watched as it licked its way around the shield she managed to pull up, pressing in closer as Finlay gritted his teeth and pushed harder. Smoke and shadow clashed in a horrifying dance. For the first time, Nemain backed up a few steps, her face contorting in surprise and rage as she was forced onto the defensive.

Darrya broke away from the rest of the group. She began pacing around the perimeter, notching and loosing arrows as she went, keeping up the onslaught even as they resounded off Nemain's shield. Kipp and Blaise began circling the expanse of flames and darkness, trailing behind Darrya as they looked for an opening to sink blade or fang into.

Rumbling underfoot told me my father had begun upsetting the ground beneath her, and I heard a hideous snarl of frustration as the goddess worked to fend off attacks from every angle. Nemain's snarl pitched to a scream, and for a moment my heart lifted at the hope of someone's magic or weapon striking true.

I doubled over and let out a harsh gasp, however, as the scream continued, expanding as if it had a physical radius. It reverberated off every nerve as though dousing me in a bucket of ice water. Every last thread of magic left my body. This was unlike the mere dimming of my magic in the human realm. No — this was...an entire shutout. Not a single scrap remained in my body. It was a pain nothing like the torture Myriam — Nemain — had inflicted on me over the past several hours. This was both physical and psychological, losing something integral to my very being.

"What the hell is happening?" I yelled hoarsely, squinting over Gray's neck at the others. Finlay's fire had completely died out; the only ones not crumpled in agony were Blaise and Kipp.

"Her screams. They nullify your magic," Blaise ground out as he spun his sword, moving lithely across the ground to close in on Nemain. Her mouth remained agape, and the wail that emerged never faltered, even as she gathered her shadows close.

Without taking his eyes off her, Blaise raised his voice, commanding us with an air of finality. "Everyone. Get out of here. Now."

The others tried to argue, but were beaten down by another, more intense, round of shrieks. I cried out as it lapsed over me in waves, like something horrible was roiling inside me and eating away at a piece of my soul.

Darrya scrambled toward me, grabbing Finlay as she went. Cas was more hesitant, shooting a look at Kipp before following. Kipp held firm, his hackles raised as he paced in the opposite direction of Blaise, the two attempting to divide and conquer from either side of the lethal goddess and her shadows.

My father was the last to retreat, fighting against the throbbing pain of Nemain's cries with everything he had. With a final hiss, he grabbed the reins of a remaining horse and dragged himself to where the rest of us stood, warring with Blaise's command and our inability to leave them to the fight.

"We should go," he said through clenched teeth. He gripped a bag of Faerie dust tightly, voicing what we all knew to be true. Yet still, nobody moved. I watched helplessly as Kipp lunged, lupine teeth bared, only to be struck away by a simple flick of Nemain's shadows. Blaise parried from the opposite side and landed an impossible strike on her. It was perfectly placed and would have found purchase directly through her chest—

—would have, had Nemain not moved a hair's breadth to her right. The sword drove through her shoulder rather than her heart, and Blaise retreated swiftly, bracing for retaliation.

But all his training — with blades, fists, and elemental magic — could not prepare him for her shadows. And it was with those shadows that the goddess of death landed her counterattack. They rose in a dark torrent to surround her and Blaise, spinning faster while closing in. Kipp hesitated, pacing around the wall of shadows uncertainly. He whined as he searched for a way to strike without inadvertently hitting Blaise.

The onslaught of screeches fell abruptly silent, and I nearly collapsed with relief as a thread of my magic returned, dim but reassuringly present. I glanced around at the others, who wore similar expressions, but the relief was short-lived as Nemain's voice rang out.

"I promised you, child of Cú Chulainn, that I would find a way to make you hurt."

Her shadows morphed into an unkindness of ravens, hurtling toward me. I threw an arm up, feeling Gray shift in alarm as they passed.

"Consider that promise fulfilled."

When the last of the ravens sailed by, I uncovered my eyes to see Nemain had disappeared, leaving Kipp and Blaise alone on the ground. Kipp's head was lowered over Blaise's body, and after a moment, he tilted it to the sky and let out a short, mournful howl. The breath left my body entirely.

"No," I choked out. I flung my leg over Gray, ignoring the way my calves collapsed momentarily as I landed. I stumbled over to where Kipp and Blaise remained, falling to my knees as I took in the sight.

Blaise's own sword had been turned against him, wedged in the exact spot where he had attempted to drive it home on Nemain moments earlier. His eyes were open, his chest heaving erratically as short breaths left his body. His face was ashen, a trickle of blood leaving his mouth. I cradled his face in my hands, wiping the trail away. It only served to smear crimson across his cheek, a mockery of my attempt to be rid of the truth of this moment.

"Cas!" I screamed, looking up to call him over. A rippling sensation behind me told me Kipp had shifted. My eyes met his, and I immediately hated what I saw there. His face was grim and sympathetic, but the *last* thing I wanted in that moment was his sympathy. I wanted hope. I wanted fight. I didn't want the answer I read in his eyes — that Blaise was too far gone already.

A rattling breath drew my attention back to Blaise, and his hand twitched at his side, as if to reach for me. I clutched his palm tightly.

"Hold on, Blaise," I pleaded. "I need you to hold on. I need you."

"You never needed me, sunshine," he rasped, every word choked out in effort.

Cas arrived at our side, and Kipp moved so he could rest his hands across Blaise's chest. Magic flared, dimly, but then sputtered out. I flailed a hand out and caught his, but despite the ease with which we power-shared before, the sensation was now locked firmly away. I tugged desperately at the thread of my magic that had returned, but it wasn't nearly enough to share. Cas cursed and removed his hand from mine, focusing once more with both palms over Blaise's wound.

"But you had me. And you always will."

He smiled weakly, and I gazed at his face, blinking away tears as they blurred the image of his beautiful hazel eyes. The eyes that had trained me, teased me, and loved me since the moment I arrived in this world. The eyes that promised to fight for me, no matter the outcome.

It was those eyes that I looked into as Blaise died beneath me.

Chapter Twenty-Four

Everything was numb by my own making. I had to force the numbness, or face the mountain of rage, guilt, and despair warring inside me, which only left the former option.

It hadn't started that way. Everything had exploded in me at once, and the only thing that kept me from lashing out at the others as they pulled me from Blaise's body was the dampening of my magic. Body and soul, I had nothing left to give, but I'd screamed as they pried me from Blaise, holding me tight as they dragged me away from the scene.

Finlay approached Blaise's body, near expressionless aside from the paleness betraying his shock. He leaned over Cas, whose horror ran rampant across his face, and murmured something inaudible in his ear. As they shifted, Darrya blocked my view, engulfing me in an embrace as she choked out unintelligible words, her own voice thick with emotion.

Even as some part of me registered the intent, I fought her, attempting to disentangle from her arms as I watched Finlay and Cas lift Blaise, placing him on Finlay's horse.

I lunged forward again, yet someone — Kipp, possibly — grabbed me and hauled me back onto Gray; my father slid up behind me and held me in place. Before I could protest, we were moving, putting distance between ourselves and the mansion. The others remained close as my father clutched me tightly, though one look at Kipp's face had me crumpling once more, and I was unable to look any of them in the eye. I gripped Gray's mane, alternating between cries and hiccups as we moved swiftly through the forest, barely noticing when he swung his large head around to nuzzle at my foot.

An indiscernible amount of time passed before we finally stopped and cast Faerie dust to portal back to the palace. I was pried off of Gray, and immediately returned to Blaise's body, now placed on the ground outside the palace.

Cas sat close beside me as my vocal cries disintegrated into silent tears. I remained still while he gradually pulsed healing magic into my body as his gifts slowly returned. At that point, I would have preferred the physical pain rather than the obvious truth that lay before me.

Blaise was dead. He had come for me — given his *life* for me — and because of that...he wasn't coming back.

I stared, crying mutely until my tear ducts ran dry, and even then, I remained with my hand in his, as if I could will my warmth into him. If the others said or did anything, I was wholly unaware — my eyes were fixed solely on him.

By the time the sun had fully set and twilight rolled in, I had just come to terms with who — or what — lay before me. It was no longer Blaise. His hand felt different, his body an empty shell; he was somewhere, but it wasn't here, lying before me. Accepting that was the only thing that allowed me to look away as Kipp and Larke approached.

Kipp communicated with a silent look at Cas, who finally moved from his position, after spending hours by my side. Some dim part of me recognized how utterly kind the gesture was, that Cas had stayed, but I couldn't manage the words to offer a polite thank you. I simply watched through puffy lids as he gave me a grim smile and slipped into the night.

"Do you want to go to your room, or stay at Cas's tonight?" Kipp asked softly, bending over me. His cinnamon-bark hair fell softly over his lupine eyes, and I was reminded of him fighting, in wolf form, side by side with Blaise. What if I had lost him today, too? Somehow, a drop of moisture remained in my body, and it sprung to my eyes unbidden at the thought. Lowering my gaze, I shrugged, and felt his warm hands on my waist as he picked me up.

"I can walk," I mumbled as I steadied myself on my feet. My voice was hoarse, and I was surprised the words even came out. I leaned against him for support, however, as I watched Larke cover Blaise's body with a large, dark cloth. The soldier looked up at me, face ashen, but said nothing. I didn't blame him — I had no idea what to say to him, either. We simply shared a long moment, exchanging all we couldn't say with a look, until finally, I glanced away.

"My room," I whispered to Kipp. "Here."

I skipped washing up — dirtying my sheets seemed like a trivial inconvenience, anyway — and curled up in my blankets. Kipp shifted into wolf form and curled up at the foot of my bed. I was grateful for the unspoken agreement to keep me company for the night.

Though it calmed my frayed emotions somewhat, it didn't help me sleep. I stared at the ceiling for hours, wondering what I could have done to change the course of history that night. Throughout the night, a wall was built, brick by brick.

On one side lay the old me: the one who felt her emotions deeply and openly, blissfully moving through life, oblivious to the consequences of each decision she'd made. The other now knew firsthand how death rode on her coattails. She would not allow it to happen again — could not allow her recklessness or emotions to endanger anyone else.

By morning, I was firmly on that side of the wall. The safe side.

Kipp didn't come back the next night, but my lack of sleep hadn't gone unnoticed. I left the bed the next day only long enough to wash up, in which time someone came to change my sheets. When I dressed once more, there was a soft rap at the door. Once I opened it, Kipp carefully slid a velvet bag into my hand.

I weighed it curiously in my hand, guessing its contents. "Faerie dust?"

My heart thrummed anxiously at the thought. I wasn't ready to venture out again, especially with the possibility of running into Nemain more real than ever. The wall inside me grew a tiny bit taller at the prospect, a tiny bit thicker.

Kipp shook his head. "Do you remember the sand I packed from the human realm, a long time ago?"

When I nodded, he motioned for me to open the bag. The sand inside looked plain, but shimmered a light silver as it shifted in my hand, as if the movement triggered its magic. I remembered Kipp's words from the day he'd packed it — the day we'd first set off for the Faerie realm. It helped people sleep soundly, he had said. My eyes shot back up to Kipp curiously, and he gave a soft smile.

"I noticed you were having trouble sleeping. I was saving this for a rainy day, and..." he trailed off with a shrug. "It's storming out now."

"Kipp," I breathed, shaking my head. "I can't take this from you. I'm sure it's incredibly valuable."

Not only did I not want to take something this precious from him, but I felt unworthy of the offer. They had all come to rescue *me* yesterday, and I was the reason things had gone so terribly wrong. I didn't deserve this compassion. I closed my eyes and extended the bag back toward him, aware of the obvious tremble in my hand.

Kipp ignored me and stepped forward, wrapping me in a hug that pushed the bag back against my chest. The gesture was so kind and selfless that my eyes stung, desperate to shed tears despite having none left to give. We remained that way for a long moment, as though Kipp knew it would take more than a quick embrace for my resolve to falter.

"You're more valuable," he murmured into my ear, and strode away before I could respond.

That night, I trickled some of the sand over my pillow, and when Kipp asked the following morning, I lied and told him how wonderfully it had worked.

Though I slept some, the sand only exemplified the nasty images from that day, replaying them in my mind. I found myself waking up sporadically, terror coursing through my veins as panicked sweat made the sand stick to my cheeks. Each time, it took me several long moments to realize I was no longer being tortured in that basement. Yet the relief was short-lived, replaced by despair as I remembered what had happened to get me out. I decided I would rather go without sleep than be unable to escape the horrors that awaited me when my eyes closed.

CHAPTER TWENTY-FIVE

I t had been a full week since Blaise's death, and I knew I owed the rest of the group answers. I'd already surmised that Nemain's lack of retaliation simply meant she was relishing her win — the one that sent me reeling with a different kind of pain than she'd originally intended. She couldn't break me externally, so her blows were now internal, breaking my very soul.

As I looked into the sympathetic eyes of my friends and family, I knew how close she was to achieving it. For as long as I — and the talismans — remained out of her grasp, everyone I loved remained a target, and she would pick them off, one by one, to get my attention. I had to actively ignore that fact if we were to continue.

I clutched the sides of my chair. The other side of my wall was fast becoming a distant memory.

"Do you recall any research that would have warned us she is a *Bean Sídhe?*" Kipp asked the group, answered by numerous head-shakes.

"I mean, maybe, at some point, but it doesn't really matter now that we know for sure." Finlay shrugged, twirling a toothpick with his tongue. He looked on edge, like he needed a real cigarette, and badly.

"Banshees really exist?" I blurted, images of ghostlike, wailing creatures crossing my mind.

"Yes and no," Kipp answered. "The Bean Sídhe race was supposedly decimated hundreds of years ago. There are still stories that crop up here and there, but mostly just to scare children. They were a race somewhere between a dark Faerie and our own kind, with both malign and good magic. They formed communities and had morals, but they also had a fierce, devastating power. The fact that their cries crippled the magic of the Aes Sídhe is why they were a threat, and therefore hunted like prey."

"Oh," I murmured. "That's kind of...sad." Nevertheless, my skin prickled as I recalled the way Nemain's had drained me to the point of utter helplessness, and part of me understood the need to fight back with a vengeance.

"If I had to guess, she's the goddess whose bloodline created them in the first place," Finlay muttered, and kicked his legs up on Darrya's chair, who shot him an irritated look.

"And it didn't affect you because...?" I asked, turning to Kipp.

"My magic is more physical. It can stop me from shifting in the moment, but it's not powered by my soul's connection to other living things, like yours, or Cas's," he replied. I nodded, feeling the raw throbbing in my heart as I remembered how Blaise had been unaffected, too, his magic being of the physical sort like Kipp's.

"And the shapeshifting?" I asked. "Is that a Banshee thing, too?"

Kipp shook his head. "Not that I'm aware of. I suspect that's just a gift specific to her as a goddess. But I sensed that power in her ages ago...I should have known."

He averted his eyes, the frustration clear in his tight expression. I opened my mouth to argue where to place the blame — to say this was my fault, not his — but my dad spoke first.

"Did you get any more intel from their place?" His voice was achingly gentle as he leaned in close. He stopped short of touching my arm, though I could tell he wished to. I raised my own hand to rest on the spot where he'd been headed. I wanted the comfort, but anyone's touch right now reminded me of Nemain's torture or Blaise's affection. Both were painful.

I nodded slowly, blinking as I forced myself to remember.

"There was a map. It had paths marked on it — army movements, I think."

Larke nodded excitedly at that, scrambling up to locate paper of his own to write on. I continued.

"And — a letter. I'm trying to remember; it said something about wanting to help, but needing reassurances, because they'd already done so much to aid Myr—Nemain."

"Was it signed?" My father asked, and I bit my lip, pulling the letter to the forefront of my mind.

"Not exactly. It had initials. A and T, I believe?"

"A and T..." My father sagged back, rubbing his jaw thoughtfully as he considered.

"It couldn't mean..." Darrya spoke suddenly, and shared a weighted look with Finlay as she trailed off. Recognition sparked between their exchange, and Finlay tensed at her side, kicking his legs back down as he straightened in his seat. She winced but finished her thought quietly. "...Aerrin and Thaddeus?"

"Holy fuck. I don't want to think so, but...it could be," Finlay responded. He stood as if the sheer idea overwhelmed him. His hands raked roughly through his hair before he brought them down and clenched them into fists. "Gods dammit, that's huge."

"Who are Aerrin and Thaddeus?" I asked hesitantly.

Darrya answered for me as her eyes tracked her cousin, who now paced the room. "Lachlan's sons. The ones I told you about a while back."

My lips formed around a silent "oh" as I thought back to the mention of them. The brothers who would someday take over his rule, never mentioned by name.

Darrya continued. "It almost makes too much sense, really. They have no real control; Lachlan's been tactfully barring them from things for a long time now." She blew out a long sigh through pursed lips. "They could have seen this as an opportunity to gain control of the narrative."

"Fuck!" Finlay roared, causing us to jump.

"Fin," Darrya said lightly, reaching out to him, but he tossed an unreadable look her way and stalked out of the room.

We all sat in silence for a moment before Larke pushed a blank paper and stylus my way.

"Do you think you can remember what the map looked like, Kate?" he asked softly, his warm brown eyes hopeful. "I'll try to guide you with the layout as much as I can."

I dragged my eyes from the doorway where Finlay had left and nodded. For the next half hour, we worked together to replicate the image in my mind, Finlay's outburst and every other dark thing temporarily forgotten.

Chapter Twenty-Six

The cold winter weather offered reprieve as I worked to heal the agony of Blaise's passing. The days shortened while the nights grew longer, and I enjoyed disappearing with the darkness.

Seeing others mulling around, laughing and joyful, ripped my insides to tatters as I remembered what I lost and those I could still lose. A year prior, I'd had only my mother to care about, but now, I loved so many more people. And Nemain had made it clear there was a target placed on every single one of their backs.

Everyone was apprehensive about the inaction from Nemain or her dark Fae army — aside from me. In the time I'd spent with her as Myriam, I understood that above all, she was patient. She had been working on her plans for centuries; a few weeks meant nothing to her. She thrived in the shadows, using whispers as her weapons as much as any magic. Her ravens gathered intel for her just as the Faeries did, and I had no doubt she was doing reconnaissance on our movements, which only solidified my choice to hide indoors as much as possible.

The only exceptions were my daily visits to Gray, to assure myself he was still okay. Now that Nemain knew of his existence — the largest threat to her plans, aside from me — a pit of worry formed in my stomach, assuming she'd find a way to hurt him.

My father accompanied me half the time, and I was sure he was doing the same with me as I was with Gray — ensuring I was still whole. He, like the others, continued to tread on eggshells around me, and I knew my demeanor wasn't helping. He remained resolutely close, though, despite me snapping at him on more than one occasion.

He began introducing me to some of the things he'd learned during his Fae upbringing. Despite my initial disinterest, it began to fill a hole I'd had long before the newer one left by Blaise's passing — one where I'd questioned how my life could have been, had I been raised here.

When he'd first knocked on my door, carrying a large stack of antique novels and donning an uncharacteristically light grin, I remembered where my love of reading came from. The realization lightened my heart, and I felt a tug on it; an invisible thread binding us, running just as deep as the blood we shared.

"See that?" he said now, pointing enthusiastically at the yellowed page of a leather-bound book. I squinted, studying the series of brackets and lines.

"Am I supposed to know what this is?" I asked, lifting my brow dubiously.

"It's the Ogham alphabet. An early medieval language, very primitive." He pronounced the word Ogham like *"oh—wam"*, his accent leagues better than my own tongue when I attempted to stumble over unfamiliar words. He traced the symbols with his finger.

"We learned it early on in grade school. We sometimes use it to aid spells, but mostly, it's to be able to read ancient headstones marking graves or land ownership. It's not the most important language nowadays, but I figured with your aptitude for reading, you'd be curious."

I nodded, flipping to the next page and tracing a symbol with my index finger. "A lot of these look like...trees. Little stick figure trees."

My dad's laugh was soft. "You're exactly right. It's actually known as the language of the trees."

I looked up at him, my lips parting in surprise. "The language of the trees?

"Mhmm. It was said that the initial descendants of the Tuatha Dé Danann spoke several different languages. They all came together one day and picked the best from each language, crafting it into a written language. The common factor being, they all believed in the magic of the trees."

He shifted closer, and I felt a protective calm in his presence. This was exactly how we would have been, had I grown up with him alongside me. In the human realm, this book could have easily been replaced with a history paper, or algebra homework.

Memories of my mom sprang to mind, the one who had truly helped me in those moments. A wave of wistfulness crashed through me as I realized how much time we had now spent apart. So much had changed for me while she was none the wiser, thanks to Kipp's enchantments. The distance between us was now larger, and much more complicated than a simple jump through realms.

I blinked away a wave of emotion and looked up at my father. Did he miss her, too? I contemplated interrupting him to ask, but he looked so happy in the moment; he leaned in close to the book, trailing his finger over specific characters. I pushed away the thought and focused instead on his explanations.

"The letters here are simply the first letter of that tree in the old languages. For example — B: *Beith,* or birch. It's one of the first trees to grow in wild areas, so it's known to signify beginnings, or overcoming challenges." His finger skipped to another symbol. "This is *Nion* — the ash tree. Ash represents our connections in the world, the way our roots go deep, and our branches reach for the skies."

I smiled as I listened to his animated talk, setting my troubles aside and taking the time to pretend this was no special moment at all; that we could always be completely — blissfully — ordinary.

CHAPTER TWENTY-SEVEN

I tugged the thick black shawl closer to my body as I walked to the stables, the light layer of snow crunching under my feet. I watched with mild interest as the heat of my breath spiraled visibly in the frigid air, welcoming the cold that had set in over the past few weeks. It numbed me until I was as cold on the outside as I was inside. Even when I was outdoors and exposed, I felt somewhat safer in my ability to hide under mounds of clothing.

Wren greeted me with a soft smile as I arrived at the stables. Gray was already indoors and haltered. She offered me the grooming pail without question; this had become our daily ritual over the past month. We worked in tandem, slowly teasing knots from Gray's mane and tail. It was quiet for a long while before Wren spoke, and I jumped slightly when she did, now unused to filling the silence with words.

"Are you going to try and visit your mother the next time the portal between our realms opens?"

I pressed my lips into a thin line and shook my head. "No."

"Why not? Isn't it almost Christmastime in your realm?"

Her question was of genuine surprise, but I felt a slight tug on the wound inside me. I had, in fact, thought about it a handful of times, but ultimately decided it wasn't possible. My mom was much safer in the human realm without me. Visiting her would only put her in danger. Anger flared, an immediate front for those deeper emotions I dared not explore.

"I can't risk her tracking us there," I muttered between clenched teeth. I pressed the brush harder into Gray as I worked the dirt from his shaggy winter coat. His skin twitched, and he pawed irritably at the added pressure. Guiltily, I softened my motions and continued grooming him, until a light hand touched my shoulder. I looked over to see Wren watching me, her eyes shimmering with a mixture of sympathy and frustration. I'd been avoiding everyone else's touches for weeks now, but hers was featherlight and soothing, like an extension of her gentle and kind personality. I found myself relaxing into it.

"I know you want to do this all by yourself, Kate, but you can't set yourself on fire just to try to keep us warm," she said, her voice soft but firm.

"What do you mean?" I asked, though I knew where this was headed.

"What I mean is, I know you blame yourself for all this happening with Nemain," she started. I tried suppressing a flinch at her name and failed. "But the truth is, she's been an issue for a very long time, and we only now have a face and a name for what's been happening right under our noses."

She leaned in close, her hand on my shoulder squeezing tight. "And even though you want to keep everyone at arm's length, this isn't a battle you can fight alone. You need to let us in, so we can help you."

Tears pricked my eyes, hot and stinging. "I couldn't forgive myself if one of you got hurt helping me, though. Not again. Not like..." I trailed off, still unable to say his name.

"We all know the risks," she answered. "You don't think I sit here worrying about my stupid brother, too? I love him, but I couldn't stop him if I tried — and I won't. We all know this is so much bigger than just us." She paused, then added, "And I know Blaise would make the same choices all over again, a thousand times, if it meant saving you."

At the mention of his name, tears spilled over my cheeks in earnest, the first I'd let loose since the day he died. Wren's hand clutched my shoulder firmly, turning me to face her. I met her warm, gentle eyes, and seeing no judgment there, lay myself bare before her. She tugged me into an embrace and I crumpled, the tears streaming like rivers until I'd soaked her tunic and was hiccupping from the force of my sobs.

"I'm not afraid to lose against her," I choked, sniffling slightly. "I'm just so scared to lose any more of you."

"Isn't it amazing, though? To be surrounded by people you love so fiercely that losing them is the most terrifying thought you can have?"

Wren, ever the damned optimist. I smiled weakly at her words.

"You're just lucky I still suck at fighting, or I'd be out here, too," she added reproachfully. I let out a quick laugh, garbled by the tightness in my throat.

"Well, you're amazing at everything else, so that's fine by me," I murmured into the crook of her neck, and her arms tightened. The wound inside me was still there, still raw, but in that moment, I felt it heal slightly.

I heard multiple voices as I approached Darrya's room the next day, and I took a deep breath before knocking. She answered almost instantly, and her look of surprise was like a knife in the gut. Wren was right — I had been keeping everyone at arm's length over the past few weeks, yet they'd understood and left me alone without question. I was grateful for that, but Wren had a point. The only way to defeat Nemain was to keep a unified front. I couldn't keep acting as though closing myself off made anyone safer.

I peered past Darrya to see Finlay, Kipp, and my father in the room, wearing matching looks of astonishment. I offered them all a tentative smile and turned back to Darrya.

"Can I come in?" I asked, and her bewildered look instantly changed to one of sheer joy. She curled a hand around my arm and hauled me into the room without hesitation.

"Absolutely! We're just plotting our next moves. You missed Samhain." At this, she paused, trying to deftly brush over my whole *being re-marked and held captive* subject. *"But,* there's always another reason to celebrate. The winter solstice happens to be coming up in a couple of weeks, and it's finally giving us an opportunity to take some action." Her grin was equal parts sly and triumphant.

"Really? How's that?" I settled in next to my father. It seemed Wren was right on this front, too. Though I held an important key, this battle was far bigger than just me. With or without me, my friends would continue the fight against Nemain. My father and Finlay were sitting next to each other, and I was surprised to find no traces of animosity between the two.

Finlay and my dad, getting along? When did that happen?

Kipp leaned forward, nodding at Finlay and Darrya. "Every year, there is a huge winter solstice party hosted at Lachlan's castle in Leven. Naturally, Lachlan's sons will be there, but all the royal families are invited, meaning these two have invites as well."

I nodded, absorbing the information. Neither of them enjoyed the sons — even before we knew of their potential involvement with Nemain, though I didn't know why. But this would be an excellent opportunity to quiz Lachlan and his sons to get the answers we needed.

"It's also one of the events where the most Aes Sídhe are gathered in one place, especially the royals. So, I've asked Larke to bring more guards than usual, just in case," Darrya added. My heart wrenched, both at the prospect of them in danger and at the mention of Larke, who had officially taken over Blaise's position as commander-in-chief. While I could think of no one better to do so, I knew he was no happier than the rest of us about the reasons why.

"Could you score another invite?" I asked suddenly, and watched as surprise rippled through the group.

"You want to go with them?" Kipp inquired. His voice was apprehensive, and I squared my shoulders, nodding.

"Given that you two don't have the most...savory history with Lachlan's sons, they might be more receptive if I'm the one asking the questions," I explained.

Finlay and Darrya exchanged looks.

"She's onto something there," Finlay admitted. "They've never seen her, much less interacted with her." He tossed a measured look between me and Darrya, as if weighing his next few words. "And we know Aerrin has a weakness for pretty women."

I blinked as Darrya cleared her throat. "Obviously. Plus, Lachlan loves her. He'd be completely fine with adding another name to the guest list." She shot me a smile, and I thought of Lachlan's jovial attitude. My heart warmed at the prospect of talking with him again.

"Perhaps it would be best if she goes in with an alias," my dad suggested, "in case Nemain shared names along with other information."

Kipp and Finlay hummed their agreement.

"Okay, so let's say I'm..." I flitted through names in my head, finally landing on my old coworker from the coffee shop. "Lynn. Lynn Smith. Can you get word to Lachlan?" I directed my question at Darrya, who nodded.

"Absolutely. Asking him to play along will only excite him more." She laughed, eyeing me mischievously. "But you know what my personal request will be."

I rolled my eyes, having expected the ask. "Yes. Pick out whatever dress you'd like. I swear I'll be good and wear it."

She released a cheerful whoop, celebrating her small victory and causing me to snort in amusement. We turned the conversation to plot how best to extract information tactfully from Thaddeus and Aerrin.

I sensed a shift, then. It was small but visceral, settling me while we schemed as a unit. The feeling of things falling slowly back into place.

Chapter Twenty-Eight

I bit the inside of my cheek in frustration, staring at the items before me. Of course, there had to be a flaw, because everything else was going according to plan.

Lachlan had been both intrigued and willing to add me to his guest list under my pseudonym, Lynn Smith. Over the past two weeks, Darrya had been coaching me on court etiquette: which titles ranked where, what — and what not — to discuss to avoid certain conflict within certain families, and which mannerisms would constitute respect or offense. She'd pestered me around the clock with information until I was finally able to categorize names and titles in their rightful places.

We were leaving this afternoon to give us a few days' time before the solstice party, which was actually a three-day-long celebration of feasting, dancing, and merriment — something I hadn't realized when I'd allowed Darrya to dress me. It wasn't just one painfully upscale outfit, but *multiple*.

"It's a high-profile royal event, and you're considered a royal lady from a distant land this week. Which, to be fair, if your family hadn't been forced to disappear for so long...you might very well have been," Darrya had firmly asserted this fact after I'd stormed to her room to question her choices. "Not to mention, there's a dress and color code for each night — *none* of which include leathers, tunics, or pants."

Verbally and politically cornered, I was forced to agree, but still, I sighed heavily as I surveyed the clothing lined up before me. I wasn't mentally prepared to pack, because I wasn't entirely sure how to *wear* half of it.

There were long, exquisite red, green, and black dresses for the main events, but also maroon, silver, and light blue dresses for other days, along with multiple accessories. Darrya had provided me with long capes, hairpieces, brooches, necklaces, shoes, and gloves to accessorize. It gave me a headache just considering how all the pieces were supposed to fit together.

I left the least complex outfit out for travel — a light silver hooded cape and a cool blue, floor-length dress, trimmed in white — then packed the rest in a large leather bag. I wasn't supposed to pack any weaponry, so swords and other large items were left to Larke and the guards accompanying us, but I strapped a small dagger to my leg...the dagger Blaise had gifted me. It was more of a sentimental comfort than a weapon, I decided, and thus didn't count.

I headed to the kitchen to grab a coffee and say a quick goodbye to the others before we left. They were a mixture of upset and relieved by their inability to attend. All citizens did their own solstice celebrations in their homes, but nothing on the scale of Lachlan's event. If anything, Cas was the most disappointed, given his proclivity for dressing up and surrounding himself with alcohol and general merriment. The others understood that while it was a party, it was also a carefully orchestrated political gathering.

Every movement and conversation would be carefully marked, weighed, and tucked away as ammunition. We were walking into a den of snakes, and I was a mouse parading as a viper. Or perhaps, I considered, a viper masquerading as a mouse — which was arguably a more precarious position to be in.

I sipped on my caffeine and changed for our travels, stifling a nervous yawn. I still wasn't able to sleep more than a few precious hours every night, though it had improved once I'd allowed myself to reconcile with the others. Our conversations during the day focused on our upcoming plans, for which I was grateful. The past came back to haunt me every night, right on schedule, and it didn't discriminate between my worst memories.

Sometimes I saw dark Faeries speared through to their very core, choking heavily on their own obsidian blood. Other times, it was my own crimson blood, dripping to the floor as I rotated in the air, awaiting the next strike of a fist or blade from Nemain. The worst, however, was seeing the life drain from Blaise's face, knowing his death was signed and sealed no matter if I fought against it with every fiber of my being.

A light rap on the door jerked me from my thoughts, and I scrambled to open it, grateful for the distraction. Darrya stood there, eyeing my outfit with approval. She wore something similar, though hers was grander — a scarlet dress trimmed in black detailing, the neckline plunging more daringly than mine. Her hooded cape was black and trimmed in beautiful silver detailing.

"I was worried I'd have to fight you more on the outfits," she said, eyes twinkling. "I'm glad to see you heeded my suggestion, *Lady Lynn.*"

I couldn't help but grin back at the use of my pseudonym. "I didn't think it was a suggestion, or I would've fought harder."

She snorted. "Are you ready to go?"

I nodded, shouldering my travel bag as she grabbed my free arm and dragged me down the courtyard.

Finlay was waiting for us, and I noted his considerably fancy wardrobe: form-fitting black pants, knee-high leather boots, and a white, button-down undershirt, which was, surprisingly, buttoned all the way. His overcoat was high-collared and made of black velvet, edges embroidered with gold.

We halted in front of him, and Darrya darted to her bag on the ground next to his. She rifled through it for a moment before cursing colorfully.

"I'll be right back," she said before hurrying off, muttering under her breath about gods-damned Faerie dust. Noting Larke's absence, I figured he and his guards had already taken off and would meet us outside of the castle, at the spot where we had arrived on our last trip.

I released a soft breath, realizing this was the first time Finlay and I had been alone since we'd arrived back from our encounter with Nemain. It had been surprisingly unintentional; I hadn't given him much thought at all, too consumed with grief and the sluggish, sleep-deprived haze.

He eyed me carefully, and I noticed the glassy look in his eyes, indicating he was already less than sober. I wondered briefly if their grandmother would be in attendance this week, and if that made him nervous. Finlay opened his mouth, and I braced myself for whatever half-cocked comment he would make.

"You look good. Tired, but good."

I blinked in surprise.

"Uh…thanks," I offered in return. "You're looking rather dapper yourself."

He smiled, and we fell into silence again, the awkwardness looming between us. I glanced down, around, anywhere but at him. Eventually, he cleared his throat, and I looked up.

"This is the exact opposite of what I'd normally say, with my proclivity for bondage," he began, "but I really hated seeing you tied up like that."

Somehow, it was exactly the line needed to break the tension, and I let out a surprised chuckle. "It felt about as good as it looked."

Silence draped over us once more, but this time, it was the comfortable kind. I took a moment to study him further, noting the attempt he'd made to tame his unruly hair. It worked — for the most part. His hair was combed back, but a few golden strands had escaped, as though hinting at his rebellious nature. I noted with a start that he was studying me, too, and we locked eyes.

"Are you sure you're ready for this?" He asked the question cautiously, as if afraid of angering me. Normally, I would scoff at such a question, maybe even be offended. As of late, however, fate had enjoyed tossing cruel things in my path. I'd much rather express my emotions with a good physical fight than any careful political dalliances.

"I think so," I admitted. "Darrya's been training me." As if on cue, Darrya reappeared, grasping a bag of Faerie dust.

Finlay pulled a toothpick from his pocket, swirling it in his fingers. "So, you're ready to meet all these royal bores? Talk, drink, dance, make merry?" He placed the toothpick in his mouth and raised his eyebrows at me.

"Dance?" I sputtered, latching onto the word and whirling on Darrya. Her head jerked back, startled. "You didn't mention dancing! What kind of dancing?"

"Oh, shit. Do they not still teach dancing in the human realm?" she asked, her face contorting into a look of genuine surprise. I flushed, though whether it was with anger or terror, I wasn't entirely sure.

"Not really, no. I mean, dancing at our parties is just — just jumping and swaying to the music. I don't think I've really danced since I was...fourteen? Even then, it was just a few classes in school. The waltz, I think?"

She paled, mouth opening and closing before she shook her head, recollecting herself. "Okay. Well. That can be fixed. We have a few days before the first day of the solstice; you can learn the basics before then."

"Fucking hell," I groaned, lifting my bag irritably. "These shoes you made me pack? There's no way I won't twist an ankle trying to dance in those!"

She smiled at me sweetly and gathered a pile of Faerie dust in her fist. "But you'll look *so* good while it happens."

We had only just arrived, but I was ready to disappear. Although only a thin channel of water separated Daersill from Muiranvia, the landscape was entirely different. The palace was surrounded by towering trees and a flowing river, but Lachlan's castle — just outside of Daersill's capital city, Leven — sat atop a hill surrounded by rolling, barren hills. That, paired with its location further north, meant a constant, icy wind screeched outside the castle walls.

It was still early in the morning when we greeted Lachlan, but he had quickly run off to his duties, greeting more families. We spent the next several hours greeting every royal with whom we crossed paths, and I relied heavily on Darrya running interference, for fear I'd trip up on their names — or worse, my own. The social obligations quickly drained my already low energy reserves, and I collapsed gratefully on my bed when I made it to my assigned room.

Darrya burst in less than twenty minutes later. "Alright. You only have three days before the solstice events begin. Your dance training starts now."

"What?" I moaned, flipping over on my bed. "Now? Where? With whom?"

"Yes, now! I scoped out an empty room, and we have a male at our disposal that, unfortunately for him, has to do pretty much whatever I say."

I raised my eyebrows at that.

"Finlay?" I guessed, and she nodded. "He hasn't already escaped to find something to drink, smoke, or sleep with?"

Darrya shook her head and laughed. "He's under strict orders to wait for us in the room. Come on, let's go."

Much to my surprise, he had listened to Darrya's orders and was ready in the open room she had found for us. The room, like all the ones in Lachlan's castle, was cozy and spacious without oozing opulence. Whereas the rooms of the palace back home were ornate — decorated head to toe in gilded patterns and intricate paintings — this room was fashioned with only two colors: the pale gray of the castle stone, and the rich red shine of the walnut boards covering the floor and raised beams of the ceiling. Whatever its original use, it now stood empty, offering us plenty of space for practice.

The prince stood in the center, and though he didn't look particularly enthused, he offered his hand to me willingly. I took it, finding it warm but not unpleasant. I stepped closer, pressing my body flush against his, and wrapped my hand around his shoulder. I expected him to grab my waist, but he simply stiffened.

"What?" I balked, pulling back.

"Most of our dances aren't this...intimate, little angel." With a laugh, he carefully plucked my hand from his shoulder, moving it away. "Those are reserved for serious couples. If you're not courting, engaged, or married, you're mostly dancing at arm's length, and switching partners regularly."

"Oh." I felt my cheeks burn. "I didn't realize."

"Not that I mind," he amended with a drawl, and my flush deepened, accompanied by an eye roll. "But if you're not looking to spark controversy, you'll want to keep things formal. At least where wandering royal eyes are involved."

"If wandering eyes are such an issue, I'm surprised you haven't sparked controversy with every eligible royal over the age of eighteen," I quipped back.

He smirked playfully. "Who says I haven't?"

Over the next two hours, Darrya dictated, mimicking the beats of common tunes while Finlay and I followed her guidance. She hopped in and out on occasion, demonstrating certain aspects of the group dances.

By the end, my feet burned and my head spun, but I could identify the basics of the main dances enough to follow general guidance. They were fun and upbeat; I found myself genuinely enjoying the jumping and twirling — when I wasn't panicking about glaring missteps giving away my 'unroyal' upbringing.

I had just changed into pajamas and climbed into bed, building a small pillow fortress to prop my throbbing feet up, when a soft rap came at my door.

"No," I complained, throwing myself dramatically on the side of the bed. "I'm done with today."

The knock came again, more tentative, and I considered waiting until the person left for a serious moment, before sighing and clambering out of bed to answer.

Finlay stood on the other side of the door, looking somewhat sheepish. He had changed into sleepwear as well, wearing simple baggy pants and a loose shirt. His eyes shone clear, the glassiness from earlier diminished. Three books were wedged under his arm, and I eyed them curiously.

"What are you doing here?"

He lifted the books pointedly. "I couldn't help but notice how exhausted you looked today, and not just from the dance lessons. I figured you hadn't been sleeping well. The best cure I know for that is reading, so I figured I'd loan you some of my favorites."

He held them out. I took them silently, shocked by both his accurate assessment and the thoughtful gesture.

I turned them in my hands to read the spines, surprised to see I recognized them all. They were classic adventure novels, and while I'd only read one of them, I'd heard of them all. I remembered the way he'd mentioned his yearning for adventure. No wonder his favorites all involved epic journeys — it was a way for him to escape.

I was admittedly a little sick of how much adventure I'd had as of late, but I clutched the books to my chest, intending to read them regardless. At least with these, I'd find a happy ending.

"Thank you," I murmured, giving him a genuine smile. He offered one in response and turned to leave.

"Wait," I called out suddenly, startling even myself. Finlay halted, then turned to face me once more, raising a brow. Before I could overthink it, I continued.

"I've been having a hard time sleeping alone. The best sleep I've had since..." I swallowed and started again. "Since Blaise...was when Kipp stayed over. When he wasn't there anymore, even his enchanted sand didn't help. Would you mind staying and reading to me for a bit?"

Finlay's lips parted in surprise. I wasn't entirely sure why I was admitting this all to him, either. I contemplated taking the words back as a sudden pang of self-consciousness made my cheeks flush. Would I make matters worse by playing it off and shooing him away?

For whatever reason though, he seemed to accept it in stride, and I was grateful he didn't push the subject. He simply nodded and came back through the door, peering around for a moment.

I followed his gaze and realized what he must have noticed — the guest room had no chairs for him to perch on. The main room had only a bed, a dresser, and a basic nightstand with a lamp, with a door leading into an adjacent washroom.

"Do you mind if I sit on the other side of the bed?" he asked hesitantly.

I swallowed a smirk, amused to see the cocky prince's bashful side. "That's fine. But you can't disrupt my pillow fortress."

"Your what?"

"Nevermind."

I shook my head, crawling into bed and extending the books to him. After a moment, he climbed onto the other side, and the bed shifted under the added weight. I brushed aside the awkward feeling of intimacy at sharing a bed with him, especially as it made my mind wander to memories of Blaise.

I steeled my mind against that dangerous line of thinking, propping my feet on the extra pillows. "Which book should we start with?"

Finlay took the question seriously, turning over each one in his hands in quiet consideration. Finally, he selected one I hadn't read yet.

"This one," he decided with an air of finality. He placed the others on the nightstand and turned off the lamp. Darkness consumed us for a moment, and I was about to question him when a small flame flickered to light in his palm, just enough to illuminate the open book in his lap and parts of his face.

I snuggled further into bed and pulled the blankets around me, giving Finlay a small smile to encourage him to begin. He studied me intently for a moment, returning the look warmly before facing the book again.

When he spoke, his voice was steady and clear, expressive enough to add life to the story without detracting from it. I listened, entranced, for three full chapters before my attention wavered from exhaustion. I struggled against it, excited to hear the hero's next move, but soon it became too tough to fight, and I succumbed to sleep.

The next morning, I awoke alone but fully rested. To my surprise, the only dreams that had invaded my mind were tendrils of the story I'd been listening to. I hadn't woken up once.

Chapter Twenty-Nine

The next morning involved more dance lessons, but only after I demanded we locate some coffee in the castle's kitchens. My sleep last night had been leagues better than the past few weeks, but the tinge of sleep deprivation remained, chasing at the corners of my mind and limbs. It would take several more nights of recovery to feel like I'd returned to equilibrium.

Still, the caffeine helped renew my energy, and my confidence grew with every turn of our dances. It seemed my athletic abilities were not limited to brute physical sports, and by the end of my second lesson, I was throwing myself feely into the motions, my mind no longer halting my steps.

"Excellent!" Darrya cried, clapping as we staggered off our feet. "Kate, you're a natural."

"Well, it helps that it's so fun," I replied, laughing, and caught Finlay's eye as he collapsed onto a nearby chair. A thin sheen of sweat lined his brow, and he flashed me a mischievous grin, white teeth gleaming against the red flush that tinged his cheeks.

"If there is anything the humans get right about us Fae folk, it's that we pride merriment above all else," he put in devilishly. Something he took even more seriously than others, I figured.

"We still have tomorrow to practice, but even if you had to dance tonight, you'd blend right in," Darrya said in an appreciative tone. I grinned at her and pushed off my chair, gathering my cape.

"In that case, I think I'm going to go for a quick walk. Cool off a bit, maybe visit the stables."

"Do you want company?" Darrya scrambled to her feet. "You shouldn't go alone."

I shook my head. "I'll make sure one of the guards comes with me. Maybe Larke — unless he'll be too preoccupied with you?"

She flushed, and I shared a smirk with Finlay. Darrya was usually as confident as they came, ready to take what she wanted and fully aware of the effect she had on others. Yet where Larke was involved, that all came to a screeching halt. I wasn't sure what they'd shared outside of our training sessions, but I was positive that if the mere mention of him had her in such a state, she wasn't making any moves with him in private.

With a laugh, I exited the room. Instantly, one of the guards posted outside the door moved to follow me, a lethal shadow. I understood that our race was endangered, and as 'royals' we were considered even more at risk, but the need for constant accompaniment still unnerved me.

Though I supposed, I used to have my own personal guard. I closed my eyes as I wandered the corridors, heading to the nearest castle exit. I summoned the courage to draw Blaise's face to memory: his hazel eyes, his full lips, pulled back in a rare, dimpled smile—

Nope. It had been almost two months, and yet, the pain of his memory still felt like a punch to the gut. I quickly diminished the image from my eyes and opened them as I approached the large, wooden door leading outside. As I stepped into the cold air, I tried to shift my thoughts to the present moment. The lack of foliage, paired with the height of the hill on which the castle stood, meant I could see all the way to the ocean in the distance. There had been no recent snow in Leven, but the ground was still frozen, and the grass crunched beneath my feet as I walked to the stables.

When I arrived, my chest decompressed from the earthy smells of hay and sweet grain, combined with soft nickers from curious horses. A grateful smile spread across my face with the feeling of home. I paced along the stalls, extending a hand to velvet noses and watching puffs of hot air from their nostrils meet the cold winter air as they whuffled at my palm. A large, dappled gray mare pushed her nose against me, and I paused to stroke her, grinning. None of the royals that came for the solstice brought their horses, so it would have been strange to bring Gray, but I missed him, nonetheless.

"How curious to see a lady out here in such cold," a lilting voice reached my ears. I turned to see a tall, dark-haired man entering the stables, leading an equally massive black horse. He wore a long, obsidian coat made of wool, paired with black riding pants and tall riding boots. He and his horse were a pair of dark storm clouds striding in together; however, his eyes were ocean blue, bright and assessing as he took me in, the same way I did him.

"Pardon me?" I asked, my tone clipped but polite. Though his riding outfit was nothing flashy, the quality was impeccable, and I readied myself for another stifling royal interaction.

"Normally, the ladies in the castle flock together near the fireplaces. There's warmth, food, and good conversation to be had indoors," the man mused, passing his horse to the stable hand. "None of which can be found out here."

I huffed a soft, incredulous breath at the idea of what passed as *good conversation,* meaning it to be inaudible. When the man's brows lifted, however, I realized I hadn't been as quiet as I'd intended.

"Apologies," I murmured, turning away to stroke a path down the white blaze of a nearby horse. "I just — I prefer being here. I grew up riding almost every day, and I find the company of horses easier to manage than most people."

A truth, to be sure, and I hoped he would take that as a hint to leave me alone. He paused, but I bit the inside of my cheek as his footsteps drew closer.

"Then join me for a ride tomorrow," he said, his voice low with a slight air of command. My eyes widened at his audacity, and I whirled around.

"You don't even know me."

"Then tell me your name."

"Tell me *yours.*"

He took a step back in surprise at my sharp response.

"You can't tell me you don't know," he began, and my eyes narrowed at his arrogance.

"Then I won't say as much. But it won't change the fact."

I crossed my arms, waiting. After a beat, the man realized I was serious, and bowed with a smile.

"I'm Thad." He extended a hand, and my mind raced as I offered mine.

"As in Thaddeus? Thaddeus Byrne?" I blurted, and watched as he laughed into my knuckles, his lips brushing across my hand in greeting.

"The one and only. And you are?"

"Lady Lynn of Ryel," I answered quickly. The land, picked by Darrya, was apparently massive and bountiful with resources. It was full of large houses that enjoyed immense wealth from their trading, and seldom left the land due to the moderate climate and location across the sea. Even Darrya couldn't name every house residing there, and as such, it made sense that this would be my first year visiting for the solstice.

I watched Thad's face carefully but saw no hint of suspicion. He simply straightened and inclined his head slightly, accepting it without question. Exactly as Darrya had anticipated.

"Well, Lady Lynn. Now that we've been properly introduced, when can I expect to see you tomorrow for our ride?" He had let go of my hand, but stood unnervingly close; the clouds from our breaths mingled in the frigid air.

I leaned back slightly to gain more space and shrugged the hood of my cape up around my ears, trying to dispel the unease of his presumptuousness. It sounded too much like a command. I figured it was simply his way, a confidence born from his rank as a son of the duke, but it was grating nonetheless. My mind flitted momentarily to Finlay, drawing comparisons between the two.

Finlay had certainly overstepped the mark in our first interaction when he'd tapped into my magic by power-sharing. That being said…for all his cockiness, shameless flirting, and overconsumption, Finlay had never presumed I would bend to his whims due to his status as the prince.

I chose my words carefully, ensuring I didn't offend Thaddeus.

"I have quite a bit to prepare for tomorrow before the celebrations. I can't say for certain when, or *if*, I'll be back out here."

A silence hung in the air; I could almost taste his astonishment at my polite refusal. But then, I thought of the opportunity a longer conversation would present and backpedaled.

"How about this…if we happen to run into each other out here tomorrow, I promise to set aside the time to go for a ride with you." I offered a small smile, one he returned broadly.

"I look forward to it," he replied, "however slim the chance may be."

With that, he turned on his heel and strode out of the stables. I waited a moment before allowing a deep breath to whoosh out of me. He left me unnerved, and slightly irritated, but I did not feel threatened in the way I'd anticipated. I wondered again what he and his brother were capable of to cause Darrya and Finlay such turmoil. If I was this ruffled by Thaddeus, I couldn't imagine the effect of his older brother.

That night, in an unspoken invitation, Finlay returned to my room. His knock was less tentative than the night before, and I opened the door wide to allow him in. His demeanor was soft and inviting, like the warmth of his flames was emanating out in anticipation of lulling me into slumber.

He came to sit on the edge of my bed, and I handed him the book we'd started. As I clambered onto the other side, he studied me intently.

"What?" I asked, my hand going subconsciously to my face.

"I didn't get a chance to tell you during our dance lessons, but you look better today. Not with dancing — well, obviously with the dancing—" He fumbled over the words. "—but more well rested, too."

"Oh." I blinked. "Thank you. Truly. It was you who helped. You have a wonderful voice."

He flushed slightly, and I was amused to see how much my compliment caught him off guard. "How did you know reading would help?" I asked.

"It's what I do every time I hear about another loss. I read until I physically can't keep my eyes open anymore," he answered, his voice so soft it was barely audible. "And my grandmother read to me often, right after my parents died."

His face was unreadable at the mention of his parents. My heart tugged, considering how the memory of them likely tailed his every action, like voices carried by the wind. "How old were you?" I whispered. "When they…"

"When Nemain killed them?" he finished for me, his voice flat. He shook his head and lowered the book to his lap. "Six."

I bit my lip. *So young.* I tried to imagine Finlay as a young child — his hair the unruly blond mop it still was, but even more dramatic on a smaller frame; his mischievous cherub-like face, punctuated by those pale blue eyes. I bet he'd been sinfully cute, able to get away with anything.

"It's funny," he continued, though his grim tone said differently. "Until your father arrived at the palace, I had no idea my great-grandmother knew who was behind the attacks. Decades, with the answer right under our noses. I can't believe she's never wished to pursue justice."

"Maybe she was worried for your safety," I supplied, my tone hushed.

Finlay's chuckle was flat. "Maybe," he answered, "but it's not like I wasn't already in danger before."

At my questioning look, he cleared his throat, eyes downcast. "I was there. When my parents were murdered."

I let out a soft gasp. "What?"

"The guards must have arrived in time to stop her before she got to me, or perhaps she decided I wasn't worth it, being so young. But again, nobody ever told me — nobody ever *talked to me* about what happened."

He paused for a long moment before continuing, his expression growing distant. "For a while, I remembered nothing of that night, but then, the nightmares started. I would wake up, screaming in terror, overwhelmed by images of dark shadows and ravens."

I sank against my pillow, eyes widening with realization. What Nemain had said to him when she saw him that day — *I didn't have the chance last time we met.*

Nemain's words had made little sense in the moment, but the horror we all witnessed several weeks ago had already visited him as a child. It had *been* visiting him, in his dreams, ever since.

His jaw flexed as he ground his teeth. "I didn't realize until I saw Nemain for myself, and witnessed the power she held, they weren't nightmares at all. They were memories."

I wasn't sure what to say, or if anything at all would help. I recalled the nights I'd woken up, sweat pooling into the notch between my neck and my collarbone, throat raw from the screams that ripped me from my sleep. We basked in a long moment of silence before he sighed and continued.

"Anyway, my grandmother eventually noticed. Whether she saw how tired I was, or was alerted by some guard who heard my screaming, I don't know. But from then on, for the next few years, she made a habit of reading to me almost every night."

Out of impulse, I put a hand on Finlay's arm. It was tense, solid as stone, and burning hot. Without thinking, I rubbed my thumb across the fabric of his shirt, willing him to relax. He met my gaze with a startled look, and I smiled reassuringly.

"So...let's read," I said quietly. "When you left off, the hero had been stranded on an island. What kind of cliffhanger is that? I *need* to know what happens next."

Finlay absorbed the question, slowly relaxing until he finally returned the grin. "Well, sometimes the wait is what makes it all the better. Now we get to experience the best part."

With that, he opened the book and took a moment to locate where we left off, then began to speak again. I lowered my head to the pillow and closed my eyes, letting his words consume me. I left my hand on his arm, feeling the way his muscles shifted with every page turn.

I was nearly asleep when he stopped, my mind lingering somewhere in the middle of the waking world and the world of dreams. I might have imagined it, but I could have sworn when he shifted off the bed, he placed a soft kiss on my forehead and murmured, "Thank you, little angel," before slipping away into the night.

CHAPTER THIRTY

I managed to keep myself busy with dance lessons the next morning, tactfully avoiding any thought of my looming stable conflict. I refrained from mentioning it to Darrya or Finlay, as I was still undecided on whether to accept Thaddeus' offer. It was an excellent opportunity to gain more information from one of the brothers, but the idea of riding alone with him was unnerving. I was certain I could protect myself, but stabbing Thaddeus Byrne wasn't exactly something that would go unnoticed — or unpunished.

I warred internally with myself as Darrya and I walked to the same room where we'd previously met Lachlan. Darrya had scheduled some time for us to talk before the solstice, and I was looking forward to learning what else he knew.

"Lady Lynn. Lady Darrya." Lachlan greeted us warmly as he entered, and shooed away his guards as we curtsied. When the door closed with a thud behind him, he bowed deeply.

"It is an honor to see you again," he said to me, oozing formality. I flushed awkwardly, but before I could say anything, Darrya tutted.

"You chide me every time I come here to be less formal, and yet look at you now. Pot, meet kettle," she said, sharply but not without humor. I chuckled.

At my laugh, Lachlan's kind blue eyes softened, and his lips spread into a wide grin.

"All right, then." He straightened, motioning for us all to sit. "I hear ye have had quite the adventure since we last met. I hope ye'll enlighten me."

I was grateful when Darrya took the lead, tactful but direct with her questions and explanations. Lachlan confirmed that the cauldron was still safely stored in the castle, and reiterated his dismay from hearing the cauldron had been in Daersill all along. His normally rosy face took on a deathlike pallor as Darrya offered a succinct account of my capture.

"By all the gods," he breathed when I removed my cloak and tugged aside the fabric of my dress to show him the scarred remains of my marks. "If she has the power to do that alone, there is no way we can allow her to succeed in reuniting with her sisters."

Darrya nodded, face grim. "There was documentation that she's died at least once before, but was able to resurrect herself."

Lachlan's lips pursed, but he said nothing. My heart sank as I realized he had no idea how this was possible, either. I leaned forward, adding, "We have a feeling that at least some of the murders have been attempts at necromancy. Which I suppose is both fortunate and unfortunate, because while each murder is devastating, it's also an indicator she's unable to resurrect anyone other than herself."

"And she's coming for Aes Sídhe because our powers are the closest to what the gods once had," Lachlan murmured, rubbing his hands together in contemplation. "Especially powerful royals."

"We think so," Darrya confirmed, voice laced with distaste. "And it has the added bonus of creating chaos and pitting us all against each other from fear of extinction."

Lachlan nodded slowly, absorbing the information, and his eyes slid quizzically to me.

I sensed the forthcoming question and answered before he could ask. "She kept me alive because of the power I'll have once the talismans are combined. She seems to think that with me wielding them, I can aid her agenda." At the mere prospect of aiding her, bile rose in my throat.

Lachlan grunted. "How inconvenient. The only thing that can raise her sisters from the grave is also what will send her there." Sarcasm dripped from his words as he fixed me with a fiery look.

"Please know, ye have the full support of both Daersill and Brytham's armies, should the time come," he vowed.

Darrya and I smiled gratefully. Though Finlay said we couldn't count on Aerrin or Thaddeus to offer their forces, Lachlan had the ultimate say. He could — and would — overrule his sons if he needed to.

"So," he continued, "by my count, ye lasses have three of the four. What's the holdup on the last one?"

I laughed, a little pitifully. "We've scoured every legend and book we can get our hands on. It's stubbornly short on information about Lugh's spear."

"Well, unfortunately, I canna think of any more stories that tie back to the spear, other than what ye've already heard. But...seeing as Lugh is the father of Cú Chulainn, I wouldna be surprised if this last one calls to ye in a way even the other talismans havena."

I turned the thought over in my head. "I've been in our armory dozens of times, and nothing has called to me there. Maybe I could look through yours?"

Lachlan nodded, but Darrya jumped in thoughtfully. "*Except,* a spear isn't something used very often these days. A sword, sure, even if its gleaming tips us off. And a stone, a cauldron — those can be hidden in plain sight. But a massive, ancient spear is too obvious."

"Aye. But the magic is likely to be in the spearhead, not the wooden shaft," Lachlan put in. "The metal spearhead is much smaller, easier to pass down through families."

I groaned. "So, what you're saying is, we're probably not looking for an obvious, six-foot murder weapon, but a tiny metal spearhead?"

The pair shot me guilty smiles, and we tossed around a few more ideas before Lachlan stood to leave, blaming preparations for the solstice. Darrya and I thanked him for his time and exited.

"So, where are you off to now?" Darrya asked as we walked. I bit my lip and contemplated my answer. We were heading back to our respective bedchambers, but to head to the stables, I would need to turn in the opposite direction.

"I, uh...I might be off to ride with Thaddeus," I said carefully, watching as her eyebrows shot up in surprise. I searched for a hint of pain or anger in her face, and added, "But I don't have to. It's probably not a good idea."

"No, no — it's a wonderful idea, actually. I'm happy to hear you've met him so fast. Some alone time could open him up and answer any questions we have before the solstice takes place. Besides, Thad is the better brother."

She smiled at me, but it was an unnatural smile for her, one that didn't reach her eyes. The sight of it stopped me in my tracks. I glanced around the hallway to ensure we were alone, and turned to face Darrya.

"What happened?" I asked, quiet but firm. She winced, and for a moment, she no longer looked like the radiant envoy, exuding confidence that filled the room. "What did they do to you?" I pressed.

"Nothing," she replied, but the answer was too quick, and we both knew it. She scanned the hallway carefully as well, then dropped her gaze to the floor. After a beat, she continued.

"Truly, nothing happened. But...Aerrin and I were engaged to be married before we even knew one another. We'd seen each other in passing, but it wasn't like we'd spent any time together. Then, the queen and Lachlan organized for Finlay and me to visit for a week so Aerrin and I could get to know one another properly."

I listened silently, as if a single heavy breath would startle her from her story. She sighed and crossed her arms as she continued.

"At first, Aerrin was nothing but charming. He made me laugh and complimented me. We stole kisses in the shadows. But then, he decided he wanted to know *everything* about what it would be like to be married, to be sure we were right for each other…"

I grabbed her arm instinctively, realizing where this was headed.

"I was still very young, and when you're always being watched and trained for court, there are…few opportunities for any shenanigans. So, when he came to my room, I had no idea what he was after," she continued. Her expression was etched with grief, as if mourning those innocent times.

"He tried. He held me down and ripped at my clothing. Even when I struggled and told him to stop, he struck me to shut me up. The only thing that finally made him stop was Finlay."

Astonishment overtook my quickly spreading anger. "Finlay?"

Darrya nodded. "He heard me and burst in before anything could really happen. He was so angry, he nearly burned down a whole section of the castle before getting it back under control. It wasn't something they could hide from Lachlan, and when he heard, he immediately called off the engagement. Since then, he's always careful to avoid putting me in direct situations with Aerrin. Events like these are the closest we get."

I reached for Darrya, pulling her into an embrace. She relaxed against me, as though relieved to finally be talking about it, and my lips tugged into a sad smile.

"I'm so, so glad you're okay," I murmured into her hair, and she squeezed me tightly.

"And even though Finlay can be a shithead, I'm glad he's protective of you," I added, and was happy to hear her laughter in response.

"It's been ages, but it's still hard to see either of them. Thad is a reminder of his brother...but he did nothing wrong. You should be fine with him."

"But he could have warned you. If he knew what his brother was like," I retorted, pulling back. Darrya shook her head emphatically.

"I can't blame him. It's easy to look for the bad in strangers, but it's much more difficult to see flaws in the people closest to us."

I couldn't argue that.

"You came," Thaddeus said, his lips curling into a small smile as I approached the stables. I was slightly surprised to see him waiting; I wasn't sure whether to feel flattered he chose to wait, or irritated by his confidence that I would come. He waved, and instantly, a stable hand sped off, presumably saddling horses for us.

"I came for the horse," I replied, then chided myself for the quip. To my relief, he simply gave a low chuckle.

"I'll take what I can get."

The horse the stable hand chose for me was a stocky bay that reminded me of Coyote, and my heart twisted as I considered how they were doing. I wondered how my mother was dealing with the snow, something we hadn't experienced growing up in California unless we traveled elsewhere to find it. I quickly shooed the thoughts away as we mounted. Thaddeus was back on his black steed, and I followed his lead as we traveled away from the castle.

He asked mundane questions at first — my age, my signature magic, if I'd ever left Ryel before this, and what my childhood was like. I answered with a mixture of lies and truth, lobbying a few of the questions back his way. His own upbringing sounded more complicated than I'd anticipated. His tone made it clear he lived mostly in the shadows of his brother, but I couldn't tell if he was relieved to not have the responsibility or chafed by it.

"What kind of hobbies do you have outside of your standard obligations?" We rode along the beach, so I raised my voice to be heard above the lapping of the waves crashing onto the shore. We'd ridden for easily an hour at this point, and I shook my gloved hands, fighting against the frigid air threatening to stiffen my fingers against the reins. Frost lined the indents of previous hoofprints in the sand, though it was not cold enough to freeze such a massive body of water.

"I'm a collector of sorts," he replied. "I have a myriad of rare creatures from around the realms."

"Like what?" I asked, leaning forward in my saddle. I waited for his answer with genuine curiosity.

"Kappas, Kelpies, Muckies, Turuls, even some Failinis off-spring...the list goes on."

My mind raced to make sense of it. I'd heard of Kelpies — some sort of aquatic horse, if I remembered correctly — but I hadn't heard of the others. I was fairly certain Kelpies were considered more murderous than cuddly, however, meaning Thad was possibly col-lecting creatures just as dark as the Fae army Nemain was amassing. I suppressed a shiver at the thought.

"Am I supposed to know all those creatures?" I asked carefully, trying not to sound too oblivious.

A short laugh escaped his lips. "I would be surprised if you did. Half of them aren't even from this realm."

My brow furrowed at the information he threw out so casually. *Not from this realm?* Either there were creatures I was unaware of in the human realm, or other realms I wasn't yet privy to. That felt like information I would know if I had been raised here, so I kept my surprise to myself.

"And what is it you do with them?" I inquired instead. "Are they just — kept in cages?"

It sounded like he was collecting creatures for his own personal circus; I could only imagine what kind of torment that meant they were subjected to.

Thad picked up on the judgment in my tone, and his eyes narrowed. He straightened in his saddle to answer. "I can assure you they are well taken care of. I don't wish to punish them; in fact, I prefer not to see them go extinct. That's the point in raising them."

"Ah," I replied, unsure what to think of his response. I reminded myself it was entirely possible he was making this all up. He'd already seen my interest in horses, so perhaps this was a simple tactic to pretend he cared for animals, to seem like a better person for my sake. My hands tightened on the reins as I leaned into that far more likely prospect.

"As far as their environments, I can assure you, I've seen people kept in far worse cages — physical or otherwise," Thad added. The flatness of his tone indicated there was more to the comment than he was letting on. "And if you don't like the fact that I collect dangerous and dark creatures, you should see what our very own queen keeps right at her palace."

*Interesting...*goosebumps threatened to pop up over my skin, but I shook off his comment and refocused on the task at hand.

"So. You're telling me growing up with everything you ever wanted wasn't always sunshine and rainbows?" I pivoted back to his upbringing tactfully, hoping to unravel some of the incentives he and his brother had for partnering with Nemain.

He shook his head, eyes downcast. "Not always. And the closer my brother gets to ruling Brytham, the more added responsibility weighs him down. Me, too."

"Would you do things differently?" I asked, and pushed my horse into a trot to close the distance between us. "If you could?"

He took a moment to think and then nodded. "I definitely see the world differently than it is now." A bit of an answer, but not a full one. Not one that told me anything. I pressed further.

"Do you think you two can change things?"

His reply was cryptic, yet held a tone of finality. "I believe a lot will change here. And soon."

My stomach dropped. I considered digging deeper, but eventually dropped the idea; my questions may have already aroused some suspicion. Instead, I deftly switched our conversation to lighter topics. When we got back and passed the reins back to the stable hands, Thaddeus turned to me.

"Thank you for joining me." His voice dropped an octave, eyes burning with voracious intent. My gut twisted as I read the hunger there, and I had to remind myself of Darrya's words. *He did nothing wrong.*

"Thank you for having me, Thaddeus," I returned, as brightly as I could muster. I made to turn, but he caught my hand.

"Please," he murmured, "call me Thad."

I felt his hand slip around my waist and froze. He turned me back to face him and my nerves stood on end. He leaned in close.

"Are you excited for the solstice?" I asked as Thaddeus stilled, his mouth a hair's breadth from mine. I pulled back slightly against the embrace and prayed he would take the hint, hoping he would be nothing like his brother.

He hesitated, face somber, before stepping back. His eyes shimmered as he regarded me closely.

"I am," he answered finally, his hands detaching from my waist. I breathed a soft sigh of relief. "Are you?"

"It's my first," I admitted, and his brows lifted. "I know, I know. But better late than never, right?"

He snorted. "Better late than never, indeed. Leven at solstice time is truly a sight to behold."

He walked around me and placed himself at my side; I was surprised when he offered his arm, which I tentatively accepted.

"Allow me to escort you back to the castle. You will want a good night's rest if you're going to experience everything the solstice has to offer."

As we walked back, I cursed the fact that, despite our brief encounter, Thaddeus was behaving like a gentleman. It was much easier to lie to him, to hate him, when I envisioned all the ways he was awful. I had to imagine it was only a matter of time before he would show his true colors.

CHAPTER THIRTY-ONE

Lughnasadh had been a wonderful celebration, full of local families, arts, and crafts. There, I'd felt togetherness, the spirit of the earth, and the creativity of our community. This solstice celebration was a different feeling entirely — elite, exclusive, but above all, beautiful.

The color scheme for the night was scarlet, and the dress Darrya had chosen for me was admittedly breathtaking. It was floor-length, a bright crimson to complement my dark hair, and though the front plunged suggestively, large silver feathers covered my chest respectably, and continued their dance across the entire front of the dress.

Darrya braided half of my hair back, and I noted her dress choice — a darker, blood-red velvet number, simple and more modest than most other dresses she wore. The fact that she would be in Aerrin's presence told me all I needed to know about her wardrobe choice, and I chose not to comment. My nervousness increased the more

Darrya talked, mentally preparing for the political gymnastics to come.

All apprehension fell from my head, however, as we walked to the great hall. I took in the exquisite décor of the castle; each door boasted a ring of holly, the red berries in each wreath a fitting pop of scarlet to match the night. Every fireplace was lit, the fires roaring and crackling their own tunes beneath the sound of music echoing from the hall.

The grandeur only heightened as we crossed into the black-and-white patterned threshold of the great hall. Holly and mistletoe wove around each stone column, reaching to the arched stone ceiling; green leaves and white and red berries offered a glimpse of holiday cheer, providing a sense of familiarity.

The setting sun gleamed dimly through two small windows, but candles hung from nearly every available surface, unlit but prepped to illuminate the cheery décor once the sun fully set. The royals were mostly centered around a massive fireplace at the end of the hall, which burned brightly with several oak logs. A harpist played a quiet but beautiful tune as the crowd grew.

Darrya motioned to the crowd and leaned in, whispering, "Each family is to bring an oak log to burn. It's like your Yule log tradition — it's to celebrate the rebirth of the sun. It brings good luck for the longer days that follow the shortest day of the year."

I looked at her, alarmed, but she waved a hand dismissively as she read the question in my eyes. "Don't worry, we've got you covered." She grinned. "Finlay, the queen, and Lachlan will put their logs on first, and the others will follow over time. The fire won't go out for the full three days we're here. I've got two in my room for us."

I nodded, and gratefully took a glass of champagne from a passing attendant as I took in the steadily filling room. The ladies all wore unique patterns with their scarlet and crimson dresses, and the men wore different shades of the color on their jackets, embellished with buttons or chains.

But none wore gold. None, that was, except Finlay and the queen. A ripple of bows and curtseys flowed out from the audience as they entered together, and I surveyed the queen with quiet curiosity.

Her crimson dress was belted with a golden lace applique, which fanned out in both directions. It followed the slit of fabric to line the bottom of her dress, as well as her neckline. A robe was cinched at her shoulders, the same color as her dress, with a long train flowing behind. With the wide berth offered by the other royals, there was no chance of it being trodden on.

She gave soft nods to certain royals as she passed the crowd, but didn't appear to notice me. For that, I was grateful. We hadn't crossed paths since she gave Finlay her blessing, aiding me in my endeavors to defeat Nemain. I didn't want to know her thoughts on everything that had transpired since. I didn't need to give her any more reason to remember me, lest I end up in her dungeons. I sidled back into the crowd, pressing behind two taller royals as I watched Finlay stride behind the queen.

The prince had donned black pants and knee-high leather boots, his ebony vest and cardinal jacket embroidered in gold swirls that made their way around its edges, leading all the way up his high collar. His billowy blond hair was piled high, styled away from his face. I was amazed to find not a strand out of place, a complete change from his usual disarray.

He stood stoically by the queen's side, one hand grasping a glass of champagne while the other was tucked behind his back. Flutters whispered a strange tune in my stomach at his serious expression, jaw sharp and firmly clenched — dutiful, even, as he embodied the role he was expected to play. While I knew he wasn't enjoying this, I had to admit he looked good, nonetheless.

Darrya nudged me. "It's about to begin," she whispered, pointing up to the ceiling. I glanced between the columns in confusion, before a massive crack resounded through the hall. I grabbed for Darrya's wrist in alarm, but she merely laughed and leaned into me.

I watched in dismay as the stone between the two small windows crumbled away and became one. The space left was impeccably placed, large enough for a solid beam of golden sunlight to illuminate the walkway of the grand hall, which led directly to the fireplace.

"It's *stunning,*" I breathed incredulously, and Darrya hummed her agreement.

"They use earth magic to dismantle and reassemble those windows every solstice."

"Does he not have some sort of ward against that?" I asked, confused. "It seems like a safety hazard to know any Faeries with earth magic can just crumble his castle at any time."

She shook her head vehemently. "Oh, no. You're totally right. This section is the only place in the castle that has its wards lifted, and even then, only during the solstices."

I opened my mouth to question further, but a voice rang out — Lachlan's voice, assuming the professional formality I'd heard the day prior. I glanced back to see his large figure looming before the fireplace, champagne flute in hand, donning a luxurious, dark red velvet suit. Despite the piercing blue eyes and facial structure, which left no room for argument that Thad was his kin, Lachlan's demeanor was warmer. He commanded the room with respect alone, obvious in the way the room hushed the moment his voice sounded.

"We welcome you all to another wonderful winter solstice. As always, we appreciate your presence, and on these longest nights and shortest days, we will make our wishes for the new year."

He turned, took a log near the fireplace, and tossed it into the fire. It hissed and crackled as the flames rose to consume it. He turned back to the crowd, and the red and orange flames behind him matched the remaining auburn in his hair, a stark contrast to the gray.

"As for me?" he continued. "I wish for the sun to fill our lives, homes, and souls with warmth and happiness. May our hearts bloom like the spring that will soon be upon us."

The sentiment was short and sweet, and he stepped out of the way to allow the queen and Finlay to toss a log on the fire, both of whom echoed his wishes in a similar manner. Once completed, Lachlan raised his glass, waiting as the crowd followed suit. Once all glasses were raised, he bellowed, "Now! Let us eat, drink, and be merry!"

A chorus of cheers resounded through the room, and the dismissal was clear. Finlay, released from his duty at last, immediately slipped away from the queen and approached us. A handful of royals hovered behind him, tittering as they summoned the courage to ensnare him in conversation, but he completely ignored their presence. He held his champagne flute, already emptied, but his approach was surefooted and clarity shimmered in his eyes. I regarded him with interest.

It seemed he was toeing a line of sobriety, likely brought on by the queen's presence. I assumed, with surprising relief, that it would keep the unruly prince on the right side of consciousness tonight. I'd grown used to his company the past few nights, and had been preparing myself for the likelihood he'd be too inebriated to partake tonight. Perhaps there was still hope — if he wasn't pulled away by one of the ravenous-looking royals who were currently casting burning looks of jealousy our way.

"You look really good," I commented, and at Finlay's miffed expression, I clarified, "I mean, you're — practically glowing."

"Ah," he replied, shifting. "That. Well, you're quite literally right."

He turned and pointed to the fireplace. "There's a reason fire is part of the celebration. The sun's powers increase as the days grow longer. It's believed that the sun stands still for several days around the solstice. All these fires constantly burning feed my magic, and it makes my soul feel positively delightful."

I smiled, a bit wistfully, and took a careful sip of champagne. I wondered if I would feel the same, had I summoned so much as a coin-sized spark of fire magic.

"Ready to dance, Kate?" Darrya inquired gleefully as the music increased in tempo. I nodded, apprehensive, and she dragged me to the middle of the hall, where others had already begun to gather. Finlay joined us, and their combined grins relaxed me, to the point that a giddy laugh slipped past my lips as I hopped with the thrums of the music. We twirled our way through the crowds, and I caught Thad's eye as I slipped by, dipping my head with a polite smile.

I drank, danced, and stood closely at Darrya's side as she navigated polite introductions and mindless conversations with a handful of royal families. The beam of light disappeared slowly as the sun set, the touch of magic returning the windows to their former shapes while the candles lit. They replaced the steady glow with a whimsical, flickering light that beat in tandem with the music.

As I stood with Darrya, discussing the profitability of the spice trade with a couple whose names I had already forgotten, I felt a prickle at the nape of my neck.

I was being watched.

I rotated, scanning the crowd. A tall man accosted me with a burning stare, his blue eyes and auburn hair marking him clearly as Lachlan's other son, practically the spitting image of Lachlan himself. He stood tall and poised, his gaze unabashed, though he made no move to approach. I realized with a start that he was likely staying put due to my company — he would not approach Darrya. I decided to test my theory and murmured an excuse to her, slipping away to a corner.

It came as no surprise when he shifted, prowling toward me like a predator locked on its prey. I steeled myself, instinctively knowing this would be a different playing field than the one I'd been on with his brother.

"Lady Lynn," he said as he grew close, his voice deep and calculated. My muscles tensed, feeling slightly threatened; he'd clearly asked around to prepare for our interaction. When he stopped in front of me, he gave a slight bow.

"Lord Aerrin," I responded with a curtsey. "To what do I owe the pleasure of this interaction?"

"Do I need a reason," he inquired, "other than the desire to speak with a beautiful lady?"

Thad's advances had been bold, but left a polite opening where I felt I could excuse myself without incident. Aerrin's speech, while equally clipped and cordial — a testament to their royal upbringing — held a more foreboding tone. Something told me he would not take kindly to rejection. I forced a smile at the compliment, despite the warnings roaring in my head. I'd been marked, like Darrya, all those years ago. My eyes traveled to her in the distance, relieved to find she hadn't yet taken notice of our conversation.

A movement of gold flickered in the corner of my eye, and I shifted my gaze to find Finlay settling himself against a column nearby. Lazily, he leaned against it, and sipped his champagne. He surveyed the room and its guests, and though he never glanced in our direction, I knew he was listening. A wave of comfort instantly washed over me.

I cast my eyes downward, feigning bashfulness. "You find me beautiful?" I asked.

"I find your beauty absolutely singular," he crooned, eyes scanning my body. I shifted at the oddly formal comment, attempting to hide my discomfort. "Red suits you. It brings out your skin, your hair, your eyes."

"I suppose it's a good thing his grace chose this color scheme, then," I replied tactfully, opting not to use Lachlan's first name. 'Lady Lynn' would not have that close relationship with him.

"Actually, I chose today's colors. After all, red is the color of...lust."

"And the color of blood," I added, sipping my champagne without meeting his eyes. I was beginning to feel a bit lightheaded from the drinking and dancing.

Aerrin raised his brows. "A bloodthirsty little thing, are you?"

I feigned a long sip while considering my next words. If I had to play this game with him, I would do my best to squeeze any information out of him that I could.

"I find conversations of trade deals and court gossip inane," I said, rolling my eyes. "Things such as battle and war are much more...thrilling."

"Unfortunately for me, my life at court involves more dull conversation than fighting," Aerrin replied, his white teeth gleaming in a broad grin. "My position requires me to adhere to sensible diplomacy."

"So, when you rule Brytham, you will be a ruler of diplomacy rather than one of action?" I asked lightly, swirling my drink innocently, like I hadn't just insinuated he was a coward. His grin wavered and his eyes narrowed as he studied me, assessing the weight of my words.

"Rest assured; I have big plans for my rule. Ones that will require serious action," he replied in a biting tone. I leaned in eagerly.

"How so?" I breathed. "What do you have in mind?"

The instant the words left my mouth, I could see that I'd gone too far. A shadow of suspicion clouded his face, and I worked furiously to backtrack.

"My apologies. It's just that — such dangerous talk makes my heart race, and my blood rush — similar to other feelings. Like lust," I threw him a sickly-sweet smile, praying it would detract from the distrust behind his gaze. I watched with bated breath as his look transformed, returning to his milder, flirtatious expression.

"Well, aren't you just a wildcat," he purred, leaning in. His eyes grazed over the feathers on my dress, and it took every ounce of my restraint not to tug back as his hand wrapped around my waist, his head dipping to press his mouth against my ear. He whispered his next words.

"I can only *imagine* what you're like in bed. Care to join me later tonight?" he asked, his eyes gleaming ravenously. He pulled back, waiting expectantly for an answer. I opened my mouth, yet struggled to find the words. His grip tightened, and I bit my lip. But before I could think up a response — one that didn't involve breaking his nose — Finlay burst in.

"Lady Lynn! Darrya is calling for you," he exclaimed, his grin stupidly broad as he shoved against Aerrin, spilling his champagne in the process. The lord snarled and stepped back, releasing my waist as he brushed off his coat.

"Apparently, one of them got their hands on some *voitín* and it's—" he paused, gesturing wildly around his head to mimic the explosive feeling it produced. I propped a hand over my mouth in a show of astonishment, attempting to hide the smile twitching at my lips from his ridiculous show. I glanced over at Aerrin, whose face had gone cold, jaw rigid and eyes dark.

"My presence alone isn't enough for my dear cousin; she desperately wants you to join. Says she needs as much time with you as possible before you head back to Ryel."

Finlay offered me his hand in invitation and I took it without hesitation, but flinched slightly as heat scorched my palm. He turned on his heel and paused, cocking his head.

"Aerrin," he stated flatly, as if just now realizing his presence. He tipped his champagne flute in brief acknowledgment, tugging me away before the lord could so much as open his mouth to reply. I was surprised when Finlay pulled me past Darrya, and the crowds, taking us straight out of the hall.

"Finlay," I ventured softly. He glanced at me, dropping my hand at the sound of his name. He continued moving through the crowds and, after a moment's hesitation, I followed until all traces of the crowd were gone.

"Finlay!" I called more forcefully this time. He finally stopped, and that was when I noticed how badly his hands were trembling. My eyes widened.

"Are you okay?" I asked.

"It's—" Finlay cut himself off, shaking his head. He paced from one side of the hallway to the other while I watched. The prince was teetering on the cusp of losing it, and I didn't have any of the right words to help bring him down. Finally, he took a few deep breaths and stopped pacing. When his gaze found mine, a deep, carnal anger shone in them.

"I will end his life if I see him touch anyone else without permission again," he growled, the corridor heating under his power. "Especially Darrya — especially *you*."

My mouth fell open at the severity of his tone; I had never seen him like this. As sparks jumped across his hands and rage bloomed on his face, I saw the person who burned down part of the castle to protect his cousin. But I knew he wouldn't let that fire hurt me.

I crossed the space between us and took his hands in mine. There was a brief moment as he reigned in his power where my hands seared, but the heat quickly dissipated. He inhaled sharply in surprise, and raised his eyes to meet mine.

"She's okay," I murmured, squeezing his hands tightly. "I'm okay."

His chest heaved as he focused on his breathing, and I continued.

"That was an impressive show back there. You're good at pretending to be sober when you're wasted, but somehow, you're even better at pretending to be wasted when you're sober."

The tease caught him off guard, and he paused. I felt the room cool a degree or two as he gave me an off-kilter smile. "I'm impressed you know the difference."

"I've had a lot of experience with the levels of Finlay sobriety," I goaded. When I turned, pulling him along, he followed willingly. "Come on. I think I've had enough dancing for the day."

We walked to my room, making small conversation as we went.

"He certainly has a way with words," I mused sarcastically, opening the door. "Apparently, I'm a *wildcat.*"

Finlay followed in, snorting. "To be fair, he also called you a beautiful lady."

"I'm no lady, either."

"Oh, I certainly know that," he replied, laughing, and flopped down on the side of my bed.

I pulled out loungewear and slipped into the washroom to change, but quickly found myself struggling to get out of the elaborate gown. My fingers fumbled around the lace that tied the back, catching and slipping time and again.

"Did you fall in?" Finlay drawled.

I rolled my eyes and attempted once more to catch the ties, but failed spectacularly. With a groan, I poked my head out of the washroom.

"Would you mind helping me?"

After a moment, Finlay appeared at my side, eyes scouring my dress. I turned my back to him and gestured to the strings. He hesitated, placing his hands on my shoulders. They were warm and broad, and I tried not to shiver at his touch.

"For someone with so much experience undressing women, you're certainly taking your time," I taunted. I heard a grunt behind me, and with a swift jerk, the dress came undone. I scrambled to catch the fabric before it fell completely.

"Hey!" My weak protestation collapsed into a laugh, and I turned in time to see Finlay's devilish grin as he left the washroom. I quickly changed and jumped into the bed, scrutinizing him. He lifted a new book to start, but I stopped him.

"No," I said. "I want to hear your stories from other solstices. You've had so many, I'm sure you have at least a few good ones."

He lifted a brow, but complied. "I suppose I do have a few good ones. Have you ever noticed the small scar Darrya has on her lip?"

I nodded and leaned into him, eager to hear more. We talked, exchanging lighthearted stories until Finlay eventually drifted off to sleep. I made no move to wake him; rather, I took the moment to study him in his sleep. He appeared just as he had when I found him sleeping outside the palace — softer and more vulnerable, as if the weight of his title and the haunting memories were lifted. A soft glow still lingered on his skin. He looked ethereal.

Like a fallen angel.

I thought of his lips, featherlight on my forehead a few nights before. Before I could think, my hand reached out, and I ran my fingers through his soft golden hair, down his sharp cheekbone, and then over his lips. When he shifted slightly, I pulled my hand back and closed my eyes, pretending to sleep until finally, I did.

CHAPTER THIRTY-TWO

If it wasn't for the fact that Finlay could still feel the touch of Kate's fingers on his lips, he would have been sure he'd dreamt it. He'd woken instantly at the touch of her hand running through his hair, but dared not breathe as she explored her way down his cheek and over his lips. It gave him something he had not allowed for months, or...ever.

It gave him hope.

Every instance where Kate had returned his affections previously had been clouded by extenuating circumstances, and he had kept a careful distance after everything transpired with her rescue. His rage had been unfathomable when he saw her in physical pain, strung up in Nemain's basement, battered and bloody. But seeing the way she'd screamed and cried, prostrate over Blaise's dying body — Finlay would have cut out his own heart and given it to the commander, if only to save Kate that pain.

But Finlay had known it would happen, of course. It happened exactly as Blaise had warned it would.

Blaise had known since his first visit with Kate to the Valkyrie, Ensley, who told him he would die. She'd prophesized his death while protecting Kate. He told Finlay he'd visited numerous times since, looking for ways to protect himself and Kate from harm. Certain things changed each time, but the result remained the same. By the time he came to Finlay, he had accepted his fate.

That didn't change the traumatic reality of the moment. As much as Finlay's pain was for Kate, he, too, ached with stunned grief at the sight of the fallen commander. He couldn't dwell on it, though — he owed it to Blaise to ensure Kate would find her way through it and survive his passing. For that reason, he'd forced his limbs to move, protecting Kate from further trauma and preserving Blaise's dignity as he removed the commander's lifeless body from the grisly scene. And on their way home, Finlay had ground his teeth to dust, fighting back surprising torrents of emotion and memories. Despite their complicated history with Kate, he and Blaise had formed a bond of sorts.

"I need to know," Blaise had asked. "Do you love her?"

It was the first time Finlay had been hit directly with the question, and his instant reaction was to deny it, especially to Blaise. But he knew, in his broken and twisted soul, that he'd loved Kate from the first time he'd set eyes on her. And so, he'd nodded.

He'd upheld the first part of his promise, telling no one else the truth of Blaise's fate. And he had every intention of upholding the second part of his promise as long as he could: to keep Kate safe.

If that meant cutting Aerrin's hands from his body to keep him off her, he would not hesitate. The mere thought of his hands on Kate's body made his fists clench, hard enough for his nails to break skin.

Finlay knew he wasn't entirely in Kate's good graces, but over the last few nights, a sort of kinship had formed between them. Keeping her safe didn't simply mean physical danger, and for once, he was glad his own experiences could help. It was merely an added bonus to watch her drift peacefully into sleep every night.

As he surveyed Kate's sleeping form in the early morning light, intending to slip away before she woke, he knew he owed it to her to reveal the full truth about Blaise. But he'd seen the way she avoided any mention of his name, instead throwing herself into training, riding, or otherwise hiding away. She wasn't ready yet, but he'd share the truth when she was. When it wouldn't hurt her quite so much.

Watching Kate at the solstice was all the entertainment Finlay needed. He observed with delight as she fumbled her way through the sit-down dinner on the second night. The first night had been small, bite-sized items passed around on trays, but this was more intimate, with only the adults of each royal home. Two long tables stretched down the great hall, and she had a place halfway down from where he was seated. Though she clearly felt out of place with the extravagance of the meal, Darrya's lessons had worked well, and she used all the right silverware, corrected her posture constantly, and never spilled a drop or crumb.

Small things still set her apart from the others, but in all the best ways. It warmed his heart to watch as she thanked all the waitstaff while they refilled her glasses or brought and removed her dishes — a thing the others had learned to simply ignore. Her confusion at having the silverware and dishes replaced with each course amused him to no end; he coughed into his napkin to stifle a laugh when she insisted she didn't mind reusing her silverware, earning bewildered looks from the waitstaff.

During the dancing, he wasn't the only one whose eyes were drawn to her. There was a reason she'd caught the attention of both Lachlan's sons, single-handedly drawing information from them without their realizing. The joy she radiated while dancing was infectious; her broad smile gleamed and her laugh, just a bit louder than the others, echoed over the lilt of the music.

Kate's dress that night was no less stunning than the red one from the evening prior. The dark emerald green was an equally beautiful color on her, detailed with sequined sleeves and a shimmering lace top. The tulle bottom flowed as she twirled, hugging her impressive muscles and delicious curves in all the right places. Her silken brown hair whipped wildly, as if it had a mind of its own.

It was all Finlay could do not to grab her and claim her on the dance floor, pulling her flush against him as she had intended in their first dance lesson. But she wasn't his to claim. He was still nothing to her, but to him...she was everything. And he would wait as long as necessary for any sign she wanted him, too. He thought back to her fingers on his lips, and the kernel of hope it placed in his heart.

He mingled all evening, saying all the right things, recalling just enough detail to impress the families that mattered most to the queen's alliances. He noticed the lingering attempts some made to flirt with him, but brushed them aside. The last time he'd been interested in sleeping with someone had been shortly after meeting Kate, and he'd been left wholly dissatisfied. When they had parted ways, he'd blinked rapidly, having envisioned Kate's own eyes, like melted caramel, in place of the dark green the Faerie actually had.

He danced, but barely drank, preferring to keep his wits sharp — not only to avoid disrespecting the queen, but to keep a close eye on Kate. She handled the brothers expertly, polite but distant. Finlay was relieved he didn't have to interfere again.

By the time the evening came to a close, Finlay collapsed onto her bed, relieving the ache in his burning feet. He was surprised, however, when Kate stayed on hers, flashing him a playful grin. He propped onto his elbows, eyeing her.

"What are you up to, little angel?"

"I smuggled some dessert," she said slyly, producing a container and two spoons from behind her dress. Her eyes twinkled and her cheeks flushed with animated joy as she beamed at him. A smile twitched at Finlay's lips at seeing her this happy — the happiest he'd seen her in a long while.

She kicked her shoes off, flopped onto the bed and handed him a spoon, which he took with a stunned laugh. "You really made an impression on the waitstaff, didn't you?"

"It costs nothing to be kind," she replied, already shoveling into the vanilla custard. He gave her an appreciative look before taking a spoonful of his own. They ate in silence, and Finlay decided he far preferred his meals like this over the prim and proper one they'd endured earlier.

"So, we finished the book," Kate said, licking the last bit of custard off her spoon. "Which one is next?"

Finlay gave her a long, assessing look, and set his spoon down on the nightstand. He outstretched a hand, and she looked at it, startled.

"I have a different idea," he said, smiling. When she took his hand, he led her out of the room and back to the great hall. The crowds had cleared and the candles were snuffed, leaving only the fireplace to brighten the space. The silence left by the late hour was punctuated only by the crackling of flames.

"I think I like it better like this," Kate breathed, taking in the quiet beauty. While she looked around the hall, he looked only at her. The blaze of the fire lit the sequins dancing on her dress, illuminating her golden eyes.

"I couldn't agree more."

He broke his stare before it became apparent what — or who — he was gazing at. He approached the fireplace and sat down, patting the ground beside him. Other ladies wouldn't appreciate ruffling their dresses by sitting on the floor, but as Kate said herself, she was no lady. Without hesitation, she plopped down next to him, not bothering to smooth her skirts. He grinned appreciatively.

"The tradition is to make a wish on the yule log." He assessed the massive fireplace while absorbing the heat and power emanating from it. "But it's hard to make an honest wish in front of hundreds of royals."

Kate hummed sympathetically, in a way that told Finlay she already knew his public wishes had been platitudes. He continued.

"We're supposed to talk about what we hope for in the new year, and what we leave behind in the old year."

"And what is it you hope for?" she asked, watching him curiously. He felt himself flush and looked away, focusing on the flames instead.

"I hope for...an end to all of this," he admitted, his voice turning rough with emotion. "An end to the murders, the bloodshed. I hope for justice."

There was a pause, and he turned to find her amber gaze still on him, head tilted as she listened. Her bare feet poked out from under her dress as she shifted with a sigh.

"I hope for the same," she said firmly. She took his hand, squeezing, and his heart stumbled over a beat. When he squeezed it in return, she asked, "And what will you leave behind?"

He took a moment to think. "It's always been hard to...see the point of everything. I never had the guidance of my parents, only the memory of their destruction. My grandmother raised me, hoping I would be a kind and just ruler someday. But she also had me trained, *relentlessly,* so I could protect myself from this threat I never understood, but constantly feared."

Finlay paused, taking a deep breath. Kate sat still, her gaze burning into his with a painful understanding. The sight of her pushed him to continue.

"Eventually, I didn't want to feel anything, so I covered it with shallow parties and any substance I could get my hands on. That lack of feeling — *that's* what I want to leave behind."

She nodded along, listening intently, and he gave her a small smile. "I have you to thank for that, little angel. You're giving me purpose. Now, feeling those things doesn't seem as hard anymore."

He felt that familiar twinge of apprehension at offering so much honesty. Kate never judged him for it, but it was still an unfamiliar sensation. As she gazed at him, he grew nervous at what her next words would be. So instead, he asked, "And you? What will you leave behind?"

It was her turn to avoid his gaze, her expression rife with pain and contemplation. When she glanced back up at the fire, tears shone in her eyes, and Finlay felt his heart twist.

"The fear of losing more of us as we put an end to this," she whispered.

A single tear dropped from the bottom of her eyelid and trailed down her cheek. He could only imagine who she was envisioning, and the memory of her screams suddenly reverberated in his skull. It was the push he needed as he gathered her into his arms, pulling her close. To his surprise, she didn't tense or pull away; rather, she sank into his embrace, a testament to the hurt she felt.

"Whatever happens, we will face it together," he vowed. "And we will protect each other. All of us."

"I'm still struggling to allow the people I love to fight this battle with me," she said, the words muffled as she spoke into his emerald blazer. He wondered fleetingly if he was included in that list.

"That's the thing, though. We all fight for who and what we love," he reminded her gently. "You can't choose to fight for us and not let us fight for you. Don't be ridiculous."

Kate considered him with an expression that hovered somewhere between surprise and distress. "I'll try to keep that in mind," she muttered.

He placed his chin on her head, mind racing. "Did you see all the kids here for the solstice, running around and playing their games?"

"Yes. They're adorable. Why?"

"If you won't let us fight for you, let us do it for them," he said gently, breathing the words onto her dark, silken hair. "And their families. To ensure no more children have to grow up without parents, and no parents live in fear of outliving their children."

Her mouth opened, but she was stunned into silence. Another tear had begun a descent down her cheek, following the path of the first. Face twisting with concern, Finlay brushed his thumb across her cheek to wipe it away. Before he could remove his hand, Kate reached up to grab his wrist, and he stilled.

"You're right. It's for them. I just — I only hope I can do this," she whispered. The slight tremble in her voice betrayed how little she believed in herself. Finlay could recite hundreds of reasons why she was entirely capable, but it wouldn't be the comfort he intended it to be. He gave a small smile, rubbing his thumb across the back of her hand.

"If only you could see yourself the way I do," he mused, and turned back to the flames. She shifted to sit next to him, fixing him with an unreadable look.

"I could say the same thing about you," she countered, words edged with her own fire as she withdrew her hand from his. He set both hands on the floor and leaned back, blinking at her in surprise before schooling his face back into a dark, humorous expression.

"Me? I'm just a...uniquely immoral man, known for overindulging in his vices," he replied carelessly, his smile turning devilish.

He hoped to goad her into a grin, an eye roll, or another one of her delightful tongue lashings, but was stunned when she lifted a hand to his face, cupping his cheek in her palm. It was soft and cool against his skin, and he closed his eyes for a heartbeat, wondering what good he'd done in this world to deserve her touch so much in the past few days.

"You're much more than that," she whispered.

When his eyes opened again, wide with dismay, she met them steadily for a long moment, hand still resting on his face. He watched as her lips parted and she leaned in, her soft mouth brushing lightly against his own.

Over the past several months, Finlay's yearning for Kate had been all-consuming. And yet, he couldn't have imagined the way the mere brush of her lips against his sent shocks down every nerve in his body. It was frighteningly intense, but quick, dissipating the moment she pulled away. She stared at him as if she also couldn't believe her actions.

For a moment, they simply gaped at one another, like two creatures stumbling upon the other in the woods, both assessing the danger. Finlay practically turned to stone with how still he became; he barely dared to breathe, as though any motion would scare her away.

But by some grace of the gods, she leaned in again, confirming the reality of the moment. Her mouth pressed against his once more, tentative at first, but then firmer, this time not pulling back. Shock waves skittered through his body again, settling into a steady bliss.

Still, he returned the kiss carefully, his hands remaining firmly on the ground, as though any quick move on his part would shatter the illusion. His thoughts grew hazy; his only focus became her mouth, and how perfectly it fit against his.

Her lips moved suddenly, demanding more, and he responded in kind, deepening the kiss. His hand lifted from the ground, trailing up her spine to rest possessively on the back of her neck.

Suddenly, restraint felt like agony. His tongue hesitantly stroked hers, relishing the delicious taste of vanilla and magic. When her hand trailed from his jaw into his hair, his soul sang. And when she sighed softly against his mouth, he came undone.

In one swift movement, he lunged forward, pressing his body over hers and pushing her gently to the ground. She fell back willingly, but their lips never left each other's, still tasting, consuming, devouring. One of his hands rested on the back of her head, fingers twisting into that dark, silken hair, the other on her cheek.

Finlay moved his hand to her chin, tipping it up to trail kisses down her neck. Her breathing hitched, and the sound sent his mind haywire. A pained groan left his throat as he moved back to her mouth, pausing a mere hair's breadth from her lips.

If she were any other woman, he wouldn't hesitate to take her right there, to taste every inch of her flesh — getting caught be damned. Any other woman, and he would ensure her screams of pleasure echoed through the great hall, rising high above the crackling fire.

But Kate was no ordinary woman, and he wasn't sure she was even his to take. Finlay vowed he would go no further, not unless Kate explicitly led the way. Part of him feared this was a mere distraction for her, a diversion from Blaise's death. She was still dealing with the endless trauma left by Nemain, and he had zero intention of causing her more pain. Love and desire were entirely different beasts, both dangerous by themselves, but even more lethal when you couldn't tell the difference.

Those two emotions warred dangerously in him as he leaned over her, their noses brushing and their heavy breathing mingling as they took each other in. He was completely, utterly lost to her, and she held all the power to crush him. If she did, he'd allow her to, and happily.

Finlay gazed into her eyes, that beautiful color of liquid honey. He relished the way her body rose and fell beneath him as she caught her breath. The evidence of his arousal pressed tight against her hip, and she squirmed slightly, causing him to greedily capture her mouth once more.

He drank her in with each kiss, enjoying the feel of addiction setting in with the taste of her. At that moment, he decided, he wanted desperately to change his solstice wish. If he could ask the gods for one thing, it would be to stop the sun from rising the next morning. It was inconceivable that the days to follow could possibly be better than this one.

Chapter Thirty-Three

My lips were still puffy and tingling the next morning. Every time I brought a beverage to my mouth, all I could think of was the feel of Finlay's mouth on mine, kissing me as though all the air had left the room, and he intended to spend his last few breaths savoring me. I still wasn't sure what had come over me the night before, or what I thought of it, even after a night's sleep — a night spent without Finlay, who slipped away once we reached the door last night.

All I knew for certain was the constant pressure I'd been carrying around, like an anvil on my chest, lifted every time I was with him. Listening to him talk about the front he put on, and the reasons behind it...they all made sense. And hearing him downplay himself after what I knew about the lengths he would go to for people he cared about — I couldn't stand it.

Call it curiosity, but as we sat, wallowing in our combined vulnerability, I couldn't help the urge to lean in and taste him. He'd made his feelings for me clear. I suspected he wouldn't be opposed, so I was startled when he didn't initially respond. Moreover, I was surprised by how much *I'd* wanted more. When he finally reciprocated, I completely lost my sense of self, desire flooding every inch of my body.

His kisses had been both gentle and possessive, his lips molding perfectly to mine. Even as his tongue sunk deeper into my mouth — even when he pushed me to the ground — he'd been immeasurably tender. The feeling was headier than I had ever experienced, and when he paused to gaze into my eyes, I swore I found something deeper than desire there. That was the only moment where I second-guessed my decision, even as my body screamed for his lips back on mine. It was the only point where I was truly terrified of where this was headed.

And now, with the morning's clarity, an avalanche of guilt crashed through me, cold and lethal. When I looked at Finlay, I imagined the ghost of Blaise hovering behind me, and my gut twisted painfully. How could I be lusting after someone else when I was still plagued with memories of Blaise's death? What kind of horrible being could do that? My sips of champagne soured as I surveyed the prince.

Thankfully, Finlay kept his distance, seeming to purposefully avoid me as much as I was him. He was impeccably dressed in all-black, aside from the gold embroidery on his blazer, stitched into a pattern of twirling branches. It was sharp and elegant, tailored to fit him exquisitely, and the combination of dark and gold made his piercing eyes and gilded hair dance all the more in the firelight.

He seemed to know I would need my space, which confused, irritated, and relieved me all at once. My present plan was to pretend like nothing happened, though every time he caught me glancing at him, he volleyed a faint smile my way, leaving me flustered.

He caught me mid-glance once more, and I ducked my head back into the champagne flute as the confusing heat spread across my cheeks. And other places.

"Lynn?"

I dragged myself back to the present conversation, noting the use of my pseudonym. "What's that now?"

Darrya beamed, a broad grin I'd long ago deciphered as her fake envoy smile. "We're wondering if you'd like to join us in the music chamber. There's a local singer about to perform. She's supposed to be extraordinary."

I plastered a smile on my face to mirror hers and took another long drink of champagne, pointedly avoiding looking in Finlay's direction. "Absolutely."

Extraordinary, as it turned out, was an understatement. The singer's voice was hauntingly beautiful, and I was glad for the interruption to the thoughts racing in my mind. I felt the rise and fall of her tunes in my very blood; the angelic vibrato of her voice echoed through the chamber, enchanting me.

The artist paused, taking a sip of water, before announcing her next song.

"Our years have been plagued with heartbreak, and as we consider our darkest days, we must remember to have hope that the sun will rise again, stronger than ever." A murmur of agreement passed through the crowd, and I straightened, my curiosity piqued. The singer continued.

"I can think of no better song to express such wishes than this." She took a deep breath and began.

> *"Whispers, secrets, heard in the dawn*
> *Our gods, our gods, are they truly gone?*
> *I fear our foes lurk out in the cold*
> *But there is a hero, if the truth is told*
> *Dear Lugh, we worship you on this winter's night*
> *Bring us the warmth, god of sun, god of light*
> *With bloodthirsty force, the spear calls to thee*
> *Use it to drive out our worst enemies.*
> *And when the spear finally is laid to rest,*
> *Upon a horse's hoof, it is to be blessed.*
> *Will the darkness once more take hold?*
> *Or is there mercy for our wandering souls?"*

Goosebumps prickled my skin, hair standing on edge. It couldn't be — but then again, what a more perfect and poetic way to ensure it wouldn't be found, until Gray was once more located? Was I the only thing that called Gray to the human realm...or had another force summoned him as well?

Kipp liked to talk about fate — how he was destined to protect me, how I was destined for Gray to find me, and me him. But there was something else that called to me before either of them. Kipp didn't know the half of it.

Fate was an ironic son of a bitch.

I must have made some sort of strangled sound, because Darrya whirled to face me.

"Lynn? Are you feeling well?" she asked, her diplomatic words measured.

"I need some air," I choked out, gathering the satin skirts of my black dress and scrambling from my seat. I was garnering attention, but I didn't care. Suddenly the room felt too hot and too crowded. I needed out.

Darrya followed me, and seconds later, Finlay slipped out of the chamber too, from wherever he'd been seated. I didn't bother speaking as they followed me; I wound through the corridors and finally slipped outside. I braced myself against the stone wall of the castle, willing my heart to stop pounding at the revelation.

"I know where the final piece is," I gasped, then remembered to choose my words carefully and lowered my voice. "It's just like Lachlan said, Darrya. It's part of my bloodline. It's *called* to me, I just — I just didn't realize it at the time. And it's not a spearhead anymore. It's been melted down."

"Upon a horse's hoof, it's to be blessed," Finlay mused, impressed. "It was recrafted into a horseshoe for Gray."

"And you know where it is now?" Darrya whispered excitedly. I nodded. My fingers twitched as I recalled the chill that coursed through me when I first touched it — in a different world, in what felt like a different lifetime.

"It's in the human realm. At my mother's place."

We packed quickly. With the solstice coming to a close, it was only a matter of time before the ley lines between our realms no longer worked.

As soon as I was back in my room, however, I realized we had to return to Sairas first.

"Are you ready to — Kate?" Finlay appeared at the doorway. "What's wrong?"

I barely registered his alarm, apparent in his use of my real name. He came up behind me, and the breath hissed out from between his teeth.

"Kate, you haven't even begun to pack, what the—" Darrya froze as she entered, hushed by Finlay, who wrapped an arm protectively around my shoulder. We stared down at my bed for a moment before I spoke.

"I need to get my dad," I whispered. "I think we have to bring my mom back here. Find somewhere to hide her."

He squeezed my shoulders as Darrya circled around us, gasping at the sight on my bed.

There, a dead raven lay, staining the sheets red with blood. Black feathers fanned out from its mutilated body and scattered across every inch of the bedspread. Darrya tentatively picked one up and twirled it in her fingers, eyes wide with terror as they rose to meet mine.

The message was clear as day. Nemain had bided her time long enough. She had spies everywhere and knew I was back on the move. Whatever action I took next, her reaction was clear. She would follow. And someone would pay.

"You're staying." I squared off with Larke, placing a reassuring hand on his arm. He sheathed his sword in frustration. "I've got the people I need coming with me. We can handle smuggling one person and a horseshoe back."

It was more than that, but the words were still a half-truth. Darrya — apologizing profusely — had been summoned back to Daersill to help wrap up solstice duties with the queen. My father, Kipp, and Finlay were all coming with me, though, so we had the numbers and fortunately, the lack of magic on our side. If we happened upon Nemain, her cries would not cripple us, since magic was rendered dormant in the human world. It would be a battle between mere humans, and our skill and rage would be a good substitute for magic.

I wondered if that was why Larke wanted to come. Perhaps he was imagining a killing blow against the weakened goddess who took the life of his friend. But he was the commander now. The army needed his leadership; he couldn't let emotions get the best of him.

"You started correspondence with our allied armies already," Finlay put in, as if he knew Larke needed the extra nudge to agree. "I fear now is the time to follow them through."

Caught off guard, Larke stepped back and sized up the prince. "You know I can't do that without the queen's explicit orders," he said hesitantly.

Finlay didn't miss a beat. "When she asks, tell her the truth. Tell her the orders came from me." The authority in his voice rang clear. "I will deal with her when we get back, but right now, time is of the essence."

Finlay stood tall and confident, donned in fighting leathers with his sword at his waist. As an extra precaution, Larke had talked him into light chainmail sleeves and a chest plate. If I wasn't so nervous, I would have been amused by Finlay's petulant reaction to Larke's insistence.

I gazed at him now, his expression as fiery as the power that burned within him, and my eyes traveled to his lips. Everything was happening so fast; there had been no time to discuss the meaning of that moment between us. The time would come, but for now, I was grateful for his unwavering support.

I caught Darrya's eye, and she tilted her head, giving me a curious look. I flushed and averted my eyes. Two conversations to have, then.

She cleared her throat. "I'll handle the queen; Larke will handle the armies. We've got things here in good hands."

She came forward to hug Finlay and me, and touched my father and Kipp's arms reassuringly. "You four, go get that talisman. And get your mom." She grinned, warm brown eyes glittering. "I can't wait to meet her."

I smiled as she left, dragging Larke with her, and as Finlay and Kipp slipped away — to locate Faerie dust and other items we needed — I realized with a start that my father and I were alone.

He looked physically pained as he shifted on his feet. His jaw was rigid, as was his posture. His eyes, though — those amber eyes I had inherited — were far away, his mind somewhere else entirely. I pondered for a moment about what kind of love still lived in his heart for my mother; what he would do when they saw one another again.

"Are you sure you want to come with?" I asked quietly. We'd never truly discussed my mom, but he hadn't seen her since he had left over ten years ago. I couldn't even begin to speculate how he must be feeling.

Whatever trance he'd been in seemed to break. He glanced my way in surprise. "Yes. I am."

"Then tell me," I pushed forward brazenly. "Do you still love her?"

He winced at the question, but his answer was immediate. "Of course. You and your mother...you two are the only happiness I've ever truly known."

Emotion consumed me at his words, forming a lump in my throat that made it difficult to breathe. My dad stared off into the distance with a wistful expression, and when he continued, his voice was soft.

"Having you back in my life makes me wonder, sometimes, what it would be like to have that again with her, too." His voice cracked, then, as did a piece of my heart. It was unexpected to see such a vulnerable side of him, but I was grateful he chose to share it with me. The admission felt like the answer to so many questions. I stepped closer, leaning into his shoulder in silent encouragement to continue.

He took a deep breath. "I wish I knew of a simple way to be — to live with you both in my world without losing something in the process. Or worse, losing one of you for good."

When he met my eyes again, he smiled, but I'd never seen a smile so sad. I glanced down, my eyes blurring. The more I dwelled on it, I realized, the more I had in common with my father than just the color of our eyes. We both burned with an intense desire to protect the life and happiness of those we loved — even if we had no hope for our own.

The resounding emptiness that came from the abrupt loss of my magic was even worse this time, likely because it had been even longer since my last visit. The only one who didn't double over in the first moments of our arrival was Kipp.

My initial reaction to being back was dread, but unlike the rumors which struck fear in those back in the Faerie realm, I knew my magic would return when I did. Darrya once told me, when I first learned magic, that the strength of this realm came from empathy and compassion. I drew on that as I thought of my mother.

"Fuck, little angel, you lived twenty years like this?" Finlay groaned, stretching his fingers and looking down at his palms like he'd never seen them before. I wondered how long it had been since he'd last visited the human realm.

"Yes. The entertainment is great, but the food is awful. And I suspect your bad habits won't feel as good here, either, so don't leave us to go find a cigarette," I jested — a pathetic attempt at lightening the tension rippling through us all.

He smirked. "I wouldn't dare."

"Take it from the decades I spent here — they don't," my dad responded. "All right. Ready to press on? We're cutting it close on time. I expect we have a little over an hour left to travel by ley line before the solstice passes."

The tightness in his expression betrayed his nerves, and I nodded, pulling my cloak in tight around me to set off.

The snow crunched underfoot, illuminated only by the moonlight. It was much deeper and heavier than I expected, and a sickening panic settled in my gut as I considered the implications. With the added weight of the weapons strapped to us all, it would not be easy to run, should we need to.

I veered swiftly from that train of thought before the apprehension grew too suffocating. Instead, I focused on the excitement of seeing my mother again — the endless positivity she exuded, the warmth of her hugs, the smell of her perfume encompassing me. Part of me worried that, despite the enchantment, she would see the change in me. And how could we begin to explain my dad's reappearance? Though…my lips curled in excitement at the thought of the two of them reuniting.

The shifting and cracking of branches under snow broke apart the silence as we strode ahead, the barn and house slowly coming into view. Yet even the relative silence of the snow was too quiet, and I slowed, stopping just before the clearing. A sickening sense of foreboding flooded my veins, and my hair stood on end.

"Wait," I murmured. The others obliged. "This isn't right."

I scanned the clearing, my eyes raking over the buildings. Though everything looked well cared for, an unnatural stillness hung in the air. No music drifted from the house, as was normal when my mother was home, and no sounds came from the barn, despite the horses and our dog.

Everyone waited for several long heartbeats, but when I couldn't pinpoint my unease, I shook my head.

"Where would your mother be?" my dad asked in a hushed tone, peering at the front door of the house intently. His fists tightened around the hilt of his sword. It gave me a sense of determination, too, as I focused back on the house.

"Kipp, go for the horseshoe," I whispered, the words more a command than a request. "We'll go find my mom."

My eyes didn't stray from the house, but the sound of footsteps in the snow told me he was on the move. My eyes scanned the windows for any movement.

"Her car is out front," I mused, more to myself than Finlay or my father. "We'd see her if she was in the kitchen — so she's either in her room or the living room."

"So, in we go," my dad said. He stalked forward, unsheathing his sword as he went. Finlay and I shared a quick look of trepidation, then scrambled after him.

As I opened the front door, however, Scout shot out. The dog completely ignored my presence and that of two new visitors, which was unusual for him. I was too busy watching him sprint outside to see my father's arm, barring me from stepping further into the house. I crashed to a halt, Finlay bumping into me from behind.

"Katie," he hissed, and I glanced up, stilling at the sight in front of us.

My mother was sitting in a chair in the living room, her green eyes wide as she took in the sight of my father. Tears flooded them, making them shimmer like two emerald jewels. She was as radiant as ever, and the simple feeling of both my parents in the same room felt like a salve on a long-irritated wound.

It should have been a beautiful moment.

It would have been one, if not for the knife at her neck, held there by Nemain.

CHAPTER THIRTY-FIVE

It took all his strength not to rush forward when he saw Nemain. But the sight of Kate's mother, sitting helplessly at the mercy of her blade, froze him in his tracks. Admittedly, it was probably a good thing he had no magic. Nemain standing there, teeth bared in a terrifying, cold-hearted grin, was enough for him to burn this house to the ground.

Kate's house.

He stole another furtive glance her way, noting the fear and resentment brimming in her gaze — a nearly identical look to the one in Pat's eyes. Finlay ground his teeth. They had to play this right, though he wasn't sure how.

There wasn't a reasonable bone in Nemain's body. Both Finlay and Kate had deaths to atone for, and he certainly didn't want Kate's dad to have to do the same. While he had once despised her father, Pat was making up for it by continuously working to keep Kate safe.

And — Finlay realized with a start — this was exactly what her father had spent the last decade avoiding: Nemain in the same room as the two people he loved most. Finlay's heart clenched.

Pat's sword was already unsheathed, and Finlay moved to join him, relishing the feel of the weapon at his side. Most of his training had focused on defense, often supplemented with his magic. But even without his powers, he had that physical training, and a blood-lust that rivaled the hounds of hell. He rolled his shoulders as he tested the weight of the sword in his hand.

Nemain tutted. "I wouldn't do that if I were you."

A breath hissed between Pat's clenched teeth, though he didn't move further. Kate clutched for Finlay's arm; he sensed the slight shake in her fingers, even as her grip remained firm. He leaned slightly into her in reassurance, though his eyes never strayed from Nemain.

"Patrick?" Kate's mother whispered.

She was stunning, a daintier kind of beautiful than her strong, fierce daughter. Whereas Kate was hard to read, her mother wore her emotions on her sleeve — and right now, confusion and panic were written all over her face. Briefly, he wondered if she knew anything about their world — though even a Faerie would be terrified in this situation. He would be, too, if not for his rage.

"Lisa," Pat responded hoarsely.

"Let her go," Kate demanded. Her grip tightened on Finlay's arm, as though drawing strength from it.

"And why would I do that? I've only just found your little lost lamb. I'm not very keen on giving her up," the goddess purred, black eyes gleaming as they slid to Kate.

"Though, I never would have guessed you were a... *half-breed*. Just like Cú Chulainn before you. Your kind never ceases to be anything but meddlesome." Her voice dripped with disgust.

Finlay clenched his jaw so hard his teeth clacked together. Kate shifted forward in anger, and he used the arm she had a grip on to tug her back.

"What do you want?" he spat.

"Such a silly question. I hope it's rhetorical." Nemain looked almost bored. "I want the last talisman and all the others returned to my possession. Oh — and her, of course." She motioned to Kate, and Finlay bristled, shifting in front of her.

Pat lurched forward, his face strained. He froze once more, however, as Nemain's knife tightened, inciting a terrified squeak from Kate's mother.

"No," he pleaded.

"A bit monosyllabic, are we?" Nemain droned, words coated with sick amusement.

In a swift movement, Kate pushed around Finlay, and though he grabbed for her arm, fingers brushing her cloak, he was left clutching air.

"I'll go with you if you leave them be." Her voice was strong, her tone leaving no room for argument. Normally, Finlay loved that defiance, but not at this moment. He clutched his sword so hard his knuckles turned white.

"Katie—" Pat began, but Kate turned, a warning flashing in her eyes.

"She needs me alive. She knows I'm the only one who can activate the talismans."

"Unfortunately, the girl is right," Nemain said flatly, pursing her thin lips. "But I'll be needing the talismans as well."

"There's only one here," Kate snapped. "You get me and one talisman. I'll tell you where the others are when you let my mother go and we're back in our realm. Consider it a promise made of good faith. Not something you would know much about," she added with venom, "but *my* promise is something you can count on."

Finlay made a small noise of reproach, but a sharp look from Kate silenced him. Fine — he would voice his opinion later, and pray Kate had a strategy to go along with this. Nemain took a long moment to consider, the air thickening around them. Finally, she plucked the knife away from Kate's mother's — Lisa's — throat. Lisa made a garbled sound of relief, and Pat shifted a step toward her.

"Okay, child of Cú Chulainn. Lead me to the talisman." Nemain allowed Lisa to stand, but the knife remained on her collarbone — a clear message she was still a mere flick of the wrist away from taking her life. They left the house first, heading across the yard for the barn.

Kate kept her eyes locked on the building, while Nemain kept hers on Kate. Pat watched Lisa, and she returned his gaze like a parched flower soaking up water at last.

Because of this, Finlay was the only one who caught the shift of the dark beast in the distance, barely noticeable as he pressed against a large stone between two trees.

Kipp lowered his head, horseshoe clutched in his large, wolfy jowls. His bright blue eyes gleamed in the setting sun, darting between Finlay and the rest of the group. Kate opened the barn, assessing, and Nemain paused as Finlay and Patrick stopped on either side of her. All waited for Kate's next move. Finlay shook his head faintly, willing Kipp to wait.

Kate didn't hesitate to enter the barn. What was that clever little angel planning?

When Kate reappeared, she held up a horseshoe and plopped it into Nemain's free hand. She met the goddess's eyes, who smiled, showing no sign anything was amiss. Finlay turned his head slightly to Kipp and mouthed a word.

Go.

The wolf hesitated, eyes unblinking as he silently defied the prince. Finlay's own eyes narrowed.

Go. Now.

Finally, Kipp slipped away, silent and graceful in his lupine form. Finlay only prayed they would be able to meet him shortly, his own senses roaring that they were running out of time. If Kate and Nemain disappeared, and the ley line closed before they could reach it, they would be stuck in the human world for weeks.

"Now. Leave my mother, and you and I can go back and collect the remaining talismans," Kate said firmly. Despite the fear twisting Finlay's insides into knots, a part of him glowed with admiration for her impenetrable ferocity. She'd withstood Nemain's capture once already, and with her unshakeable confidence, she almost had him believing she could do it again. He would fight and burn his way back to her, no matter where she went.

Nemain tapped the knife thoughtfully against Lisa's neck, and a whimper slipped from her lips. Pat tensed, and the goddess whipped her head to him, inky black hair flying. He instantly stepped back and lowered his sword.

"Just let her go," he pleaded.

"You promised," Kate added as a real look of panic flashed across her face, the first since their deal had been struck.

"You see, now, I didn't," Nemain said blandly. She took a step back, dragging Lisa with her. Finlay reached instinctively for his internal flame, feeling momentarily off-kilter as his magic evaded him. Kate bared her teeth, sliding a dagger from within her cloak.

"Honor, promises, good faith... those are all such human things," Nemain continued disdainfully. Ravens circled above her now, partially covering the moonlight, caws echoing ominously throughout the trees.

"It's time you learned this lesson for good. I will take what I want — if not willingly, then by force." The cawing of the ravens loudened. "And by blood."

The blade at Lisa's neck glinted in the remaining moonlight as it sliced through her flesh. Pat roared, lunging with his sword, but Nemain had already disappeared in a cloud of darkness, headed skyward with the ravens, somehow retaining a scrap of magic. Lisa stumbled forward through the remains of the shadows, clutching her throat as red liquid spilled from between her fingers.

"Mom!" Kate shrieked. She leapt forward with her father as Lisa collapsed. Finlay was left to watch, powerless, as she took giant, gasping breaths. The white snow quickly turned crimson as blood spurted from her windpipe. Pat fell upon her, clutching his hands against her neck. He folded against her body, willing the pressure of their combined hands to staunch the flowing of her blood.

Kate buckled on the ground, hands twisting in her hair, her breathing high-pitched and rapid as she helplessly watched on. Finlay dropped to his knees and gently gripped her shoulders, though he doubted she even felt his presence.

He remained, unmoving and chilled to the core as he listened to Pat's pleading as Lisa's panicked expression slipped quickly into unconsciousness. He wished desperately to turn Kate to him and shield her from this. But he knew what it was like to watch your parent's final moments. If she needed to see it to make sense of it, he would not take that from her.

It was less than a minute before Finlay knew Lisa was gone. He sensed the moment the same revelation hit Kate and Pat, the pain radiating off of them. The sensation was so strong, it mixed with the metallic tang of blood in the snow — just as physically present.

They knelt for what seemed like ages, yet no time at all, given what had happened. Eventually, Finlay knew he had to say it. He despised the words, despite the necessity of them.

"We have to go," he murmured, his voice low. "We can bring her with us, but if we don't leave now, we won't get back to Muiranvia."

Pat drew a ragged breath, then looked at Finlay, eyes glassy with tears. Kate didn't acknowledge him.

"We can't let Nemain have that advantage," he added quietly, hoping those were the words to pump a seed of motivation back into their bodies. He watched as the seed took hold, blossoming with rage and understanding.

"We can't take her back," Pat said, his voice thick with emotion. "She belongs here in the human world. She deserves a proper burial. An afterlife untainted by...our misdeeds."

Kate nodded and reached for her father, tears still streaming down her face. He clutched her hand tightly. Finlay took some solace in the fact they would share their grief together, even as he warred with the images in his own mind.

Three parents he had now seen taken by Nemain. He prayed he wouldn't see another. Vowed she wouldn't take another, not if he could help it.

CHAPTER THIRTY-SIX

No matter how many cold winter days passed, the pain never lessened.

It wasn't acute like the pain I'd felt from Blaise's passing; rather, it was a deeper, more visceral ache than any I'd experienced before. It was as if my entire soul throbbed from the despair of it all.

One week dragged by, then two. Most days I felt seconds from breaking. The only solution was to retreat into myself, steering far from any conversation that could sever those wounds open and bleeding once more.

It was also different from losing Blaise in that I saw the loss of my mother mirrored in my father as well. At first, the sight of him felt like a shot to the diaphragm, bringing up flashes of memories that rendered me gutted and breathless. I think I had the same effect on him, too. We hovered around each other like opposite magnet poles; if we flipped some things around, we would never let go, yet some invisible force was repelling us.

It was a loss that could have taken me for all I had. Like my father, I had been doing everything in my power to protect her — enchantments and distance to keep us apart. Then, in one fell swoop, I'd stupidly led Nemain right to her and cost my mother everything. The guilt nearly suffocated me most nights.

But in the blindness of that pain, my dad was the only one I saw. And surprisingly, he ended up being my saving grace. I watched as the circles under his eyes grew with the passing days, until I finally approached Kipp, returning the bag of sand to him. When I ordered him to give it to my father, the purpose it gave me — to aid my father's grief — was a beacon of light.

For the next several days, I followed that purpose like I was clutching to a lifeline. Once the dark circles under my father's eyes lightened, I wandered through the library until I found the ancient text I was looking for.

"What's this?" I asked without preamble, plopping down next to where my father sat in the dining hall, drinking a coffee alone. He looked startled, but glanced down with a faint look of intrigue at the book I set on the table before us.

I pointed, tracing the circle drawn on the page. The page was uneven from wrinkles and felt fragile under my fingertips. I lifted my hand away from the discolored pages, scared to injure the text. "This."

It took only a moment for him to reply. "That's the Ogham Wheel."

"Is that different from the alphabet?" I asked, puzzled.

A corner of his mouth lifted at my question — not quite a smile, but the first semblance of one I'd seen since we'd returned from the human realm. Something pleasant tugged in my heart at the sight, and I listened intently to his explanation.

"It's like a calendar. Our ancestors prided living in harmony with nature's cycles above all else. With that in mind, our lives are considered only a small part of a much larger pattern. That pattern is laid out here."

He motioned to the inner circle, calling out the increasing numbers in a Fibonacci sequence.

"One — the singular center of all things. Two — the spiral within the cauldron. Three — the Triskele."

He shot me a guilty look before continuing, and I felt the phantom of the mark burn into my collarbone. Yet as I observed him, I couldn't help but smile as he grew more animated with each explanation. It felt like the first step toward normalcy — a different kind of normal, but one I could live in without feeling like I was suffocating under the weight of grief.

"The outer circle ties the order of Ogham letters together to form a calendar of tree magic. So, each tree in the calendar has its own lunar cycle representation," he continued. "Yours, for example, would be the hazel tree, because of your August birthday."

"Like the zodiac," I realized, and he nodded eagerly.

"The magic of hazel trees is regarded as perfect for divination. They carry wisdom and knowledge, helpful for providing inspiration."

I snorted. "And what's yours?"

He glanced down at the page once more, inspecting the artful designs and notches making up the calendar within. "I was born in October. So mine would be...ivy."

"And what energies does that possess?"

He pursued his lips, considering. "Well, some would say it's only good for binding and restricting. But...it's known for its perseverance. It conquers and climbs high...in fact, it can bloom even amongst ruins."

We were silent for several heartbeats.

"I guess we could all use a bit of ivy," I murmured, leaning into his shoulder. He peered down at me for a moment, expression unreadable, before shifting to slide an arm around me. He tugged me into a tender embrace, and I melted into it, welcoming the familial warmth and love it offered. He rested his chin on my head, and we sat like that for a long moment. When he spoke again, I could hear the hint of a smile in his words.

"Yeah, Katie. We really could."

Chapter Thirty-Seven

The trancelike state we'd been drowning in was officially broken. The next day, I dragged my dad out into the training ring and urged him to spar with me.

We began cautiously, volleying blows and strategic spurts of magic at one another. However, as days passed, our sparring grew frenzied as we both used physical exhaustion as an outlet for our grief. Like father, like daughter, I suppose. If it weren't for Cas's constant hovering, I was certain we'd both be painted black-and-blue from mottled bruises.

The others sometimes joined our training. Darrya taught Wren the fundamentals, and Kipp and Finlay dueled. Finlay, however, had been joining Larke more often as they navigated in and out of the queen's throne room.

At this point, I had all four talismans in my possession, yet I felt no different. I chided myself internally, knowing it was likely because I had not mastered all four elements. Larke had offered to have pieces of the talismans taken to a smith and crafted into the sword of Nuada, so it harnessed the power of all four. It was a good idea, but one that would take a while. So we practiced, biding time as they were all crafted into the Whisperer.

Nemain's little birdies probably knew all this as well, which explained why we were not currently overrun. She was weighing her odds, especially now that she held none of the talismans. We assumed she would wait until I managed to activate the celestial magic. Only then would she strike again, timing it so she could steal it from me and force my hand, then kill me once I was no longer of use. It was difficult not to constantly envision her target on the backs of those I loved.

In a moment of unwelcome quiet, I sat down on the stone bench in the courtyard and gazed up at the maple tree. Leaves littered the ground, dotting the white snow with colors of brown and burnt orange. The tree was a dull brown as well, the branches extending like claws with snow blanketing their tops. The angry fire I'd felt against the world had dissipated, leaving me as cold as the surrounding air. The negative thoughts I'd held at bay surged through the quiet.

My mother had been the target I had not anticipated. She played no part in this; she hadn't willingly knocked on death's door, yet death took her nonetheless. Or at least, the goddess of death had.

I kept rewinding the scenes in my mind, wondering if there had been any way to change the outcome. The 'what-if's' surged in my mind: what if I had told her the truth? What if our family had reunited? Memories that would never come to pass.

The thought of my mom sent me spiraling, and the wall I built had crumbled, leaving a clear opening for me to barrel down a dark path.

We'd retrieved all the talismans, sure, but we had no idea how to quell Nemain's screams. With that weapon in play, every soldier of ours with elemental magic would be crippled on the battlefield — easy pickings for Nemain and her dark Faerie army.

To add on, I had not figured out how to activate the talismans — and even if I accomplished that, Nemain might find a way to resurrect herself once more. Finding the solution to all *those* problems wasn't even going to aid the biggest pit in my stomach — the one left by the unnecessary death of my mother. It was becoming hard to see the point in trying.

I wasn't sure how long I sat there, consumed by the negative thoughts and outcomes. Eventually, a crunching indicated someone's approach, and I turned as Darrya came to sit next to me with a faint smile. She was bundled in gray faux fur, the paleness of the snow complementing the light blonde streaks in her hair. I could see, then, her relation to the winter goddess. I didn't return her smile, though. Sighing, I leaned back into the bench.

She remained silent until I could no longer deal with the uncomfortable lapse in conversation.

"Everything feels dead," I stated, my voice flat.

Darrya looked surprised at my comment. "What do you mean?"

"It's winter," I replied, scanning the courtyard. "The leaves, the grass, the tree — everything looks and feels dead."

"Well, that's just not true," she argued. "Pull at your magic. Can't you feel it?"

I shook my head. "Even when I reach out with it, the earth feels less alive than usual."

Darrya's smile turned sad as she leaned into me. "If that's the case, it's something else," she said gently. Catching my dubious look, she continued, and motioned upward. "The earth is always alive; I promise you that. It's alive in different ways. Take the tree, for example."

"The tree?" I echoed, glancing back up at it. "You mean it has its own energy?"

I thought back to my recent learnings about the Ogham Wheel and tried to picture the unique, alleged magic within the tree. The dull brown and vivid white of the snow-covered branches were a stark contrast to the bright blue of the sky beyond. All I saw was something that appeared as exhausted and muted as I felt.

"It seems most alive in the summer, yes?" she questioned. At my nod, she continued.

"But that's just because the leaves are doing their job, converting light energy into fuel. In the fall, the tree seals that fuel — those nutrients — into itself, and thus the leaves fall. It no longer needs them."

I blinked, wondering where this was headed. Darrya pressed on, unfazed.

"But even then, the leaves on the ground will decompose into the earth, becoming nutrients for the tree to use again in spring.

It'll grow buds that eventually unfurl into leaves, before the whole process starts again. It never truly stops."

I dug the toes of my boots past the snow into the dirt, absorbing her explanation. I tried to reach out, to feel that connection between the earth and my soul, but something still felt...broken. I exhaled loudly in frustration.

Darrya's mild, warm expression turned troubled as she assessed me; she pulled back, her brow knitted with worry.

"Like I said. It's not a lack of life in the earth that's making you feel disconnected. But the lesson is the same."

I raised a brow in confusion. "What lesson?"

"Impermanence," she stated simply. "Things only last for a short period of time. As much as I want you to grieve, Katie," she hesitated, eyes flashing with concern. "You can't just stop your life or try to go back to how things used to be. You need to take what life is giving you, now. Even if it looks shitty, at least it's something useful. And it'll be less shitty again, eventually."

My head ducked down in astonishment. "It's...it's not that easy," I ground out, choking on the words. I'd lost both Blaise and my mom in a matter of months, and Nemain was still out there, plotting her next move against me and everyone I loved. It was impossible to imagine life dealing me anything but a shitty hand. Life was a sadistic bitch.

Darrya grabbed my hand and squeezed it tight. "I know it's not. And that hole eating away at you? It won't go away. But you'll learn to grow around it. Your mother would want that for you — to keep moving on, evolving, and growing."

I bit my lip, considering her words. She looked ready to press the issue further, but a familiar laugh drew our attention. Finlay appeared from around the corner, walking alongside a beautiful blonde Faerie. He noticed us, and before I could stop her, Darrya waved him over.

He hesitated, and then said a quick goodbye to the Faerie, gently kissing her hand before parting from her. My gut twisted strangely at the sight. It wasn't like those lips were supposed to be mine — hell, we'd barely spoken in weeks — but seeing them on another female made my own lip curl, like I wanted to claim his instead — claim *him*. I shoved the ridiculous thought aside as he approached.

"She's stonewalling us," Finlay said through gritted teeth. He plopped down with a thick piece of bread in hand, next to where Darrya and I sat. He tore viciously at the loaf with his teeth, chewing angrily for a moment. Darrya and I exchanged curious glances.

"The queen," Finlay clarified as he finished chewing. "She'll hear no more of it. She's refusing to see me. She has appointed a liaison to speak with Larke about every other military matter — except the gathering of allied troops."

"Does she not see Nemain as a threat?" I asked, aghast.

Finlay grimaced. "She now sees a common cause. She believes if we simply give Nemain what she wants, it will be over, and we'll no longer be threatened. She believes Nemain will leave our race alone once she has her sisters back."

I glanced at Darrya's face, painted with disgust — a look surely mirroring my own. My stomach churned at his words.

"But Nemain still despises the other races. She's made that abundantly clear. That leaves hundreds of thousands at risk — if not more!" I exclaimed, struggling to keep my voice down. My hands trembled at the prospect, and I clutched them between my legs.

"She'd rather risk the 'lesser' Faeries than the 'more important' races that make up the armies and royal decision-makers," Darrya spat, using air quotes as she referenced how other royals leveraged the terms.

"But — with the power of the triple goddesses, they'll be obliterated!" I sputtered. "I thought she spearheaded a new initiative? One that believed in equality between races?"

Finlay looked down at his hands in his lap, his expression pained.

"Only insomuch that she can see the benefit for herself. If the cons outweigh the pros, she'll side against it." Darrya's words were hushed, and she glanced around to ensure no one could overhear. "Don't mistake her progressive movements over the past century or two as anything other than selfish political gain."

Though I agreed wholeheartedly, they were traitorous words to speak in the palace, especially from the queen's envoy. I was impressed by her bravery in voicing them aloud. Finlay nodded, concurring, and my brows shot up in surprise.

"I've known for a long time that she's not nearly as progressive as she claims to be. Think about it. My grandmother could have a claim to the throne. Yet my great-grandmother has never made a motion to put her in the path of succession, which she could have done through her marriage. But she chose not to." Finlay's tone was bitter, picking at the bread in his hands. "She thinks my grandmother is too weak-hearted, too sympathetic to the plights of others."

"Empathy is not a weakness," I hissed. Darrya and Finlay looked at me with soft smiles.

"I know that, little angel. We both know that." Finlay murmured. His hand moved to mine, but I pushed him away, standing from the bench.

"Where are you going?" Darrya asked, eyeing me quizzically.

I tossed her a determined look before I took off. "It's like you said. It's time to move forward, evolve and grow. And I'm taking the queen with me, whether she likes it or not."

"Katherine," the queen said. She practically floated in, her hound on her heels.

"Your Majesty," I responded, tipping my head respectfully. I'd changed into a pine-colored velvet dress appropriate for the visit, but I was still too worked up to offer a full curtsey. The narrowing of her pale blue eyes told me she marked the disrespect, but chose not to comment.

"To what do I owe this spontaneous visit?" she asked, settling onto the throne. She wore a deep red, floor-length gown made of velvet; the scarlet color stood out against the golden embroidery. It was the same color red that stained the snow the night my mother died — the red of the blood that would surely line the streets of countless cities if Nemain ever succeeded.

"I have heard things," I began, willing my voice to remain clear and steady. The queen tilted her head, and I continued.

"I have stood in front of you, Nemain, and the common folk. Every one of you has a different angle in this war, but regardless of intent or desired outcome, I see only one way which will avoid the most bloodshed. If you allow Nemain to come into her full power, endless numbers of Faeries will die from all races. It doesn't have to be that way, not if you allow us to bring the armies from the other lands here to fight alongside us. To fight against Nemain."

The queen scoffed, her shoulders hunching in exasperation. I stiffened.

"You too?" She sighed dramatically. "You are just like my great-grandson. Soft-hearted. Although, probably worse, as your time in the human realm has made you weak — sympathetic, always hoping to see the best in people."

"Perhaps. But if I can see the best in people, I can also see the worst. And while my time in the human realm may make me more sympathetic, it gives me the opportunity to see shades of gray that others may not. You, for instance, are thinking in black and white. You're allowing your greed for the crown to overtake your rationale."

The queen's eyes instantly became chips of ice, glinting dangerously at the bluntness of my words. Her hands clutched the sides of her throne as she took a deep breath. I pressed on before she could reply.

"What I mean to say is, perhaps Nemain will leave our race alone if she gets what she wants by resurrecting her sisters. But that says nothing for your crown. Do you really believe, with the return of a triple goddess, you'll still be the one in power?"

The icy glare melted slightly as hesitation clouded her features. I seized the opportunity.

"You may not see it as your issue if she chooses to eradicate other races, but let me pose it this way: if she begins down that road, the 'lesser' Faeries will know *you* did nothing to prevent it. They'll be screaming for your head as repayment for their lost loved ones. And mine, and Finlay's."

The queen's face paled slightly at the thought, and I waited breathlessly, hoping I finally struck a chord. However, she quickly schooled her features back into place, and her retort was flippant. "Let them try. I have my army."

With a dismissive flick of her wrist, she signaled to the guards, indicating the end of our conversation. I eyed them as they drew closer, deciding on a different approach.

"Except they won't follow you. They will follow me."

"And whyever would they do that?" she asked, incredulous.

I hesitated, grappling with the weight of my next move. I had kept the truth close to my chest for so long, fearing the repercussions. But now... it was the only card left in my arsenal. And it was time to play it.

The queen shrugged her robe around her shoulder and lifted a brow, waiting. I straightened, rolling my shoulders back and raising my chin defiantly.

"Because I found Lia Fáil. I touched the Speaking Stone, and it cried out to me." I said, allowing the words to settle. I hoped she understood their weight. The way she shot up abruptly from her throne, skirts whirling, told me she did. Even the guards hesitated, and I continued, empowered.

"I, and I alone, can command the four talismans of the Tuatha Dé Danann. And with that power, the armies will answer to me."

"You lie," the queen hissed.

"Look at your hound. Tell me, am I lying?"

We all looked, and there the magical hound lay. Its eyes were fixated on me, but it remained unbothered, offering no more than a casual flick of its ear. The queen's lips parted, staring between both me and the hound. Her eyes eventually stilled on the guards, gaze narrowing into daggers. Panic seized me.

Would she kill me for this? To cover up the truth?

"There are many who know it to be true, including Lachlan. So unless you want political warfare from multiple sides, you will let me go safely from this room. But rest assured — I do not want your crown."

The queen frowned but glanced quickly at her hound. Again, it made no move, and her face relaxed as she witnessed the truth in my words.

"But," I added, "I do want to avoid as much bloodshed as possible. So, I assume we have a deal?"

The pregnant pause hung in the air as the queen weighed her options. I felt nauseous, having laid all my cards on the table. If this didn't work, there was nothing I could do, short of a coup — a coup that would only work once I activated the power that supposedly lay in my veins along, bringing the armies to my side.

"Fine. You may tell Larke to resume his military correspondence. But I will not be held responsible should things go south. Their fates rest entirely on your shoulders."

I bobbed my head in understanding, even as my heart squeezed painfully at the thought. I turned to exit, ready to end this interaction as quickly as possible.

"Oh, and Katherine?"

I stopped and glanced back, fists clenched to hide the nerves that had finally reached their fraying point. A sly grin spread on the queen's face; she knew I had played my very last card.

"I look forward to our unique partnership. And I expect your full cooperation from here on out."

I nodded, because what was the thinly veiled threat of a queen when you were heading out to face the goddess of death herself?

CHAPTER THIRTY-EIGHT

The sun was now setting slightly later, the days growing longer thanks to the recent solstice — but it was still bitterly cold once the sun dipped behind the skyline. Normally, I'd try to be tucked in by sunset to avoid the chill, but I was invigorated now. I darted throughout the palace, my success with the queen filling my veins with an electric kind of energy. It was a win I'd desperately needed, a rekindling purpose to fight and change things for the better.

I immediately sought out Larke, who had huffed in amazement at my victory. He had not stuck around to celebrate, however. He transformed into commander mode at the news, stating how he needed to get things in motion. Full armies couldn't travel by Faerie dust, he explained, and it would take some over two weeks to travel by ocean and land to arrive from their various locations.

I chewed on my lip as I made my way hurriedly to the library, considering that timeline. In some ways, it seemed too slow, considering

Nemain likely had every soldier of hers already at her disposal. On the other hand, if I still couldn't activate the talismans, it would not be nearly enough time.

I rounded the corner to the library and yelped as I ran into something solid, biting through my bottom lip hard enough to draw blood. Books clattered to the ground, but I didn't see who I'd run into as I blinked, eyes watering.

"Shit, I'm sorry—" Finlay's voice rang out, and he stopped once he realized it was me. "Little angel! Wait — are you bleeding?"

"Yesshf," I muttered, pressing my fingers to my lip. I blinked once more, and as my vision cleared, his concerned expression peered back at me. His hand came up to wrap around my wrist, the other pulling my arm away gently to assess the damage of what I was certain was a slightly puffy, reddened lip. I smiled in embarrassment, laughing softly at his intense scrutiny.

"You've seen me bound and beaten. I hardly think this makes the top ten on my injury list," I teased. Though his face hardened for a moment at the memory, his mouth eventually curled into a smile, the corners of his eyes crinkling with amusement.

He brushed his thumb across my bottom lip, his touch softer than a butterfly wing. He asked...*something*, but I was instantly transported back to Lachlan's castle when he devoured my mouth like it belonged to him — when the only sounds were the crackling of the fire and our heaving breaths. I raised my eyes slowly from his lips to see him studying me expectantly, and realized I hadn't responded to his question.

"What?" I asked, shaking off the memory.

His eyes darkened with lust, as if he knew where my mind had gone. "I said," he repeated, "what were you doing, barreling into the library like you were being chased?"

"Well, I figured I should probably see if I missed any research on the talismans — something to help me activate them. And if I couldn't find that, at least I'd be able to grab something mindless to keep me preoccupied while we wait for the other armies to arrive."

At Finlay's aghast expression, I realized I hadn't yet told him the news.

"Oh!" I exclaimed, jumping excitedly and grabbing his hands. He jolted with surprise but went with it, returning a confused, lopsided grin. "I was able to convince the queen that uniting the armies against Nemain would be beneficial."

Finlay's jaw dropped, and he let go of one of my hands to run it through his hair in disbelief.

"How?"

"Well, it wasn't easy. It didn't scare her enough to know Nemain would eventually come for her throne, or that the common folk would rebel against her. I thought they were good, valid arguments, but neither swayed her."

Finlay nodded. "I'm sure, in her mind, the throne is too stable to even consider the possibility of that."

I rolled my eyes in agreement. The queen was equally as confident as she was stubborn. Those were certainly good qualities for a leader — unless someone had a valid argument opposing their beliefs. It was hard for the queen to imagine her citizens turning on her, so she refused to acknowledge the possibility.

"Finally, I used the one thing she couldn't argue with," I continued. He cocked his head in question.

"I told her the truth. I would have the final say, seeing as I'm the one meant to command the four talismans, and she doesn't want to be on my bad side."

He stilled, his pale eyes growing wide. "Are you...sure that was the best thing?" He asked the question haltingly, his tone laced with concern. "You might have just become her number one enemy."

I shrugged. "Honestly, what's the worst she can do? Once I figure out how to defeat Nemain, taking her on will look like child's play."

Finlay shook his head with a small laugh. "You're truly, utterly amazing."

The compliment made my heart bloom, and I grinned broadly at him. He caught my look, and his lips parted in surprise, staring at me.

"What?" My grin faltered.

Finlay shook his head once more, then looked away. "I just wasn't sure I would ever see that grin again," he replied, his voice low. I blinked, caught off guard by the remark.

He avoided my gaze, and a hesitant silence hung between us as I absorbed his words. A dozen questions sat on the tip of my tongue. Was he worried I wouldn't grin anymore because of my mother's death? Or because he didn't *want* to see me anymore after our moment in the castle?

Eventually, the silence persisted for too long, and I blurted, "Why haven't you kissed me again?"

Finlay's head jerked, startled, and his expression was unreadable as he narrowed his eyes. My heart sank, sensing the impending rejection. I backed up to press against the wall beside the library entrance, ready to make a quick exit if need be.

"Is...is that woman you were with earlier someone special?" I pressed, a pathetic attempt at understanding where he stood. If I knew his feelings without admitting anything on my end, then perhaps I could come out of this conversation unscathed.

His expression turned incredulous, and he barked a short laugh. "Delilah? She's the wife of the commander in Reviere, here for a brief visit. I thought it would be a good workaround to discuss things with her, and have her take information to her husband and his army. But I shouldn't have underestimated your determination — I should have known you'd take matters into your own hands."

"Oh," I breathed, feeling my face flush as I took in the information. Finlay noted it, chuckling deeply.

"Little angel," he purred. He pressed a hand on one side of the wall, leaning in close. "Do my ears deceive me, or do I detect a hint of jealousy?"

My heart thrummed unevenly in my chest, but I raised my chin high. "I think you should have your hearing checked."

"Mmmm," he murmured, and brought both arms up to either side of my head. "You know, if you want to be kissed again, all you have to do is ask."

He leaned in and pressed his nose against my neck, trailing it up to my ear. I trembled as desire flooded my core, but the words caught in my throat.

Once was easy to explain. Curiosity had gotten the better of me, and the whole moment had been rife with emotional vulnerability. It was easy to blame that on a moment of weakness, but this — this was an active decision. One of his hands moved to cup my cheek, his thumb brushing against my lips. I squeezed my eyes shut as he spoke once more, his hot breath fanning against my cheek.

"I'm waiting. Is that what you want?"

His tone, husky and deep, had my thighs tightening in anticipation. I was a goner. Desire was natural, I reminded myself — essential, like breathing, eating, drinking, and sleeping. It didn't need to mean more.

Decision made, I opened my eyes to meet his burning gaze, and nodded.

His mouth crashed against mine, and the relief was instant. I found myself dimly wondering why I had even fought the urge. His lips explored mine; they were warm, soft, and inviting, and he used them in a way that was somehow both tender and demanding.

His tongue ran over my wounded bottom lip, and I invited him in, our kiss deepening as we tasted one another. My body arched forward in response to the sensation of our kiss, and his hands trailed to my waist, instantly pulling me flush against him. He stepped forward, slamming us both back into the wall as every inch of our bodies touched.

One hand slid its way back up to cup my face, tipping my chin up so he could make his way down my neck, nipping as he went, then kissing over each area to soothe it before returning to my mouth. My skin felt alight at his touch, igniting as his hand slid down from my face, brushed over my breasts, and stopped at my ass, which he gripped tightly. I still wore the dress I'd donned to visit the queen, and he twisted the fabric in his hands, shortening it as he wound it higher to expose my bare legs. He broke the kiss, pressing his cheek against mine.

"May I?" he rasped, his voice dropping a full octave. I struggled to formulate an answer, but every inch of my flesh knew what I wanted. I simply parted my legs, reaching for his hand and guiding it under my dress. I reclaimed his lips with mine.

He groaned against my mouth, finding evidence of my desire in the damp fabric, which he traced for a moment before pushing it aside. He slid two fingers forward and back, teasing and feeling how wet I was. I was forced to break our kiss as I let out a soft moan, throwing my head back. Finlay's hand stilled, and when I met his gaze again, he was staring at me.

"W—what? What's wrong?" I gasped.

"By the gods, Kate," he whispered hoarsely. "That *sound.*"

I blinked in confusion, so he added, his voice near pleading, "Do it again."

My lips parted in surprise, and then I flashed him a wicked smile. "Then make me."

His brows lifted, but he grinned at the challenge. He moved his fingers against me once more before finally plunging them inside me. This time, I fully cried out, tucking my head in the nook of his shoulder as he wrung the pent-up sexual frustration out of me. He cursed at the sound and added his thumb to the mix, circling and massaging me as his two other fingers pumped inside me. He curled his fingers as he thrust them, hitting the sweet spot that sent pleasure radiating through my every nerve.

I clutched his shoulders as he continued ravishing me, certain I was leaving indents through the fabric of his shirt. I gripped for dear life to avoid collapsing, and he moved his other hand to brace against the wall once more as his nose pressed into my neck. My breathing became ragged, and he quickened his pace. Desire built inside me as I rocked my hips, wringing more pleasure out as I ground against his hand.

"Please," I begged, unsure what I even meant with the word, and Finlay hissed softly.

"Gods, you're so tight," he muttered through gritted teeth, and curled his fingers a touch more. The slight movement, perfectly placed, sent me spiraling. If it weren't for the support of the wall, I was certain my knees would have buckled. Finlay groaned in satisfaction as he felt my muscles tighten around his fingers, capturing my mouth to absorb my cries of pleasure as I fell apart in his hands.

We stayed frozen in that moment for several long seconds, both breathing heavily. I felt a pang of disappointment as he slowly removed his hand; he placed it softly but firmly on my waist.

My head raced as I considered what had just transpired. I still tingled with pleasure, yet a part of me was horrified I allowed such pleasure to be wrung out by Finlay — the man I had danced this game with even while Blaise was alive.

Blaise...

I bit my lip and winced at the soreness of it. With everything that had happened, should I even be doing this? With anyone? Even as

I was mentally shutting down, my gods-damned body betrayed me, whispering how it wanted more of Finlay's touch and kisses., the greedy little shit that it was.

Finlay ran a hand through his hair as he studied me. His jaw twitched.

"You're thinking so loudly I can practically hear it." His voice was soft and apprehensive. "Do you...do you regret this?"

I met his gaze as he waited for my answer and his remaining hand fell from my waist. He stepped back, his pale blue eyes shimmering like the shallow edge of an ocean reef.

"No," I whispered, my gut dropping further as I realized the truth of it. I felt guilty — I felt *dirty* — but in my heart, I still couldn't make myself regret it.

And that was the horrible, awful truth.

He opened his mouth to reply, but before I could hear what he had to say, I turned on my heel and dashed out of the library.

Chapter Thirty-Nine

I tugged my shawl up tighter around my ears, my mad dash having slowed to a fast-paced walk as I hustled along the path to Sairas.

The sun had dipped below the horizon, and my eyes struggled to adjust to the dusk. Despite the distant glow in some homes, nobody milled the outskirts of Sairas. It was uncomfortably chilly at night, and the curfew was more or less still in effect. Though the flock hadn't been seen since I'd been recaptured from Nemain, the threat loomed, nonetheless.

I cupped my hands to my mouth and exhaled deeply, allowing the warmth of my breath to heat my cheeks and the tip of my nose. The wind scattered leaves, twirling in little dances across the snow. Thanks to Darrya, I had learned to use my air magic to cast a bubble around me, so at least the chill of the breeze no longer bothered me.

My emotions whirled recklessly, and I dropped the leash on them, allowing them to flit through my head without abandon. I didn't bother to make sense of them, instead hoping to work through them with Cas and Wren — maybe Kipp, if he'd opted to stay there tonight.

Wren's advice was always levelheaded, and Cas had experience and wisdom far surpassing my own. I was desperate to hear their non-judgmental takes, as I truly had no idea where to go from here. There was only one thing I knew for certain: it had definitely been a dick move to run out on Finlay after coming on his hand. My stomach clenched pleasantly at the memory — *damn* my body for having a mind of its own — but I would deal with that apology later.

The packed snow crunched softly underfoot as I scurried along the path toward town, the soft glow of town lights illuminating the darkness of the sky. I had nearly reached the first stretch of homes when a chill journeyed up my spine — one that had nothing to do with the winter cold. Thinking back to my experience with the Nuckelavee, I stopped short, fingers clasping around the hilt of my dagger.

I heard nothing, however, except the gentle breeze. After a long moment, I continued forward a few more steps, but a sudden flash across the sky halted me again. I peered up at the dark clouds, moving erratically against the moonlight. It seemed like a murder of crows, or perhaps a flock of bats, but as my eyes focused, I realized they were much too large to be either. They swallowed the dark of the night, and a sickness settled in my stomach.

"What the...?"

A large screech tore through the silence of the night; it was a garbled sound too human to be a bird, yet not human enough.

Realization hit me like a tidal wave, and my skin broke into a cold sweat. I stumbled backward before turning on my heel, running as fast as I could for town.

The Sluagh were back.

I sprinted as fast as my bundle of warm clothing allowed, willing the small air shield around me to harden, so it would be effective against more than just the breeze. Though I knew now that a Sluagh had *not* attacked me when Soren claimed to 'find me in the forest', they were still Nemain's creatures — creatures that hunted at night.

Stupid, stupid, I thought as I ran. How could I have let myself so easily become prey? They were more fearsome than any other dark Faerie I had encountered, fighting in small flocks and feasting on souls for sport.

I focused on the empty sight of Sairas ahead, acknowledging the small blessing that at least nobody else would be hurt. As the swooping of wings drew closer, my breathing grew ragged and panicked.

A loud thump resounded above my head, and the air around me shook. A low gasp ripped from my throat. Though the air shield held, it was followed in quick succession by three more thumps. I felt my magic waver.

In a split-second decision, I whirled, holding my shield steady as I clutched the dagger. I took slow, measured steps backward while facing the creatures, hoping I could dispatch them one at a time, switching between magic and blade.

They flapped above on giant, leathered wings, like dark undulating shadows in the sky. Between the glow of the moon and the town's lighting, they were easy to see as they swooped in close to assess me. Each dive made me shiver as I made out more of their features.

Beneath their wings, they had human-like bodies, but they were emaciated creatures. Wrinkles of bluish-brown, haggard skin hung from lean frames, and they possessed long, bony claws for fingers and toes. A few greasy, dark strands of hair clung to their nearly hairless heads, and they had birdlike beaks where their mouths should be. Long, serrated teeth became visible when they opened their mouths to screech.

As another swooped in to test my shield, I winced. It bared its teeth as its claws glanced off the shield. Had Nemain finally decided to dispose of me once and for all? Did she believe her odds were better with me dead, rather than alive to activate the talismans? All questions left my head, however, as they took turns — now two at a time — to try and shatter my shield. There were at least seven of them, and if they all dove at the same time, I knew I wouldn't be able to hold it.

The next time they dove, I lunged, catching one in the middle of its wing with my dagger. Its screech hit a new pitch, and as it tried to flee, my dagger dragged through the entirety of the wing, cleaving it in two. The Sluagh collapsed to the ground, unable to fly.

My mouth twisted into a feral grin, hoping the sight of the fallen dark Faerie would be a lesson to the others. My stomach plummeted, however, as I watched their shadows swirling in the dark sky, intensifying instead of dissipating. The Sluagh on the ground recovered enough to crawl after me, emanating a dark hissing sound as it approached. Its leathery wing scraped against the snow, leaving a trail of inky blood behind. It no longer seemed to notice; its vile, empty eyes were fixated only on me. I stumbled back a few steps, willing the earth to shoot up around the creature.

The Sluagh went tumbling as the ground bucked beneath it, but with my mind focused on the earth magic, I didn't notice the dive from another airborne Sluagh. I cried out as the force of three beasts shattered against the shield, stretching the extent of my air magic. It held, but barely, and when another three dove from the other side, it finally collapsed.

I scrambled to fashion something from the earth, but the winged brutes were too quick. I felt a tug as I was snatched up in the claws of one of the Sluagh. It began lifting me off the ground, but I whirled to fight its claws off, the fist holding my dagger connecting with bone and skin. As I pulled the blade out, it howled and flew off, taking parts of my clothing with it.

Before I could reorient myself, another came from directly be-hind, claws digging in hard enough to grab through my clothing to the skin on my back. My breath left my body as it whisked me into the air. We ascended quickly, the intention of the Sluagh becoming clear — they had no plans to take my soul, only to transport me to another location.

I twisted and writhed, ignoring the burn as my skin tugged against its claws. I worked to get a good view of the ghastly creature, sum-moning all the strength in my core as I took my dagger in both hands and flung my body up, hoping to find purchase in something vital.

Though it didn't have the impact my broadsword would have — something I vowed to carry everywhere from now on, if I survived this — it hit true and it hit deep. The creature shuddered, lurching to a stop before its talons abruptly released me.

I tumbled toward the ground, panic and bile rising in my throat. I tried to make sense of my distance from the ground in the dark winter night, willing the scraps of remaining air magic to slow my descent. But with my disoriented state and weakened reserves, it wasn't much help.

I hit the ground with a force that cracked everything inside me, and the agony was immediate. If it weren't for the adrenaline coursing through me, I was certain I would have lost consciousness. But my barest need for survival was at an all-time high. I had enough time to shake the blackness away from my vision, hacking as blinding pain shot through my sides, before the Sluagh swarmed again.

"Fucking beasts," I seethed, my anger acting as a temporary pain relief. I fumbled for my dagger but found nothing, and realized with a start that it was likely lodged in the beast I'd struck. Using the last scraps of my magical reserves, I summoned water instead, fashioning a large icicle as I waited for them to get within striking range.

I lunged at the first one to do so, and even as I burned inside at the pain, the Sluagh staggered back from the force of the strike, its wing fully impaled. My laugh was maniacal, borderline delusional, as I watched the Sluagh circle, growing uncertain now that three of them had been injured.

The manic laughter dissolved into a cough, and I glanced down in surprise as a warm, sticky substance soaked my hand.

Blood...normal, crimson blood. That's interesting. Is that mine?

I collapsed onto my knees, my mind suddenly hazy. The creatures screeched in victory as they realized I had fallen, but before they could launch themselves at me once more, the area around us grew warm.

Snow melted instantly as the temperature around us skyrocketed. Someone stepped into my line of view. *Finlay.*

Fire roiled over every inch of his flesh as the entire sky lit up; flames exploded from his very being like one massive, lethal firework — the true extent of his power on full display. The Sluagh raced for the heavens, attempting to escape. I watched as flames licked out to attack the airborne Sluagh, incinerating them two at a time. The whole ordeal lasted a matter of seconds.

A solitary creature tried desperately to escape, flying haphazardly with an injured wing; it barely made it a few yards before it, too, was engulfed in flames. The screeching went silent, and I choked as the scent of burnt flesh hit my nostrils.

The action sent white-hot pain searing through my body, and the choking dissolved into coughing. I wheezed, panic setting in as warm liquid filled my mouth. My breathing became gargled as I searched for air that wouldn't come, and the last thing I saw was Finlay's frenzied expression as he bent over me.

CHAPTER FORTY

All my other senses came back before I found the courage to open my eyes. I tasted the coppery tang of blood in my mouth and smelled the distinct scent of various herbs and spices — an indicator I was likely at Castille's. Soft murmuring sounded all around me, the voices strained and tense.

I took a tentative deep breath, anticipating the rush of blinding pain, which blissfully never came. My eyelids fluttered, and I found myself on the couch, looking at Cas's ceiling. When I turned my head, I saw Kipp dozing off in the chair next to me. His hair was tousled in complete disarray, an elbow propped on his knee, and his head rested in his palm. His eyes were closed, but as I shifted, they flew open.

"Kate," he murmured, his eyes shimmering as he clutched my hand. "Thank the gods. You're awake."

"How long have I been out?" I asked, wincing at the hoarseness of my voice.

"A few hours. Cas tried to convince us you'd be okay, but we wanted to wait to be certain of it ourselves."

I remained silent as I took in the information, taking stock of my body. I wiggled my fingers and toes before testing the larger parts of my body, though everything seemed in working order. Slowly, I sat up and glanced around. The room was empty, and I wondered briefly who the 'we' was that Kipp referred to.

As if in answer to my question, Cas strode in. He wore a long silken robe, boldly patterned in burnt orange and black. Despite his usual bright fashion, he looked more tired than usual. Still, he caught my eye as he poured a glass of brandy and grinned broadly.

"Ah, Katie-cat! You're awake. How do you feel?" He came to sit on a nearby chair, throwing one leg over the other as he surveyed me.

"A little nauseous," I admitted. When Cas looked alarmed, I added, "I woke up to some pretty intense dog breath."

Kipp let out a small whine of complaint, and then we all dissolved into a short fit of laughter. I was relieved to find my chuckles were painless.

"Ah, so you're just fine, then," Cas concluded warmly. "I'm glad to hear it."

The sound of our laughter brought Wren into the room, who was followed shortly after by Finlay. Wren scrambled to my side, but Finlay hung back, his expression taut.

"I'm so glad you're okay, Kate," Wren said. "When Finlay brought you in, you were nearly—"

"Wren," Cas snapped, but I straightened, locking eyes with her.

"Nearly what?" I demanded. With a guilty look, Wren finished the sentence.

"Dead."

I blinked in surprise. I'd felt the blood and pain, but for whatever reason, I had always expected to sense death – to be *aware* if it was happening. I turned to Cas.

"And you were able to...bring me back?" I asked.

He nodded. "With some help. Finlay power-shared with me."

I glanced at Finlay, noticing for the first time how disheveled he looked, too. His face was drawn, hair unusually flat, like he had run his hands through it several times over. Suddenly, a memory of hurtling through the open air resurfaced.

"I fell from the sky," I said as realization dawned on me, and Finlay nodded.

"From at least forty feet." He spoke for the first time, his voice strained. "I saw from a distance and that's when I came running. I—" his voice wavered. "—I wasn't sure I got to you in time."

"You had a concussion, fractured hip, and several broken ribs. But it was the internal bleeding that was the immediate issue." Cas rattled the injuries off mechanically, propping his feet up as he stretched. I twisted subconsciously, searching for any aches or pain, but finding none. It was mind-boggling to think I'd come back from the brink of death only hours earlier.

"What would we do without you, Cas?" I asked earnestly.

He simply beamed in response.

"Let's try to never find out, shall we? I have many more plans for my gods-given life." He took a deep swig of his drink. "Which is hopefully a bit longer now that Finlay killed those pesky Sluagh."

"They usually don't travel in packs bigger than four or so," Wren mused, picking anxiously at her hair. "The fact you saw seven at once tells me Nemain was behind this. It was planned."

I bit my lip as Wren confirmed my suspicions. My mouth opened as I pondered admitting to my other suspicion — that the Sluagh were sent to capture me, and drag me back to Nemain alive. Another glance at everyone's distraught expressions had me clamping my jaw shut again. Capture or kill made no difference. It was a targeted attack — one I'd barely survived.

"Maybe she heard the news of the armies gathering. She may have figured they'd be less likely to rally around us if she was able to take care of Kate beforehand," Finlay ventured, grimacing as he spoke. Kipp let out a deep growl.

I sighed. "That just means I'll have to be more cautious from here on out. I've got a new target on my back."

We all absorbed the news in silence, and I fought the wave of hopelessness threatening to drown me. How had the day come to this? It had started with a strong victory, only to end with my near demise. It was certainly a reminder of Nemain's reach and influence. I yawned nervously.

Cas noted it immediately and set his glass on the nearby table with a loud thwap.

"As *delightful* as this doomsday talk is, Katie-cat needs some rest. Now, everyone, shoo. Except you—" he pointed at me. "Just because I'm a miracle worker doesn't mean I won't need to do some touch-ups. You're staying here for the rest of the night so I can keep an eye on you. I'll be sure to keep everyone updated, though," he added, clocking the complaints on Kipp and Finlay's faces.

I waved goodbye to Kipp who, after sharing a pleading look with Cas, sulked his way outside. He transformed, and I was certain he would simply sleep on the ground outside. Cas and I were both too smart to argue against it. As Finlay passed by, I grabbed his hand and squeezed.

"Thank you, Finlay," I whispered. He gave me a tired smile that didn't quite reach his eyes, but squeezed back, nonetheless.

"Please don't thank me, little angel," he murmured. Before I could question his response, he slid out the door. Cas flitted over me once more, checking for any residual damage, and Wren disappeared to her bedroom.

"He's upset with himself, you know," Cas muttered while twisting my arm. The warm, soft glow of his magic trailed over my wrist. I looked at him in surprise, and he raised his face to meet my gaze, puffing to clear the hair falling over his brows. His warm dark eyes assessed me as he considered what to say next.

"He said he'd decided to follow after you, but if he had followed sooner — or not let you leave as you had — this wouldn't have happened," he explained, setting my hand down and patting it softly. "He didn't go into any more detail, but I can assume."

I lowered my eyes, unable to meet his gaze. "I didn't want things between us to happen so fast, or get serious, at all. It just...it feels wrong to do that to Blaise."

"I think Blaise would want you to be happy," Cas replied gently. "He was protective, but I don't think he'd want to hold you back from experiencing life on his account."

I hummed noncommittally in response, unsure what to think or say. Every interaction between Blaise and Finlay had been tense, bordering on hostile. I couldn't help but think he would view my actions with Finlay as an even deeper betrayal.

After a moment, Cas gave my hand another pat. "Is it just physical, or is there something more?"

My eyes flew back to his face, and I replied with alarm, "How can it be more? When a part of my heart still beats for someone else?"

He shrugged and rose from his chair, moving to find me a blanket. "Honestly? I'm probably not the right person to ask. I've never given my heart to anyone. But I've seen two loves with my parents — both happy, fulfilling types of love, just slightly different."

He paused, mulling it over for a moment as he handed me a folded duvet.

"Think of it like your magic. Your soul has room for multiple types, each serving a different purpose at a different time. It's not all or nothing. Your soul makes room for all of it."

I chewed on his words, trying to figure out if there was any room in my heart for *more*.

That was what made me run – the fact I didn't regret what I had done, and that every fiber of my being begged to welcome Finlay further into my life. But trying to decipher what that meant for the piece Blaise held in my heart had sent me spiraling. I unfolded the blanket and spread it over my body before clutching it close.

"My mind can make the room, but can my heart?" I whispered, more to myself than Cas. Still, he came to my side and rested a hand on my shoulder.

"I can't begin to answer that for you, Katie-cat, but I do think you should know one thing. I've power-shared with both you and Finlay now. And do you remember what I said? About how it's like holding up a mirror to your soul?"

I nodded, remembering the difference between my power-sharing with Cas, and my power-sharing with Finlay. With Cas, it had been like two old souls, settling into their comfortable friendship. With Finlay...I sank further into the blanket, waiting for Cas to continue.

"You both felt so similar when our souls touched," he began. "Boundless power, but also endless empathy, resilience, and an overwhelming desire to protect. I've never felt two souls that seem more perfect for one another. What that means for your heart, you have to decide yourself."

With that, he said a brief goodnight, leaving me reeling. He'd given me his opinion on the matter, but somehow, I felt deflated. I'd been hoping he would say the opposite. Now that he'd nudged me in that direction, I had to face the ugly truth...that perhaps what I felt for Finlay was more than just physical. That I cared for him — maybe even loved him, a little bit.

Or more than a little bit.

The next morning, I set off with nervous determination toward the palace. I knew I needed to have the conversation with Finlay to see where he stood on the matter, but the memories of countless women flitting around him last summer popped into my head unbidden. I hated the way the insecurities gnawed at me. If I was just a random prize for Finlay to win, I wasn't sure what I would do. Then again, I wasn't sure what I would do if I was not — if he wanted us to be more.

As expected, Kipp was waiting outside Cas's front door when I opened it in the morning, but I was grateful for the company.

"What do you think, Kipp?" I asked, holding a mug stolen from Cas's place as we walked. He'd made coffee and added a generous dollop of brandy inside, along with a knowing wink. Now, the sharp scent of alcohol, mixed with the earthy tang of coffee, rose in the cold morning air. I sipped slowly, willing it to calm my nerves.

"I don't think it matters what I think," he replied easily, and I snorted.

"That's a copout, and you know it. But I'll admit, I feel a little bit like a schoolgirl with a crush."

"It's a crush, is it?" Kipp cut in, smirking. My face flushed, and I took another long sip of my spiked coffee. The morning sun provided a soothing touch as we passed over the site of last night's attack. In the light of the day, it was obvious there had been a scuffle — claw marks dragged across the dirt, and patches of blood dotted the grass and snow, both black and mottled brown. I could see where Finlay had been, too. The snow had melted clean away from his footsteps.

Despite the heat warming my cheeks, I shivered and glanced quickly away.

"I don't know," I admitted. "I've never really had this happen before."

He hummed curiously but didn't comment. Instead, we walked silently for another few moments.

"I plan on telling Cas that I love him," he said suddenly, his voice wavering. My eyes shot to his, and he gave me a serious look, laced with trepidation.

"Kipp," I exclaimed, a grin spreading across my face. "That's wonderful!"

He looked startled at my response. "You really think so?"

"I do," I replied earnestly. "Honestly, I've wondered about you two before...you just, I don't know. You make sense together."

Kipp lit with joy at my words, beaming. As soon as the dimpled grin spread across his face, however, it dissolved into one of concern.

"I'm not sure if he feels the same, though," he admitted. "He's not the relationship type."

I bumped his shoulder as we walked. "Maybe not for strangers, but for the right people, I know he can be. Just look at the lengths he goes to for me. And you have...oh, a few hundred more years of history with him."

Kipp snorted, and I ruffled his hair affectionately, the unruly locks shining copper in the sun. "Let me know how it goes either way. I'm so happy you found someone to love."

He smiled warmly, and I took a moment to sip my coffee again, considering my own predicament.

"Did you love Blaise?" he asked.

I mulled over my answer. Now, as many months had passed without Blaise in my life as I'd had with him, which left me feeling disoriented. The sharp edges on my heartache had dulled, but never disappeared, still trying to cut at me when I allowed myself to explore his loss.

Our time together had mostly involved moments of passion, losing ourselves in each other as we forgot the problems of the outside world. It had been intense, but never that openly...*intimate*. There were a few times when unspoken, vulnerable words had hung in the air during our silences, perhaps experienced but never voiced aloud. If he had said it first, and opened up to me, would I have done the same with him?

"Yes. At least, I think I could have," I amended, "and that's what hurts the most. We never really explored what we were to each other. He was taken from me before we got the chance."

My voice cracked as that part in my heart where Blaise resided throbbed. I would never know what could have been.

"That's completely understandable," Kipp said gently. "But you'll have to make room for someone new eventually, whether it's him or someone else. You can't stay stuck in the past, never willing to move forward."

"You sound like Darrya," I said, rolling my eyes and swallowing another mouthful of coffee. A soft, warm fuzziness had begun to set in, and I found myself wishing the mug would magically refill.

"Well, here's the thing," Kipp began, pulling his coat tighter around himself. "I lived in the human realm for most of my life. Humans constantly worry about the next part of their lives, trying to achieve some ambiguous version of success before they die."

I nodded, seeing the truth in that statement. He continued.

"Faerie lifetimes, though, are so long, we often don't even consider that they have an expiration date. We find ourselves stuck reminiscing over happy times in our past. So, while humans look forward, we look back, and none of us realize we are right in the middle of what we should be enjoying."

I gaped at him as he fixed me with a stern, teacher-like look. The eye contact became too much, and I glanced away, refocusing on the palace entrance instead. I drained the last drops of my coffee.

"What are you, the fucking Dalai Lama?" I muttered, and a sidelong glance told me his stern expression had cracked. He laughed as we crossed into the palace, and pulled me into an aggressive hug.

"Just a friend who wants their other friend to remember to live in the moment, especially if it means she will be happy," he said. I squirmed in his embrace, pretending to complain before returning it.

"Thank you," I replied earnestly. He looked down at me with a warm smile, dimples flashing.

"Now go get your happiness," he urged, turning me and giving me a push.

I laughed and waved goodbye, setting off for Finlay's side of the palace. I took a roundabout way, though, stopping by the kitchens to top off my coffee, laced with more liquid courage.

By the time I reached Finlay's room, I was slightly tipsy, but the warmth was due to more than the alcohol. I buzzed with anticipation as I knocked on his door, ready to admit my feelings to him once and for all — even if I hadn't quite sorted out what the hell they were yet.

Chapter Forty-One

Finlay opened the door before I could even consider turning to run away. His brow furrowed as he looked down at me, and my gut dropped at the reality of the moment.

I'm really doing this.

"Hey," he said softly, scanning me from head to toe. Though his eyes bore circles under them from a clear lack of sleep, he was dressed in new clothing. He wore tan pants and a deep indigo long-sleeved shirt, rolled up at the arms. A dark brown leather vest was atop it, and his hair looked freshly washed, back to its normal fluffy volume. With a start, I realized I still wore the dress from yesterday, and a wave of self-consciousness hit me. I ducked my head, wondering briefly what my hair looked like.

"How are you feeling?" Finlay asked, opening the door wider.

"Fine," I answered automatically. "But, um, I wanted to talk with you."

"Yeah, understandable," he murmured, and motioned for me to enter. "Come on in."

I stepped inside, and Finlay moved to perch on the side of his bed. I opted to remain standing, nerves suddenly coursing through every inch of my body. Before I could think of how to start the conversation, he spoke.

"Look, I need to apologize," he began, running a hand over his face. "I took things too far yesterday, and I know it upset you."

I stared at him, too stunned to respond. My head felt fuzzy, though I wasn't sure if it was from the situation or the alcohol — probably both.

Finlay pressed on. "You need to understand. I never wanted to push you into anything," he pleaded. "I lost control for a moment, and what happened after…"

He halted, shaking his head and burying his face in his hands. "I'll never forgive myself."

My heart wrenched as I came to sit on the bed next to him. I took his hands in mine, forcing him to meet my eyes as I spoke.

"That had *nothing* to do with you," I insisted, praying he understood. "It was my own doing. I got inside my own head; I wasn't sure how to deal with it, and…"

I trailed off, my words slightly slurred. His expression grew curious, and he tilted his head and asked, "Have you been drinking?"

The corner of my mouth twitched. "Only some apple juice."

He huffed out a soft laugh at our running joke, that signature half-cocked grin spreading across his face. I realized with a start how much I'd come to love that smile. Taking a deep breath, I continued.

"I left last night because I was afraid."

His face turned stony. "Look, I know I took things too far last night. I understand if you want time apart from me—"

"—I was *afraid*," I interrupted before I lost my nerve, "because I could feel myself falling for you."

He inhaled audibly, lips parting, but said nothing. Instead, he pulled back and turned away from me. My heart plummeted.

When he faced me once more, he held a hand to his mouth. After a moment, he shifted it, running his thumb over his fleshy bottom lip in silent contemplation. His expression was unreadable.

"Say something," I pleaded.

"And now?" he asked, his voice hoarse with all the emotion I couldn't see on his face. "Are you still falling for me?"

I let out a faint, breathy laugh. "Why else would I be here, Finlay?"

His face transformed, becoming deadly serious. "Say that again."

"Say what?" I asked, confused.

"My name."

I paused, my smile widening. "Finlay."

He lunged for me, hauling my lips against his as he slid one hand around the back of my neck and the other around my waist, tugging me flush against him. My mouth opened, offering immediate access; he took it instantly and his tongue swirled, tasting me. Our kisses grew more demanding, but when his hand moved down my face to trail over my neck and chest, I broke away, squirming against him.

"I need to get clean," I blurted, already breathless. "Can I use your washroom?"

He chuckled and nodded, letting me go a little reluctantly. I made my way to the bath, beginning to fill it and setting soap on the edge. I shrugged my dress off, my underwear following shortly after. I hovered in the corner of the washroom as a recklessness flooded through my veins — hot, delicious, and bold. Finlay had teased, taunted, and flirted with me for so long. It was time to return the favor.

"So listen, there's something you should know—" Finlay began, just as I stepped out into the bedroom, stark naked.

He stopped short, mouth gaping as he took me in. The scrutiny had my nipples peaking, and it was all I could do not to cover myself with my arms. His gaze grew dark and heated as he drank me in, however, and my confidence grew as I watched the clear approval spread across his face.

"Brave of you to assume I can wait until you wash up, now," he growled, a carnal hunger flashing in his gaze. I grinned, feeling devilish at the power of harnessing his desire. I turned, glancing over my shoulder at him as his gaze dropped to my bare backside. A muscle in his jaw jumped as I strolled back into the washroom.

"If you play nice, you can help me get clean," I teased, and his response was instant. He shucked his vest off, followed shortly by his shirt before coming up behind me. His body was smooth and hard, and I felt the heated planes of his muscles press against my back as his arms closed around me. His hands reached up, skimming tentatively over my bare stomach before tracing my breasts. My body instantly tightened, and my head rolled back into his neck.

"Only if we can get absolutely filthy after," he answered huskily, his breath fanning against my ear. I chuckled and pried myself slowly from his embrace, dipping into the bath.

The water was warm and welcoming. I reached for the soap, scrubbing at the dried blood under my fingernails as Finlay knelt beside the tub. I took him in as I scrubbed, enjoying the rounded flex of his shoulder muscles and the dips of his abs. He noticed my inspection and grinned, dipping a finger into the bath.

"How's the temperature?" he asked, and I felt the water warm further with his magic.

"Perfect," I replied with a smile, moving to wash my hair. Finlay's arms tensed as he restrained himself, blonde strands of hair flopping across his burning blue gaze. He scanned my naked body like it was his last meal.

"You're absolutely breathtaking," he murmured, moving his hands from the edge of the water to massage my shoulders.

I hummed in contentment and leaned back, dipping my head into the water to rinse my hair; he took advantage of the arch in my back to skim his hands over the peaks of my breasts, swirling my nipples in his fingers. I shot back up, a soft moan escaping my mouth. His hands wandered back over my breasts for a moment before dipping lower.

"Talk to me, little angel," he urged, his voice low and gravelly. "Where do you want me to touch you?"

"Everywhere," I whimpered, already breathless. I watched his eyes darken at the sound, a deep noise of approval forming low in his throat. The power I had felt over him earlier was gone. I was putty in his hands.

His thumb moved in circles as he reached the sweet spot at the apex of my thighs, teasing his fingers between my legs for a moment before stroking them into me. I let out a small, desperate cry as I reached for him, clutching his shoulders and digging my nails into his back.

He increased the tempo, eyes piercing into mine. Every sweep of his fingers was a blissful kind of torture; I lifted my hips with his movements, desperate to draw more pleasure as he urged me toward the edge.

"Come for me, little angel," he purred. His mouth widened into a feral grin as he watched me and with that, I was driven completely off the edge. One hand dropped from his back to his bicep as my nails bit into skin, clutching for dear life as I cried out, giving Finlay exactly what he asked for.

I had hardly caught my breath before he whisked me from the bath and carried me to his bed. I reached out as he laid me on the sheets, desperate to feel more of him. He obliged, climbing over my naked body. Instantly, I placed the flats of my palms against his chest. He shuddered, my cold hands a stark contrast to his natural heat. I traced the smooth hills of his muscles, starting at his shoulders and working my way down to his pants. I began tugging at them, and he chuckled and grabbed my wrists. His grin was gentle as I made a small noise of complaint.

"Not yet," he murmured, moving his hands from my wrists to lean his entire body over mine.

"There isn't a single part of you I haven't dreamt of kissing," he continued, lowering his head to drag his warm lips across my neck. He worked down my chest, teeth grazing my nipple gently. I gasped. "I plan on bringing that dream to life."

He continued trailing kisses down my stomach, and I clenched with desire as they brushed my hip bone. "But there's one place, in particular, I've wanted to taste for so long."

His warm hands slid behind my knees, spreading my legs so he could settle between them. He trailed more kisses along the inside of my thigh, starting from the knee and working his way up.

My breath caught as his mouth stopped just before touching my core. We locked eyes, and his glinted devilishly as he looked up at me, burning with an intensity that had nothing to do with his magic.

"So I plan on starting here." The warmth of his breath hit my sensitive core, and I shivered.

"Oh..." was all I could say before he dragged the warm pad of his tongue against me, sending all thoughts flying from my head. It was all I could do to keep from combusting as he nibbled and sucked, spreading me with his tongue and flicking playfully back and forth. My hips bucked, grinding against him. He chuckled, the sound vibrating into me and sending more waves of pleasure through me.

"Finlay," I breathed, trembling as the ecstasy mounted. He glanced up. "I need you."

"You have me," he said, but I shook my head.

"No, I need you. In me. *Now,*" I moaned, a cross between an order and a plea.

He lifted his head, grinning broadly. "Greedy, are we?"

He wiped his mouth and sat back, eyes glued to mine as he removed his pants. His movements were far too slow for my liking, considering he was clearly as ready for this as I was. I bit my lip in anticipation, fixing him with a demanding stare.

He settled back, his expression suddenly serious. His hands trailed over my legs before lifting one. There was an intense pause before he slowly guided himself inside me, and we both groaned, growing accustomed to one another.

"Fuck, Kate," Finlay moaned. I jolted, surprised at his use of my real name. "You're perfect."

I didn't dare voice it, didn't want to make it real, but...he felt perfect, too. And as he started moving inside me, I knew I would never get enough of him. Each stroke from him was a different sensation burning through my body. We were a mess of hands and heavy breathing, working to draw as much pleasure from one another as possible.

As he increased the pace, I threw back my head and moaned his name, causing him to thrust even harder. The next time his name passed my lips, it drew out in three syllables as my body shook from the force of his thrusts. Our kisses grew more dispersed and frantic between our heavy breathing, and when I bit down on his lip in a fit of passion, he groaned against my mouth, clutching the nape of my neck tightly and biting right back.

"Don't — stop," I cried out, meeting his thrusts. I reached up, clawing at his shoulders as I tightened around him, willing him to come with me.

"Never, little angel. Never," Finlay rasped. He clung to me as we finished together, ending with a last deep thrust that left me gasping for air.

We rode the final waves of pleasure out in unison, and while I knew I should have mixed emotions, in that moment, I felt only bliss.

Finlay had always referred to me as his fallen angel, but I had never really believed him until now. I had completely fallen from any grace, and I was forced to admit I loved every second of it.

CHAPTER FORTY-TWO

"So, let me get this straight. You've talked with pretty much everyone else about your feelings toward me...except me?" Finlay shook with laughter. I ducked under the covers in embarrassment, but he lifted the blanket, grinning down at me. "For all of your strengths, little angel, I have to say — communication isn't one of them."

"You may be right," I admitted, "but in my defense, it's because I don't even know how to make sense of my own thoughts, let alone voice them with others."

Finlay laughed once more and pulled me close. I wore only his blue shirt as we lay under the covers, but the heat almost surpassed a comfortable temperature as it radiated from him. I squirmed, which only caused him to chuckle and clutch me tighter.

"So tell me," he breathed in my ear. "What are you thinking of now?"

I turned to face him, drinking in his features: the stunning blue of his eyes, the smoothness of his skin, and the sharpness of his jaw. I reached out and stroked a hand across his cheek, relishing the lopsided grin that spread across his face at my touch.

"I think I've been denying my own feelings for a long time," I whispered. His smile broadened as he leaned further into my touch. "But I'm not entirely sure what those feelings mean yet. It's...still a bit of a jumble, here."

I pointed to my chest, and Finlay snatched my hand, kissing it gently before he spoke.

"I want your love when and how you're willing to give it," he said. "But just know, mine is here, waiting for you when you're ready."

I flashed him a nervous smile, my heart rate rising at his use of the word 'love'. I didn't know how long he'd be willing to wait until I was ready for more, but I had to admit, there was nobody else I wanted to be with while I sorted myself out.

"Are you ready?" Larke asked, offering me the large scabbard. The leather was a deep chestnut with gold adorning its mouth, trailing in intricate, circular patterns down the seam. It was gorgeous, but my eyes were drawn instantly to the blade inside.

The Whisperer had been sent off to be reforged by the palace swordsmith weeks ago — under the strict supervision of Larke's best men, who were all sworn to secrecy— and was now masterfully fortified with all the talismans. The entire blade still glowed softly from the preternatural remnant of flames burning inside. A round piece of the Speaking Stone made up the pommel while Lugh's spear-turned-horseshoe had once more been melted down, now adding an intricate design to the grip and crossguard. The entire hilt was plated in gold, thanks to a portion of the cauldron.

Simply put, it was a work of art.

Larke handed the scabbard over, which I gingerly took, my fingers clutching the grip of the sword. I held my breath as I unsheathed the Whisperer, listening to its dull rasp as it left the scabbard.

Everything went silent for a long moment. Finally, I exhaled and lifted my eyes to Larke's.

"I thought something might happen when you touched it," he admitted, sagging back slightly.

So did I, I thought, but kept the defeated thought to myself. Instead, I tested the weight of it in my hand and forced a grin.

"I suppose it's just one more thing I'll have to learn," I said. "So, I better get started."

CHAPTER FORTY-THREE

The following days were a blur. Darrya and Larke were nearly inseparable as they worked together to accommodate the influx of armies from various lands. So, I was left to steal Jasper, Larke's new second-in-command, who trained with me and taught me the basics of military tactics every evening. He was incredibly skilled with the blade, but I still felt an occasional pang of grief when I found myself comparing his movements to ones Blaise would have made.

I trained every morning, this time with the Whisperer, though it still didn't activate with any unusual magic. It was heavier than the broadsword I was used to, but I was determined to learn the weight of it until it was as familiar to me as an added limb.

I kept the Whisperer strapped to me at all times, with the hope I would unlock the mystery of activating it — and also for added protection. Though, I now had constant shadows in the forms of

Kipp, Finlay, and my father. They were determined to never leave me alone for longer than absolutely necessary.

The funny thing was, I didn't *want* to be alone. My free moments were spent with Finlay, practicing my magic with him as I attempted — and failed — to summon fire magic, which often resulted in him distracting me from my failures with his hands or mouth. The same thing happened every night, with me reading some of my favorite books aloud to him until he eventually captured my lips with his, effectively ending any nighttime narrations.

"What are you thinking about over there?" Kipp asked, narrowing his eyes as we walked through town. My face flushed as I attempted to play it off.

"How I'm going to persuade Ensley to join us. And if she has any more information on the battle now," I squeaked. Kipp rolled his eyes, not believing me for a second.

"He's good for you," he said. I jerked my head to him in surprise. "I can't remember the last time I saw you this happy. Even with everything happening," he added.

I considered his words for a moment, and then smiled to myself. Kipp hummed in approval while watching my face. "Exactly."

"And you?" I retorted, fixing him with a stern look. "Have you told Cas how you feel yet?"

He paled slightly. "I — with the war coming up, I just—"

I couldn't help but snort at the sight of him so flustered.

"Were you not the one who told me to focus on the happiness we can gain from the present?" I teased, and he ducked his head with a guilty smile.

"Fair enough."

I grinned triumphantly, but didn't push the matter further as we walked. The hushed tones of passersby, paired with the gray, overcast sky, invited an uncomfortable sense of foreboding. The cobblestone streets of Sairas were far emptier than the last time we'd visited Ensley — likely due to the colder weather, but I was certain recent events played a part, too. Though the citizens of Sairas were not entirely sure of the reasons behind the curfews or increased military presence, the intent was clear enough. They had every reason to be on edge.

When we arrived at Ensley's shop, I pulled at the dark curtain tentatively and peered inside. The Valkyrie spoke before I could call for her.

"Come on in," her voice rang out from inside, just as strong and crisp as I remembered.

I looked back at Kipp, motioning for him to follow as I entered. The space was dark, with only candles offering light in the rest of the shop. But Ensley's presence was impossible to miss. She sat expectantly at the wooden table across from us, surrounded by weapons and clairvoyant items. Her strong, falcon-like wings were on full display behind her.

Those tawny wings shifted expectantly as she folded her dark, toned arms across her chest. Kipp hesitated, clearly intimidated by the strong warrior before us, but I tugged him forward. Despite the Valkyrie's daunting presence, she was good-natured and honest — someone I'd trust with my life.

"It's good to see you again, Ensley," I said earnestly, and she dipped her head in response. "This is my friend, Kipp Callaghan."

Kipp flushed and mumbled a greeting, and a corner of Ensley's mouth lifted in amusement. I wondered if she was used to having this kind of effect on Faeries, or if this was a new experience for her.

"Pleased to meet you, Kipp. And likewise, Katherine," she returned with an air of professional warmth. She motioned for us to sit. "I sensed one of your questions the moment you decided to ask it of me. And the answer is yes. I will have myself and my forces ready to accommodate you in this battle."

I released a breath as the weight lifted from my shoulders. "Thank you. It means more than you can ever imagine."

"I can imagine how much it means, actually." She smiled. "But Katherine?"

"Yes?"

"Do not make such requests a habit."

I grimaced, tossing her a guilty smile. "I'll try my best to make this the only war I ask you to participate in."

Ensley snorted and offered her palms to both of us. I took one and motioned for Kipp to do the same. "We were hoping you could provide some additional clarity on the battle," I requested.

The Valkyrie nodded, inhaling deeply as she closed her eyes. When she opened them again, it was just like before — her eyes were no longer a deep brown, replaced instead by churning ripples of glassy gray, moving like animated marble. She looked around, her expression hardened, and I knew she saw a battlefield rather than the inside of her shop.

"Five days," she said. "It is happening in five days. That much is certain."

I sucked in a sharp breath and exchanged a fearful glance with Kipp, seeing the same expression mirrored in his own eyes. This was what we had spent so long preparing for, withstanding so much hurt and devastation for exactly this moment. In five days, for better or worse, we would face Nemain and her army.

"There will be many surprises. I can't quite see what...but the surprise is felt on both sides," she mused, and I restrained the urge to roll my eyes. *Unhelpful.*

"Nemain's screams can cripple a large part of our armies. Do you see a way for us to remove that obstacle?" Kipp asked, leaning forward expectantly. Ensley's brow furrowed as she sorted through what I presumed were near-endless outcomes.

"An enchanted arrow to the throat," she mused. "She will have a healer at her side, so it will not kill her, but it will permanently cripple her powers."

"Darrya," I breathed, glancing at Kipp who nodded his agreement. I'd heard multiple people claim her as the best shot in Muiranvia, and while I didn't relish the thought of putting her close to Nemain, I knew her. She wouldn't hesitate to do it. I turned back to Ensley for my final, burning question.

"And do you see the talismans activating?" I pleaded. Ensley's face pinched once more, her hands squeezing ours as she navigated her visions.

"It will take much heartbreak, and so many decisions that I can't even begin to point you in the proper direction...but under the right circumstances, yes. The sword will be imbued with your power."

Kipp and I shared a look of utter relief. Not at all easy, then, but *possible.* And with that hope, we could work with the unfavorable odds.

"Thank you, Ensley," I said. "We really appreciate it."

She nodded, closing her eyes and removing her hands from ours. When they reopened, they had returned to their normal, chocolate brown. We stood together as Kipp and I made to leave.

"I suppose we'll see you again on the battlefield," I mused, with more than a touch of anxiety laced in my tone. "I would try to hug you, but I'm not entirely sure how, with the whole..." I trailed off, motioning to her wings. "Feathered situation."

Ensley laughed, warm eyes twinkling. Her laughter was rich, bordering on ethereal, and I felt flattered, knowing it was a delight not many experienced.

"I'm glad to see you doing so well, all things considered. Blaise hoped you would find peace after his passing."

My mind cracked at her words. Did she have the power to communicate with the dead? "What do you mean he *said* that?"

"Oh," she tutted, her face etched with concern. "I only saw him a few times after his prophecy. Once he was certain he couldn't change his fate, I urged him to tell you. Did he not?"

"P—prophecy?" I sputtered. "His fate? Tell me what?"

Ensley looked uncomfortable. "During your first meeting here, I saw his death, at the hands of Nemain, protecting you. It was impossible to say when, but it was inevitable. He tried desperately to find another way, but nothing altered the course of his fate. He knew it was inescapable."

Something inside me shattered at her words. "He *knew* he would die...protecting me?" I whispered, my voice breaking as I spoke.

I had always known Blaise would not hesitate to kill on my behalf — hell, we'd even joked, *laughed* about it — but I would not have expected him to die for me. Never would I have asked that of him. Grief and anger rose in me, causing my throat to constrict. I suddenly knew why he'd refused to tell me. I would have talked him out of it, if I had known. I would have distanced myself from him. And by taking that choice from me, he'd offered his life to save mine.

Ensley was watching my face closely and offered a sad smile at whatever she saw there.

"He tried changing everything else he could, but on that, he remained firm. If he had to die to protect you, he would."

I shook my head, as if that would force her revelation from my memory. "No, no, no..."

"He knew you were the key to winning this war," Ensley added softly. "He did it for his people, but he also would have done it just for you."

I whirled on Kipp.

"Did you know? Did he tell you?" I demanded. I could no longer blame Blaise for withholding such information, but I felt as though I needed someone to blame.

Kipp raised both palms helplessly, eyes wide. "I knew nothing of this, I swear."

"There was only one other person I'm certain he told, though I still am unsure why," Ensley offered, turning a thick golden bracelet on her wrist as she spoke. "He said he told the prince."

It took several long moments for the pieces to come together in my head. Once they did, my despair twisted into something else — betrayal. And pure, white-hot rage.

Chapter Forty-Four

I stalked back to the palace, Kipp hot on my heels. I wasn't sure where I was headed. I debated between going straight to Finlay's, or to my room instead, to lock everyone out. I figured I would make that decision when we arrived.

My feet slammed against the stone palace steps, angry slaps echoing off the walls. I stormed up, the decision made to reach my own room. Kipp hesitated at the top of the steps before slipping away, deciding to give me my distance, for which I was grateful.

I flung the door of my room open, but before I could enter, I heard *him* behind me.

"Little angel," Finlay said, surprise flooding his voice. "Is something wrong?"

I froze, ice and flame somehow both swirling dangerously in my veins. I whirled to see him in the hallway, and before I could think, my feet had me striding forward to face him. He cocked his head down at me curiously as I approached, but was completely unprepared as I pummeled my palms directly into his chest. He stumbled back.

"Is something *wrong?*" I seethed. "Oh, I don't know. I would say something is wrong, but you might not. Is that why you never bothered to tell me Blaise *knew* he was going to *die?*"

He paled, his mouth dropping open. "Kate, I—"

"You know, I can't believe you. All this time, I thought underneath that exterior of drugs and alcohol, you were actually good. But it was all just a game to get in my pants, wasn't it?" I fumed. Finlay flinched as though he'd been burned.

He stepped forward again, but I held up a hand to stop him. "And all at the expense of my relationship with Blaise, nonetheless," I spat.

His face crumpled.

"It's not like that," he sputtered. "I tried to tell you, really, I did—"

"When, exactly?" I cut him off. "When your cock was inside me?"

I spun on my heel before he could answer as my rage hit boiling point. I stormed straight past my room, desperate to burn off the emotions crackling violently through my veins. I heard Finlay calling after me, so I picked up the pace.

I raced down the steps, spiraling through a maze of hallways until I reached the lowest level of the palace. It was dark and cool, a nice contrast to the heat roiling in my veins. Not another soul around.

Slowing my pace, I strode to the end of the next hallway and tested the door. Locked. I remembered it dimly from one of my first attempts looking for the palace library. I turned to navigate back upstairs, my anger somewhat dulled, but then the sound of footsteps reached me. I heard the echo of Finlay's voice, calling after me.

I gritted my teeth and turned back to the locked door, reaching in my hair for a pin. As a teenager, I made it a point to learn how to pick locks. I figured it may come in handy when I was older, though I could never have guessed it would prove useful when evading a Faerie prince.

I cursed as I found my hair without pins, but after a moment, my eyes fell to the floor. I had traveled far enough down the palace that we were clearly on the lowest level, something akin to a dungeon. The floor was not smooth limestone, but rather loose gravel and dirt. Squinting, I summoned my magic. I willed pieces of gravel to hover in the air, fashioning them together into something long and skinny, resembling a hairpin.

With a triumphant grin, I knelt in front of the lock and began to work. Though I was certain the door would be enchanted against direct magical entry, crafting a lock pick from magic was certainly an unexpected loophole. The footsteps grew closer as I worked, indicating Finlay's approach. I clenched my jaw, concentrating on the lock.

"Work, damn you," I muttered. As if in answer to my angry request, the click of the lock sounded as it turned over. I breathed a quiet cheer and slid through the door, twisting to lock it again upon my entrance.

An ominous silence filled the air, heavy in a way that told me, even before I turned, that I wasn't the only one in the room. The hairs on the back of my neck and my arms rose as I considered how ridiculous I had been. My inability to handle one situation quite possibly landed me in a much more sinister one.

What would the queen keep locked in the dungeon? My mind latched onto Thaddeus' words from when we rode along the beach before the winter solstice party.

If you don't like the fact that I collect dangerous and dark creatures, you should see what our very own queen keeps right at her palace.

"You're new."

A female voice rang out, the chime of it dancing through my ears deliciously. The inviting tone caught me off guard. Slowly, I turned, pressing my back against the door.

A small, lean woman stood in the middle of the room, wearing nothing but a simple cream nightgown. The first things I noticed were her piercing eyes, a unique pale green that glowed despite the darkness. They widened as she inched closer, assessing me with a curious look.

Then I noticed the chains. Both her hands and legs were shackled, with one even wrapped around her neck, like a grotesque iron collar. They strained as she reached their end, bringing her to a stop several feet away.

In spite of all this, the woman barely seemed to notice them. She tilted her head curiously at me, long, dark hair tumbling down one shoulder. It gleamed against the faint streaks of light the room allowed in through a small slit in the wall. The room was otherwise nothing but thick black slabs of stone. In stark contrast to her sleek hair, the woman's skin was smooth and silver-white, like marble. Despite her thin, shackled frame, the Faerie was breathtaking. *A Siren*, I thought. *Only a Siren could have this strange effect on me.*

"You're not what I expected to see when I broke in here," I ventured cautiously, refusing to move from the door. The woman wore chains for a reason. While they seemed to be working, I didn't want to test my luck.

Surprised, the woman straightened and offered a radiant smile.

"A break-in? What a delightful turn of events! Hundreds of years, and I cannot say that's ever happened."

She giggled to herself before a frown abruptly took over. "Unless you're here to kill me. Though I suppose that may be a nice turn of events as well, albeit a different one."

"Hundreds of years?" I blurted, eyeing her with trepidation. If I were smarter, I told myself, I would turn and leave. But Thad's ominous words, paired with this startling discovery, had me intrigued – and if I were completely honest, I had already proved I wasn't the smartest by putting myself in this position to begin with.

She nodded, nostrils flaring. "No, you're not here to kill me," she decided. "I smell death on you, but no deaths intended with malice."

I froze, bewildered. She *sensed* that I had killed before? Furthermore, she could *smell* the intention behind my kills? I'd never heard of such an ability.

"What are you?" I asked as apprehension and fascination warred in my gut. "Are you a dark Faerie?"

The woman smiled, tilting her chin up slightly. "Ah, yes, I can see you're young, too. That explains it. To answer your question, child, I am no dark Faerie, but I am no regular Faerie, either. I am Clíodhna."

"Clíodhna?" I echoed, the name coming out more like *'Cleena'.*

"Yes," she answered. "Queen of the Bean Sídhe, mother of Sirens."

My eyes widened, and I scrambled to find the lock on the door again. My mind flashed to memories of the crippling nothingness in my soul from Nemain's cries, and the images of Blaise's lifeless form before me. I refused to suffer through that again.

"Calm, child! I will not hurt you. I could not, even if I wished to," the banshee said. She tugged at the chain around her neck. Angry marks marred the skin of her throat — bright red marks, indicating the truth of her claim that she was not, in fact, a dark Faerie.

"Enchanted chains," she explained. "As long as they are here, I cannot summon my magic."

I relaxed somewhat, but kept one hand on the lock. "My only experience with a banshee was Nemain's torture," I threw back at her stiffly. "Forgive me if I don't have much trust in your kind."

Clíodhna hissed.

"Nemain," she spat, "is *not* what we Bean Sídhe strive to be. While some of my powers may come from her — much to my disdain — monsters are borne of deeds done. I am *nothing* like her."

She straightened in her chains, seeming proud as she spoke. "She is all darkness, while my kind strives for light. She is a goddess of destruction and terror, whereas I am a goddess of love and beauty."

I blinked in shock. "You're a goddess?"

"I once was," she sniffed, turning away. "But my decisions rendered me otherwise."

I scanned her once more. Even under the grime and torture that had clearly dimmed her light, she was stunning — certainly a goddess of beauty. I also believed her hatred for Nemain. I had no idea why she was being held captive, but I sensed there was more to the story that may not put the queen in the best light.

"The decisions that landed you here?" I ventured.

She shook her head. "Oh, child, no. But in a way, I suppose the lingering effects of those choices allowed Queen Egan to capture me. It was my love of a mortal that lost me my status as a goddess."

My brows shot up at the information. "A mortal? As in, a human?"

"Keevan," she murmured, her green eyes glimmering with affection, and some sadness, at his name. "I was given a choice: remain a goddess without him, or be with him and lose my immortality and many of my powers."

"And you chose him," I whispered. She nodded.

"But then the young Queen Egan took him," she continued, her mouth twisting into a snarl. "And she used him to lure me here and trap me. She had his memory wiped right before my eyes, then sent him back to the human realm."

My heart plummeted at the thought of such cruelty. I didn't want to believe her, yet a small part of me whispered it could very well be true. I knew firsthand the queen put her interests above all others, especially those she considered 'lesser Fae'. It wouldn't surprise me if she held just as much disdain for humans, if not more.

"Why? Why did she capture you?"

"She believes that with my wail, I possess songs that can cure any illness. An opposite side of its normal destruction." She sighed, tilting her head upward as her expression turned defeated.

My breath caught as I asked, "Can you?"

She laughed, the sound short and humorless. "I've told her endlessly that I cannot, but once she had me, I suppose she didn't care to let me go. So, here I stay."

I opened my mouth, but fumbled to find the words for the horror I felt. My mind raced with the prospect of her words. Surely if someone had such power to cure illnesses with song, they should be commended — not imprisoned. Instead, it seemed, the queen's answer was to lock her up and isolate her, forcing a truth she couldn't give. And when that didn't work, the queen tortured her down here — whether from fear or malevolence, I wasn't sure. I couldn't even begin to understand her logic.

"And it's been hundreds of years?" I asked at last, mortified.

"At least. I lost count of the exact number ages ago." She tapped her fingers on her chains. "It's an ironic curse to be a goddess of love, all while being deprived of it."

My lips pressed into a firm line as I considered her words. All I could think of was her mortal lover, lost and unassuming in the human realm. Even if she escaped, he'd be long gone now, at one with the earth once more. My heart ached at the thought.

"And you?" Clíodhna asked, interrupting my thoughts. "I never got your name. How did you come to cross paths with Nemain? I'm surprised to hear she is still messing in Faerie affairs."

I shifted on my feet, wondering briefly if the banshee could be an asset, considering her knowledge of Nemain. Perhaps my chance meeting with this goddess was a positive twist of fate, for once.

"Umm...I'm Katherine. And as far as Nemain — she's looking to resurrect her sisters to become a triple goddess once more. I just happen to be the key to that, but also a descendant of someone she's vowed to destroy. It's all very complicated."

"I've never known anyone interesting who didn't have a few complications in their life," she said seriously, then flashed me an infectious smile.

The corners of my lips tugged slightly, wanting to smile back. Realistically, everything she said made sense, but could I really trust the word of a banshee shackled in the pits of the palace? I recognized how ridiculous it sounded as the thought crossed my mind, but shoved my intrusive thoughts aside and chose to trust my instincts.

I dropped my hand from the door and moved to her side. To my surprise, she backed up, as though afraid. I wondered what my own mental state would be like, had I been locked up for several hundred years. As a goddess, she was blessed with immortality, which meant the queen likely intended to leave her down here...forever. I shuddered at the thought and lifted my hand, revealing the thin, makeshift hairpin in my grip.

"What do you plan on doing with that?" she asked, eyeing me with a slight look of panic.

"I plan on freeing you, Clíodhna. No one should be locked up and tortured like this, especially not you." I gave her a tentative grin, and her eyes widened at my words.

"You believe me?" Her question came out choked with emotion.

"I believe that in both the human and the Faerie realm, there is a lot of inequity and narrow-mindedness." I dropped to my knees, inspecting the lock that held the chain on her ankles. "Unfortunately, the most ignorant are oftentimes those with the power. I'd like to change that."

I fiddled with the first lock, and she gave me a dubious look. "I don't think Queen Egan would make it that easy," she ventured.

"Her enchantments prevent magic, but I have a mortal workaround," I replied. The lock sprang open as if to punctuate my point. I moved to her other ankle, and she watched, astounded, while I worked. When I came to the last one on her neck, I chuckled to myself.

"What's that?" she asked, twisting to see my face.

I gave her a smile. "Nothing. It's just — you were captured for loving a human, and now you'll be released by someone part-human. An ironic end to a tragic curse."

"I like that," she mused, and paused. "How can I ever repay you, Katherine?"

I mulled over the question for only a moment. "There will be a war. In five days. If you think of anything — *anything* — that could help us defeat Nemain, I just ask that you send word somehow."

"I will," she vowed. "Trust me."

The final lock sprang open, and as the chains fell from her neck, Clíodhna groaned happily and rubbed her hands against her neck. She gave me one final, appreciative smile, and before I could react, she dissolved into thin air, like beautiful silver ashes floating in the wind.

I sat for several long moments, staring at the dark empty room and the large, heavy chains piled in front of me. Perhaps I should have wondered if I'd just released another dangerous goddess into the realm, but in my heart, I somehow knew I had done the right thing.

CHAPTER FORTY-FIVE

Finlay was no stranger to disappointing others. From a young age, he'd practically made it his life's ambition to do the bare minimum requested of him, from tutors to political dalliances. Then, he graduated to spending most of his time alternating between training, reading, and partying — all simply means of keeping his mind busy from the vicious thoughts and emotions threatening to suffocate him if he allowed them in for too long.

He'd never truly minded letting anyone down if his lifestyle didn't meet their standards, but Kate's words had cut him to the core.

"All this time, I thought underneath that exterior of drugs and alcohol, you were actually good."

She'd seen him as more, as better, and tried to convince him of the same. But in one fell swoop, she ripped that away, reaffirming that she shared the same feelings as everyone else. And while she hadn't quite hit the mark with her accusations, she wasn't entirely wrong, either.

He hadn't intended to withhold the information from her, and certainly not so he could sleep with her. Finlay had never believed she would return his affections. But once they kissed for the first time at Lachlan's castle, he knew he was ruined for anyone else.

It had never been like that before. It was like she had captured everything that was his the moment she claimed his lips. He would gladly give it all to her. And when they slept together — he realized every time he had slept with another, it had only been his body going through the motions. It had been a distraction; brief entertainment. With her, it consumed his entire being — his body, soul, and mind.

He shook his head. He'd had every intention of telling her about Blaise, but the thought of beating her down when she'd already experienced so much heartbreak kept him at bay.

He'd attempted to tell her once, before they planned on taking things all the way. But every sentence left his head the moment she'd stepped into his room, undressed and taunting him. A hot tide of desire had swept through him; he could think of nothing else except his hands on her exquisite body — rounded, toned, and inviting.

He'd tried to follow after she shoved him, desperate to apologize and explain himself. Yet as he chased after her, he slowly realized it would only anger her more. So, he let her be. He'd waited a whole day and night, allowing her time to cool off. But the battle was quickly approaching, and he'd be damned if he let this continue until then.

So here he stood, summoning the courage to knock on her door. With a deep breath, he rapped his knuckles against it.

"It's open!" she called.

She sounded happy, so obviously, she was not expecting him.

Fuck.

Well, here goes.

He opened the door and slid in. Kate was sprawled across the bed, dressed in dark leather pants and a loose, cream linen shirt. She lay on her belly reading a book, bare feet kicked up. She turned to greet him, and he watched carefully as her amber eyes transitioned from curious to venomous. She shot up from her relaxed position, slamming her book shut.

"You should leave. Now," she ordered.

He slid his hands into his pants and leaned against the wall, assessing her. "Well, we both know I won't do that."

"Then what do you want?" she seethed. "Is this another shitty attempt at seducing me?"

"I wouldn't dream of it," he replied easily, making a show of scanning the room. He removed his hands from his pockets, using them to cover his groin instead. "You have far too many weapons within your reach for me to entertain that idea, and I know exactly where you'd aim first. And I've seen your training lately — you'd definitely succeed."

She gritted her teeth so hard he heard it, but crossed her arms and said nothing else. His chest lifted somewhat; she was enraged, but even in her feistiest moods, she was put off-kilter by a well-timed compliment — especially one regarding her skill with weapons.

Still, those piercing eyes that usually managed to throw him off-balance shuttered now, devoid of the emotion and vulnerability from the other day. His heart twisted, wrung out as someone would squeeze a soaked shirt dry. He only had one chance to explain everything in the hope she might, someday, understand and forgive him. He took a deep breath.

"After today, if you never want to speak to me or see me again, I promise to leave you be. But you have your side of the story, and while I know it's too late now, I owe you mine. I hope you can find the truth of it all somewhere in the middle."

She fixed him with a steely glare, but motioned for him to take a seat.

"Fine," she conceded gruffly. "You have five minutes."

He tossed her a grateful smile and sat. Under her scrutiny, he rested his elbows on his knees and wound his hands together while considering how to start. Finally, he steeled himself, deciding to speak as plainly as possible.

"I did know Blaise was going to die."

He paused, giving Kate a moment to digest the bluntness of his information. Her face contorted with pain, and Finlay was overcome with the desperate urge to get on his knees and beg for forgiveness. But an apology right now would only make her feel worse. Finlay knew that, because he knew her. So, he twisted his hands together again and continued.

"But I made him a promise, bound by blood and magic. I promised not to tell a soul until after he passed. He wanted no one to know, least of all you."

A strangled sound left her throat. "Why not? I could've — I —" Her words trailed off as she answered her own question. She hung her head at the revelation, then, and Finlay confirmed the answer.

"He wanted every last moment with you to feel as normal as possible. If you knew, you would've thrown everything else aside to find a way around it, when he just wanted to spend the time he had left with you."

He tried to make the words as gentle as possible, to soften the blow, but he saw the way they cut at her, opening nearly healed wounds. Hell, he'd come to appreciate and respect Blaise as well. And — there it was, that familiar sting of grief, raking its claws down his conscience. He acknowledged it, pressing into the ache as he continued.

"I could have told you after he passed, and I'll never forgive myself for not doing so. I thought if I could wait until it wasn't so fresh, it would hurt less to hear, but...I still kept it from you. And I've had so many opportunities to tell you since then, but you're right. I was caught up in my own selfish agenda over the past few weeks. And it's devastating to know that while I kept one promise, I broke another one I made him."

Her head whipped up. "What other promise?"

"To keep you safe," Finlay said flatly, pain laced in every word.

Kate's lips parted in surprise. "But...I am safe?" she replied, confusion furrowing her brow.

Finlay shook his head. "Physically, now, maybe. But I've hurt you in other ways. I had no right to try and make you feel things for me when you're still in love with him."

He glanced away, and in a low voice, asked, "Can you ever forgive me?"

He didn't dare look, even as he heard her blow out a long, defeated sigh, bracing himself for her answer. He expected her to cast him out and never look back — she was determined that way. Could he really blame her if she did?

"If we keep going around apologizing and forgiving, pretty soon it won't mean anything," she said with a sigh. "I think it's better if we just learn to be honest with one another."

His eyes met hers in surprise, taking in her firm expression. He nodded eagerly. "Absolutely."

"I was angry with you, sure. And hurt. I still am," she continued. "But I was also angry because...right now, there are so many choices that are not my own. This secret about Blaise was just another choice I had no say in. I'm not even sure I loved him, but maybe if I'd known the truth, I could have explored my feelings. We might have had different conversations. We could have been more honest with one another."

Finlay sagged at her words and hung his head. It pained him, knowing how he'd hurt her. Lacking control in life was something he understood all too well.

"What can I do? To make it better?" he choked out.

She zeroed in on him, her eyes burning the color of melted caramel. "I want the truth. Always. I don't want there to be any secrets between us."

"I'll give you all the truth you want, little angel," Finlay said. "Every truth, right from the beginning."

She tilted her head as he carried on, the words spilling desperately from his mouth. She was right. She deserved the honest truth — every twisted, vulnerable piece of it.

"Truthfully? I don't care if you always carry a piece of Blaise with you. There is enough space in our lives for more than one love, especially in a semi-immortal life like ours. I never wanted to stand in your way because if I were in his position, I'd want to cherish every last second I had with you. I think that's part of the reason he entrusted me with his secret. I really hope you can believe that."

He paused. Kate leaned forward, her attention rapt, and he knew then that she did — she believed him. An invisible weight lifted off his shoulders.

"But he also trusted me because he knew I loved you. I do, and I have, for longer than you both know. The reality is, I fell for you the moment I saw you riding that very first day, arms flung wide and laughing as if you'd take on the world with a smile on your face. And I knew at that moment, you would. Even when you careened into the river, like a fallen little angel, seconds later."

He smiled at the memory and glanced at Kate once more. She had stilled, her eyes growing wide as she absorbed his every word. Encouraged, he continued.

"And I knew that even if I spent the rest of my days never tasting you, never telling you, never even *knowing* you...at least I'd have that memory in my wasted heart to cherish for the rest of my life."

The temperature of the room increased with the intensity of his words, and he prayed Kate heard the truth in them. Her lips had parted slightly, but her expression was unreadable. He wrung his hands nervously, ducking his chin.

"Finlay..." she whispered, but stopped herself.

"It's just...if anything happens in the next few days — you're right. You deserve to know the truth." He shrugged, and the room lapsed into an uneasy silence.

Then, Kate exploded.

"How can you say that...? Why — why would you do this to me?" she demanded, springing from the bed as tears welled in her eyes. Finlay's head jerked in surprise, and he opened his mouth to question it, but she stopped him.

"You can't just say all — all *that* —" she gestured wildly, before running her hands through her hair. "And then talk like I'll *lose* you."

She sucked her bottom lip into her mouth, biting down, and then turned to stalk for the door. Alarmed, Finlay jumped up and barred her exit.

"No, Kate! No more running away. Talk to me." He glanced down at her. A single tear had worked its way loose, streaking its way down her cheek. He lifted his hand automatically to her face, wiping it away with his thumb.

"Damn you, Finlay," she whispered. "And damn all this talk about dying, and Blaise, and...and *love.*" Her voice cracked on the last word, and he raised a brow. A stark realization dawned on him, then.

"Are you trying to run away because you loved him, or because you're afraid you might love me more?"

Finlay's voice was low and hushed, yet held a fierceness he rarely used. She stared up at him, trembling. Her body betrayed every mental barrier she had, even, it seemed, against her own thoughts. She didn't answer, but the brazen honesty of his own words was written clear as day on her face.

"I've never loved anyone before, aside from my parents," she whispered. "I don't know how to do it. I'm so scared this will only lead to me getting hurt — or hurting you."

He gathered her into his arms, and as she collapsed into him, his heart felt like it was melting into liquid ecstasy. He nestled his chin on the top of her head and breathed in her delicious scent for a long moment before speaking.

"I made this promise before, and I'll make it to you now, too. I'll do my best not to hurt you, but please — don't run from me again," he pleaded, his words muffled against her hair. "All the hurt, all the rage — we're in this together."

Kate nodded, snuggling in closer, and whispered so softly he barely heard it.

"Together."

CHAPTER FORTY-SIX

Despite a new quiet settling in my heart about my feelings for Finlay and Blaise, my unease about everything else only heightened as the battle quickly approached.

Two days.

If we took into account the day of travel, this was our last day in the palace.

After my morning workout, I paced through the halls all day, looking to burn off any nervous energy, but no amount of physical training could quell the endless list I was checking in my mind. I tried to avoid talking to anyone, except the necessary cohort. We were under strict orders not to let the queen know Finlay planned to join us, and he'd made himself scarce on the off chance she found a way to keep him from leaving the palace when we did.

We'd also been in a constant battle with Wren to convince her to stay behind. She was adamant that if her brother could join, who lacked the basic training she now had, she should be allowed, too. She pointedly ignored the constant reminders that he would be hanging back in a healer's camp rather than joining the fray.

According to her, Gray had also been sensing my anxiety during my drop-ins at the stable. He had trotted a distinct, embedded path through the snow and dirt of his pasture.

Luckily, things were going as smoothly as could be anticipated with the joining of the armies. Thousands of troops from various lands were encamped from here to the edges of town, and the citizens of Sairas were clearly unnerved. The queen, ever the manipulative diplomat, had spun a story about new training and rekindled camaraderie between lands. It chafed my morals to hear, but even I had to admit, it did no good to scare the citizens when there was nothing they could do.

Though the occasional scuffle ensued between the new arrivals, Larke had humbly but firmly established himself as the general, commanding respect from all. It was a good thing they listened to him, considering they all awaited a show of power from the mysterious descendant of Cú Chulainn — one that hadn't yet appeared.

"That's not the face of someone ready to take out a goddess of death." Darrya's voice rang out behind me, her tone as glib as ever. "Maybe you should take a few warm-up shots on someone. I can get you a Pixie with a smart mouth. I've heard he heals quickly."

Slowing my pace, I glanced over my shoulder with raised eyebrows as she joined my side. Together, we walked toward my room. Darrya had been training nonstop, and now constantly wore a leather arm guard and archery finger tab. Today, she also wore tight black leather pants and tall boots, with a matching leather corset over a flowing white shirt. Her golden blonde hair was braided down one shoulder. While I was used to her royal attire, I had to admit, she pulled off the warrior look better than anyone I knew.

Her bright grin faltered as she took in my tense expression. "Okay, maybe that wasn't my best attempt at cheering someone up. But you should know, I have complete faith in you."

I tried for a smile, brushing over the compliment. "And I have complete faith in you." My mind wandered to the arrow made specifically for her quiver, prepped with an enchantment to nullify Nemain's screams — or so we hoped. "As long as you, you know, shoot straight."

She burst out laughing. "That won't be a problem. The hardest part will be making sure Lachlan doesn't try to protect me. I swear, he treats me like a granddaughter. He's threatened to sneak along with his army more than once."

I groaned and rolled my eyes. Though the duke had surely been a force to be reckoned with in his earlier years, and still had a lively personality, he was an elderly man — physically slower than most. If I could bubble-wrap him and strap him to a chair to keep him here in Sairas, I would. It still wasn't out of the question.

"Everything else seems to be in order, though." I mused. "If her dark Faerie numbers are still similar to what we learned earlier, and if I can get the talismans to activate...we have a real chance."

I wrung my hands nervously, and Darrya caught them in hers, giving them a tight squeeze. "We have more than a real chance here, Katie," she said. "We can do this, and we will."

Her confident words settled over me, calming me somewhat. "You are a godsend, you know that, Darrya?" I said as we reached my room.

"Goddess-sent, actually," she corrected, and as I turned to enter, she smacked my ass. "Now go get some sleep. I'm going to need to see your game face tomorrow."

Laughter bubbled up from my throat, and as I lay in bed for the night, I clung desperately to that feeling of lightness, praying we would have many more days of laughter to come.

I woke to the sound of waves crashing and birds singing, and blinked rapidly to break through my disorientation. Where was I?

I lifted onto my elbows, glancing around. The ground beneath me was hard and cool, but stretches of green grass extended around me, a bizarre contrast to the late winter snow we'd been peppered with recently. Three birds circled above, brightly colored against the milky clouds as their beautiful songs resounded. Rolling over, I pushed myself to my feet and studied my surroundings.

Confusion and apprehension nagged at me as I determined I was entirely alone, atop what looked like a tall cliff. A dark, navy ocean clashed with tawny bluffs below and spread for miles. There were no signs of civilization anywhere to be seen. I padded my way across the surface, breathing in the salty ocean air as I came to a stop just short of the edge. As I peered down, the sound of toppling waves against rock grew louder, slamming against the cliffside stretching hundreds of feet below.

A cold sweat broke out over my palms, and I scuffled backward a few steps. Had Nemain somehow gotten to me in my sleep? If I was here...where were my friends, my family? I spun on my heels and looked around frantically, my eyes catching on a tall, female figure. She stood where I had been laying moments before, the breeze gently blowing her dark hair.

"Katherine," she said pleasantly. Her green eyes twinkled like twin gemstones, and I instantly relaxed, even as I raised my brows in surprise.

"Clíodhna."

Though it had been a matter of days, she looked even more stunning than she had in the dungeon. The marks where the chains held her captive had disappeared entirely, and the slight sunken look of her cheeks had filled out once more, giving her silver-white skin a radiant, ethereal glow. "Where are we?"

She grinned. "We're in a dreamscape, child. A unique power only I possess, and one that's proving particularly useful, given the fact you remain in my prior prison. This is the safest place to meet you."

"So...I'm asleep?" I wondered aloud. She nodded, striding to the cliff's edge. An elegant, layered white dress swished gracefully behind her as she walked barefoot.

"I'm glad I was able to catch you." She stopped, peering down the overhang. I stayed back several steps, the sight of the drop still burned behind my eyes.

"It began to bother me, thinking about Nemain, and how her sisters had died while she was still alive. I was certain I'd heard of her passing."

I nodded. "We read that as well, but after enduring her torture, I can confirm she is very much here," I said, shivering.

Clíodhna flashed me a look that hovered somewhere between anger and sympathy.

"Well, I did some digging, and I have a theory. Do you see those birds above us?" She gestured upwards at the vibrant birds swooping in graceful patterns above us, singing cheerfully.

"Are they yours?" I asked. She nodded with a fond smile, her eyes still locked on them.

"Yes. They are mine, and I am theirs. I'm tied to them in a way only certain celestial beings can be. If I were to die, there would be a way for me to return with their help — a long shot, to be sure, and not one I've deigned to explore. But it is still possible."

"And Nemain has her ravens," I said, "which means she could have died, but with her knowledge of death... she came back through them."

"Exactly," Clíodhna affirmed. "So, I wanted to warn you. If you kill her now, there is still a possibility she may return through that piece of her, unless you eliminate it as well."

I nodded. That was something I very much feared. "But she doesn't just have three birds. She has hundreds." My tone was rife with hopelessness, but the goddess simply tsked.

"This is where I hope to help you. Yes, she harnesses the spirits of ravens, the same way I harness the songs of my birds. But I happen to know only one raven is with her consistently — a unique one, large and piebald in color."

The description tugged at a distant memory. Had I seen this bird before? Yes — yes, the night Nemain had first revealed herself to us. The large, piebald raven had come soaring from the skies to perch upon her hand. Soon after, it became nothing more than a shadow, aiding her lethal magic like it was a part of *her*.

My heart quickened at the enormity of this revelation. We had a way to rid Nemain of her banshee screams, and now, a firm assurance we could rid every piece of her, ensuring she would truly be gone for good. Despite all odds, this could be our fighting chance. I let out a disbelieving laugh.

"Clíodhna, you have no idea how much this helps. Thank you."

She sniffed. "It's hardly anything. I wish I had more to repay you for what you did."

"I just did what was right," I replied, baffled, but she turned from the cliff with a gentle shake of her head.

"You're doing far more than that. You're one of the good ones, Katherine. I will be praying for you to win."

With that, the landscape became hazy, and I blinked, confused at my clouding vision.

"Wait — are we leaving the dreamscape?"

"Yes, child," she answered. "It's time for you to go back to your normal sleep. Rest assured, you will remember this conversation, and I will find you if I learn anything more that can help."

I nodded in understanding. "Thank you," I repeated, causing her to shake her head emphatically, though her outline was becoming blurry and distant.

"Do not thank me. Kill the piebald raven. Kill her, and this will be ended once and for all."

CHAPTER FORTY-SEVEN

Gray's warm, steadfast power underneath me gave me confidence; we stood in the dim light of dawn, facing the army, fully gathered and ready to face Nemain. I held my head high, surveying the masses of bodies surrounding us.

The troops that stood with us were a beautiful, intimidating testament to the queen's power as the ultimate high ruler. Multiple lands had answered Larke's call on her behalf — many I hadn't even heard of. The distinct atmosphere of their lands was clear, etched in their individualities.

Their skin tones varied like a stunning canvas, various shades blending as the lines of soldiers stretched beyond, hair colors ranging from onyx black to cornflower white, and everything in between. Some faces were pale and wind-beaten, clearly used to the cold, while others were tanned from the constant sun, their faces pinched at the unexpected chill in the air.

Despite most of the soldiers being Daoine Sídhe, almost every troop had multiple Aes Sídhe in their ranks. I felt the touch of their magic, fueling my own with a tense excitement now spreading like wildfire. Every soldier wore some variation of fighting leathers and chainmail, adorned with the colors of their land underneath. The small pops of color came in nearly all shades of the rainbow — aside from mauve. That dark purple was reserved for the queen's royal army behind us, of which I was now an honorary member.

My father sat astride a large bay mare on my right, Darrya on a black stallion to my left. Larke was positioned in front of us on a large chestnut horse nearly the size of Gray. He, like the rest, wore the dark mahogany fighting leathers with a deep violet tunic peeking out from underneath. His sword was belted at his side, the scabbard boasting the golden royal seal to reaffirm his status as commander-in-chief.

Larke pulled a glove off, and the ring he wore glinted in the bright sun. The ring was enchanted, crafted alongside Darrya's brand-new arrows. It was made to project his voice. He pressed the ring to his throat, his voice now booming loud and clear, laced with authority.

"Fellow soldiers! While I am proud and humbled to see you all here today, I do not relish seeing us use our power and skill for such terrible things. But the threat to our peace demands it. As you know, the goddess of death, Nemain, is alive. She has assembled a terrible force, with every intention of crumbling what we have worked so hard to achieve."

My lips pressed into a thin line at the honesty of his words; a rumble of unease emanated from the masses, echoing my own feelings. Larke continued.

"Our peace will remain. Of that, I have every faith. But it may come at a high price, one we've never paid before. I do not want to ask this of you, but injustice is knocking on our very door, and we must answer with our own convictions."

He paused, and I gazed out at the soldiers beyond, transfixed by his words. I knew how capable Larke was, but I had never heard him speak like this. It was extremely effective, and I watched as resolution solidified in the eyes of every soldier. Where fear and apprehension had been a moment before, now, a determined bloodthirst shone.

"As we send our souls to battle, may light stay near, and darkness afar. May we have the power to persevere and not be met by exhaustion. May our swords stay sharp, and our arms strong enough to wield them. May fear be banished, and justice brought. And may the gods protect us all."

He took a deep breath, then, and settled back in his saddle. The war blessing had now been delivered. I felt the ache of my new Shield Knot as it burned pleasantly in the crook of my elbow. The thought of its additional safety both soothed and invigorated me as I thought back to my first mark with Blaise. This battle was as much for him as for me, for my family — for everyone.

After a heartbeat, every soldier brandished their sword, lifting them to the skies in eerie unison. Larke answered in turn, unsheathing his own and raising it high. His head turned, nodding to someone in the distance. A horn sounded, and the echo of it rang in my ears long after it quieted. Larke turned his horse, starting a chain of movement. We were off, marching to meet Nemain and the inevitable bloodshed that would follow.

"Where are the soldiers from Brytham?" I asked as we rode, leaning over to whisper to Darrya.

We had been traveling eastbound for the last two hours, the sun now high in the sky. It didn't quite get rid of the chill hanging in the air, but it provided ample light to survey our surroundings. The forested areas had given way to rolling plains and lakes, giving us intermittent breaks to water the horses and stretch our legs. While I'd surveyed the colors of the soldiers on our last break, I remembered the distinct orange and blue of Brytham, but I couldn't place them in the sea of colors marching with us now.

"We're not sure," Darrya replied, her tone equally hushed. "They arrived with Lachlan and his troops from Daersill days ago. Those soldiers are here." She motioned to the soldiers boasting shades of crimson and silver. "But the ones from Brytham were nowhere to be found this morning."

I frowned as unease settled low in my stomach. "Thaddeus and Aerrin are up to something."

Darrya nodded, her expression equally dark. "Unfortunately, I agree. But we can't afford to wait around and hunt them down. Speaking of lost soldiers — can we still count on the Valkyries?"

I nodded. "They're going to fly in to join us tomorrow morning. They can travel much faster than our soldiers on foot."

Darrya grinned. "That's so badass. My air magic has nothing on wings. I wish I had some."

I breathed a faint laugh in agreement, but before I could reply, the sound of trotting pulled my attention away. Finlay appeared from within the ranks of Muiranvian soldiers, making his way through the troops on a large bay stallion.

We had all met up briefly before leaving so I could relay the information I'd learned about the piebald raven. But Finlay hung back with Cas and the other healers as we embarked, waiting to join us up front until we had put several miles between the army and the palace.

He grinned as he caught sight of Darrya and me, guiding his horse to us. I watched as recognition flitted across the soldiers' faces. They instantly scrambled to bow, either on foot or upon their horses.

I raised a brow at the display of respect, and Finlay caught the look, winking as he pulled his horse back into a walk alongside us. He made a show of sighing dramatically. "I've spent decades trying to convince them it was unnecessary. Apparently, it hasn't stuck."

"I see that," I replied drily, and Darrya rolled her eyes at him.

"If only they knew who their real leader should be," she added softly, tossing a sly look my way. I grimaced and put a hand on my full-length scabbard, ensuring the sword remained hidden, the wooden guard muting its soft glow.

The murmurings had spread throughout the army — curious gossip as they tried to figure out who the soldier was that supposedly harnessed the power of the talismans. Most had decided it must be my father, a new face in their ranks; they openly stared his way, waiting for a sign.

He pointedly ignored them, giving nothing away as he rode. A map was sprawled open across his horse's neck. I smiled as I watched him now, noting the color and animation in his face. In the weeks we'd spent together following my mom's death, we'd relied heavily on one another to get through the pain. But I was happy now for him to be my scapegoat.

Though I'd felt confident when we set out, as the hours passed, the sun that had been high above the clouds came back down, and that small voice started in my head again, whispering doubts in my ears.

The sword won't activate for you. You'll fail. You're leading all these people to their deaths.

"Hey," Finlay said, snapping me out of my thoughts. "You okay?"

I glanced over at him. He wore a long velvet coat over his leathers, a deep purple with lavish golden embroidery along the edges. I could see the distaste written across his face as he fiddled with the buttons. He hated the attention it brought him, but he knew it boosted the army's morale to see the future king in all his glory, joining them in this fight.

"Yes. As much as can be expected," I replied, a half-hearted smile tugging at the corner of my mouth. "I just..." I thought back to our discussion on honesty, and the smile faltered as I sighed. "I'm just not sure I can do it. I shouldn't be the one to lead them. All their faith in me feels misplaced. I should be down there, just another soldier blending in and following Larke."

Finlay shook his head. "No, little angel. You were not made to blend in. You were made to lead."

I opened my mouth to disagree, but he cut me off. "Don't get me wrong, I agree with sitting back and letting Larke do his thing here. You see Larke's strengths, and you see Darrya's, and mine, and Cas's — we're all in the best position to win this war because of it. You're the kind of leader who will listen to others and allow them the freedom to excel in their own ways. You're everything that she is not."

He didn't have to say anything more for me to know he was referring to the queen.

I gave him a grateful look, and we shifted atop our horses at the sound of hoof steps announcing my father's approach. Kipp padded alongside in his wolf form. My dad waved the map at us, curled in one hand.

"We're stopping to make camp here," he called out, and we nodded, pulling up short. We decided to take a longer, more winding route to where Nemain and her army awaited. At our current pace, we would arrive tomorrow — the day Ensley had prophesized. A surprise attack was nearly impossible, given her avian spies, but it seemed even more ludicrous to charge head-on against her.

Finlay and I decided to share a tent, and I wondered briefly where Kipp was planning to sleep as Cas set one up for himself and Darrya. Either he'd told Cas how he felt, or he'd decided to keep it to himself for the time being. Once this was over, I'd have to collaborate with Darrya to see if it warranted us adding a little fuel to the flame.

Cas gave me a sly wink. "Better keep it down tonight, kiddos. As much as I'm a firm believer in everyone being properly pleasured, D and I need our beauty sleep tonight."

Darrya cackled, giving his shoulder a whack, while Finlay ran a hand over his face. I snorted, too, though we all knew nobody's sleep would be restful at all.

True enough, as we settled in for the night, and I listened to the gradual slowing of Finlay's breathing, my mind was wide awake. I traced my fingers gently across the hand he'd draped over my hip, relishing the warmth he emanated. I squeezed my eyes shut, trying to draw every ounce of peace from the moment in the hope that after tomorrow, I would be able to enjoy nights like this again.

Somehow, it allowed me to fall into a fitful sleep, because when I awoke, it was to someone vigorously shaking my shoulders.

"Katie! Katie!"

My eyes flew open. My father kneeled above me, his hands gripping my shoulders while the whites of his eyes shone with panic. Finlay was rolling up groggily at our side, blinking the sleep away.

"Wha — what? Dad? What's happening?" Panic rushed through my veins, waking me completely. I shifted up to my elbows as he handed me my sword, still sheathed in its scabbard. My eyes adjusted rapidly to the dark. It was still nighttime, but I made out the grim expression on his face.

"They found us. Nemain is here. The battle has begun."

Chapter Forty-Eight

The cold darkness that hung over the night disoriented me, and I was forced to rely on my other senses as I scrambled to tug on my fighting boots and leathers. I glanced up, catching my father's eye once more.

"How far out are they?" I asked.

"Our scouts spotted them about two miles out. Probably a mile now. We have to hurry."

I nodded, turning to Finlay.

"Go make sure Darrya's awake. I'm not sure if she can shoot properly in the dark, but I need her by my side as we work to get to Nemain, regardless."

He nodded and slipped away. I buckled the belt that held my sword hastily, noting the soft glow attempting to force its way through my scabbard like a night light. I cursed. Unsheathing it in the dark would draw attention to me, labeling me as the clear target. I strapped a second sword to my other side, doubling my belts.

As I strapped my dagger to my leg, Finlay flipped the opening of the tent aside, bringing Darrya with him. She must have been awake already; she was donned in her full gear, hair braided with her bow and quiver slung across her back.

"Are you all ready?" my dad asked, his voice low. We nodded, following him to retrieve the horses.

Kipp and Cas both waited outside the tent. Kipp was already in his wolf form, a dark shadow against the night, and Cas was fully dressed, concern etched across his face. He grabbed each of our hands as we passed, sending a warm glow of healing power into our veins as he held them, just enough to ensure we were in perfect fighting shape. I was beyond grateful we'd been able to convince Wren to stay behind, and though Cas was hanging back from the action, a pang of worry still shot through me as I held his hand. I gave his hand a soft squeeze.

"Stay safe, Cas," I murmured. He withdrew his hand from mine, only to press it to my cheek, smiling.

"Likewise, Katie-cat," he answered.

The sun had begun to rise, a soft glow stretching out atop the snow-covered land and lighting the sky a dusky blue. The carmine glow it cast upon the still, white ground would have been beautiful if not for the impending battle. Now, the reddish hue bathing the snow only reminded me of the blood soon to be shed here. My heart leapt painfully to my throat.

I shook it off as we approached the makeshift paddock; the curious nickers eased me slightly. Gray was already pacing when I caught sight of him, his stature and demeanor worrying the other horses, who maintained a wary distance.

"Someone's amped," Darrya said with a slight shake to her tone — the only indication she felt the same tension I did.

I choked out a feeble laugh.

"That makes one of us," I replied, and went to catch him. He tossed his head at first, picking up on my emotions, but allowed me to bridle him. I exhaled a small sigh of relief, taking it as a good omen. If things were going to end badly, I had hope that he'd warn me, like he had my great-grandfather before me.

My dad guided us to a high, tree-lined embankment, indicating it would be a good vantage point; we could remain relatively hidden as we waited and scoped for Nemain. My jaw dropped, however, once I realized we wouldn't be joining the rest of the troops.

"You can't be serious," I said, miffed. Finlay and Darrya remained silent as we rode, even as I continued pressing the issue. Kipp padded along silently as well, though his tail hung low. For several minutes, my dad pointedly ignored my complaints, before whirling around in his saddle to fix me with a glare.

"Your job is *not* to get in the middle of the battle. Your job is to go directly to Nemain, and her alone. It does no one any good if you die before you're even able to use your sword on her."

His words were harsh, but despite the severe tone, exhaustion and concern lived in the lines of his face. It betrayed the fact that he likely had not slept at all last night, worrying instead about this very moment. The sight made me clamp my lips shut. I scowled my disapproval, but said no more on the matter.

When we reached the top of the embankment, I was forced to admit we had an excellent bird's-eye view of the battleground. Our troops had almost all gathered, stretching out past the hill we stood upon. They adjusted their positions as Larke used his knowledge, dictating where they went based on their strengths and weaknesses. Darrya's hand shot out to clasp mine as she noticed him.

"He's right at the front," she said, fear filling her voice. I bit my lip, feeling the same, but squeezed her hand in reassurance.

"He's a true general. He doesn't expect his troops to be cowards, and he won't be, either," I responded. She nodded unhappily, and with that, the five of us fell into an uneasy silence while we waited.

It wasn't long before the dark Faeries arrived.

We heard them before we saw them, a cacophony of hoofbeats, footsteps, claws, and wings, punctuated with bloodthirsty yowls. I tensed, anticipating a solid line of creatures to come charging through the snow, but let out a disbelieving laugh when the first of them appeared. Just as Blaise had once said, the dark Fae were not, by nature, creatures who cooperated.

They did not form an impenetrable line; rather, they scrambled sporadically toward us from all angles, approaching alone or in pairs. Whether it was intentional or not, the chaos startled our troops, and the lack of sleep brought on by their ambush only added to it.

A ripple of confusion passed through the army, and they shifted and glanced at one another in bewilderment. Larke noticed and boomed orders at them, regaining their attention just as the first of the dark Fae descended on them.

I leaned over Gray's back, watching helplessly as the creatures made impact with the first of our army lines. My mind flicked back to a conversation I'd had once with Blaise.

I'd asked him once in passing why there were no guns in this realm. He'd simply fixed me with a bleak look as he answered, twirling a dagger in his hand.

"We watched as humans endured so many wars, causing so much unnecessary carnage. It's one of few things that seemed to truly take away their empathy — the thing that usually makes humans so unique. It's wrong to be able to take so many lives, so quickly, sometimes without even facing the enemy. It was one of the things that scared the leaders of the lands enough to band together, to cast a strong enough enchantment to render them useless in the Faerie realm."

I'd turned over his words in my head, confused. "But you still allow knives, swords, spears, bows — all of those?"

Blaise chuckled darkly at that. "Trust me, sunshine. Enough damage can still be done with those. If we must kill, we should have to think about it — question it for more than a split second. We should have to look directly into the eyes of our enemy to do it."

It was a distinctly Faerie-like answer, and yet, I agreed. Even though I saw the evil coursing through the dark Faeries as they delighted in taking lives and stealing magic...they still screamed like us, fought like us, and died like us. It wasn't easy to kill them, and it shouldn't be. To kill so easily would make us no better than Nemain.

And Blaise had been right on another front — plenty of damage could still be done with other weapons. My mouth went dry with shock as the soldiers clashed with a growing number of dark Faeries.

Ours were specially trained to dispatch the dark Fae, and for the most part, they cut through them like a knife through butter.

Bodies began falling, mostly the misshapen forms of the dark Fae. A rainbow of colors flashed as our soldiers began clambering over the fallen creatures to fight more. But despite the beasts' disorganization, several fearsome creatures held their own, including a handful of Sluagh circling above. The sight of them made my heart clench.

Sheer numbers worked against us. Nemain had convinced a handful of our kind to fight on her side, interspersed throughout her masses. The sound of metal colliding with metal reached us alongside a symphony of screams. Blood splattered the snow in a canvas of red and black, and as the body counts grew, it pooled together, making it hard to know if there was more black blood, or if it just overpowered the red. I'd seen us fight a small number of them before, but this...all those bodies gathering. How many of ours would die before this was over?

My heart started beating irregularly, and I sucked in rapid breaths, but it still felt like I was being deprived of oxygen. I hunched over for a moment, closing my eyes. I willed myself to breathe in slowly through my nose before the others noticed.

Focus. Calm down. It's happening, whether you like it or not. Now, it's important you stick to your part of the plan.

When my eyes reopened, the blood-splattered snow was melting, and I realized elemental magic was now in play on both sides. The strange fire I'd seen when the dark Faeries invaded the palace now clashed with our fire elementals, and left scorched earth in their wake. Sporadic mounds of earth sprang up and sent bodies flying;

arrows flew with blinding speed, propelled by air magic. They struck true, causing Faeries to collapse instantly.

Larke was still holding steady in the throes of the action, and I watched with morbid fascination as he fought: ducking, spinning, and striking with his sword without so much as a look in the direction it went, as though he simply sensed who was placed where. Watching him caused my brain to tug at memories of Blaise. He hadn't relished the feel of the fight, not like Larke, but he'd had the same battle sense.

I gave a sidelong glance to Finlay, whose palms twitched, sparks dancing across them as he watched the gruesome display below us. His focus was intense, but he held firm — not to protect his own royal bloodline, I knew, but to stay and protect me. My heart softened as I watched him, but he suddenly straightened in his saddle and paled.

"What?" I asked.

He didn't look at me as he answered, eyes locked on the battle below. "It's Wren."

"No," I gasped.

He pointed, and I spun to follow the direction of his finger.

Part of me hoped he was mistaken, but as I squinted, I found her amidst the ducking and weaving bodies. She wore the purple of our troops, but her slender body was noticeably thinner and shorter than many others. Her ebony hair whipped as she twirled, using her quickness to her advantage as she fought.

Kipp snarled, taking a large leap toward the battleground before halting and swiveling to face us. Emotions warred in his lupine eyes, but I nodded.

"Go," I said firmly. "She needs you."

He gave a slow blink of understanding and disappeared with a flash. I turned back to watch the battle, eyes locked on Wren. She alternated between using a small sword and twisting her palm, crafting vines that snuck out to ensnare weapons or the feet of dark Fae.

To her credit, she was holding her own, but mostly due to her position within the ranks. She was not a natural fighter and had barely begun her training. My throat constricted as more dark Faeries infiltrated the lines, and she slowly became overwhelmed.

I was about to suggest Finlay try to reach her with his flames — to literally trap her in a circle of fire until Kipp arrived — when the screaming began.

I doubled over instantly, my sight blurring with tears of agony. When I was finally able to glance up again, about a quarter of our army was doubled over, too.

"Gods, that never gets any better," Darrya groaned from my side, gritting her teeth. Finally, she managed to straighten and notched an arrow with a wince. "Where is that nasty bitch?"

I blinked the tears away, scanning the area for Nemain. As I looked, my eyes dragged back to where Wren had been; she was struggling against the agony of Nemain's wails, barely able to lift her sword. A dark brown blur moved in the distance, skirting through the entangled soldiers, making a beeline for her.

My heart lifted as I anticipated Kipp reaching her and dragging her back to her brother.

But as I held my breath, willing her to fight for just a minute more, I watched an arrow strike her chest.

CHAPTER FORTY-NINE

Even through Nemain's screeching, Kipp's enraged roar reached my ears. I watched Wren's face go blank, her lips forming a silent "oh" as though surprised. She collapsed, falling to one knee, and then the other.

My heart stumbled, and I followed the trajectory of the arrow back to its archer. He was a creature with wings almost identical to Cas's, aside from the color — a mottled mixture of black and purple, dull whereas Cas's shimmered with light. He turned slightly toward us, still loosing arrows, but as my eyes zeroed in on him, an arrow pierced his chest directly where his heart would be. Thrown back, he landed on his wings and remained there, unmoving.

My eyes slid to Darrya, who lowered her own bow, face grim. She met my gaze for a moment, fury I hadn't seen before simmering just under the surface. *Good.* I knew she saw it in my expression, too, as I nodded, turning to locate Wren once more.

I exhaled with relief to see Kipp had reached her, helping her onto his back. She moved slowly, but still, she was *moving,* clutching his fur as they took off. I prayed desperately they would reach Cas in time.

Dark shapes appeared in the sky, flashing across the slowly rising sun. I peered up in time to see the Valkyries arrive. There were at least forty of them, stunningly beautiful and equally lethal. Their striped wings were magnificent, large enough to completely block out the sun as they descended.

The circling shapes of Sluagh faltered as they took stock, fleeing across the skies at their arrival. The Valkyries didn't bother to slow as they landed, targeting the dark Fae preying on our soldiers with elemental magic, crippled by Nemain's cries.

A shudder rippled through the dark Fae as more decided to retreat, despite outnumbering our own forces. The Valkyries didn't need numbers, and as they began to fight, that was more than clear.

"Kate," my father said. I looked at him, and he jerked his head across the field. "There."

I sat up on Gray's back, as best as I could with the ache carving away at my soul, and followed his line of sight — straight to Nemain. She stood at the opposite end of the battlefield, the entirety of her army before her. A soldier, presumably her healer, stood by her side. She donned a black dress with equally dark leather pants, stark against her pale skin. She was a sizable distance away, but I could see she had smeared black war paint across her face, turning her already onyx eyes into an endless, ominous pit.

My eyes lifted to the skies in search of her piebald raven, but there was no sign of it. Perhaps she kept it restrained within her magic for now.

"Can you reach her from here, D?" Finlay asked, his voice strained as he struggled against Nemain's power. Darrya tilted her head for a long moment, deliberating, then shook it.

"Without my air magic, I need to get closer," she decided.

Finlay exchanged a look with me. I met his eyes, and he knew my decision before I even voiced it.

"Finlay, you should cover Darrya while she gets closer. My dad and I will go down on the field to get as near as possible to strike. That'll also keep her focus on us, instead of anticipating you."

My dad nodded slowly. "It's a good idea," he said, turning his horse. Darrya and Finlay bobbed their heads in agreement.

Before they took off, Finlay leaned over, clutching the back of my neck to drag me into a frantic kiss.

"Be safe, little angel," he rasped.

"I will," I promised, and leaned back, looking at Darrya. "And Darrya? Shoot straight."

She laughed, giving me a mocking salute, reminding me again that she and Finlay were related. I drank in the two of them for a long moment before turning to join my father amid the battle.

I wiped at my nose, stuffed with blood, not bothering to check if it was black from my enemies or red from my own. My cheeks flared as I heaved deep breaths, thanking the gods for how much I'd been training.

Pain was no stranger to me; in fact, it was a close acquaintance. We had walked hand in hand for the past several weeks. My soul had felt empty, and I'd physically beat myself into the dirt to escape it time and again. The ache raging inside me as Nemain drained my magic was not so different, and I used it to my advantage, giving over to muscle memory as I parried and struck with my regular sword, grinding my teeth to dust as I tried to ignore her wails.

I'd long since dismounted from Gray, unused to fighting from his massive height, but he held his own, stalwart at our sides. Mounted soldiers on Nemain's side were promptly unseated as their steeds bucked and ran, escaping his glowing stare. The soldiers on foot foolish enough to get within his reach were met with his bone-shattering hooves, or a fatal bite as his neck snaked out to ensnare their flesh in his teeth. Those who recognized him fled, witnessing the truth of his prowess.

My father remained on his mare, attempting to carve a way through the colliding bodies toward Nemain. I did my best to follow suit from the ground.

I braced, using the flat edge of my blade to halt the slash of a sword overhead. My arms complained as I used both hands, and the dark Faerie pressed further. It sneered, its eye sockets hollow and teeth carved to points. They gleamed with crimson blood, and I shivered as I realized what the creature was. An Abhartach — a vampiric dark Faerie known for feasting on the blood of the living. It was likely overjoyed to be a part of such slaughter.

With an angry grunt, I braced back on one leg and kicked out with the other, landing it squarely against the Abhartach's chest. It stumbled back in surprise, but I allowed no time for recovery. My blade plunged straight through its throat. Red and black blood gurgled back up out of its mouth as it fell to its knees.

I put a foot back on its shoulder, clutching the hilt of the sword to tug it back out, but was knocked off my feet before I could remove it. Two Faeries parried with one another, leaping back and forth as they searched for an opening.

The dark Faerie was much smaller than the royal soldier, its haggard skin boasting a sickly greenish hue, and its bare hands and feet formed grisly talons. Fresh red blood dripped from the cap it wore, making me gag. *A Redcap.* Despite its stature, it was quick, and as the royal soldier pivoted, it anticipated the move and used its short pike to cut straight into the soldier's chest. The soldier collapsed, blood spurting from his wound. The dark Faerie bent over, and I watched in horror as it removed the cap to dip it in the wound. It turned to me, then, red eyes gleaming.

I scrambled to my feet, backing up as my fingers searched for the hilt of the Whisperer, still safely tucked into my other scabbard.

The Redcap grinned and advanced, and my heart thrummed its way wildly up my throat, threatening to exit my body.

Just then, an alleviating silence settled over the battleground, and several crippled soldiers shot up straight. Groans of relief were heard all over the field, and I sighed as I realized what had happened. *Darrya.* I hadn't doubted her for a second, and now, I was open to take my shot.

The Redcap paused, sensing the shifting tide, and I took full advantage of the hesitation. I thought only of Larke's training as I summoned every available scrap of my water magic. The Redcap's eyes watered as it doubled over, choking and coughing up water.

I didn't relent, pressing harder as more magic slowly returned to me. I heard his drowning gags even as I turned, not bothering to look back as I located my father.

He met my eyes as I found him, and we exchanged a long look. He gave a firm nod.

"Let's get you to Nemain."

Chapter Fifty

With our magic and Gray at our side, it took only a matter of minutes to cut through the remaining masses. We didn't have to worry about any surprise attacks — Gray's fearsome hooves and teeth prevented that from even being an option.

As our magic returned to us, slowly seeping back into our souls, my father and I summoned as much earth magic as possible, willing the ground to wrap around the feet of any dark Fae that came close.

It wasn't with the intent to kill; rather, it rendered them immobile and allowed the soldiers coming behind us to finish them off. I had a far more important target, and she locked eyes with me, waiting with aggravating calm as I approached. Her throat bore no mark from the arrow that had rendered her cries powerless, but another arrow was lodged in the chest of the healer, now on the ground beside her. It looked like his last act had been healing Nemain before Darrya was able to target him.

Clashing and screaming raged around us, but it slowly faded from my mind against the adrenaline of this moment. My father hung back with a grim nod, turning to fend off any dark Fae that dared turn back to protect their goddess of death.

I stopped a few feet from Nemain, unsheathing the Whisperer as I awaited her first move.

She unsheathed a sword of her own and raised her palm, releasing dark plumes of shadow into the air. I tensed as the shadow transformed into a cloud of ravens, squawking frantically as they circled above her. My eyes found the largest of them, and there it was — the piebald — soaring a careful distance away. My gaze snapped back to Nemain, however, as she cleared her throat.

When she spoke, her voice was scratchy, and dark satisfaction coursed through me.

"I'm impressed you've made it this far," she taunted, "but I am disappointed to see nothing has happened with that sword." A pointed look at the Whisperer told me she knew all the talismans were contained within the blade.

She cocked her head, twirling the tip of her own sword in the ground thoughtfully. "Perhaps it was for the best that I let you go all those months ago. You've proven to be nothing but useless."

I bared my teeth at her as I raised the sword. "You'll be the one feeling useless when you're lying on the ground, dying and begging to join your sisters."

She snarled at the mention of them, and with a twitch of her fingers, her ravens dove to attack. I braced, summoning my air magic into a shield, but several ravens burst into flames before they could reach me. A strangled cry came from Nemain — nowhere near her banshee levels, but enough to make her horror apparent.

"Come on, Nemain. At least let it be a fair fight," a voice drawled. Finlay appeared, stepping out from the trees that lined the field. He must have taken a shortcut from the other side of the embankment.

Flames licked across his body in a show of power. Though his stance was lazy, I saw the emotion roiling in his eyes like the blaze that lit his body. I didn't see Darrya, but I assumed she remained at a high vantage point with an arrow notched and ready.

Nemain pursed her thin lips, considering whether it was worth the fight. Suddenly, she raised her sword. Her remaining ravens dissolved into her shadow magic, rising into a column of black tendrils that surrounded us.

I heard Finlay curse loudly, unable to decipher between Nemain and myself now that we were encircled in her darkness. It was reminiscent of her battle with Blaise, and for a moment, I saw red.

"All right, a fair fight," she hissed. "But this fight is between you and me, child. Let's end this."

"I couldn't agree more." I lunged, closing the gap between us as our swords met.

I threw everything I had into the fight. The rapid movements allowed no time to think, let alone leverage magic into the fight — but neither could Nemain, as she struggled to maintain her shadow blockade while fighting with her blade.

Our strikes and slashes grew sloppy as we went, and I overshot, taking a precious moment to right myself. Nemain took advantage, her blade catching my side and cutting through my fighting leathers.

I gasped, but used the burst of adrenaline that came with the pain to spin around completely, catching the opposite side she blocked on and slicing through her arm. She shrieked and stumbled back, but her recovery was quick, and we began our deadly dance once more.

Our blades clashed, and in a rash decision, I dropped one hand and went in for a punch, which she caught with a free palm. I strained against her grip for a moment before an idea flickered through my head, tucked in a long-ago memory of my first lessons with Blaise. I bucked my head forward and slammed my forehead into her nose with a satisfying crunch.

She cried out and dropped my hands, her own moving to clutch her face. I grinned as I blinked the pain away, gathering my sword in both hands and throwing all my weight behind a final blow.

Somehow, Nemain's hands moved with blinding speed, catching my strike with an earth-shattering ring of metal against her own blade.

I panted as we both strained against each other, neither giving way. I could hear my teeth screeching against each other as I gritted them, and my arms throbbed. Sweat blurred my vision, but I would not blink, instead glaring into the sneering face of Nemain, whose teeth were bared in a similar strain. My feet, back, core, and shoulders all cried out in agony, threatening to succumb to exhaustion.

Long seconds passed, and the trembling worsened. I let out a sharp gasp, and Nemain's sneer turned to a sickening smile. She was winning, she knew she was winning—

I couldn't let her win—

But she *was* winning—

I couldn't let their deaths be for nothing, all these soldiers—

Blaise—

My mother—

Wren—

I cried out as their images flashed through my mind, my body burning with despair and rage. Looking into her eyes, I saw the reflection of my own gaze, burning with hatred. Before I comprehended what was really happening, I saw I was *actually burning*.

My eyes shone with a golden glow, and the Whisperer burned as well, a white light dancing across it. Nemain's eyes peeled from mine to watch the white light, and a wary confusion flickered in them. In a flash of realization, I pushed that white-hot rage toward Nemain's sword, before she could fully grasp what I'd discovered. With a hiss, she was forced to drop it, and in the same breath, I struck.

White lightning cracked down on the edge of the Whisperer as I slammed it into her chest. It found deep purchase, and I was propelled backward by the intensity of the strike, completely engulfed in light. Somewhere in the distance, I heard Finlay yell my name.

I landed with a tuck and roll, scrambling to my feet before the light cleared. I squinted, desperately trying to locate Nemain. As the light slowly faded, I held my breath and braced for the worst.

When it cleared, the shadows cleared with it, and there she lay: the fearsome goddess of death. Slain.

The Whisperer remained lodged in her chest, no longer glowing, and her eyes were frozen open, hauntingly pale against the black war paint darkening her lids and cheekbones.

Footsteps approached rapidly while I stared. I heard Finlay swear as he came to a stop beside me. His eyes dragged from the scene in front of us to me, running up and down my body, checking for any signs of injury. I saw my father appear from the corner of my eye, lithely moving over Nemain's body for inspection.

"The heat you were able to summon — the magic that hadn't emerged—" Finlay began, shaking his head in disbelief.

"It wasn't fire magic," I murmured. "It was...light. Lightning."

My dad looked up, emotion shimmering in his eyes. "You did it," he breathed. "She's dead."

I collapsed.

Both Finlay and my father rushed to my side, picking me up. The battle still raged on behind us, slow to disperse despite their leader perishing. It was no matter to these two men in my life; they moved me behind a rock and remained on either side of me, allowing me space to gasp and sob. Wet tears streaked my cheeks as I processed the enormity of what had happened.

I closed my eyes and willed myself to breathe through my nose, forcing my breaths to slow and calm. Finlay's warm hand found its way into mine, while my dad placed a protective arm around my shoulder. My heart squeezed and slowed, even as the remaining ravens circled above, unsure what to do without their master. My father glanced up as they cawed, his brow furrowing.

"As long as the raven lives, her spirit can still come back," he murmured. I nodded, and he pulled me against him protectively.

"Let's finish this off once and for all, kiddo."

CHAPTER FIFTY-ONE

Plenty of ravens gathered around Nemain's body, but none of them bore the distinct piebald pattern Kate had mentioned. While we scanned the skies, a soft thump announced Darrya's arrival as she jumped down from a tree onto the battlefield. She ran up to us, throwing her bow across her back.

"Kate! You did it!" she exclaimed, wrapping her in an embrace. Finlay watched as Kate winced, pulling back to clutch at her side. When she drew her hand back, it was wet with blood. He stepped forward.

"You're hurt," he said in alarm, but she waved him off.

"I'll be fine," she replied, and turned to smile at Darrya. "I couldn't have done it without you, D."

Finlay's eyes remained locked on Kate, and narrowed as he took in the weakness of her smile and the pallor of her skin. The skies roiled with storm clouds, and Darrya looked up.

"A thunderstorm in the middle of winter?" she asked, bewildered.

Kate gave a guilty shrug. "Yeah, uh...I think that's maybe my fault."

"Look, there will be plenty of time to explain later, but right now, we need to find the piebald raven," Pat cut in, his voice tense. He had removed the sword of Nuada from Nemain's dead body, and eyed her corpse suspiciously, as though he expected her to spring back up at any moment.

"Is it that one?" Darrya pointed to the skies, ever the markswoman. Everyone followed the direction of her finger to an abnormally large raven tucked in the swarm of black, tufts of white splattered across its chest.

"Yes!" Kate exclaimed. She bit her lip, focusing as she summoned her new magic. Static filled the air, and a bolt of lightning shot across the sky. The ravens scattered, feathers flying as they took off in a panic. Her new magic was untested, though, and her aim was off.

A clap of thunder followed the electric charge, and Kate cursed as the piebald raven twisted in alarm, swooping in a circle before flying off. "We have to follow it," she said, and whistled.

Gray came running, but as she tried to mount him, she stumbled back. Blood gushed from her side with renewed vigor. Her father was at her side in an instant, and she slumped in his arms.

"You can't ride like this," he spoke quietly.

She shook her head, struggling against him. "But he's the only one fast enough to keep up with the raven," she demanded weakly.

"We'll ride him," Finlay said, and Kate looked up in surprise. "Darrya and I can do it. We'll get the raven. You just get to Cas."

Kate paused for only a moment before nodding, an alarming indication of how hurt she must be. It took everything in Finlay not to grab her and drag her back to Cas himself, but he knew Pat would take care of her. Right now, they needed to end this.

He mounted Gray, momentarily disoriented at the stallion's height, then leaned over to pull Darrya up behind him.

"You ready, cuz?" he asked. His eyes locked on the spotted wingspan of the raven, getting smaller by the second.

"Let's ride," she answered, tugging her bow from her back. With one last worried glance at Kate, Finlay urged Gray forward. It took all his strength to stay latched onto the stallion as Gray exploded, leaping forward with such speed that his teeth clacked together. Darrya's arms shot out to clutch around him, nearly unseating them both.

True to Kate's word, Gray's speed was unnatural, and it took several seconds for Finlay to adjust before he even risked glancing up to track their gains on the bird. The battlefield was quickly left behind as they reached an empty clearing, growing even with the raven. Finlay waited until they were directly underneath to pull Gray up, dropping the reins entirely to summon his fire.

Within seconds, columns of flames ignited, rising taller until they surpassed the height of the raven. It flew in a panicked circle before shooting upward, but Finlay had already fashioned the fire into a cage, trapping the raven in. Gray tossed his head, clearly unnerved by the flames, but stayed put.

Despite the chill in the air, the dome of fire Finlay summoned created instant heat. Beads of sweat dotted his brow as he held it together. Tongues of flame licked out from the dome, chasing the raven as he attempted to singe it, but the bird was too fast.

"Darrya," he began, his arms starting to tremble. She must have heard the request in his voice, because she shifted behind him, nocking an arrow.

"On it," she replied. He heard the soft thump from the bowstring as the arrow left its mount. She hissed as it skirted past the raven, taking a chunk of feathers with it but not striking true. The blaze swallowed the arrow whole, and she cursed.

"I only have one more arrow," she said, her voice shaking slightly.

A bead of sweat trailed its way down his spine, though he wasn't sure if it was from the heat, exertion, or both.

"Then make it count," he ground out. He had full faith in his cousin, but he lacked the same faith in himself.

He felt her adjust, and after a moment, he heard a deep exhale, followed by the sound of the last arrow being loosed.

The raven fell, spiraling to the earth, and seconds after it landed, Finlay consumed it in flames. He took a long moment to watch the creature's body burn, smoke curling toward the skies. He was dismayed that something so small was the key to ending it all. Nemain could never return.

He twisted to look at Darrya and saw the same shock and relief mirrored in her eyes.

"You did it," he breathed.

"We *all* did it," she replied, eyes flicking from the raven back to him. "It's over."

Finlay thought a victory march back to the palace would be more cheerful, but it was an incredibly somber experience. Soldiers grieved and whispered quietly about their experiences on the field. Finlay listened carefully, attempting to fill the gaps, as he had not been involved in most of the fighting.

After Nemain died, Larke leveraged Kate's storm to his full advantage, wielding the rain to supplement his water magic. Apparently, it had been a terrifying sight, as he'd willed the water to climb the dark Fae and freeze them whole. Gossip was already running rampant that he'd even created an entire sea serpent out of the water, and when Finlay stole a glance at the commander, the faint smirk told him Larke particularly enjoyed that one.

No matter what the truth of it was, it had boosted the morale of the remaining troops. Between that and the Valkyries, the tides had rapidly turned, causing most of the remaining dark Faeries to flee. By the time Finlay and Darrya had reemerged on the battlefield, the soldiers were collecting their dead or assisting the injured.

They'd helped carry the wounded back to the healer's tent, where Finlay nearly collapsed with relief as he saw Wren, healed and whole, helping Cas work on the remaining injured soldiers. Kate was there as well, and Finlay had rushed to gather her against him, feeling her collapse against his frame. Larke had declared victory, earning a volley of cheers that seemed to shake the trees to their very roots.

Heads hung in relief, backs were clapped, and tears were deftly wiped away as everyone warred with the realization of triumph, combined with the cost. Many embraced, and from where Finlay stood with his arms wrapped around Kate, he watched as Kipp and Cas threw their arms around one another. He grinned, murmuring for Kate to turn, and when she did, they both observed the tender moment from a distance.

Kipp was the one to pull back first, a shadowed look in his expression, but Cas held firm, moving his hand to Kipp's face. Kipp's look of surprise caused Cas to falter, but they stood frozen like that for several long seconds while Finlay and Kate watched. Kate's hand ventured to his, squeezing as if she could encourage them with her own faraway energy.

Come on, Kipp, he urged in his mind.

As if he'd heard Finlay, Kipp moved forward, closing the remaining space between the two of them. His own hand reached for the back of Cas's neck, and he pulled him forward to capture his mouth in a heated kiss. Finlay's breath caught as he waited for Cas's reaction, but there was no hesitation from him. They melted into each other as though they'd been drowning, like the only air they could find was with one another.

A tiny sound of excitement peeled past Kate's lips; Finlay tried to hush her, though he was grinning broadly himself. It didn't matter, however, because a loud whoop tore through the moment. They all looked up to find Darrya a tent away, a raised mug in hand, cheering loudly for Kipp and Cas.

Gods spare me, Finlay thought. *How did she even get that?*

Kate laughed, the sound full and rich and with abandon. It brought him back to the first time he'd seen her, looking so beautifully joyful and carefree. For the first time in a long time, he realized, that's exactly how they *could* be — happy, carefree, and wholly in love. In an instant, he turned Kate back to him and captured her soft, beautiful lips with his own.

His heart soared when she didn't hesitate to return the kiss, melting into him. A contented groan built low in his throat as he savored the taste of her, losing himself in their kiss. When they reluctantly separated to find their breath, her eyes held a heated promise of what would come when they returned home.

Now, he looked over, watching her out of the corner of his eye as they rode. Most of the soldiers didn't know what had happened with the talismans, and he watched, bemused, as they all paused in her presence, feeling the pull to her power but not knowing why. Those who did know, however, were spreading the word quickly; he had no doubt by the time they returned to the palace, they would all be bending the knee to her. He looked forward to it, and would willingly bend his own — though with a different end goal in mind.

She was clearly still energized from everything that had happened, her golden eyes wider than usual as her fingers tapped anxiously against Gray's mane. She took off a leather glove and turned her palm, sucking her bottom lip as she concentrated. After a moment, a spark lit in her palm, growing into a small web of white-gold electric currents. She let out a delighted laugh, one that sounded like actual music in his ears.

Gods above, he was entirely lost in her. He couldn't wait to love her for the rest of their days.

She didn't relent for the remainder of the ride home, testing small bouts of her new magic as they rode, until they finally reached the palace.

As they approached, however, Finlay frowned.

Even though they had traveled for hours, and it was well past sundown, there was a distinct lack of guards in front of the palace. In fact, he realized, there wasn't a single one in sight. He pulled his horse up short to dismount, and Kate turned to him curiously.

"Finlay?" she asked, and he shot her a quick look of caution.

"Something's wrong," he murmured, striding forward. Kate was off Gray in seconds, following closely behind as he stalked into the palace with no one to stop him.

Once inside, he heard a commotion but saw no one. He marched through the corridors to follow the sounds of racing footsteps and frantic exclamations, and finally, a flash of red hair dashed past. He blinked as he recognized the palace worker.

"Corryn!" he barked, causing her to stumble in alarm. She whirled to face him. "What's happened?"

"Th—the queen and the duke. They have been — murdered," she choked out, her face pale and lips trembling. She blinked as she realized who she was talking to and collected herself to offer a low curtsy. "Your Majesty."

Before he could ask what she was doing, more staff came rushing through the halls in a panic, stopping short to curtsy or bow as they came across him. He blinked in confusion at their exaggerated respects, until he finally *heard* what they were saying. Their exclamations echoed through the halls in a unified chorus, repeating the same eight words.

"The queen is dead! Long live the king!"

More From Jayme Hunt

Stay tuned for the epic conclusion to Kate's story in the final *Marked* book, planned for late 2023. Please follow the author for more updates!

Acknowledgments

Something I find absolutely wonderful is the fact that everyone I know has some sort of unique passion or hobby.

For my brother, it's anything to do with guitars – from playing them to building them. For my husband, it's landscaping. I could lose track of him for hours, only to find him outside building a new garden bed (which our dogs will promptly run through and ruin). My friends have hobbies ranging from the most standard Colorado hobby of hiking to things like knitting and traveling. These things will all bend the construct of time for them, causing them to do things others might find ridiculous ("You get up at 4 am to go mountain biking? Are you crazy?!"). But the fire it sparks in them is one of the greatest things I've ever seen, and I love watching people chase that spark and find their purpose in life.

The fact that you can find me up at 2 am many nights, squinting at my screen to make edits, says quite a lot about my spark. And I appreciate all the people who either completely understand that (or don't understand it at all, but still love me regardless).

To my father, who will tell everyone he knows about how I'm an author now — thank you for always being proud of my work, even if it's something I may forbid you from ever reading. You'll always be in a bit of every father-daughter scene I write.

To my friends stateside, Hannah and Megan — thank you for putting up with all of my feverishly excited text updates about my books, and for reading them with equal excitement. Not everyone can say they have friends so supportive of their passions, so be warned: I'm never letting either of you go.

To my friends abroad, Sarah and Lea — thank you for bringing a baby book from an American author into your book club in Germany. Ich bin unendlich dankbar.

To everyone in my newfound reading community — especially Charlie, Michaela, and Beca — thank you for restoring my faith in the supportive, loving side of social media that proves its worth. Love you long time!

To Aamna and her wonderful design team at Etheric Tales, for taking all my wild ideas in stride and making something beautiful out of them. I appreciate you all!

And to all the other indie authors, who hustle in the wee hours of the morning to get the stories from their souls out on paper — just like anyone else with their hobby, I see you doing it for the sheer love of it. Keep that spark alive!

About the Author

Jayme Hunt studied marketing and data analytics in college, and continues working a full-time job in the marketing field. In early 2022, she rediscovered her love of reading and writing, and has barely put down a book since. *Marked by Fate* is her debut novel, followed by *Marked by Gods*. She resides in Colorado with her husband and two dogs, who often make cameos in her social media posts.

@authorjaymehunt
www.authorjaymehunt.wordpress.com